WHERE
THE RIVERS
MERGE

NOVELS FOR ADULTS ALSO BY MARY ALICE MONROE

WHERE
THE RIVERS
MERGE

A NOVEL

MARY ALICE
MONROE

𝓌𝓂

WILLIAM MORROW

An Imprint of HarperCollins*Publishers*

WHERE THE RIVERS MERGE. Copyright © 2025 by Mary Alice Monroe LTD. All rights reserved. Printed in the United States of America. No part of this book may be used or reproduced in any manner whatsoever without written permission except in the case of brief quotations embodied in critical articles and reviews. For information, address HarperCollins Publishers, 195 Broadway, New York, NY 10007.

HarperCollins books may be purchased for educational, business, or sales promotional use. For information, please email the Special Markets Department at SPsales@harpercollins.com.

FIRST EDITION

Endpaper art courtesy of Shutterstock/ColorMaker

Library of Congress Cataloging-in-Publication Data

Names: Monroe, Mary Alice, author.
Title: Where the rivers merge : a novel / Mary Alice Monroe.
Description: First edition. | New York, NY : William Morrow, 2025.
Identifiers: LCCN 2024043718 | ISBN 9780063249424 (hardcover) | ISBN 9780063249455 (ebook)
Subjects: LCGFT: Domestic fiction. | Bildungsromans. | Novels.
Classification: LCC PS3563.O529 W47 2025 | DDC 813/.54—dc23/eng/20240924
LC record available at https://lccn.loc.gov/2024043718

ISBN 978-0-06-324942-4

25 26 27 28 29 LBC 5 4 3 2 1

This book is dedicated to Liz Stein
for your insights, faith, and heart

WHERE
THE RIVERS
MERGE

BOOK ONE

Part One

HOMECOMING

If sleep has a smell, it grows here
When flowers raise their heads in the mist
To eat the light pulsing at the edge of the sky
Where tapered tails of wind unwind
Like roots stumbling through darkness.

After the green silence of dreams
I rise and drink the warm rain falling,
Dig two holes in the ground
To plant my tired feet,
Because I need to live for awhile

—MARJORY WENTWORTH, "HOMECOMING"

Prologue

⟡

1908

The child stood in the enclosed garden as the sun lowered into a crimson sky. The moss-draped oaks stood watch and the countless white camellias seemed to shimmer in the twilight as the world held its breath. From the distance came the first, faint, nasal calls of ducks. She imagined them coming in as a great cloud, their dark wings flapping against the sky, from the river to roost in the rice fields.

Fly away, her heart cried out.

In the next breath she heard the five-note artificial duck calls from her daddy and his friends sitting in the blinds, enticing the ducks closer, their guns poised. In counterpoint, a burst of high-pitched laughter rang from the house behind her. Looking over her shoulder, as great shafts of light shone from the tall windows, she could see her mother and friends standing in long gowns, their red lips moving. The girl shivered in the twilight air. She hated these parties and the way her mama acted when she drank from those long-stemmed glasses.

As the sky darkened and duck calls filled the sky, their number appeared as a shadowed cloud approaching the rice fields. Suddenly the evening's peace was rent by explosive shots. Songbirds cried in the surrounding trees, and the girl's heart fluttered with unspeakable sadness. She started to run, her bare feet pattering over the brick walkway, escaping the confined garden walls to sprint across the manicured lawn that stretched far out toward the ancient rice ponds, surging now with the rising tide. With each pump of her arms her mind called out,

Fly away . . .

She darted into the deep woods, farther from the dull cracking noises in the sky and the frenzied laughter. Lightning flashed, urging her to push through the thick shrubs at the lawn's border into the woods. Branches scratched her face and arms and twigs tugged at her hair, pulling dark strands from the ribbon's hold. An inner voice scolded that she shouldn't wander so far off the path. Still, she ran as the night thickened and familiar signposts disappeared. Never had she run so far.

When the sounds of guns changed to the soft rumble of thunder, the child stopped to listen, as still as a fawn, her ears cocked. Once her breathing calmed, she heard the wind rustle the leaves and rattle palmetto fronds, heralding a storm. A moment later came the soft thuds of a slow rain falling on the thick tree canopy overhead. Then one drop hit her forehead, fat and wet. She ran again, her bare feet skittering over the matted leaves of the forest floor. She burst into a large clearing and stopped, hands on her chest, panting. The meadow was unexpected and vast. A field of wild grasses swayed in the wind like waves across the ocean.

Standing in the middle of the meadow, like some regal queen, was a giant live oak tree. The biggest she had ever seen. The enormous outline was silhouetted against the purpling sky like a mountain. She couldn't count all the thick, muscled boughs that spread far out over the grass before gracefully drooping to the earth. The limbs snaked along the ground and narrowed at the tips, where they curled like cragged fingers, beckoning. At the great tree's base, she spotted a large hollow.

A fierce crack of thunder spurred her on, instinct guiding her across the meadow toward the tree's shelter. Yet when she reached the hollow, she didn't rush in. She paused, as hesitant as any wild animal before entering the cavernous darkness.

"Shoo!" she shouted and clapped her hands. Silence from within. The brown resurrection fern that grew thick along the jagged edges of the hollow was changing to a bright green right before her eyes. She took a step closer then paused again, poised for flight. Suddenly a cloudburst dumped a torrent of rain. Its iciness stung her tender skin, sending her scurrying inside the belly of the majestic tree.

The darkness smelled of moldy leaves and mushrooms and earth. The girl breathed deeply and was comforted. Chilled to the bone, she curled her legs to her chest and wrapped her thin, scratched arms around her bony knees. She tugged the hem of her wet nightgown to blanket her bare legs, but it offered scant warmth. Inside the hollow, she heard the rain as the beating of a drum.

Gradually, her eyes acclimated to the dark and she could see the long, rough folds of the inner hollow. She smiled as it dawned on her that she was sitting inside a tree. The ridges of wood reached skyward like the arches of the church her mama brought her to on Sundays in Charleston. In the corner a cluster of daddy longlegs were racing around in a panic.

"I won't hurt you," she told them. Her voice echoed in the cavernous space. A sudden tickling across her toes caused her to start, then giggling, she brushed away a shiny green beetle. There was nothing inside this old tree but a few bugs, she thought.

The girl yawned, feeling the pace of her run, then stretched out on the mossy ground, which was as soft as a feather bed. She rested her head on her arm and breathed in the heavy fragrance of petrichor. She was safe. The rain had slowed to the gentle pattering of a lullaby. Closing her eyes, the young girl fell into a deep sleep.

Chapter One

EAST BAY STREET is an iconic street in Charleston created nearly 350 years ago. The fabled Rainbow Row of pastel-colored, historic mansions is located on East Bay along the Battery, across from the seawall of Charleston Harbor.

1988

I dreamed again that I was nestled inside the hollow of a great tree. I could smell the green earth. Feel the fuzzy moss. Hear the rain battering the ancient oak's trunk. Someone was calling my name.

"Miss Eliza. Wake up!"

I blinked, my senses sharpening.

"Rise and shine! It's your birthday," the determinedly pleasant voice persisted. "Eighty-eight!"

I sighed as the last vestige of the dream faded. I wanted to stay in the dream. "Go away."

A small hand tentatively nudged my shoulders. "Good morning, Miss Eliza!"

Prying open an eye, I saw the slight figure of my assistant, Hana Nakamura. She was dressed in gray baggy pants and a shapeless brown shirt, her tiny hands clasping a clipboard. Her dark hair with a single wide streak of white was pulled neatly back in a bun, making her look like a sparrow tilting its head in curiosity.

I dug deeper into my pillow. "What's so happy about being another year older? Everyone I knew and loved is already pushing up daisies. Yet here I am, persisting aboveground for another year."

"Celebrate that you woke up, Miss Eliza. God gave you another day. Each day is a gift."

"A gift I never asked for," I mumbled as I folded back my blanket. Hana quickly moved to assist but I brushed her hands away. "I may be old but I'm perfectly capable of rising from my own bed, thank you very much."

I swung my legs over the bed's edge as Hana pulled open the heavily fringed silk curtains from the expanse of windows, revealing a rainy Charleston morning. A gust of wind rattled the windows, and from a dreary sky, drops of rain streaked the glass with a pattering noise. I thought again of my dream.

I rose and slid into the silken fabric of my robe. "It seems to me if it's my birthday, I should be able to stay in bed on this rainy morning. And dream . . ." I sighed and tightened the sash. "It was such a lovely dream. Of a place I knew as a child. I've had it often of late."

"The best way to make your dreams come true is to wake up and make it so."

I chuckled quietly at Hana's unswayable optimism. "Today I have to make my dreams come true, don't I?"

"Yes ma'am."

The lingering dream discarded, I focused on the day ahead. "What's my schedule?"

Hana heard my tone shift, squared her shoulders, then lifted her clipboard. The petite woman had a backbone of steel. "At nine o'clock you meet in the morning room with your lawyer. The shareholders meeting begins at eleven in the ballroom, followed immediately by the family luncheon at the Yacht Club. You approved the menu and wine selection."

"That dreadful affair," I muttered as I walked to the bathroom. Every year on the seventeenth of June my family swarmed in from all over the country to roost at my home, gawk at the historic house, enjoy my wine, and natter at one another, each deeply suspicious that someone else was getting more money from dividends they did nothing to earn.

"You'll have everything ready for my departure to Mayfield? I don't want any delays."

"Of course. You are already all packed."

"Good," I said, feeling relief at the prospect of leaving Charleston for my home in the countryside. At the door I turned and asked, "Is my son here?"

Hana's smile fell and she nodded. "Arthur is in the dining room. With his family."

"Counting the silver, no doubt."

Hana had the grace not to smile.

I descended the sweeping staircase like a general would approach a battlefield. I'd made countless sacrifices over many years and was prepared to face the enemy today. My strategies were set, my players were in place. I smoothed the knit skirt of the carefully selected black Chanel suit—my ceremonial armor. The insignia gold buttons shone like medals.

Today I was neither a wife nor a mother. Or even a friend. Today I would make no apologies. Today's meeting would decide the continuation of my life's work.

Hana awaited me at the bottom of the stairs, her ever-present clipboard tucked under her arm. Arthur's booming voice emanated from the dining room. My hand tightened around my cane as I walked down the long hall. From the row of windows overlooking the veranda, sunlight peeked through storm clouds, promising a better day. Storms often rolled in fast along the coast, dumping cold rain to flood the streets and stir the mud before heading out to sea. *People could be like that too,* I thought.

Approaching the dining room, I heard the words *conservation easement* and stopped abruptly. Leaning slightly forward in the shadows, I peered in. It was a substantial room. The celadon wallpaper and raspberry silk drapes were an elegant backdrop for the long Chippendale dining table and chairs. Mother's portrait over the fireplace dominated the left wall. Sitting beneath the portrait, in my usual chair, was Arthur. I noticed that his blue blazer was straining at the seams and his once-reddish hair was now gray and thinning. When did my son get so old? I wondered.

To his right, I recognized his wife's helmet of blond hair. Carolina was saying, "Arthur, don't go flying off the handle again."

Arthur angrily skewered a breakfast sausage. "I can't help but get riled when I think of it. What did she expect? Giving away all that land is the same as picking my inheritance straight from my pockets." He set his tableware down with a clatter. "You're right. Why should I get upset? I should be used to it by now. She never listens to me. When Mother has her mind made up, heaven help anyone who gets in her way."

"Daddy, why do you even care? You're always complaining about how bored you are at Mayfield. You never even go there."

I couldn't see Ashley, but I recognized the honeyed voice of my eldest granddaughter.

"What are you saying?" Arthur huffed. "I took several groups of friends for hunting."

Carolina laughed. "But did you actually go out in the weeds and shoot?"

Feminine laughter sounded from the room.

Arthur picked up his fork, mustering dignity. "I was managing the hunt the house. Taking care of my guests."

"Darling, no need to explain to us," said Carolina. "We all know getting down in a boat and sitting for hours in the damp cold isn't your idea of a good time. What Ashley means is why are you so upset about your mother putting the land into a conservation easement? You will still own the land. You will still be able to take your buddies out there to hunt."

A new voice entered the fray. "Daddy, I'm confused. What even *is* a conservation easement?"

This was the voice of my younger granddaughter. Savannah was eighteen years old. Her debut at the St. Cecilia Ball last winter was all Carolina could talk about. I'd offered the ballroom upstairs for her coming-out party.

Arthur leaned back in his chair and placed his elbows on the armrest. "Simply put," he began with a voice tinged with annoyance, "a conservation easement is a deal between the land holder and a conservation group that ties the holder's hands so the land can't be sold."

I scoffed. That was hardly a definition. The land could be sold. But the covenants would go with the deed so the protections would continue under the new owner.

"*Ever?*" Savannah asked. I heard the youth in the high-pitched, petulant tone.

Arthur nodded perfunctorily. "In perpetuity."

"That doesn't sound fair. And it doesn't sound like Grandma Eliza. She's a businesswoman. It's not like her to just give it away," Savannah said.

"She's not quite giving it away," Carolina replied. "There are tax advantages. You know, Arthur, you might want to look there. Consider the inheritance tax alone."

"The land is an asset, first and foremost," Arthur said. "Really, children, this is elementary, so listen carefully. You asked why I am upset. I'll tell you. My darling mother has joined a group of land-owners to create some sort of task force intent on creating a wild-life refuge. They got Ducks Unlimited and the Nature Conservancy involved. Smacks of a government takeover, if you ask me," he said derisively. "That Ted Turner started it off by putting St. Phillips

Island in conservation a few years back. Now he's put Hope Plantation into conservation easement, which is smack dab in the ACE Basin. Sampson Island and Botany Bay Island were next. The governor is praising it all, calling it a model of how state and private groups can work together. It's turning into a damn domino effect."

Carolina tapped her chin. "The ACE Basin? I never heard of that. Where is it?"

"It's an acronym," Arthur replied testily. "For the rivers in the estuary—the Ashepoo, Combahee, and Edisto."

"That's where Mayfield is," Carolina said.

Arthur gave a long, annoyed sigh. Yes. Exactly." He shook his head. "She and that Brusi Alexander from the Nature Conservancy are thick as thieves, and you know my mother. She's front and center, trying to save the land. She already transferred four thousand prime acres into conservation. With the final thousand acres held in reserve. That's where the plantation house is." He paused to let those numbers sink in. "I mean to stop her."

I inhaled sharply, feeling a mother's heartbreak that my son, my only child, was a stranger to me. Worse, an opponent in my efforts to protect Mayfield. I'd always recognized that Arthur had different dreams and goals than mine. I had turned a blind eye to his insatiable greed and accepted him, with all his faults and attributes, with a mother's resignation. But I could listen no more.

I straightened my back, lifted my chin, and entered the dining room. The clatter of silverware silenced as all eyes turned to me with surprise.

Arthur was the first to recover. "Mother! At last. The birthday girl is here. Sit down," he said, rising to his feet. "I hope you don't mind we started."

"Grandma Eliza, hello," sang the chorus from the two young women.

I met Carolina's eye as I passed, and we shared a womanly understanding that I'd overheard all. Carolina looked down as I walked to the opposite side of the table, Arthur following closely. He gallantly pulled out the chair for me.

As I sat, my maid, Camila, appeared with a fresh pot of coffee and poured a cup, then walked around the long table refreshing everyone's coffee.

"Would you like breakfast?" she asked me.

"Some toast would be nice, thank you, Camila." I picked up the napkin from the table. "I don't have the stomach for more." Laying the napkin on my lap, I breathed deeply, willing myself to not let them see me upset.

I gazed up at my two granddaughters, the only children of my only son. They were tolerably pretty, as my mother would say. They had the Chalmers oval face and short forehead. Ashley, at twenty-five, had more of Carolina's classic Southern belle genes in her features—wispy blond hair, slightly protruding, large blue eyes, full lips. But I could clearly see my ex-husband's features in eighteen-year-old Savannah. She was small and fine boned, like her grandfather Tripp. She also had his ginger hair. I held my smile at seeing she wore the round eyeglasses that Tripp had worn too. I wondered if some of Tripp's gentle spirit lived on in the girl as well.

I smiled magnanimously. "I must confess. With every passing year I feel all the happier seeing you. Thank you for coming."

"Of course, Mother. Where else would we be, today of all days?"

My gaze returned to my granddaughters, and I felt a twinge of love . . . and regret. "I really must make more of an effort to find time to be with you, my darling girls. My mother would have doted on you, I'm sure."

"I wish I'd known her. I love her portrait," said Savannah. "She was so beautiful. I wish I had her dark hair."

"And that waistline," Ashley added with a laugh.

"Sloane Bissette was considered the season's beauty when she made her debut," I said. "Poems were written about her, as she often reminded me. When she moved back to Charleston from Mayfield,

this house was always filled with artists, musicians, and writers, especially poets." I looked up at her portrait behind Arthur. She stood
dressed in white, her dark hair adorned with pearls and roses. In her
hand she carried a plumed pen. "Mother's greatest passion was poetry, you know."

"And you, Grandmother Eliza?" The corners of her lips rose faintly.
"Your passion is business?"

I turned toward Savannah and offered a languid smile. "Business?"
I considered that a moment, then shook my head. "No. I'm good at
it, but it's not a passion. Horses, perhaps. Wait, that's not right. Mayfield. That place is my passion. The land, rivers, animals . . . all of it.
Always has been. I'm happiest there. Which suits me. I've never been
the celebrated beauty my mother was. And I didn't care one whit for
parties."

"You still don't," said Arthur.

"True enough. Which is why I prefer living at Mayfield. This
house is beautiful, even grand, but Mayfield is home, rich with our
family history and heritage."

"Then why did you put an easement on the property?" asked Savannah.

The question shattered the sweet moment of nostalgia.

"Oh, do shut up," snapped Ashley.

"For God's sake, let's not spoil breakfast," Arthur muttered. "It's
your grandmother's birthday."

I studied my younger granddaughter's face. Savannah's eyes were
wide, and I saw no malice there.

"This has everything to do with my birthday," I said, looking at
Arthur. "Because Mayfield stands for everything I've fought for all my
life." I set my hands on the table, one over the other, then turned to
Savannah. "It sounds to me that you've been listening to your father."

Savannah bit her lip.

"There is often misunderstanding about what a conservation easement is. I've been able to control what happened to Mayfield for as

long as I owned it. With the easement, I can continue to protect the property from development after I'm gone. It's that simple. I realize your father feels the easement will tie his hands. Make it impossible for him to sell. Or develop. And for what, he asks."

I glanced his way and saw his eyes widen. Now he knew that I'd overheard their discussion.

"To preserve Mayfield for you, your children, and their children."

There followed a long silence.

I turned again to Savannah, "Why don't you come with me to Mayfield? I'd like to help you understand why I must protect the land."

Savannah blinked her pale lashes. "For how long?"

"As long as you wish."

Her eyes brightened at the possibility. "Well, sure. I suppose I could. I mean, I don't have much planned this summer."

"What about that internship at *Charleston Magazine*?" Arthur pointed out. "Your mother pulled strings for that."

"I haven't gotten it yet," Savannah replied with a frown. "Besides, that's what *she* wants me to do. I'd rather be with Grandma Eliza. And I haven't been to Mayfield in ages."

"It's best you stay in Charleston," Arthur said with finality.

Savannah stared at her plate, her eyes narrowed.

"This is important, Arthur," I said, annoyed at his interference. "In fact, why don't you come too? The whole family. I can't remember the last time we were all together at Mayfield." That sounded close to the pathetic plea of a lonely old woman. "I regret we haven't spent more time there together, all of us. And . . . it's lovely this time of year," I added.

"Not a good time, unfortunately, Mother," Arthur said, smoothing out his napkin. "The shareholders meeting and all. Perhaps in the fall."

"I'm sorry, Grandmother, but I couldn't right now," Ashley said in a rush. "I'm tethered here. The twins are a handful, and Roger's family expects us in the Highlands."

"Perhaps for a weekend?"

"We'll try . . ." was Ashley's half-hearted response.

"Daddy, please, I'd like to go," Savannah tried again. She cast me a sidelong glance of commiseration.

"We'll talk about it later," Arthur said. His tone made it clear she wouldn't be allowed to come.

I closed my eyes, feeling profound disappointment. Did my son never feel the pull of the tides to Mayfield? Or to hear the call of the curlew at dawn? Or see the sunlight dapple through the twisted boughs of a live oak? Or smell the pluff mud after the rain? Why was it at the end of one's life, when time was so precious, that one understood the importance of legacy? How could a legacy continue with no steward to tend to it?

A soft cough at my side drew my attention. I opened my eyes and saw Hana.

"Excuse me, ma'am, but it's almost nine o'clock. You have your meeting."

"Yes, thank you." I turned to my family and fixed a smile. "It was lovely seeing you all this morning. Thank you for coming so early to celebrate my birthday. Do finish your breakfast. I'll see you later."

"Who are you meeting?" asked Arthur, straightening in his chair.

I rose slowly then said, "Bobby Lee Pearlman."

Arthur made a soft choking sound like he had a hair caught in his biscuit. "Should I be present?"

I studied my son. He looked older than his sixty-two years. His face sagged at the jowls, the top of his head was balding, and he had the pastiness of skin that came from a sedentary life. We had endured some hardscrabble years, just the two of us. Yet he'd also shared in the great wealth that came later with the DeLancey Group. Given the choice of being rich or poor, I allowed rich was better. But there were important lessons to be learned in poverty. Hard-won building blocks that forged character.

"No," I replied with a perfunctory smile. "You are, as you so often tell me, a busy man. Tend to your family. I'll see you later at the shareholders meeting."

Some fifty years earlier, I had come to the Charleston office of a young man I'd known since childhood. Bobby Lee Pearlman was a newly fledged lawyer in Charleston, and I needed to seek his counsel. Bobby Lee was already gaining a reputation of being brilliant in his field of estate law. After a long meeting, he had nervously confessed he'd been in love with me since the first time he had seen me at cotillion at Hibernian Hall. I was flattered and touched by his surprising declaration, and if times had been different so might have been my response. But at that particular moment in time, I had my sights set on another target.

Instead, we'd formed a long-lasting, trusting relationship that delicately danced between devotion and friendship. Over the years, Bobby Lee used his vast knowledge of the law to protect me. Now, though formally long retired and having handed down the law firm to his son, Bobby stayed on as retainer exclusively for me.

Bobby Lee waited patiently as I settled in the chair opposite his at the table in the morning room, then he cleared his throat to speak. "Happy birthday."

A small laugh escaped my lips. "Bother that. We all know the vultures are circling under the guise of celebrating my birthday."

He chuckled then handed me a navy blue folder with the DeLancey Group logo embossed in gold. "And this, my friend, is my gift to you."

I took hold of the folder and opened it, glancing at the fifty-some pages enclosed. "Why don't you just give me the bullet."

"The bullet will sting, I'm afraid."

"Go on."

"What you're holding is the result of several months of quiet investigation. It appears your son has been attempting to garner support on the board, as well as with shareholders." He paused. "To remove you as CEO."

I sucked in my breath. He was right. The words stung. Yet I was not completely surprised. "Let me guess. His search began after I opposed him and put Mayfield into conservation." It was more a statement than a question.

"Yes."

I shook my head wearily. No amount of money, no measure of love, was ever enough for Arthur.

"I believe he will make his move at today's meeting," Bobby Lee said grimly.

"Is he going for incompetence?"

"Not overtly, but implied, perhaps. Arthur intends to introduce mandatory retirement at sixty-five. There is a strong precedent in other companies."

I pondered the implications. "But if he succeeds, Arthur is already sixty-two."

"He does not intend to remain chairman for long." He paused again, weighing his words. "Arthur intends to sell the majority interests."

I sat back, stunned. "He wants to *sell* the DeLancey Group?"

Bobby Lee nodded.

I exhaled, letting the pieces settle in my mind. In this way too, Arthur was just like my brother Lesesne. Eager to sell to the highest bidder without loyalty. Money had always been the crux of my troubles. Being land rich and cash poor forced difficult decisions. Yet I worked like a beast in the harness until we were wealthier than I'd ever dreamed.

"So. Arthur has no intention of entrusting the company to his daughters." I laughed bitterly. "Primogeniture continues strong in the family."

Bobby Lee offered a slight shrug.

"I'm old and I'm tired, Bobby Lee. I've been fighting all my life. And this breaks my heart. I don't know if I have fight left in me."

"You face two battlefronts. One, the takeover of the DeLancey Group. Second, the conservation easement for Mayfield."

"Mayfield is the entire war."

"Then we must secure it."

"I thought the conservation easement was a fait accompli."

"Not quite. You've settled on the terms for the four thousand acres. I expect to hear from the Nature Conservancy any day regarding their approval. It's a mere formality. Once the papers are signed, the final step is for them to be recorded at the county courthouse."

"But they are not yet signed," I said, understanding the threat.

"Exactly." Bobby Lee gathered his hands on the table. "Eliza, I am not overly concerned about the land you have already placed in conservation." He paused. "Arthur has his sights set on the final thousand acres of Mayfield. Your house."

"That thousand acres is not controlled by the DeLancey Group. It is mine, and mine alone."

Bobby Lee paused. "And your inaction there has left that land vulnerable."

"I've designated that it become the Mayfield Wildlife Foundation."

"The foundation exists only on paper."

"I know," I said softly. I raised my gaze. "I want a Rivers family member to head the board of trustees. And if my family is to avoid paying exorbitant inheritance tax, I must leave the land to the foundation"—I smirked—"upon my death."

"No need for that now," Bobby Lee replied with a wry grin. "A signature is enough."

"Is it? Bobby Lee, I can lose the corporation. Lose my fortune. But to lose Mayfield is unthinkable. It cannot happen. Mayfield isn't business. It's personal. I do not own the land. The land owns me. I am merely the caretaker for my generation." I touched my brow. "It just breaks my heart that I do not have one member in my family who will take on the responsibility that has been unbroken for generations."

"Even so," Bobby Lee said in a tone that brought reason back to the discussion. "You've run out of time. You must make your move. Or lose Mayfield to Arthur."

I dropped my hand and, straightening my shoulders, looked Bobby Lee in the eye. "Have the papers ready."

"They are at my home in Green Pond."

"Good. I'm leaving for Mayfield today. Let's finalize them as soon as we can."

"And the votes?"

"We shall soon find out."

Chapter Two

⟡

SWALLOW-TAILED KITES (*Elanoides forficatus*) are striking raptors with narrow, pointed wings and a long, deeply forked tail. Their bright-white head and underparts contrast dramatically with gleaming black wings, back, and tail. The swallow-tailed kite soars effortlessly, swooping and gliding, a joy to watch. The species is listed as endangered in South Carolina.

1988

At the door of the ballroom, I paused to collect my wits. The appointed hour for the shareholders meeting had arrived.

I looked down and gazed at the walking stick in my hand. It was one of my most precious possessions. The head of the stick had been painstakingly carved into a swallow-tailed kite by the father of my beloved childhood friend Covey. Wilton had been the caretaker and manager of Mayfield for as long as I could remember, serving both me and my father with unwavering loyalty.

But—the image of an old woman needing assistance to walk was not one I wanted to present at this important meeting. I tucked the cane under my arm, straightened my shoulders, and nodded. The heavy wooden doors were opened.

Twenty-some DeLancey and Chalmers family members were already gathered in the elegant room. But it was the whispers of the past that enveloped me. Portraits of family ancestors stared at me from the cream-colored walls. Echoes of DuBose Heyward, Josephine Pinckney, Alice Ravenel Huger Smith, George Gershwin, and others who'd been entertained in this room swirled under the enormous chandeliers.

Happy birthday! You're looking so well. This is my favorite day of the year. We love to visit you in this lovely house. I was besieged by guests offering birthday salutations. I spotted Arthur and his family clustered near the front of the room. Arthur was moving from group to group, shaking hands, pausing to laugh, patting backs, and guiding people to take their seats. He glided over to my side and kissed me on the cheek.

"Mother, you're here. Are you ready to begin the meeting?" He offered his elbow and escorted me to my chair near the podium.

At my seat he leaned over to kiss my cheek. *Et tu Brute?* I thought.

Arthur stood in front of the podium and the chatter subsided. I listened as he welcomed the family to Charleston and offered the requisite opening joke. This was followed by the acknowledgment of the board of directors, and finally the board secretary's reading of the previous year's minutes. When finished, as CEO, I was scheduled to deliver the state of the corporation. But as I prepared to rise, Arthur began speaking again.

"Before we get into the details of business," he said, "I'd like to take time to sing my mother's praises on this special day."

I glanced across the room at Bobby Lee. He knitted his brows and shook his head.

"Eliza Rivers was born at the beginning of this century at Mayfield, a place of singular history and importance to everyone in this room. In her lifetime, she has gone from a world of unpaved roads and horse-drawn carriages to automobiles and to space travel. She has lived through two world wars, the Great Depression and its crushing poverty, and then like a phoenix rose to untold wealth. After the passing of my dear father, James Livingston DeLancey, more than thirty years ago, my mother took the helm and turned the collection of businesses my father had started into a conglomerate of corporations and subsidiaries that today is the DeLancey Group."

He turned toward me and said with gravity, "Thank you, Mother. Well done."

A murmur of agreement and mild applause sounded in the room.

Dear father? I thought with incredulousness. In truth, stepfather . . . James didn't care one whit for Arthur as a child. Barely knew he was alive. He'd wanted his own child, his own bloodline. Something I could never give him.

Arthur cleared his throat. "Today, as we celebrate Eliza Rivers Chalmers DeLancey's eighty-eighth birthday. . . ." He paused, then said again in the manner of announcing a great achievement, "Eighty-eight years! Isn't that a triumph?" He joined the applause, smiling back at me.

I see what you're doing, I thought. *Hammering the point of my age.*

When the group quieted, Arthur continued. "At this crossroads, as her son, I have to speak up. . . . I believe my mother has earned the right to step away from the harness *at last*. To enjoy a peaceful life of retirement." He paused to begin clapping.

The family responded with weak applause, turning to me with questioning glances. I sat ramrod straight, expressionless.

Gripping the sides of the podium, Arthur said in a daring voice, "With that view, I am proposing today that we vote to create mandatory retirement at sixty-five years of age for every CEO, effective immediately."

A stunned silence followed, then a rumble of discontent and shouts for Arthur to sit down. I perched like an eagle on my chair as I scanned the crowd, taking mental notes of who did what.

"We, the DeLancey Group, are at a crossroads," Arthur declared, bringing the meeting back to order. "As I'm sure most of you are aware, the majority of Mayfield's vast acreage has recently been placed by Mrs. DeLancey, as a trustee, under a conservation easement with the Nature Conservancy. This effectively removes the land as an asset of the DeLancey Group. In perpetuity," he added with emphasis.

"What this means for all of you is, you will not receive the dividends from the sale of this land."

The audience leaned forward, listening acutely now.

"And there is still the matter of the final thousand acres as yet *not* placed under conservation. The value of which, in today's market, is in the millions." He paused again, looking at the board. "Will this land also be allowed to be put into conservation and thus removed from the DeLancey Group's assets? Forgive me, Mother, but I say it should not!"

He paused to let that sink in.

I was enraged. That thousand acres was not held by the DeLancey Group. Arthur knew that and was outright lying. I could feel the change in the mood. Smelling blood, the vultures were circling.

Then a voice came from the back of the room. I looked up to see a tall and slender woman, dressed in a modest black skirt and white blouse with a strand of small pearls at her neck.

"You speak of the conservation easement as though it were a stupid decision," the woman began in a clear tone that demanded the attention of the room. "This, I assure you, is not so. I am a director of the Nature Conservancy in Pennsylvania and well versed in easements. In truth, Mrs. DeLancey was using a powerful tool at her disposal to protect the property from future, unwanted development and damaging land use. As for the value of this piece of land, it cannot be measured simply in terms of dollars. Mayfield holds significant historical and ecological value. Mrs. DeLancey understands that." She looked at Arthur. "Even if some do not."

I covered my smile with my hand. I was intrigued by the woman's composure in the face of such obvious antagonism. *Who is she?* I wondered. I had many dealings with the Nature Conservancy in the past years, but this was a private shareholders meeting. How did she gain access?

The woman continued speaking in a clear voice. "I might add, for those of you who have not read the easement on Mayfield, the final thousand acres is not owned by the DeLancey Group. It is the private property of Mrs. DeLancey. And her intention to put *all* of the land, including the final thousand acres, under a conservation easement is clearly stated. This is not open to debate or discussion."

Her gaze swept the room. "This is a good thing for all of us. Why?" Her hand motion included everyone in the room. "Because all of us, as family members, will be able to enjoy the land for hiking, boating, hunting, or just the pleasure of taking family out to a legacy that has been in our family for hundreds of years. To share equally our proud history. Rather than it being the private property of the privileged few."

The crowd murmured, this time in her favor. Heads tilted in thought. I felt hope stir in my breast as I looked again at Bobby Lee. He responded with an unknowing shrug.

Arthur couldn't restrain his frustration. "*Our family?*" he shouted from the podium. "I've never seen you before. Who are you?"

All heads turned to regard the young woman.

She lifted her chin. "I am Norah Davis. Daughter of Desmond Davis. Granddaughter of Covey Wilton Davis and Heyward Rivers. Grandniece of Eliza Rivers Chalmers DeLancey. And"—she smiled—"I am a shareholder."

The room erupted in mayhem.

I sat back in my chair, my heart beating fast as the ballroom erupted in voices of surprise and utterances of disbelief. Repeated over and over I heard the phrase, *The scandal was true.*

The young woman was Covey's granddaughter. My grandniece. My brother's child's child.

Arthur stood in stunned silence. He'd lost control of the meeting. It was time to act.

I rose and walked with grace to the podium. By the time I reached the center of the room, the family had noticed and quieted, wondering how I would respond to both Arthur's proposal and this strange outburst. Arthur hesitated, then cleared his throat and stepped aside. I was accustomed to being in charge and smoothed the papers on the podium in a powerful pause. Then I looked up and smiled.

"Well, this certainly has been a lively meeting." I waited until the laughter subsided. "First, thank you all again for your warm birthday wishes. I'm truly grateful. And to Arthur for his expansive, though altogether unnecessary, history of my life. However, he got a few of his facts wrong." I slipped on my reading glasses and looked at the papers handed to me by Hana.

"You should all receive a printed report . . ." I looked up, then smiled seeing Hana handing out the company reports. "Ah, there they are. You'll see that though it was a difficult year, I am pleased to report that the DeLancey Group did realize a profit again this year." I removed my glasses and nodded in acknowledgment of the applause.

"While I appreciate my son's concern for my health and well-being, I assure you I am in good health, my mind is sharp, my wits keen, and my outlook positive." I turned to look at Arthur, who straightened in his chair, his face mottled.

"As for my history"—I set the papers down and kept going—"I have managed Mayfield for over fifty years, longer than any other Rivers family member in our long history. With my husband James, I doubled the acreage to six thousand four hundred acres. I have maintained the historic rice crop as a nod to our history and overseen a strong and steady truck market. I've continued my father's legacy, breeding Marsh Tacky horses and increasing the number of that rare South Carolina breed. I've been a good steward of the land, both in farming and managing hunt clubs. I oversee the running of two large houses, each fully staffed. And"—my steely gaze swept the room—"I have served as chief executive officer of the DeLancey Group since James's death thirty-two years ago, expanding its mission and growth substantially in that time. Currently, I have two thousand and seven people in my employment."

I waited for the applause to stop.

"You shouldn't be surprised to learn that I have already thought ahead to the future and taken my retirement under advisement. Retirement from *my* company. Of which I own fifty-nine percent of the stock." I paused for effect.

"We will not waste our time today to vote on any mandatory retirement. Instead, I am announcing that I, Eliza Rivers Chalmers DeLancey, being of sound mind and body, will retire at the year's end. To secure the company, I have initiated a revised shareholders agreement that offers *all* the shareholders of the corporation a vote in the election of the board of directors, who in turn will select from themselves a chairman of the board. A term that will last no longer than three years." I looked at my son and drove the dagger. "The position of chairman of the DeLancey Group will not be inherited."

Astonished mumblings erupted in the room.

"I leave it to Bobby Lee to come to the podium and explain the details. Thank you. That is all."

Without another word, I walked with dignity from the podium and strode the center aisle between the rows of chairs. When I neared the last row, I slowed and searched for my grandniece among the family members, all sitting with their mouths agape.

Norah stood and met my gaze.

Up close, I saw the woman's large eyes were an unusual hazel color and rimmed dark brown. They were Covey's eyes. My heart fluttered and I put my hand to my chest, feeling my breath come short. I discreetly wagged my fingers, indicating she should follow.

Norah nodded, bent to grab her purse, and slid out of the room behind me.

Hana was waiting outside the massive wooden doors, pacing nervously. "Are you all right, Miss Eliza?"

I kept walking toward the elevator. "Perfectly fine."

The elevator doors opened and the three of us entered. When they closed again, Hana spoke. "The doctors were firm you are not to get overexcited."

"Those idiot doctors, what do they know? For the past three months I've stayed in the city, against my will, and subjected myself to every test known to man. Only to be told to not get overexcited."

Hana followed closely, keeping her voice low. "You had a heart attack."

"Do not use those words," I whispered sharply, glancing at Norah. "It was not a heart attack. If Arthur were to get hold of that idea . . ." I waved my hand in dismissal. "The doctors said it was a warning. A mild hiccup. Nothing a lean diet and a quiet life can't fix. I intend to slow down."

"You've been saying that for years," Hana said flatly. She met my eyes. "You never do."

I laughed at the truth of that. I had worked tirelessly for decades, transforming my husband's sleepy company into the conglomerate it was today. I did not have the personality to sit back and rest when there was work to be done. Truth be told, life never granted me that luxury.

"I will," I replied.

"I've heard that before."

"Why do you think I've had all the meetings with my lawyers these past weeks? Bobby Lee is painting a picture of what retirement might look like. No agenda, no schedule. Free to wander the fields of Mayfield." I felt a moment's exhilaration at the prospect. "Perhaps, Hana, you were correct. Each day *is* a gift. And I intend to live each one fully. With purpose." A smile played at my lips. "But not yet. And certainly not today. Now I must scoot, before the hordes of well-wishers descend on me."

The doors slid open to the ground floor, and I was pleased to see my car idling out front. I spoke quickly as we walked. "Now, I am making my escape and heading home to Mayfield."

Hana looked shocked. "B-but you were supposed to leave after the luncheon. They will be disappointed you're not there."

"They will survive. We gave them plenty to talk about. Most importantly, I mustn't meet Arthur. He'll make a fuss, be sure of that.

I have work to do before I talk with him again." I turned to Norah. "My dear, have you ever been to Mayfield?"

"No. But I've heard stories of it."

"Would you like to come with me?"

"Me? To Mayfield?"

"Yes dear."

Norah thought for a moment. "I want to see Mayfield," she began cautiously. "But I admit I have reservations. . . ."

"What are they?"

"My grandmother was born and raised there, but she left broken-hearted and never wanted to return. My great-grandfather Wilton was the manager of the plantation for most of his life. But in fact, he was among the first generation of freemen in the family. My African ancestors were enslaved there. So, while going to Mayfield is important for me to learn my family history—" she took a breath "—it's also difficult." Norah lifted her chin and looked directly into my eyes. "But this is why I came to Charleston. To meet you, and to learn about my family history. So yes. I would like to come with you to Mayfield."

Not for the first time I felt a wave of shame of my and my family's part in the Wilton family history. "I'm so very glad you will, my dear."

"Grandma Eliza!" A voice rang from the house.

Looking over my shoulder I saw Savannah rushing toward us, clutching her purse, her red hair flying. Her blue eyes shone brightly.

"I'm coming with you."

"You're what?" I asked, stunned.

"I'm going to Mayfield. That's where you're going, right?" She grinned. "Escaping."

I let out a short laugh. Clever girl. "And if I were?"

"I want to come with you. Like you asked. I don't care what my daddy said. Please?"

A thousand questions formed in my mind, but time was of the essence. We had to leave before people came out.

"Yes, all right. Hop in the car. Hurry now!" I slid into the sedan after the girls, fastened my seat belt, then took a deep breath as the big car drove out of the driveway onto East Bay Street. We'd escaped. Arthur would be furious. I chuckled. That was a bonus. I was returning to Mayfield.

I turned to eye the two young women sitting behind me in the backseat. My granddaughter and my grandniece. Two branches of the Rivers family.

"My darling girls. I have so many stories—a lifetime of them—to share with you."

Chapter Three

⊰≡⊱

THE ACE BASIN is the watershed of the Ashepoo-Combahee-Edisto (ACE) rivers. This vast and ecologically significant area is located across four counties in southeastern South Carolina. It is comprised of pine uplands, hardwood forests, freshwater swamps, former rice impoundments, salt marshes, and estuarine tidal creeks that converge into St. Helena Sound.

1988

I always believed the essence of a house was captured from the moment one crossed the property entrance. The choice of gate, driveway, trees, plants, flowers, the sunlight, the shade—all were as intrinsic to a house's presence as the architecture.

The large black car rolled through the discreet entrance then slowly made its way down a long gravel road that wound under an allée of majestic, centuries-old live oaks dripping long tails of gray Spanish moss.

"There," I said with excitement as they caught glimpses of a white structure through the dappled shade. "Mayfield." The house grew larger until the space opened up to a sunlit grand entry.

"It's like I imagined it," Norah said in a soft voice.

Savannah lowered the window and put her head out, looking up at the trees like a pup.

Mayfield was magnificent in its stature and architectural detail. Two symmetrical buildings flanked the main wooden house like the wings of swan about to take flight. My heart lifted at the sight. I thought it the most beautiful plantation on the Combahee River.

"Look there," I said, pointing with some excitement to a redbrick wall to the right of the house. "That is my camellia and rose garden. Umberto Innocenti designed it." I didn't mean to sound pretentious. I was simply stating the fact. Then more to myself, "I really must check my roses."

I gazed at the grounds, assessing, hungrily devouring details. The grass appeared lush, the shrubs neatly trimmed, the live oaks mulched. The camellias were past bloom, but the roses were showy. The property had been well managed in my absence, I noted.

The driver circled around a fountain then parked at the front of the imposing white house. I couldn't wait and pushed open my door.

I stood with my hands on my hips and took a deep breath of the country air. It seemed to me to be softer here, more sweet smelling. Exhaling, feeling terra firma under my feet again, I turned to the women staring at the house.

"Girls, welcome to Mayfield. The original house was burned by Sherman, like so many others. My father rebuilt it in 1895 when he married my mother. He needed a home, and she had the family money to build it." I paused and smiled to myself. This was a point my mother had made to my father at every opportunity.

"Daddy built the center house, which is where I grew up. It seemed plenty big to me as a child. Mama insisted on a big kitchen," I added as memories flittered back. I saw in my mind the old kitchen dominated by the brick fireplace with an enormous wood-burning oven, the long farm sinks, and copper pots and pans. Another small building out back was used for cold storage. I was often sent scurrying to one or the other to fetch something for Clementine or Mother.

"When I married James, the house had been neglected for a long while. We didn't have the money for repairs, and it needed so much work. James loved to build and renovate. He had lots of opinions." I smiled again, remembering the arguments we'd had over each detail. "We added the two additions on either side of the house. Pretty, aren't they? And like my mother, I redid the kitchen and bathrooms with modern electric appliances and indoor plumbing. That was about 1930."

"Wait," said Savannah, her eyes wide. "You didn't have electricity or indoor plumbing until 1930?"

I shook my head. "After the turn of the century, we were struck hard with hurricanes and the boll weevil. That made for difficult times in Beaufort County. Though, to be honest, we children never really felt poor. Life was good. And we didn't know what life with indoor plumbing and electricity was like." I grinned and added, "But I can tell you, we were pretty excited when we got our first self-flush toilet inside the house. Going to the outhouse I was always afraid of snakes, so indoor plumbing was high cotton. Baths were held every Saturday, and let me tell you it was a major event. The water had to be heated in a big boiler pot on our stove then carried upstairs by hand. We had to share the water, of course, and we kids always fought over who got to go in first. Being the girl, I often won that battle."

Savannah's mouth slipped open.

I was glad to see it and know my granddaughter was hearing the real family story other than the facts recorded on ledgers. How had I never found the time to talk to my granddaughters of the past like this? I resolved to do better.

"Let's go inside." I grasped the black iron railing and began walking up the stone steps to the front door, feeling breathless by the time I reached the top. The door swung open and a woman with blazing dark eyes and a brightly colored head wrap rushed out to greet us.

"You came home, Miss Eliza! This house was pining for you."

"Mariama!"

In her sixties, Mariama had the vitality of youth. She loomed a vision of beauty in a denim skirt and a crisp scarlet blouse. Her wide smile outshone her sparkling eyes. We reached out to grasp hands and held tightly. Mariama was the grandniece of Clementine, our beloved housekeeper when I was young. I'd known Mariama since she was a baby and watched her grow to become a fiery young woman, mother, and now grandmother. Like her great-aunt, Mariama was a renowned cook and owned a popular Gullah restaurant in Beaufort. Over the many years, Mariama had catered my parties and family gatherings and become a trusted confidante.

"Seeing you here is both a surprise and a delight. How did you know I was coming home?"

"Hana called, so I scooted over to see you. And I brought food from the restaurant. We can have gumbo for lunch."

"I can't even tell you how good it is to be back," I said. "I missed you. Honestly, I couldn't bear to stay in the city another day. There was always one more appointment, one more meeting, one more thing needing doing. But I'm home, at last."

Mariama's gaze moved from me to Savannah, prompting another burst of joy. "And welcome back to you, dear girl! It's been way too long. Lord, look how you've grown. You're a young woman now."

Savannah stepped into Mariama's outstretched arms and the two embraced.

Then Mariama's gaze moved to Norah. Curiosity flickered in her brown eyes.

"Mariama," I said, "I'd like you to meet Norah Wilton Davis. Covey's granddaughter."

Mariama's eyebrows raised, and, in a rush, she stepped forward to wrap her arms around Norah's slender frame. Norah stood with her arms at her side, eyes wide.

"Child, you are a welcome sight!" Mariama exclaimed. "So, you're kin of Wilton and Covey. God rest their souls." Mariama stepped back, her hands still grasping Norah's shoulders, letting her gaze sweep over the woman, catching details. Satisfied, she dropped her hands, but not her smile. "Norah, you said your name is?"

Norah collected herself and her smile was genuine. "Yes."

"How old are you?"

"Forty."

"Married?"

"No."

Mariama made a face. "As pretty as you are?"

"I didn't say I wasn't asked."

Mariama's grin widened with approval. "Well, what are we stand-ing out here for? Lettin' the mosquitoes in. Come in, come in." Mariama moved aside and waved her arm.

I stepped into the center hall and exhaled long and slow, feeling every neuron being reassembled into its rightful place. How many times had I crossed this threshold in my many years? Each time the sensation was the same. Nothing felt as good as home.

The elegant living room was to the right and the large dining room to the left, looking the same as when I'd left them. "Let me show you around," I said to Norah.

"I'll meet you in the dining room with lunch," said Mariama. "I need to check on my gumbo."

The front rooms of Mayfield were formal with many family antiques, paintings and portraits, and rugs. But here and there I'd selected armchairs for comfort. Nothing was harder to sit on than horsehair cushions.

I led the way down the main hall and stopped at double doors that offered a sweeping view of the vast, fallow rice fields in back. "Those rice fields built this house," I said, knowing full well it was an understatement. We moved on to the east wing of the house, passing the gun room to a paneled family room with large windows, two fireplaces, and several leather sofas and chairs.

We returned to the main hall, and I led them to the dining room. One footstep into the room was akin to stepping back in time. A magnificent mural covered the walls of the dining room that de-picted dozens of scenes from Mayfield's history.

Norah gasped when she saw it. She walked slowly around the room studying all the scenes with soft exclamations of wonder. "These are incredible. When was the mural done?"

"Long before I was born," said Savanah with pride and a hint of proprietorship.

Memories gathered as I scanned the scenes of the mural painted across three walls. "Savannah's right. It was the 1960s," I began. "James had died, and I was feeling my own mortality." I sighed, remembering that low point in my life, how I'd felt a pressing need to share personal stories about Mayfield. To somehow document my memories. "Arthur lived in Charleston at the time and had little interest in Mayfield. He rarely visited and made it clear he wasn't interested in the family stories. The names of the Rivers family, mine included, have been duly recorded . . . but what about their lives? Their stories? I had no one to tell them to who cared to listen."

I glanced at Savannah, whose expression reflected some hurt. "I'm sorry, but it's true. Though," I added in an upbeat tone, "you're changing that by being here now. Of course, the house is on the historic registry." I looked at the mural. "But the real stories, those oral histories that go from one generation to another . . . told at dinner tables. From mother to daughter while cooking, or when taking long walks." I smiled at Savannah and Norah. "At a grandparent's knee."

"These stories are important," said Norah. "I want to know what inspired every scene."

"Me too," said Savannah.

I walked across the room and pointed to a scene. "This one shows the construction of the rice fields in the 1700s," I began. "I may be old, but that was before even my time."

I moved on to one portraying a young girl riding a horse, hair flowing behind her like a flag. "This one depicts a very important horse race. That's Capitano, our prize Marsh Tacky stallion. What a fine boy he was. And that young girl riding him—" I laughed lightly

"—is me." My gaze traveled to another scene of a hayloft and a young girl and a blond-haired boy holding hands. My smile fell as I felt a stab in the heart that was too fresh for reason.

"There are so many stories," I said and turned from the wall. I stopped and rested my hand on the back of a chair, feeling light-headed. I swallowed hard and tried again to speak. "I feel a sudden urge to tell the family history, to pass them on before, well . . ." I paused for a breath, not wanting to appear maudlin. "Before I'm gone. Or . . . I don't remember them anymore. I don't want the family stories to die with me." I looked up and smiled brightly, trying to lighten the mood.

"I'd like to hear them all," said Norah.

Savannah nodded in agreement.

"It will take all day. Days, perhaps." I looked at the young women, concerned that their attention spans would endure that long.

"Grandma," said Savannah, her voice urgent. "This morning, at breakfast, you asked me to come to Mayfield. You said you wanted to show me what was important to you here. And then I saw you at the shareholders meeting. . . . What you said, how you took over." She laughed shortly. "Grandma, you rock. I was so proud of you, and I knew . . ." She paused. "I want to get to know *you* better."

"Thank you, Savannah. Hearing that means the world to me. I wish I'd spent more time with you when you were growing up. It seemed I was always filling my days with work. But now I intend to retire. That will give me time . . ." I shook my head. "Oh, that precious, fleeting commodity. Let me just say that I hope I'll have the chance to get to know *you* better."

Norah said, "That's why we're here, isn't it?"

I looked at the woman before me and felt again the connection to Covey. "Indeed, it is. It's a start. Perhaps it isn't a coincidence that you two girls are here with me now. Look at you. I see you both and realize I'm witnessing the next generation of Mayfield. Both of you carry the history within you. It's in your DNA. Maybe my stories and your being here will stir up that genetic memory a bit. I wonder what will happen then?" I extended my arm toward the chairs. "Let's try, shall we?"

We moved to sit at the long mahogany dining table. I sensed the presence of those who had passed gather around as though waiting to hear my telling of a tale in which they were all players.

"Where to begin. . . ." My gaze scanned the many scenes then settled on one of a strapping blond-haired man in a frock coat beside a dark-haired bride, their hands held under a curved floral awning. I walked to the scene and let my fingers trace the joined hands. "This is my mother and father. Rawlins and Sloane Rivers. I guess my story begins with them.

"Theirs was a great love story—and not. A comedy and a tragedy. I've learned that life is really a combination of both. As a child, I was often caught in the crossfire between them. Finding humor in a harsh situation, and being able to laugh about it later, was my way to survive. You could say my childhood prepared me for the difficult future I was to endure. By taking the long view, I was able to distance myself from tragedy.

"My father was an original good ol' boy—boisterous with a hearty laugh and always a story to tell. Oh, he could spin a yarn. Daddy loved Mayfield over all things. It was his north star. In second place was Mama, or maybe it was a running tie between her and his horses. The horses were easier to manage.

"When they met, Rawlins's daddy had already passed and Rawlins was running Mayfield, though barely scraping by. Being good-looking and a landowner, his only choice was to marry money. My mother's family was relatively new to Charleston. They had made a fortune in trade and trains, but no amount of money would open the doors to the city's closed society. Pedigree alone was the key. So, Sloane Bissette set her sights on a husband from a founding family that would grant her entry. To be fair, Mama wasn't just another pretty face. She was educated. She had studied at Converse College, though she never graduated. In her junior year, a friend introduced her to Rawlins Heyward Rivers. My father declared that he fell head over heels in love with her at first sight. When he invited her to the St. Cecilia Ball, she accepted and that was that. They were married a year later. My father's dream was to restore Mayfield to her former glory. The house had fallen into disrepair after the Civil War and subsequent years of neglect. Sloane's parents generously provided the funds as a wedding gift. Rawlins made certain the house had the same grand architecture as the original built on this knoll in the mid-1700s. Not long after the new construction was finished, my eldest brother, Heyward, was born. Mama had proved her worth by financing the restoration of the house and giving my father his heir."

"Heyward Rivers. That was my grandfather?" Norah asked.

"Yes," I replied, searching for any sign of my older brother in Norah's features. She had a pleasing face with Covey's unusual hazel eyes. I didn't remember Norah's father, but the girl's high, chiseled cheekbones had to come from my brother.

"Heyward was, quite simply, the absolute best son and brother. A finer man was never born. I won't say he was perfect. What man is?" I chuckled softly. "Of course, he lost his temper from time to time, and I'm sure I gave him cause, but Heyward was genuinely kind, not just to me, but to everyone. A natural athlete too. There wasn't anything he couldn't do—ride a horse, climb a tree, fish, shoot. I tried to keep up with him and he knew it, but rather than tease me, he'd encourage me, saying, 'You can do it, Lizzie.'" I felt a gentle twinge in my heart at the memory. "That was his nickname for me. He liked to give nicknames. Heyward gave our younger brother the nickname Les. True, it was the obvious abbreviation for Lesesne. But he claimed it also fit because he was *less than Heyward*."

"Isn't that a bit mean-spirited?" Savanah asked.

"Perhaps. But it was true," I said. "His full name is French Huguenot and is pronounced 'Le Zane.'"

"That's an unusual name," Norah said.

"Lesesne is an old family name," Savannah said blithely, as though Norah should understand how common that practice was in the South.

"He was born two years after me and was a sickly child. Mama doted on him."

"I've never heard anyone talk about Great-Uncle Lesesne," Savannah said. "Was he like, the black sheep of the family or something?"

I shook my head. "No," I replied quickly. There were stories about Lesesne that were best left untold. "I daresay *I* was my mother's biggest disappointment as a child."

"Really? Why?" asked Savannah, leaning forward on the table. These personal stories were clearly more appealing to her than the historical ones.

How to make a young girl of this modern era understand the constraints on women at the turn of the century? "To be fair, my mother had the normal expectations for her daughter at that time. She wanted me to be trained in domestic arts, proper dress and behavior, modesty, and social etiquette. I didn't want any part of that. Today you'd call me a tomboy. But at the turn of the century, I was an enigma. At the very least, I was not, shall we say, feminine."

I sighed. "Back then, I was the opposite of my mother. Mama was a lady who loved poetry, her roses, and entertaining society. She had a curvaceous body that filled out a dress. I was, as my brothers often told me, as flat as an ironing board." I smiled devilishly. "Though I confess I was satisfied with that appearance, back when I was a girl who wished she'd been born a boy."

"Were you always a trailblazer?" Norah asked.

"Hardly," I said with a short laugh. "I just did what had to be done."

"Then what were you like?" asked Savannah.

"As a child?" I considered her question and searched my memory for the headstrong girl I once was. "In truth, I was more like the ancestor I was named for, Eliza Pinckney. I'm proud to bear her name. Even in the colonial period, she was a little powerhouse. And capable. While her father was called away to Antigua, she ran his three plantations and brought indigo's success to South Carolina." I looked at Savannah. "And she was but your age, Savannah."

Savannah's mouth slipped open then curved into a wry smile. "Cool."

"She was my role model. I suppose because I was small and dark haired, like her. But also because I loved botany and farming. And horses. And my dream always was to manage Mayfield. But unlike Eliza Pinckney, I had a father who believed firmly in primogeniture and eschewed the idea of his daughter running his plantation, no matter how qualified." I heard the bitterness in my voice.

I paused to sip my tea, setting my glass onto the table with care. "Still, I have to say, my early years were happy ones in the Rivers family. *All happy families are alike, but every unhappy family is unhappy in its own way.* Tolstoy was right about that. For the Rivers family, the tragedies came later."

I had to look away from Norah's face, from the sympathy I saw etched there. I wasn't looking for pity. It was too late for that, and unnecessary. I was simply telling a story. How the listener judged it was not something I could modify.

My gaze sought another mural scene and settled on one depicting the hollow of a large tree. From its dark center, one could see three children peeking out—myself, Covey, and Tripp.

I closed my eyes, and suddenly the intense dream of the night before burst forth again. In my mind I was back in the tree hollow, enveloped in a humid, heavy cocoon, sleeping on a cushion of moss. I could smell again the pungent earth, hear someone calling my name.

I opened my eyes and gasped, seeing Covey looking at me, concern etched in her hazel eyes. My eyelashes fluttered and as my senses returned, I realized it was of course Norah's face before me. My hand went to my temple, and I took a calming breath. I was too old to believe in coincidences. *God works in mysterious ways,* I thought. I searched the young woman's face and wondered, *Why is Norah here at this important moment in time?*

Lowering my hand, I thought I mustn't get ahead of myself. I was here to tell a story of my family. My life. To share the memories, good and bad. Looking into the faces of the two women, I realized that this could be my last chance to do so.

"I warn you, I can't help but shade the story with my own perceptions," I said. "I'm sure if they heard my telling of it, Mama and Daddy would shake their heads and tell you I had it all wrong. My brothers would agree. Especially Lesesne, who always saw the world through his own peculiar lens."

"This is your story," said Norah. "Your family, your life. As you see it."

"Very well, then. I suppose my first true memory of my childhood is the day I met my dearest friend, Covey." I looked at Norah. "Your grandmother."

Part Two

HALCYON DAYS

I saw in Louisiana a live-oak growing,
All alone stood it, and the moss hung down from the branches;
Without any companion it grew there, uttering joyous leaves of
dark green,
And its look, rude, unbending, lusty, made me think of myself;
But I wonder'd how it could utter joyous leaves, standing alone
there, without its friend, its lover near, for I knew I could not.

—WALT WHITMAN, "SOUTHERN LIVE OAK"

Chapter Four

⟨◆⟩

TREE HOLLOWS are cavities formed in the trunk or branches of a live or dead tree. Such hollows are usually more characteristic of older, mature to over-mature trees but may form in earlier-growth stages depending on tree species. They are a natural feature that can be important for wildlife.

1908

You in there, girl?"

I felt someone grip my shoulder and shake me hard. I didn't want to awaken and moaned softly, feeling groggy. My eyelids felt heavy and gritty when I tried to open them. "Go away."

"I said, wake up!" The voice was more insistent. "We're both gonna get in a mess of trouble unless you come outta there. So come out, hear? If'n you don't come out, I'll get my daddy to come get you out."

There was a tone in the girl's voice that bordered on a fight. I was too tired to muster anger, so I forced open my eyes. The world was dimly lit, and I was lying on the ground, curled up against the chill. I looked to be in some kind of nest.

"Where am I?" I sat up so fast my head started spinning.

"You're inside a hollow," the girl called back. "Don't you know that? I ain't goin' in there. Ain't you scared of spiders and snakes? Come on out."

"I'm not scared." I hated to be called scared. My brothers used that against me all the time, me being a girl. I idly scratched an itch on my arm that had scabbed over and looking down saw several angry red scratches from my elbow to wrist. As I scanned the dark wooden crevices surrounding me, memories of the night before flashed through my mind. I was running in the woods. I was lost. It was raining. I remembered seeing the tree, and the hollow. I'd run into it for protection.

I'm inside the tree. The thought filled me with wonder. Now I could make out the sharp, crooked ridges of the inner belly of the great tree rising high up into the darkness. My hands felt the soft layer of moss that had been my bed. To my relief, there weren't any snakes and spiders I could see.

"You coming?"

"All right."

"You sure taking your sweet time."

She seemed peeved, so I shifted to all fours and, one hand after another, quickly crawled out from the darkness into the brilliant light of day. I scrunched up my face and shielded my eyes with my hand, realizing I must've slept in the tree all night.

I swiped away the twisted hairs from my face. *Rat's nest*, Mama called my hair. I was outdoors in the broad daylight still in my nightgown, and worse, it was muddy and ripped at the hem. Mama was going to scold when she saw that.

"You're Miss Eliza Rivers, ain't you?"

"Uh-huh," I said and rubbed my eyes as I studied the girl kneeling on the earth beside me. She was a Negro girl and looked to be about the same age as me. Her black hair was tightly braided past her shoulders. And her eyes were a wonder. Orbs of green, gold, and gray were locked inside a dark perimeter, drawing you in. It was like looking into the woods on a sunny day.

"Your daddy and mama are lookin' for you," she said with a scold. "My daddy told me to go and search you out. Shoot, most of Beaufort County is out lookin' for you. You been missing since last night." Her eyes sparked with import. "They even checkin' the rivers."

I heard this with both a thrill that I was the subject of so much interest, and fear of the whupping I'd get when I got home. "I got lost."

"I reckon," she said, looking me over. Then shaking her head, she said with sympathy, "You got scratches all up and down your arms. They hurt?"

I shook my head.

"Well, come on, then," she said, rising to her feet. "My house is just around the bend, over by the river."

I balked. "I got to go to *my* house."

"It's too far. Wilton ought to be by soon. He'll know how best to let your folks know you're okay."

"You know Wilton?" I was surprised she knew the manager of the plantation.

The girl made a face and waved her hand. "'Course I do. He's my daddy."

Daddy? I scratched my head. I didn't know Wilton had a child. He didn't have a wife. "You call your daddy 'Wilton'?"

"That's what everyone calls him."

"How come I never met you before?"

The girl merely shrugged. "How come I never met *you* before?" With that, she turned on her heel.

I thought it odd that she called her daddy by his given name, but I didn't have time to think about it because the girl was already walking off. I didn't want to be lost again, so I scrambled to my feet, brushed myself off, and ran after her. We walked single file along a worn path toward the river. The grass was still damp from the rain and was soaking the hem of my nightgown, but the sun shone brightly in a brilliant, cloudless sky. Ahead of me the girl swung her arms and took long, confident strides with skinny legs. Her feet were wrapped in brown lace-up boots and her yellow dress swirled around her knees. I was having a hard time keeping up being barefoot, and my nightgown kept getting snagged in every branch and spur I passed. Frustrated, I hitched the trailing nightgown in my fists up over my knees and trotted quickly to catch up.

"Hey, I don't know your name," I shouted.

The girl turned her head and called back over her shoulder. "Covey. Like a flock of birds. My daddy told me he gave me that name because that's what we are. A flock that sticks together. On account my mama died when I was a babe."

"That's real sad."

"Not really. I don't remember her none."

She spoke so matter-of-fact about it that I took her at her word.

"How old are you, anyway?" I asked.

"Eight. Near nine."

"Me too."

Covey's lips twitched. "You're pretty scrawny for eight."

I scowled. "You seem pretty bossy for a girl the same age."

Covey merely shrugged then turned and continued walking. I felt ready to explode but I wasn't about to argue with her now. I shook my head and skipped to catch up with her. We both walked on in silence.

I heard the river before I saw it. The water was rushing swiftly, high along the banks from the heavy rain. Dappled sunlight played with the current, creating sparks of light that revealed clouds of midges hovering over the water. Even though it was fall, everything was still lush green, from the grasses that climbed the banks to the scrubby shrubs and trees. Here and there I spied specks of gold in the leaves, hinting change was coming. Daddy always said that fall was his favorite season. I was never sure if it was because of the colors or because it was the beginning of hunting season. We turned the bend, and I spotted a tidy white cottage sitting prettily on the rise.

"Wait here," Covey told me.

I obliged. She walked toward the house where the grass was trimmed low, then climbed the few wooden steps to the front porch. Moving closer, I saw a pair of men's boots beside the front door that I figured belonged to Wilton. I watched as she passed the door and headed straight for a small wooden table nestled between two ladderback chairs. She pulled something out of a tin box. Covey didn't talk as she came back to the front yard. She headed straight for what looked to me like the frame of a teepee set on a bed of gravel. Three tree limbs were joined together at the top over a platform with some kind of firepit.

I drew closer and watched as Covey struck the match. My mouth slipped open in awe. Mama didn't even let me touch matches. Covey seemed right handy with them. As soon as the match caught flame she bent to light the dried grass and leaves under the kindle wood. I was mightily impressed when the fire sparked.

"Now we gots to get some green," Covey said. "Let's try to find some cedar. That works best."

I didn't tell her I didn't know what cedar leaves looked like, but once again I followed Covey and gathered the flat, feathery leaves she did from the nearby woods. We hurried back to add it to the fire. The wood was burning real good now. Every time we tossed more green leaves onto the fire it devoured them like it was a hungry beast, then belched out plumes of smoke high into the sky. I laughed at the sight.

"There," Covey said, looking at the smoking fire with satisfaction.

"Why'd you do that?"

Covey peered at me like I was a fool. "It's a smoke signal. Wilton made it so if I ever needed him in a hurry, he'd see it and come running. I reckon this is just such a time." She wiped the soot from her hands on her apron. "All we got to do now is wait."

"You mean, he'll come if he sees the smoke?"

"Sure will. Just look and see how high the smoke is going. Everyone who's searching for you will see it."

I craned my neck back and saw the dark smoke billowing high up over the tips of the tallest longleaf pines. For sure Daddy ought to see that!

"You're covered with dirt," Covey said, giving me a good once-over.

Embarrassed, I scowled. "So?"

"So, do you know how to swim?"

"'Course I do," I answered, lifting my chin. "My brother Heyward taught me. He's a good swimmer. Fact, he's good at everything."

She didn't look like she believed me. "Not many girls know how to swim. Boys neither."

"*You're* a girl," I fired back. "Do you know how?"

"I sure do. Wilton said living near the river, and me being alone a lot, I needed to know how to swim so I didn't drown. See, his daddy drowned in the river and Wilton said that wasn't ever going to happen to him, so he took it upon himself to learn and he teached me."

There was truth in what she said. "My mama doesn't know how to swim," I conceded. "She says a lady doesn't never go near the water, except to observe its beauty." I felt obliged to share that in defense of my mother's lacking. Then added, "Mama doesn't know that I know how to swim, neither. She thinks only my brothers go to the river. She'd be mad as a hornet if she found out I went with them. Doesn't seem fair only the boys get all the fun. Still, she'd say it wasn't ladylike."

Covey laughed at that. "I don't think it's ladylike to drown, neither."

Her laughter sounded sweet to my ears. I was glad that she took my side on matters of being a lady.

"I'm all sweaty from searching for you all morning. And you're all covered with mud. I reckon if we jump in the river, that's the quickest way to get cleaned off. You want to?"

"Sure." I followed Covey down the slope of sparse grass spotted with patches of blue mist wildflowers along the bank. She took off down the long, rickety dock that reached far out over the river. The old wood was warm under my feet, and we were careful to avoid the rotted patches. I walked with my arms out over bits so narrow I feared I'd fall into the river.

At the dock's edge I carefully peered over. Below I saw the river racing furiously, like some ferocious beast. The water wasn't clear like in the shallows that me and Heyward swam in. Here, the river was deep and roiling, the color of Mama's tea. I couldn't even see the bottom.

"You sure there aren't any gators down in there?"

Covey drew near and casually looked down into the river. "Nah. Wilton says they like it best in the rice fields where there's lots of grass to hide in and ducks to eat. They don't come way down here. I never seen even one, not ever. Leastways not here by our dock. But I always look, just in case." She studied the water for a while with her hands on her hips. She straightened and shook her head. "Nope, nothing there."

I was skeptical. I'd heard tales of gators as big as a boat in these waters. "Daddy lost a hunting dog to a gator once. That's one of his most popular stories to tell." I looked doubtfully at the murky water. "You sure?"

"Cross my heart. I go swimming here most every day." She bent to take off her boots then looked up at me staring back at her, unmoving. "You coming or not?"

She saw I hadn't moved and began unbuttoning the row of buttons on the front of her dress. "You scared?"

That did it. I slipped the nightgown over my head and dropped it on the dock. The river breeze cooled the sweat on my bare chest. When Covey pulled off her dress, we looked at each other standing on the dock in our cotton drawers and laughed.

Covey held out her hand. "Hold on to my hand and we'll jump in together."

Covey's hand was near the same size as mine, but when I grabbed it, I felt the strength of it as she tightened her grip around my fingers.

"Ready?" Covey asked in a high voice.

I swallowed hard, then nodded. "Ready."

Holding hands, we took off running toward the end of the dock. With a squeal and a single leap, we were airborne. In that instant I felt I was flying! Then my feet hit the water. Cold. My breath whooshed out in a flurry of bubbles. I'd never gone under so deep before. It was strange the way my hair floated out from my head and my legs flailed in the murky water. As the river swallowed me up, I lost my grip on Covey's hand. I kicked hard upward, gasping when my head broke the surface. The sun was on my face and blinking, I saw a blue sky.

"Eliza!"

I turned toward the voice. With a start, I realized I was being carried in the current, farther away from Covey and the dock. On instinct I began dog-paddling toward the dock in the way my brother had taught me.

"Eliza, swim harder!" Covey was clinging to the ladder on the dock and waving to me to come.

The water was so cold my chest felt tight, and my breath came in choked gasps. My arms thrashed wildly as the current pushed me farther from Covey. Fear gave me strength. Stretching my arms out like I'd seen Heyward do, I kicked and dug against the current, gaining inch by inch. Water splashed my face and down my throat. I coughed and spat out the muddy taste. I couldn't catch my breath. Panic struck. My legs felt numb, and the river pushed me back as easily as if I was driftwood.

"Covey!" I croaked.

"Grab my hand!" Covey reached out toward me.

I saw her hand as a lifeline. Fixing it in my sight and mustering my strength once again, I paddled with everything I had, kicking furiously against the river's icy hold. When I drew close, Covey lunged for my hand. I felt her fingers tighten around mine, then with a firm tug, I was at the ladder. I grabbed the wood, slimy with algae, and hung on for dear life.

Inches from my own face, Covey was panting like me, eyes wide. I reckon we both knew, without saying words, that we'd been in trouble.

"Last night's rain made the current strong," she said, wiping water from her eyes.

I could see Covey was shaken. But oddly, though I'd been scared a moment ago, I now felt elated. Even triumphant. I wasn't fool enough to lose my grip of the ladder, but I let my legs float out behind me. The water flowed and swirled around them, and I felt a heady sensation. I laughed out loud.

"Girl? What's so funny?"

"I never swam in water so deep before. My brother only lets me paddle around in the shallows. But I did it!" I added, grinning with pride. "Let's do it again!"

"Girl, you crazy?" Covey snorted, shaking her head. "Let's go up."

Reluctantly I climbed up the ladder behind her. We stretched out on the dock, arms at our sides and faces to the sun. The wood was warm, and the September sun set to drying our skin.

"The water was too strong," Covey said on a ragged sigh. "I shouldn't have said to go in."

"I got scared," I confessed.

"You got the mud off, at least," Covey replied with a laugh.

I guffawed and raised my arms, seeing that indeed she was right. The flesh of my arms showed red scratches, but they didn't look as angry. Suddenly, my stomach let out a loud growl. Embarrassed, I turned my head to look at Covey. We both began laughing again.

"Come on. I'll fix something to eat."

We slipped our garments back on and made our way barefoot to the cottage. I think we both felt something had shifted between us. Having confronted death together, we were no longer strangers. It was like we'd been friends for a long time.

"Why are your door and window frames painted blue?" I asked as we approached the front door. I'd never seen such a bright blue painted on a house before.

"That's to keep the haints away."

"You mean ghosts?"

"Sure. Ghosts, haints, boo hags. Everyone knows that."

I didn't.

The inside of the cottage was as tidy as a pin. The living room wasn't near as big as Mayfield's, but it didn't feel small. An old blue sofa sat under the front windows with a lively colored patchwork quilt draped over the back. Two mismatched wood chairs and a coffee table were in front of it. On the other side of the room a multicolored rag rug lay underneath a round table with four ladderback chairs, each with a cherry-red cushion. The only other furniture was a glass-paned gun case. Beside it was a tall sweetgrass basket that held carved walking sticks, and a hat rack from which hung several straw hats. The walls were void of any pictures.

Covey returned carrying two pottery plates. "Come eat."

My tummy rumbled again, so I hurried to the table. Covey set a plate before me. On it was a thick piece of white bread smothered with honey. I took a bite and almost groaned out loud, it tasted so good.

"I don't think I've ever ate anything as good as this."

"That's Wilton's honey from his bees. He's real good to them and he says they're real good to us right back." She took a big bite and, smiling, said, "I'm mighty hungry too. I didn't get to eat this morning 'cause I was out looking for you."

"Sorry."

"Reckon that's why it tastes so good. Wilton says food always tastes better when you're hungry."

I took another big bite. I thought back and realized I hadn't eaten since supper the night before. It was meager fare. Clementine was flustered getting the fancy dinner ready for Mama's guests. Pots were simmering and clanging on the big iron stove, making the kitchen hot and sweaty. Heyward and Lesesne grabbed most of the meat leftovers before I even got my plate.

Peeved, I left the table and crept into Mama's room. I always loved to watch her get all prettied up. I crouched in a corner like a mouse, mesmerized by the way she tilted her head and dabbed at her face at the mirror. My daddy stepped in, dressed for hunting. He went to kiss Mama's cheek, saying she was pretty enough she didn't need the war paint. He always said that to her, and Mama always slapped his shoulder and laughed. When Mama finished doing up her face and went downstairs to confer with Clementine, I sneaked over to the vanity table. All Mama's makeup lay before me in sweet little painted jars.

Looking in the mirror, my face was tanned after a summer in the sun, something Mama had told me was a disgrace. "No lady lets her skin get dark," she'd scolded. Hoping to mend that, I reached for her face powder first. It smelled sweet, and the small puff made of goose down tickled as I tapped my cheeks. The powder fell over my face as soft as snow. I swear, it did make my face appear lighter. Next, I reached for the pot of rouge. It looked like cherry jelly. I dabbed it on the way I'd seen Mama do it. Two red dots bloomed on my cheeks. I turned my head from left to right, admiring my reflection. Using my fingertip, I smoothed more of the sticky red stain on my lips. I giggled at the sight of me, thinking I looked like my doll.

"Wretched child!" Mama cried out from the doorway.

My heart froze in my chest. I dropped the rouge in a clatter and slunk from the vanity stool.

Mama rushed to her vanity. "You horrid, ugly girl. Look at what you did," she shouted, putting the pot of rouge inches from my face. I could see the center was gouged by my fingertips. "Do you know how expensive these are? Look at you. You look like a clown!" She was as riled as I'd ever seen her, and she wasn't done yet.

"And your hair." She tsked in disgust. "Your hair is like a rat's nest. I've told you over and over to brush your hair, but you won't. You're mean-spirited and stubborn, just like your father." Her face crinkled with disgust. "Get out of my sight. Go sleep in the barn with the rest of the animals."

All I wanted to do was be as beautiful as she was. I thought Mama would be pleased I was trying to be pretty. But now I knew I never would be. Shame bloomed in my chest, and I ran from her room straight to the bathroom down the hall that I shared with my brothers. I poured water from the pitcher into the bowl. Grabbing the soap, I scrubbed my face. The soap stung my eyes, and my cheeks burned as I heard my mother's words again in my head: *You horrid, ugly girl.*

I lowered the towel from my face and stared at my reflection in the mirror. My mouth was set in a firm line and my eyes blazed. If Mama said I was like an animal, then that was what I would be. I'd run away and live in the wild where I belonged. I'd show her.

Across the table, Covey was waiting for me to say something.

"Huh?"

"Eliza, you've been woolgathering. What you thinkin' about?"

My shoulders slumped. "I was thinking I had to go back home again."

"Don't you want to?"

"Sure, I guess. I mean, there's nowhere else for me to go. Unless . . . could I live here with you?"

"Live here?" Covey burst out with a short laugh. "Go on. You've got a big fancy house to live in. Why'd you want to live here?"

"My mama will be really mad at me this time. I'll get punished for sure."

"Aw, I'm sure she's just worried. You been gone since last night, after all."

As though on cue, from outdoors I heard the sound of hooves and a man's voice calling urgently, "Hey there!"

"That's Daddy!" I crammed the last bite of bread into my mouth and rushed from the house, Covey close at my heels.

Two horses trotted to the front porch, Wilton riding a dun, my daddy on his favorite bay. He no sooner reached the cottage when, spying me on the porch, Daddy tossed the reins, slid from the horse, and took the stairs in a single leap. Once on the porch he scooped me into his big arms and swung me around like a rag doll, holding me so tight I couldn't breathe. I clung to him, smelling the sweat on his neck, feeling the roughness of his denim jacket.

When Daddy set me back down on the porch, he crouched low so his face was inches from mine. His scruffy blond hair, which always looked unbrushed, fell over his forehead, and he was grinning ear to ear. But his blue eyes were brimming with tears.

"Lizzie, where have you been?" he asked, his voice raspy with emotion. He brought his arm up to swipe his eyes. "We've been looking for you all night. Folks are combing the rice fields and Mama . . ." He paused. "Well, she's collapsed in bed. We feared the worst."

"Am I in trouble?" I croaked out.

Daddy barked out a laugh. "Trouble? You're worried you're in trouble? Hell, we'll all just be singing God's praises you're alive. Where were you?" he asked again.

"I got lost," I blurted out. "I wandered too far, and it started to rain, and I found this tree, and hid in it till Covey found me." The words came tumbling out in a rush. Then, I burst into tears. Daddy brought his calloused hand to my head and pressed it to his shoulder.

"It's okay," he murmured.

Wilton walked up the stairs. "You done real good to light the signal," he said to Covey. "We spotted it and came straight here. Glad to know the system works."

Covey grinned with pride.

"How come your hair's all wet?" Daddy asked me.

I leaned back to look in his face. My tears dried up real quick as I brimmed with pride. "I jumped in the river!" I crowed.

His eyes widened. "You went in that river? It's wild from the rain. You could've drowned."

"But I didn't. I swam, just like Heyward taught me. We jumped in and I beat the current."

Wilton's smile slipped to a scowl as he turned to Covey. "Child, you know better than to swim in a river that's angry."

Covey looked to her feet. "Yes sir. Sorry, sir."

"Don't be mad at them," Daddy said, rising to his feet. He rolled his shoulders, releasing a night's strain. "I think they've been pretty darn grown-up to survive a night in the woods alone, light a signal fire, and swim in a raging river and live to tell the tale." He put his arm around my shoulder. "Let's go home, Lizzie."

He guided me down the porch stairs, but I balked and ran back up to Covey. I wrapped her in a hug and squeezed tight. "Thanks for finding me." I looked to Daddy and said, "Can I come back here to play with Covey?"

Daddy half smiled and put his hands on his hips. "So, you found yourself a friend. I'll wager your brothers will be relieved."

He was teasing me, but I needed to know. "Daddy," I pressed. "Can I?"

"Sure, we can arrange that. 'Course, we'll have to teach you the way back home," he added with a light laugh. "We can't have half the county hunting for you each time you go visiting your new friend." Then he looked over to Covey. She straightened under his gaze, but Daddy smiled warmly. "And you're welcome up at the house anytime. Thank you kindly for helping my girl."

Covey relaxed. Her eyes were bright.

Our gazes locked. As I stared into her mercurial hazel eyes, I felt a strange surge of emotion—like I was back in the river, deep and marshy green—rushing through me, brimming with promise.

Chapter Five

—◆—

JEWELWEED (*Impatiens capensis*), also known as touch-me-not, is found in the moist, shady woodland edges and stream banks of the ACE Basin. It is known to be a natural remedy for symptoms of poison ivy and oak, and stinging nettle.

1908

Mayfield loomed large in the distance, sitting on the hill. Its multiple redbrick chimneys rose high above the tree line. I was cradled in my father's arms, secure in the scents of his leather and sweat and the gentle rocking of the bay as we rode at an easy gait. Despite the warmth of his arms, however, I shivered, knowing what faced me inside those stately walls.

When we drew close, the back door sprang open and my brother came bolting out, calling my name. Heyward was tall for ten years old, and his long legs covered the distance in no time.

"Lizzie!" His voice mingled joy with worry, and hearing it, my heart filled with love for him. Heyward resembled my father with his blond hair and piercing blue eyes. His shoulders were already beginning to broaden.

He reached up to catch the reins our father tossed. "You okay?" His eyes searched my face.

I nodded, my throat dry.

Behind him, my younger brother, Lesesne, leaned against the house door, watching. Lesesne's hair was wispy, near white, and fell low over his forehead, shadowing his eyes. Scarlet fever ran through the family years ago, and the fever hit Lesesne hardest. He barely survived and grew up a sickly child. He was shorter than most boys his age. Though small, he had a way about him that made him seem older. I reckon it was his eyes. When he looked at you in a certain way, there was a coldness that set one ill at ease.

Daddy swung his leg around and slid off the horse. He was a big man, with shoulders like a mountain, but he moved as smooth and swift as any stallion. I felt his strong hands grip my waist, and with one swing, my feet hit the ground. Immediately Heyward's arms wrapped me in a bear hug.

"Let loose, Heyward," I cried. "I can't breathe!"

Heyward released his hold but kept his hands on my shoulders as he stared into my eyes. I was surprised to see his were as watery as a summer lake. I couldn't remember ever seeing my big brother cry except for the time Daddy had to put his horse down.

"If you run off like that again, I'll whup you," he said gruffly.

Though Heyward was only two years older than me he sometimes acted more like my father. In addition to teaching me how to swim, Heyward helped me muck the stalls in the mornings, took me riding, and taught me the trails and which critters and snakes to be wary of.

"I didn't run off," I said, pushing Heyward off. "I got lost."

"Same difference."

I didn't think it was at all the same, but I said nothing because Daddy's hand was on my shoulder, gently pushing me toward the house.

"Time to pay the piper," he said. "Your mama's waiting on you."

Lesesne smirked as I passed him into the house; we both knew what was coming. As I walked up the long flight of stairs, my legs felt as weightless as they did in the murky river. But I pushed on, following my father.

Upstairs, we each had our own room, including Mama and Daddy. We kids ran in and out of our three rooms, but we entered Mother's inner sanctum with trepidation. She often closed her door to us. When I asked Clementine why, she told me Mama was a fragile sort and needed her quiet time.

At the end of the hall, my mother's bedroom door was now closed. Daddy and I stood before the door and my heart took to hammering.

"Go on in," Daddy said in a low voice.

I gave my father a pleading look, but he opened the door and gave me a gentle nudge. The curtains were drawn, and the bedroom was as gray as dusk. I stepped forward, my eyes fixed on the four-poster bed. Mama was lying there, propped on pillows like the Queen of Sheba in the stories she read to us. Her long black curls fell over her shoulders and her arm covered her eyes like she was sleeping. When the floor creaked under my foot, Mama moved her arm from her face and her gaze captured mine. For a moment neither of us moved. Then, in a swoop, Mama was on her feet, rushing to my side to engulf me in her arms.

"Baby girl," she crooned, near hysterical, rocking me from side to side. "Sweet baby girl."

I closed my eyes, encircled by the smell of roses. My stiff bones relaxed, and I leaned into her softness. For a precious moment, I felt safe. Then, just as fast, the moment ended. Mama pulled back abruptly. Opening my eyes, I saw in her face the shift of emotions, as quick as flicking a switch. I braced for the onslaught.

"Where'd you run off to?" Mama demanded. "I've been worried sick. We all were. The whole town is out looking for you. Reverend Sykes is offering prayers. I don't know how I'm going to thank them." She put her hands to her cheeks and shook her head.

"I got lost," I mumbled. I'd lost count how many times I'd said those words, and each time they felt more and more feeble.

Mama's eyes flashed. "Lost? You're always running off somewhere like a wild thing, paying no mind to who might be worried. Selfish child. Did you think about how I'd feel?" Her hand slapped her chest. "I'm a wreck! I thought you were hurt. Or worse. I daren't even say the words."

"I'm sorry."

"Sorry!" she cried and shook her head with disgust. "You're always sorry. Do you know all my guests left? My weekend was ruined! And you're sorry." As her gaze raked over me, I felt my skin prickle. I knew what attack was coming next. "Look at you," she said, her tone laced with disdain. "You look like a ragamuffin. Your gown is torn and muddy. And your hair . . . I swear you're going to kill me with that hair."

I looked down. I had my mama's hair.

"Always in knots," she said. "It's a gift to have those curls but look at you. A rat's nest. Day after day, I beg you to brush it, to be ladylike. But you never do."

"No, Mama," I cried. I hated to see her upset. To be such a disappointment to her.

Mama turned her head to call out, "Clementine!"

Clementine, who had been hovering in the hallway, stepped into the room cautiously. "Yes'm?"

Mama fired off orders, waving her hand dismissively as though shooing me from her sight. "Take this child and give her a good bath. She's filthy. And wash. That. Hair." She grimaced. "See if you can do anything with it."

Daddy, who'd been standing nearby during the onslaught, suddenly stepped closer. "Sloane, you ought to give her the bath. After what she's been through."

"What *she's* been through? Don't you mean what *I've* been through?" Then, looking at me, she gave a parting shot. "I know you do this deliberately. Do you hate me to vex me so?"

I buried my face in Clementine's chest and shook my head as she wrapped her arm around my shoulders. She smelled of biscuits.

I could see Daddy's fists forming at his thighs. "You're talking crazy, now," he said. "Eliza didn't get lost to *vex* you. That child spent the night sheltering from the storm. *Alone.* We're lucky, damn lucky, she's alive. Do you think how scared *she* was? If you were any kind of a mother, you'd smother her with kisses, not scold her."

Mama rose up, facing him like a bantam rooster. "How dare you!"

Clementine swiftly led me from the room, closing the door after us. We all knew the shouting would continue for a long time and the best thing was a safe retreat. When I passed the boys, Heyward was looking out for me. He gave me a reassuring smile. Lesesne was lying on his bed with a pillow over his head, drowning out the sounds of Mama and Daddy's fighting.

Clementine hummed loudly as she ushered me into the washroom. "I got everything ready. The water's heated nice and warm. Go on, now. Climb in."

I sat in the big clawfoot tub, silent and slump shouldered, clasping my knees close to my chest as she poured cupful after cupful of steaming water over my head. My tears mingled with the cascading water. Clementine lathered up Castile soap and, with firm hands, began washing my hair, using her fingers like a comb to gently pull the soap through the strands.

"Child, don't you fret. There ain't no blame in being lost." Her voice came from her like a song. "We're all grateful you've been found, safe and sound. A biddey biddey like you could get hurt in the woods."

"I weren't afraid," I told her.

"Well, you should be. Lots of things to be afraid of out there." She shook her head.

"I've never been that far out before," I confessed. "I just ran and ran like the devil was chasin' me. I'll ask Heyward to teach me the way to and from Wilton's house."

"That's good."

I turned in the bath to face Clementine. She was kneeling beside the tub, her muscled arms resting on the porcelain. Steam rose up to frame her round face, tightening the curls that escaped from the bun at the nape of her neck.

"Clementine," I said with a hint of accusation. "Did you know Wilton has a little girl? Same age as me?"

Her face broke into a smile. "Why sure I did."

"Well," I sputtered, "why didn't you tell me?"

"Why would I tell you?"

I couldn't believe she was asking me that. "Because I would have a friend!"

Her face softened. "So, you and Covey are friends now?"

I nodded, thinking how Clementine knew the girl's name. I felt a tap on my shoulder and turned to allow Clementine to scrub my head. "She's the one who found me in the tree hollow." My words tumbled out as fast as the water flowing down my shoulders. I told her all about waking up confused in the tree hollow, meeting Covey, seeing Wilton's cottage for the first time, how I felt brave jumping in the river, the smoke signal, and finally how Daddy and Wilton came to fetch me.

"Now that's a story you're going to remember all your life, I reckon."

"I still can't figure why you didn't tell me about Covey."

"I knew you'd find each other when the time was right."

"Who takes care of her?"

Clementine chuckled low in her chest. "Covey takes care of herself. She as bright as a shiny penny. Wilton, he checks on her, of course. And I go to their house most every day on my way home. I make sure they have provisions and I bring dinner on days I have extra." She chuckled again. "Which is most days. Anyhow, they do just fine. Now tilt your head back."

She rinsed my hair with warm water that smelled of apple cider vinegar and herbs that would help take out the tangles.

"Clementine, what happened to Covey's mama?"

"That's a sad story. Her mama died back when Covey was just a little child. A fine woman, she was. Cheerful as a spring day." Clementine sighed heavily. "Covey lost her mama and a brother that day."

I blinked hard and tried to imagine what it would be like to lose

Heyward. My heart twisted in my chest at the thought. When I wondered about losing Lesesne, however, I thought I could live on. The vexing question was: How would I feel if I lost my mama? "How come Wilton never got married again?"

Clementine wrapped me in a towel and guided me from the tub. "Sometimes a man don't want to jump the broom twice. A woman neither. When you get older, you'll come to understand that sometimes what you need most is a good friend."

"You're Wilton's friend, aren't you?"

A smile spread across Clementine's face that made her look young somehow.

"Yes, I surely am. A good friend. To him and to Covey." She wrapped the towel tight around me then paused to look into my eyes. I felt the love clear to my bones. "You're my good friend too." Her expression shifted and once again she was no-nonsense. "And you listen, hear? You're a good girl. Brave and true. Don't you be doubtin' that." She cupped my face in her palms. "You're right pretty too. You're a child yet. You just got to grow into your beauty. You have good bones, nice teeth. And your eyes are like full moons. They lift one up just to gaze in them." She dropped her hands and continued drying my body. "Your hair is a bit wild and untamed, like you, but it's beautiful. You'll be glad for it one day."

I blushed at hearing such compliments from Clementine. Rare as hen's teeth.

Clementine raked my hair with a wide-toothed comb. The vinegar did its work, and I didn't yelp and complain as much.

"Let's you and me try to manage this better," Clementine said, studying my hair. "I sometimes braid Covey's hair. Maybe we could try braids on you, to hold your hair when you're outdoors. I think it'll look real nice. And we'll brush it, every night, till it's soft as silk."

"Aw, Clementine, you know I hate that stuff. And Lesesne will start teasing me that I'm a girl and ought to do girl things."

"Honey, you *are* a girl. Ain't nothing going to change that fact." She wrapped the towel around my body, then held me in my cocoon as she looked into my eyes. "We Gullah have a saying: *Mus tek care a de root fa heal de tree*," she said. "Child, I ain't telling you to change *all* your ways. You are who you are. Be the girl you want to be. Don't fight it. Show everyone what a girl can do." She straightened, releasing her hold. "That's what I tell Covey."

"You do?"

"Mm-hmm." Clementine returned to my side with a jar of her special ointment. She bent over my arm and, squinting some, began to gently dab salve over the long scratches. I watched, mesmerized. I couldn't remember my mama ever doing that for me. I didn't hold it against her. I just loved Clementine all the more for her tenderness.

Clementine spoke as she administered the ointment. "This here is jewelweed. It's best for poison oak or poison ivy. You let it set for fifteen minutes. Don't move, hear?"

"Yes'm." Then I asked in a hesitant voice, "What does Covey do?"

"Do?"

". . . I mean, you know, about showing what a girl can do?"

Clementine kept dabbing. "Covey don't have time to ask herself what does a boy do or what does a girl do. That child just does what has to be done."

Her words stung more than the ointment. "So, what does she *do?*" I persisted.

Clementine slowly put the lid back on the ointment. "Well now. . . . She tends Wilton's sick birds. Cooks. Cleans. Minds the garden. When she has spare time, she goes into the woods. Trees, plants, critters—she knows 'em all. Goes out to ponder them." A smile spread across her face. "Wandering, she calls it."

Wandering. My heart beat quicker. Just like me.

"But Covey's mighty tidy about herself too," Clementine continued, getting back to the point at hand. "If that busy child has time to brush her hair, I reckon you can brush yours a mite more too."

"I have my chores too," I said, feeling the need to remind her.

"I know. You a good girl." Clementine reached over to put her hands on my shoulders. Her look was tender. "Just sayin' you can do all you want to do as a girl. Don't try to be like your brothers, child. Be yourself. That's enough."

Chapter Six

—❖—

OSPREYS (*Pandion haliaetus*), locally known as fish hawks, are medium-size raptors with a dark brownish back and a white breast, and a distinctive, mask-like stripe that extends across the side of the face. Ospreys live near water and excel at fishing. Their oily plumage enables them to dive into the water to grab a fish with their long, curved talons and unique toe pads.

1908

A farm doesn't run itself," my daddy always told us.

Our animals needed to be tended, even when we were sick. Even on Sundays. Even on Christmas. "It's a pact we make with the animals when we take them into our care," Daddy said. He wasn't much for churchgoing. Lord, there were fights with Mama about that. He often said how this land was his church and he prayed there regularly. Daddy held that to abuse an animal was a sin not only against nature, but against God.

Mayfield had two barns. One barn for the farm animals was kept on land a ways from the house. We had a few cows, pigs, and chickens, enough to keep the family fed. The main barn, however, was near the house and strictly for the horses. In particular, Marsh Tackies. Daddy believed the small but valiant South Carolina Marsh Tacky was the perfect horse for farming, transportation, and sport. Bringing the breed back into popularity would secure his fortune.

Barn chores meant mucking stalls, fetching feed and water, and doing whatever else Daddy and Wilton told us needed doing. My mama never reconciled that I had chores in the barn rather than the house, me being a girl. But I rebelled against being stuck in the house. I loved the smell of hay, leather, and horses. That scent felt more home to me than anything cooking on the stove or Mama's potpourri in the living room. Plus, my favorite people worked in the barn with me—my brother Heyward, Daddy, and Wilton. My brother Lesesne didn't care for barn chores and grudgingly helped out only when made to. Lesesne helped Mama with her errands, carrying parcels, polishing the silver. Daddy told Mama she got things mixed up with us two.

Heyward and I lingered and listened to Daddy and Wilton talk about most everything, from the horses to weather to what was happening in Beaufort County. I think I learned more about horses and life in those hours in the barn than ever I did in a classroom. As much as I liked people, I loved horses more. They never found faults in my looks or the way I did things. I'd look into their liquid brown eyes and a kind of peace would settle in me.

That next day, I couldn't wait to meet Covey. But of course, I had to finish my chores first. I gulped down my breakfast of grits and applesauce, pleading with Heyward to hurry. He was as good as his word and saddled up our Tackies, Sparky and Queenie, then guided me to Wilton's cottage. I rode with my grinning face to the sun, noting how leaves were beginning to turn near as yellow as Heyward's hair. He took a path that followed the river, because it would be the easier route to find my way home. It wasn't long before I once again spied the cozy white cottage on the rise by the river. Covey was hanging sheets on the clothesline. My heart leaped, and I spurred Queenie on faster and shouted out her name. Covey turned and did a little hop of joy, then waved back. When I neared her, I slid from my horse, and we ran toward one another and gripped each other's hands tightly.

"I wasn't sure you'd come," Covey said, squeezing my hands.

"I told you I would," I said, giddy at seeing her again.

Heyward dismounted and tied the horses to the hitching post. Covey's eyes shifted to gaze at him and nervously released my hands.

"Hey there, Covey," Heyward said, sauntering toward us.

"Hey," Covey murmured back.

I was surprised at their casual greetings. "You know Covey?" I asked my brother.

"I seen her from a distance when I was out with Wilton," Heyward replied. Then to Covey he added, "Nice to meet you."

Covey stammered something as she looked at her feet.

Heyward walked about the property with a proprietary air. I frowned with fury at him acting like the lord of the manor. The cottage might have been on Mayfield land, but it was still Wilton and Covey's house.

"I've not been in this corner of Mayfield much," he said. "I heard tell your daddy has a bird hospital out back."

"Yep, he does," Covey replied, squinting in the sunlight. "I can show it to you, if you like."

"You don't have to show him nothing," I said.

"I'm just curious," Heyward said.

"It's out back. Follow me." With a final glance at Heyward, Covey led the way, straight-shouldered proud, toward the rear of the cottage. Heyward's grin was smug as he passed me. Covey was near as tall as Heyward, and I thought they both looked regal as they strolled through the tall grass. I hurried behind them, feeling small by comparison.

It was plain to see that Wilton was as organized at his own place as he was at Mayfield. But I remembered Clementine told me how Covey was the one who kept everything swept and tidy at home. A whitewashed fence bordered a rectangle of land that was divided into four sections. On the left was a brightly painted chicken coop where six hens pecked at the earth. In front of this, a garden was overflowing with an abundance of vegetables and herbs. The right side of the property was dominated by a white farm shed. The door was painted haint blue, and it held a wooden knocker in the shape of a hawk's head. I recognized it as Wilton's work. Attached to the shed was a narrow cage that was twice the length of the shed. Perched inside was an eagle.

Heyward whistled softly under his breath as he slowly approached the eagle.

"Don't get too close," Covey called out.

Bird and boy eyed each other warily. "So, it's true about Wilton taking care of sick birds," Heyward said, stopping ten feet away. "I figured he took in songbirds, maybe a hawk or an owl. But an eagle." He turned, his face incredulous. "He handles this bird?"

Covey lifted her chin. "Sure does. Ain't a bird Wilton can't handle. Though he's partial to eagles."

Heyward gestured toward the eagle. "What happened to him?"

"He was shot by someone."

"Why, who'd shoot an eagle?" I asked, horrified. "He doesn't do naught but hunt rodents and fish. He don't bother farmers' fruits neither, like the Carolina parakeet. And it ain't good to eat."

Heyward shook his head. "They bother the ducks, but some people shoot things just 'cause they can. Don't have to have no reason."

I knew Daddy would have an opinion about that. "He going to be okay?" I asked Covey.

"Yeah," Covey replied. "*She* was in real bad shape. Wilton worked on her for seven months. She's in the flight cage now. She's healed but needs to have room to get strong flying and catch prey before Wilton will let her go so she don't starve."

I studied the long coop, figuring it would take but a flap of that eagle's eight-foot wingspan to cross the distance. "Where'd Wilton learn to take care of injured birds?"

"Clementine says he's got the gift. Like his daddy did before him. That's who he learnt all his healing skills from. And he's passing it on to me."

"But you're a girl," said Heyward.

"What difference does that make?" I retorted.

"I don't mean nothing by it. Only, aren't you afraid going after a bird that big?" asked Heyward. "I know I would be."

Covey shook her head. "First off, I don't get to handle the big birds yet. But I will when I get older." She looked at the eagle. "I respect the bird, but I don't fear him. Wilton says animals can smell your fear."

I took a step closer, listening intently. I knew that was true with horses.

"It's the same with the bees," Covey said.

We bit the bait. "Bees?" we both said in unison.

"We've got hives over yonder in the woods." She said to me, "You tasted his honey yesterday."

"So, Wilton's a bee charmer too?" I'd heard about people who could work with bees without getting stung, but I wasn't sure it was even a real thing.

Covey's eyes crinkled with a laugh. "I don't know I'd call him that. He has bees and that's enough to say, I reckon. I'm learning that too."

I looked at her with awe.

Covey motioned with her hand. "We've got a few birds healing inside. Come on, I'll show you. But you have to be real quiet."

Stepping inside the shed, I breathed in a pungent scent I couldn't name. Not that the shed was dirty. It was as clean and tidy as the cottage. Hand-hewn wooden cabinets lined one wall, and a long wood table sat in the center under a single light bulb hanging from a cord. Beside it was a tray covered with small knives and other tools.

"What's that smell?" I asked, pinching my nose.

Covey looked puzzled. "Smell?"

"You don't smell it?" I asked with disbelief.

She took a sniff. "Oh. That. I reckon I don't notice it anymore. What you smell is their breakfast."

"What're you feeding them?" I asked. "Manure?"

"No. I just cut up some rats."

"Rat guts?" I yelped, raising my hand to cover my nose.

Heyward and I looked at each other. He attempted to act like it wasn't a big deal, but he looked like he was about to lose his own breakfast. I knew that distinct odor would be forever imprinted on my brain.

Covey snorted. "What do you think an eagle eats? Grits? When they get healthier we put them in the flight cage outdoors. We toss in live prey for them to eat, to be sure we can let them loose. They've got to hunt in the wild."

She led us through the treatment room to the rear door. "This is the hospital," she said, then put her fingers to her lips in the universal sign for silence. Nodding, we followed her to the rear room.

I could smell the pungent rats and something else, something musky, which must've been the birds. It was dim like a sickroom. Cages of different sizes were stacked on a wooden shelf that ran the length of the room, six on each side. All save three were empty. These were covered with old fabric so only the front was open for viewing.

"You can look, but don't touch the cages or make noises," Covey instructed us. "They're mighty sick and can't be shocked."

I bent to peer into the first cage. It was one of the largest. I immediately stared into the big round eyes of a great horned owl. When it raised its foot with long talons, I bolted back. "That owl didn't look sick. It looked fit to kill me."

"That's just its way," Covey said. "Wilton says we don't want to make friends with them. They need to stay wild."

In the second cage was a black bird crouched in the back. As I looked closer, the bird raised its white head and I saw the mask around its eyes. "It's a fish hawk!" I exclaimed. Hearing my voice, the bird commenced flapping its wings in a panic, banging the cage noisily.

"I didn't mean to startle him," I cried, backing far off.

"Hush now!" Covey rushed to cover the front of the cage with the fabric. We stood frozen till the flapping subsided.

"What's wrong with the fish hawk?" Heyward whispered. "He sure seems pretty strong in there."

"He got himself tangled in fishing line. Wilton says he's good enough now to go to the next station." Covey cast an assessing glance at Heyward. "And he's not a fish hawk. That's just a common name. It's an osprey."

"I knew that," said Heyward defensively.

Glancing up I saw Heyward's superior attitude slip away, replaced with admiration for the tall, slender girl. I looked at Covey with a world of respect.

She guided us out the back door into the yard. I breathed deep the fresh air, happy to leave the pungent scent of cut-up rats.

"How old are you?" Heyward asked Covey.

"I'll be nine before Christmas."

Heyward scratched his head with a silly grin on his face I'd never seen before. "Well, we best be off," he said to me. "Daddy will have our hide if we don't show up at the barn soon. I'll take you back here again."

"I'm grateful, but you don't have to worry. I'll be fine on my own tomorrow." I turned to Covey. "If'n I can come back. I'll help you with your chores. I'd like to learn about birds too."

Covey brightened and opened her mouth to speak, but Heyward interrupted.

"Can't tomorrow," he said to me. "Did you forget Mr. Coxwold has already arrived? No way Mama is going to let you skip out on the first day of school."

"I don't want to be stuck inside the schoolroom all day."

"You've got to. It's part of growing up." He smirked. "And being a lady."

I slapped his shoulder. "Don't you call me that."

"Who is Mr. Coxwold?" asked Covey.

"He's our tutor," replied Heyward.

"He's your tutor, not mine. I can already read and write and do numbers. Daddy said I'm the smartest girl in the county."

"That's not saying much," Heyward replied with a snort. "Half of the girls can't read."

"Half the boys neither. Besides, I'm every bit as smart as you," I shot back.

"Aw, don't be that way, Eliza. You're eight now and you have to start school and there's not a darn thing you can do about it. Why you always got to be so contrary?"

"I'm not," I said, hurt. "I just don't like everyone telling me what I've got to do and what I have to be all the time."

Covey looked at me. "You can already read? Like books?"

"Sure." Then a new thought took root. "Can't you?"

Covey's face was uncertain. "Wilton taught me my letters. And to read words on paper. But I'm hungry to learn real books."

"Don't you go to school?" asked Heyward.

"'Course I go to school," Covey replied with heat. "I go to the Sheldon School." Then, looking at her feet, "When I can. It's too far to walk regular. Wilton needs to be at the barn early, so he can't take me there every day."

"Daddy don't want to take us to Beaufort, neither," Heyward said in a way to mollify Covey.

"And because Mama won't have it any other way." I added. "She blames the school for Lesesne catching the fever."

"Hush, Liza," said Heyward with a nudge.

"Fever?" Covey's eyes widened.

Heyward signed with resignation. "Scarlet fever swept through the school a few years back. Eliza and I didn't get it bad, but Les was the youngest and he's never been strong. He was as good as dead. But somehow he pulled through."

"Mama still coddles him," I said with a snort.

"Mama never sent us back to public school and hired a tutor for me," Heyward explained. "This year, she's having Eliza and Lesesne join me."

"Covey," I exclaimed, an idea brightening. "Why don't you come to the schoolroom with us? Your daddy can bring you with him and Mr. Coxwold can be your tutor too."

A light sparked in Covey's eyes. "Could I?"

"Hold on a minute," Heyward said, shifting his weight uncomfortably. "You'd better check with Mama about that first."

"Sure, I will," I replied, then turned to Covey. "But she'll say yes. I mean, why wouldn't she?"

Covey cast a doubtful look at Heyward, who simply looked away.

⊸⊶

That evening, Clementine served a fine dinner of pork chops, applesauce, mashed potatoes, and beans. We always gathered in the dining room for the evening meal, washed and wearing clean clothes, Daddy in a jacket and the girls in dresses. Mama wouldn't tolerate the smell of the barn at her table. Hungry as I was, I barely made it through grace before I blurted out my question.

"Mama, can Covey come to the schoolroom with us tomorrow? She wants to go to school something fierce."

Mama was reaching for her biscuit and looked at me like I'd grown two heads. "Covey? You mean Wilton's child?"

"Yes'm."

"Don't be silly, child. She can't join Mr. Coxwold's class."

I stared back in confusion. "But why not? We have plenty of room in the library."

Mama set down her biscuit and looked at Daddy with exasperation. "Rawlins, can you explain it to her?"

Daddy looked up from his plate, his face blank. It was clear he'd been enjoying his dinner and paying no mind. "Explain what?"

Mama gave one of her long-suffering sighs. When she spoke, it was determinedly slow, as though to a child. "Please explain to Eliza why we cannot ask Wilton's daughter to join the children's tutoring class."

Daddy wiped his mouth and leaned back in his chair and gave Mama the stink eye. My stomach clenched, sensing a change in the air. "Why can't she? I think it's a fine idea."

Mama's mouth slipped open. "You are not serious?" It was more an accusation.

Daddy shrugged in the country way that irritated Mama. "I don't see where there's a problem. Covey is a right fine girl, sharp as a tack, and she's part of the Mayfield family. We pay Coxwold enough to take on another student."

"*I* pay Mr. Coxwold."

In the following silence, Daddy worked his jaw but no words came out.

Mama turned and spoke to me with a chilly calm that told me her temper was running hot. "Eliza, you have a unique ability to stir the pot. Just yesterday you returned home after causing mayhem in the entire county, and here you are, causing a disturbance again at my dinner table."

"I apologize, ma'am." I muttered and ducked my head. Lesesne snorted beside me.

"And I'm sorry," Mother said in way of conclusion, "but you cannot invite your new *friend* to the schoolroom."

My head shot up. "But she wants to learn," I countered, feeling if I could just make Mama understand she'd see I was in the right. "Don't you always tell me folks should study hard to better themselves?"

"I'm not saying Covey shouldn't study."

"But she can't get to her school, not regular. It's too far."

Mama picked up her cutlery and began slicing her pork chop. "It's just the way things are."

When I looked back at her uncomprehending, Mama sighed and

set her cutlery down. "You know very well there are schools for white children and schools for Black children. Everyone knows their place. How would it look?"

Daddy sat forward and put his elbows on the table. "When did I ever give a damn how it looks?"

Mama looked up sharply. "You know as well as I do we don't mix with their kind. They have their schools and we have ours. It's the way things have always been. It's all well and good for the girls to play together—here at Mayfield. Nonetheless there are lines that must be drawn. To allow Covey to be tutored here would be, well . . ." Mama groped for a word that would not inflame Daddy ". . . inappropriate. For us, Mr. Coxwold, and even for Wilton." She took a breath, and said more firmly, "As I said, it's best for everyone to know their place."

Daddy clasped his hands together, leaned forward on the table toward Mama, and looked directly into her eyes. He said in a low voice, "Do you think I didn't hear similar arguments from my family as to why I shouldn't marry you? That you should've known your place?"

Mama paled and furtively glanced at us. "Rawlins . . ."

Daddy put his palms on the table and roared, "I didn't listen to the harpies then and I'm not going to listen now."

I looked at Heyward, nervous that my father was raising his voice at the table. Heyward sat ramrod straight in his chair.

"You're going to talk about that in front of the children?" Mama said in a threatening voice.

Daddy paused to calm himself. "Wilton has served this family well all of his life, and his father before him. He's done right by his daughter, raising her on his own. She's capable, hardworking, and honest. And that girl might very well have saved our daughter's life yesterday. If that child joins our schoolroom, I say our children would be all the better for it."

"I don't think—"

Daddy pushed back his chair and rose abruptly, throwing his napkin on the table. "For God's sake, Sloane, don't think. For once, just do the right thing. Mayfield is my land and I'll be damned if I can't do what I want to do on my own land. This is my decision. And my final word on the subject. Covey can and should come to school here tomorrow morning. I'm just sorry I wasn't the one to think of it." He looked at me with appreciation. "Education is the greatest gift anyone can give a child." He took a breath and looked at Mother. His face was set in stone. "I'll ride over to inform Mr. Coxwold that he has a fourth pupil. Then I'll call on Wilton and invite Covey to the schoolroom." He paused, then said, "How you tell anyone else—if you need to tell anyone—I leave to you. I'll be late coming back. Don't wait up."

Mama's lips were tight, and she stared straight ahead until he left the room. For a moment, my brothers and I sat motionless, gazing at our plates. Then, Mama swung her head toward me, eyes glittering. "Eliza, what are you thinking, bringing a Negro child into my schoolroom?"

"She's my friend," I said softly.

"You see what happens when you try to make a Negro girl your friend? Trouble. That's what happens." Without another word, she tossed her napkin on the table and quickly rose, her dark eyes shooting anger at me like an arrow, then left the room. I shrunk in my seat as the rustle of her long dress swept past me.

"Ooh, you're in for it now," Lesesne said in a low teasing voice.

I stuck my tongue out at him, then shot a glance at Heyward. He was looking at the door. Swinging my head, I saw Clementine standing stock-still, a bowl of mashed potatoes in her hand. From the look on her face, I could tell she'd heard it all. She walked straight to my side and served a heaping spoonful on my plate, knowing how much I loved them.

"You want anything more, child, you just let me know."

I was too surprised to answer as she walked from the room, my gaze following her.

"Hey, Clementine," called Lesesne. "I want more potatoes too."

His cry went ignored. I held back my smile as I picked up my fork and made a show of eating the mashed potatoes. Mama was mad at me, but that was nothing new. Inside I was glowing. Covey was coming to school at Mayfield.

Chapter Seven

—◆—

CATTAILS (*Typha latifolia*) are one of a genus of some thirty species of tall, reedy aquatic plants that grow in fresh to brackish waters. They have many uses but are sometimes considered a nuisance as they can interfere with water flow and crowd out other seed-producing plants that are food for waterfowl.

1908

Our "schoolroom" was in the Mayfield library. Books—old, dusty and moldy—filled the shelves floor to ceiling. Stepping into the library was like walking in the deepest, darkest woods where the smell of composting wood tickled your nose. Maybe that was why the library was always my favorite room in the house.

Mama stood at the door beside Mr. Horace Coxwold, her hands folded and her back straight, looking like a teacher herself. She'd said to be educated was the mark of gentility, and come hell or high water, her children were going to be well educated. Even if we did live far from Charleston.

Mr. Coxwold was tall and thin and stood erect in his gray-striped suit and starched shirt. He wore a gray waistcoat that had tiny pockets. Heyward quickly gave him the nickname *Mr. Highpockets*. His head looked like an overripe melon. I figured it was too much area for his thinning hair to cover, so he combed long strands over the scalp. He was very particular that those hairs never got mussed and checked on them during the day, his long fingers tapping the top of his head. He smelled of mothballs and the licorice chips he sucked on. I thought he was near one hundred years of age, but Mama laughed and said he was but half that.

"Welcome, Miss Eliza," he said in a formal manner when I approached. His body was still but his eyes flickered like a cat's tail when about to pounce. I took a step back. Mama gave me a hooded *be a good girl* look.

"Thank you, sir," I mumbled.

"You'll find my Eliza is as bright as a shiny penny," Mama said.

I was startled hearing that, like I'd been given some award. Beaming, I added, "Daddy says I have horse sense."

Mama's face mottled and she hustled me into the library. I saw Covey already sitting at one of the desks, her hands tightly clasped and her brow furrowed. She wore a sun-colored dress with a round collar so crisp she must've soaked it in starch. Her hair was slicked back in tight braids tipped with bright yellow ribbons. Her face brightened when she spotted me. I hurried to her side, and we hugged tightly.

"You're here!" I exclaimed.

"Wilton brought me first thing. I rushed to get my chores done. I didn't want to be late on my first day."

"You look real pretty," I said.

"So do you," she said.

My dress was new. Pink gingham flowed loose to the sash at my hips, then fell in pleats below my knees. I wore black stockings, like Covey, though I wore black strapped shoes and she wore her usual brown lace-up boots. But they were polished till they gleamed.

Heyward approached the library sauntering like the conquering hero of some novel. Mr. Coxwold greeted him exuberantly and escorted his prize pupil to the largest table.

Lesesne followed and was also warmly welcomed. Mr. Coxwold put his hand on Les's shoulder and offered a squeeze. Lesesne rolled his hand off with a sneer.

Mr. Coxwold closed the library door and sat behind his desk. His smile swiftly disappeared to be replaced by a sour expression, like he was sucking a lemon. His gaze swept the room and landed on Covey. He narrowed his eyes, then looked at me.

"Miss Eliza."

"Yes sir?" I responded.

He tapped his desk. I thought that was an odd way to call us up, but I obliged. I drew close enough to catch a whiff of mothballs and spy a thin line of perspiration on his brow. I reckoned he pulled his wool suit out of the cedar closet for the season. It was a hot September day and I would've felt sorry for him, except he was so mean. He looked down at me from his height like we were bugs that he was considering smooshing.

"So, Miss Eliza, you're to be in my class this year." There wasn't any joy in that statement.

"Yes sir."

"I understand you've brought your—" he paused "—*friend* with you." He cast a disdainful glance toward Covey.

I felt my blood chill and replied in a low voice, "Yes sir."

He cleared his throat and looked down his long nose. "I am not accustomed to teaching Negro children." Plucking lint from his sleeve he added, "And I'm not particular to teaching girls. I expect you both to work especially hard and try to keep up with the boys."

"They can try and keep up with us," I snapped. I regretted my words when I saw his eyes flicker. Mama told me to be good and she wouldn't take kindly to a bad report on my first day.

He parted his lips to speak, then they closed in a sarcastic smile. "Indeed. You can take your seat." He gave a dismissive wave of his hand.

With assumed dignity, he passed out the new schoolbooks. These were prized and handed out with pomp—arithmetic, geography, and history. There were workbooks for writing, numbers, and religion. He gave one set to me. "These are yours." He paused. "You can share them, if you wish," he added with a sniff.

"Why do *we* have to share?" I asked indignantly. "Lesesne is only six and he can't read one bit."

Mr. Coxwold eyed me warily. "And you *can* read?"

I didn't care for the sarcasm in his voice and lifted my chin. "Of course I can read." I chuckled and looked at Heyward with a smug smile.

"Is that so? Who, may I ask, taught you to read?"

"Well." I hesitated, looking at my older brother. "Heyward helped me when I asked him. And I like to sit by him when he reads out loud so I can follow the words. It just happened. It's not that hard," I said with a shrug.

I heard Heyward stifle a laugh.

Mr. Coxwold studied me for a moment. "Please oblige me, Miss Eliza, and read a paragraph."

"Yes sir." I was happy to have the chance to show Mr. Coxwold that I could read. I noticed Covey was watching with keen eyes. She handed me the McGuffy Reader from our pile of books. I ran my hand over the cover, appreciating the feel of my first schoolbook in my hands. Opening to one of the first pages, I selected a random paragraph. The words seemed easy enough, I thought. I began to read.

"'Good morning, little children. I hope you are all well. It is a bright, sunny day. The birds are singing and the flowers are blooming. Can you hear the birds chirping? Can you see the pretty flowers in the garden? Look at the sky. It is so blue. What a beautiful day it is.'"

"That will be enough, Miss Eliza," Mr. Coxwold said dryly.

I closed the book, looking at him, expecting him to be pleased. But instead, he looked annoyed by my reading. Confused and worried I'd made some error, I glanced at Heyward. He rewarded me with an approving nod.

"You done real good," Covey whispered to me.

That was all the praise I needed. The day progressed slowly, with Mr. Coxwold deferring to the boys and almost ignoring Covey and me.

After school was dismissed, Covey and I darted to the door like buckshot, but stopped short when we heard Mr. Coxwold call out. "Girls!"

"You," he said, pointing at Covey. "Come to my desk."

We shared a worried glance as Covey went to stand before Mr. Coxwold, her hands clasped and her eyes wary. I watched from the doorway.

"Yes sir?"

He folded his hands on his desk. "From today forward, after class it will be your duty to clean the erasers and the blackboard." He waved his hand indicating the room. "And any other cleaning that needs to be done. We must keep our schoolroom tidy. I'm sure that would be appreciated," he said, smiling thinly, "by your most generous patron, Mrs. Rivers."

"Yes sir," Covey replied softly, her eyes downward.

Satisfied, Mr. Coxwold got up, swept his books from his desk into his arms, and regally walked toward the door. I abruptly stood in front of him, blocking his path.

"'Scuse me, Mr. Coxwold, but it ain't . . . isn't . . . right to tell Covey to clean the boards. I mean, shouldn't we all help?" I saw his sour expression and added, "Sir?"

Mr. Coxwold peered down at me in thought, then surprised me by nodding in agreement. "You make a good point, Miss Eliza."

I smiled, encouraged. "Thank you, sir."

"Indeed, cleaning is women's work. 'She looketh well to the ways of her household, and eateth not the bread of idleness.' Proverbs 31:27. It seems fitting that you assist in the cleaning of the room. Every day after school. Understood?"

I gasped in protest. "What about the boys? Don't their minds go idle?"

Mr. Coxwold's lips twisted into an amused smirk, as though I'd told a joke. "Good day."

He turned and exited from the library, unaware of the dirty look I shot his way as he passed me. My blood was boiling, and I was about to pounce after him when I felt Covey's hand slip into mine. I swung my head around to face her, unprepared to see her smiling.

"Please, don't cause no trouble."

"But—"

"Eliza, I don't care, if it means I can stay in the class. And you were kind to offer to help, but don't feel obliged. I'm fine doing it on my own." Her gaze lifted to the books that lined the shelves of the library. Her expression was filled with wonder. "I like being in here. I feel like I'm in church, you know? It's a holy place. All these words surrounding me, just waiting for me to read them—they're like gifts from God." She leaned closer. "When he's gone," she said conspiratorially, glancing at the door, "and no one else is in here, it's like my own secret place."

My eyes gleamed and my fury seeped from me like a balloon that released air. I knew what Covey meant, but for different reasons. The library had long been my secret hideaway in the house to escape my mother's criticisms or glances of disapproval.

"Tell you what. I'll help you do the chores," I offered, squeezing her hand. "We'll stay here after we finish and read. Together. No one will come looking for us here. Not Mama, not Lesesne—"

We both smiled and said at the same time, "—and not Mr. Coxwold."

❖

Cool fall days turned to long chilly months of winter. Covey and I became very best friends. Inseparable. We made a clapping game of cleaning erasers, talked as we washed the blackboard and straightened desks. Then we prowled the shelves, discovering books and sitting shoulder to shoulder on the cushy sofa reading. Some days, we made up stories of our own, laughing as we created villains and heroes of people we knew. No faint-hearted teacher could keep Covey from learning. By winter's end Covey had not only passed me in her level of reading, but she was also catching up to Heyward in poetry. On occasion, Heyward joined us in the library after class and I watched as they recited poetry to one another, challenging each other to know the author. I admit I was jealous when I saw Covey's and Heyward's heads bent close over a book.

Winter changed to spring, and the library windows were flung open. The stuffy smells of chalk and licorice were replaced with the giddy scents of yellow jasmine and Mama's roses.

The promises of warm weather could be felt on the gentle breezes and seen in the soft green grasses and leaves budding on trees.

Once the spring planting season commenced, we bid farewell to Mr. Coxwold and began farm chores. Covey was sorry to see the school season end. But for me, summer meant freedom to roam the acres of my beloved Mayfield.

Chapter Eight

RED TAILED HAWKS (*Buteo jamaicensis*) are abundant residents in South Carolina. They are birds of prey often spotted soaring or perching on telephone poles. Red-tailed hawks are very territorial. The male patrols for intruders while the female guards her nesting site, screeching out challenge calls.

1909

Spring cleaning was a seasonal ritual that turned Mayfield topsy-turvy. While the men worked outdoors in the fields, the women tied their hair back in scarves, donned aprons, and attacked the mess and clutter of the house.

Brooms, mops, and feather dusters were put to work cleaning baseboards and shutters, washing stair railings, shaking out dusty curtains. Rugs were beaten outdoors, windows washed with vinegar, and the heart pine floors polished till they gleamed. The larder was filled with fresh cream, and enough ice was secured to churn for butter and the rare treat of ice cream.

Clementine set pots of soup on the stove served with cold chicken and crusty bread to fuel our labor. There was always much to be done yet this year in particular—Mama was in high spirits in anticipation of the arrival of Arthur Middleton Chalmers to Mayfield.

The Chalmerses were one of the Charleston families Mama declared "important." Mrs. Leila Pringle Chalmers had been her dearest friend. For years, every time Mama went to Charleston to visit the Chalmerses, which was as often as she could, she brought me along with her. Probably hoping to civilize me. Mama and Mrs. Chalmers spent most every day together while her son, Tripp, and I played. Born the same year, Tripp and I had been friends since the cradle. Our mothers thought it was cute to declare that the two of us were betrothed.

Mrs. Chalmers had recently passed. Mama was distraught and sobbed in her room for a week. When she got word that poor widower Mr. Arthur Chalmers was at a loss with his poor motherless child, she immediately wrote and invited young Arthur, nicknamed Tripp, to spend the summer at Mayfield.

We finished our cleaning just in time for the arrival of the great guest and his son. On that late May morning we rose early, as usual, had breakfast on the large, scrubbed table in the kitchen and awaited the appointed hour. Daddy was grumbling that he wasn't out in the fields, and the boys chafed in their Sunday best. When at last a horse-drawn carriage was heard clip-clopping up the oak-lined alley, we moved to the entrance to welcome them. The late spring sun beat mercilessly as we set welcoming smiles on our faces.

When the carriage halted at the front step, only a boy sat in the rear. He bolted up, whipped off his straw hat, and waved it with a whoop of excitement.

Mama called out, "Welcome, Arthur!"

My mouth slipped open. I looked at Heyward, who stood equally astonished. We had expected *Mister* Arthur Middleton Chalmers II from Charleston, not just this pip of a boy. Outrage simmered at all the folderol for young Arthur Middleton Chalmers III.

"You mean Mama made us get all prettied up just for *Tripp?*"

Heyward rolled his eyes and shrugged.

Tripp jumped from the carriage and ran up the stairs, making a beeline for Mama. He wrapped his arms around her and pressed his face to her belly. Tears came to Mama's eyes as she embraced him.

"Thank you for inviting me," he said when she released him. "I'm right grateful to be here. I was feeling mighty lonely, and my daddy is so sad."

Daddy cleared his throat and slapped his back heartily. I thought Tripp would fall over from the blow. Heyward shook his hand, and so did Les, which surprised me because he didn't much care to touch other people. Finally, Tripp approached me. We studied each other for a moment, neither of us moving. It'd been a year at least since Mama last took me to Charleston and in that time I'd grown, but he must have quit because I'd caught up to him in height, which was surprising given I was small for a girl. His hair was the same shade of light red, only now it was trimmed so short his ears stuck out. Freckles smattered across his nose under soulful eyes as blue as the sky.

Tripp lunged forward and wrapped me in a tight hug. "I'm right glad to see *you* again, Eliza."

I pried him loose with an unladylike shove.

He kept smiling at me, brimming over with excitement. "You always talked about Mayfield and now I'm here at last," he said. "The rivers, the fields, the horses . . . I want to see everything. We're going to have such fun together."

I'd counted on having this summer just for me and Covey. Alone time from the boys. But seeing the adoration and eagerness in Tripp's eyes, I thought, a bit begrudgingly, that maybe his being here for the summer wasn't going to be so bad after all.

⟡

Mama intended for Tripp and Lesesne to be playmates and put Tripp in Lesesne's room. It had two beds and shelves filled with books and various collections of toys. Les was as territorial as a hawk about his room. Of all his possessions. He kept his door closed and patrolled for intruders, eyeing me suspiciously whenever I tried to peek in. Lesesne took claim of our guest as though Tripp were just that, something that belonged to him. I was astonished by how he allowed Tripp entry into his room at all.

Lesesne proudly showed Tripp his extensive collection of glass marbles and regiments of tin soldiers. Lesesne spun his top with a fervor, glancing up often to gauge Tripp's reaction. Tripp was kindly and tried to seem interested, but I could tell he was just being polite.

"Come sit on the rug," Lesesne called out, grabbing a deck of cards from his bed table. "Do you know how to play Snap?"

"I like that game a lot," I exclaimed from the doorway, rushing into the room.

"You can't play," Les shouted at me so meanly I was taken aback. "It's just me and Tripp."

"Aw, don't be like that, Les. You know I'm a good player."

"Get out of my room!" Les leapt up angrily and pushed me.

I stumbled back, barely catching myself from a fall.

Tripp's face colored, and he gave Lesesne a fierce push right back. Les fell to the floor then stared up with demon eyes of fury.

I looked intently at Tripp, stunned that someone beside Heyward defended me.

"You don't push girls," Tripp told him in a grown-up tone, brows knitted. Then offering an olive branch, he said, "Sorry I pushed you. Come on, it'll be more fun to play with three." He extended his hand.

"Get out," Lesesne yelled as he slapped Tripp's hand away. Then he lunged for a marble and threw it at Tripp. His aim was true. The big bonker hit Tripp smack in the middle of his forehead.

Tripp let out a yelp to wake the dead and slapped his hands over his forehead. I stood mouth agape. Mama came running with Heyward at her heels. When she learned what had happened she lit into Lesesne like I'd never heard before. Lesesne sat on the floor, stone-faced. I didn't see one lick of remorse on his face.

Daddy must've heard Mama's shouts clear from the barn. When he walked into the room, he stalked over to Lesesne and grabbed hold of the neck of his shirt and proceeded to drag him to his feet. "To the shed, boy," he told him.

Heyward and I exchanged knowing glances. We'd both visited the shed to meet Mr. Flog, the long piece of hickory Daddy used as his switch. I felt its sting only once.

I thought back to that time a year earlier. I'd been ashamed to be taken to the small shed behind the kitchen where Daddy kept his tools.

"I didn't do anything wrong," I had cried to my father. "Just 'cause I don't want to help make jelly? You don't make Heyward do that."

"Because your mama says so." He let out a long, weary sigh. "Why must you frustrate your mama so? You have to learn the female arts. It's expected of you."

"I don't want to learn that stuff. It doesn't suit me. I can do barn chores. Wilton says I'm right good with the horses. Near as good as Heyward. And a site better than Les."

Daddy put his hands on his hips and studied me. His face was tanned and leathery from long hours out in the fields. "I know it. It's a shame you weren't born a boy."

In the following silence I heard the batting of wings against wood. Looking over, I saw a Common Grackle trapped indoors. I said, "I wish I was."

Defeat washed over his face. "Eliza, you are my only daughter. I value that, even if you don't. And as such, you have responsibilities that the boys do not. Your mama knows this and she's doing her best to raise you proper." He blew out a plume of air. "I suppose the fault is mine. I spoil you and let you stay in the barn with the boys, and truth be told, I like having you around. You're a tintype of your mama." He snorted. "Only easier to handle."

He cleared his throat, and his face grew stern. "But you listen here, Missy. You'll do your indoor chores. And brush your hair. Because if your mama wants it so, then it will be so, hear?"

"Yes sir."

"Good. Now turn around."

My eyes widened. Daddy had never laid a finger on me, and now

I was to meet Mr. Flog. I swallowed hard and turned around, gritting my teeth and clenching my fists. To my surprise, I felt two light taps on my behind. Barely a sting. Still . . . I'd been whipped. I exhaled loudly and my shoulders slumped.

"Eliza . . ."

I turned, shamefaced.

"That near killed me. I never intend to strike you again. I don't expect you'll give me cause. Are we in agreement?"

"Yes sir."

He nodded and turned to leave. As he opened the shed door I called out.

"But . . ."

He stopped and looked over his shoulder, brows raised.

"I can still help in the barn?"

His lips twitched but he forced a stern look. "Yes."

Now here it was, Lesesne's turn to meet Mr. Flog, and I didn't think Daddy was going to go as light on him as he did with me.

Mama was contrite and her face contorted in regret as she reached out to take Daddy's arm. "Rawlins, I don't think this calls for the shed."

"It's long past time," he told her and marched Lesesne from the room as he howled in protest. Heyward and I looked at each other, satisfied that the day had finally come for Lesesne's comeuppance. Mama had been able to save Les from Mr. Flog in the past, but this time Daddy was firm.

Flustered, Mama took a slow breath and wiped her hands on her dress. Then she inspected Tripp's wound. Heyward and I crowded in to see an angry bruise already swelling up like a bull's-eye in the middle of his forehead.

Mama stroked the hair back from Tripp's forehead with tenderness. "You're awake and there isn't any blood. You'll be all right," she said with relief. "I'm sorry for what transpired on your first day. Lesesne has a fearful temper, but rest assured he'll think again before acting so rudely toward you. Now go on with Clementine and let her put some ointment on your forehead." She met Clementine's eye. "Send Wilton up, please. I'll need him to move a bed upstairs."

———

I wasn't joyful spending the first day of summer in Heyward's attic bedroom helping Mama ready it for Tripp. Heyward sat on his bed, a book in his lap that he wasn't reading, not lifting one finger to help.

"Why are we doing all this work just for Tripp?" I asked as I laid out the linen.

"He's our guest," Mama replied.

"Why, Tripp's no guest. He's just Tripp."

Mama was spreading the log cabin quilt over the bed. She paused and brought her hands together to look sternly at me. "Eliza Pinckney Rivers, as my daughter you must learn that anyone who spends time at Mayfield is a guest."

"Yes'm," I replied somberly. Whenever she used my full name, I knew she meant business.

She sat on the bed and tapped the mattress for me to join her. Her tone changed to conciliatory. "Tripp's mama, Leila, was my dearest friend. I was maid of honor at her wedding, and she was mine. Why, you and Tripp were born just weeks apart. You were christened Eliza Pinckney Rivers, and he was Arthur Middleton Chalmers III. Such fine names." Her face softened with memories. "After you were born, I didn't return straightaway to Mayfield but stayed with my parents in Charleston for some time. For recovery," she hastened to add. "You played together as babies, did you know that?"

I nodded.

Mama said wistfully, "You looked so adorable together. Leila and I always said that you and Tripp were betrothed." She chuckled at the memory.

"You mean like we're going to get married?" I asked, horrified at the prospect of marrying anybody, much less someone I liked like a brother.

"At the very least, we agreed that Tripp would be your escort to the St. Cecilia Ball when you come of age. You know, only a male descendant of a member can extend an invitation to that ball. The Chalmerses are one of Charleston's finest families. Why, they're connected by marriage to just about everyone important. I want that for you, Eliza. To secure your place in society. You are a Rivers, after all." She looked into my eyes, and I saw a longing I'd not seen before. "It is important that you and Tripp remain friends."

"All right, Mama. He can be my friend."

From the other side of the room, Heyward grumbled aloud, "But why does he have to sleep in *my* room? I'm sure as H not going to marry him. He should sleep downstairs, with Les. That was what you'd planned."

Mama turned to her eldest son. "You saw what happened."

"But he met Mr. Flog." Under his breath he added, "About time."

Mama ignored that. "Heyward, look at me," she said. When my brother obliged, she folded her hands in her lap and spoke only to him. "You will be the master of Mayfield one day. It's the mark of a gentleman to be kind to those in need. Tripp is an only child. He just lost his mother. Don't you think it would be nice for him to have someone to look up to now? Someone he could see as an older brother?"

Heyward was a good soul, and Mama knew to play to his tender side. He groaned, tossing his pillow, but said, "All right."

"Thank you for your generous spirit."

Wanting my generous spirit to be acknowledged as well, I tugged Mama's sleeve and blurted out, "And I reckon I could marry him."

Mama burst out with a light laugh, said, "Dear girl," and bent to kiss the top of my head.

I looked up, and seeing her smile, wondered what in heaven had come over her.

Chapter Nine

⟨⟩

RESURRECTION FERN (*Pleopeltis polypodioides*) is an epiphytic fern species that is native to the southeastern United States. The name comes from its remarkable ability to seemingly resurrect itself after periods of drought, its withered, brown fronds transforming to lush green within hours. It typically grows on the trunks and branches of large hardwoods, like live oak.

1909

After a rough start, Tripp's first summer at Mayfield began in earnest. Summer was a time of ease, and we'd have plenty of fun together . . . once Daddy got the June planting done.

Rain or shine, the fields were planted. Daddy rose before the sun to work on the land, managing the animals and fields. He worked side by side with his team as stout oxen lumbered slowly through the muddy fields, planting the rice seed. The swampy low country could not bear the weight of the new mechanical equipment that boosted rice production in other states.

Mama would shake her head and say, "That man's no better than a beast in the harness." She complained how rice production in the low country was dead and gone and how they should just give up and move to the city.

We knew Daddy never would leave Mayfield. He said his family's blood ran in the creeks and rivers here. Some days he'd come back quick in his step, praising the Lord for such bountiful land. Other times, like after a full moon tide inundated the fields, he came back to us walking like a man twice his age and asking the heavens why the Prince of Darkness continued to plague him.

There were magical moments too. The family gathered when the floodgate, called a trunk, was lifted. We watched in awe as the water slowly seeped into the fields, enough to cover the seeds. If it weren't for the water, the ricebirds would claim most of the seeds and it would be a loss. Daddy watched, a gleam in his eye, and said with satisfaction, "That's the way it's always been done."

After the planting, the whole household breathed deeply in relief. He and Mama took long, slow walks alone in the soft evening air. Sometimes we'd hear their laughter ring out when the sun started sinking in a hazy, fiery red. Clementine commenced making lemonade and sweet tea in ample amounts to assuage our thirst. Mama didn't mind if we wore our field clothes or how dirty our nails were, at least not as much. She professed she was glad we were old enough now to take care of ourselves. She opened the windows and doors and let us loose to play in the fields and swim in the river while she sewed or read poetry in the shade.

The earth also eased up as the days warmed. The sun shone hotter, baking the muddy, gooey soil that tired one to walk in, turning it into loam that sprouted green shoots and wildflowers. The streams ran full of bream and trout. We kids were warned of snakes—hoary old copperheads, rattlesnakes, and coral snakes—and took off with fishing gear in our hands. We barely had to drop a line in with a wiggling worm to have a fine catch.

It took a while for Tripp and Covey to become friends. I expected them to get along like peas and carrots, but it turned out there was some pepper in that mix.

The day after Tripp's arrival, I sneaked out to play with Covey. The midday sun beat down on the lawns and dusty paths. Covey and I sought shade under a large oak tree. I sat cross-legged on a patchwork quilt. Beside me, Covey giggled as we threaded stems of clover to make crowns. Our weaving was interrupted by the arrival of Tripp.

He strode across the grass in his city clothes, in stark contrast to Covey's and my worn cotton summer dresses and muslin aprons.

His eyes narrowed in puzzlement and he cleared his throat to announce his presence.

I looked up with a bright smile. "Tripp! Meet my friend Covey. Covey, this is Tripp." I held up the ring of clover proudly. "You've come just in time. Covey and I are making crowns."

Covey glanced up, her dark eyes meeting Tripp's gaze with a mixture of wariness and curiosity.

Tripp shifted uncomfortably, glancing around as if expecting someone to reprimand us. "But . . . shouldn't you be playing with . . . the other children?" he asked me cautiously, struggling to articulate his thoughts.

"Covey and I play together all the time."

Tripp seemed taken aback. "But . . . well, she's a Negro. We can't play with Negroes. Least while, not in Charleston," he mumbled, his gaze flickering between Covey and me.

"Well this is Mayfield. And she's my best friend," I replied, my gaze steady as I met Tripp's uncertain stare.

"Huh. Then okay, I guess, if your mama and daddy say it's all right." Tripp stood there meekly, holding his hands in front of him, as though wishing to stay yet uncertain.

I reached out and placed a hand on his arm. "Covey's the best at making up stories. And she knows the names of most all critters and trees and plants on Mayfield. You should hear the adventures we've had."

Tripp managed a small smile in return. He glanced once more at Covey, who regarded him with caution. "Okay," he said, this time with more gusto as he planted himself between me and Covey. His eyes brightened with his smile.

As the afternoon wore on, both Covey and Tripp seemed to relax as the three of us played together under the shade of the oak tree.

For most of the days that week, we got together and, pretty soon, were inseparable. When we weren't fishing or playing games of make-believe, Covey, Tripp, and I spent hours filling metal buckets full of big, sweet berries and, in late summer, the large, musky scuppernong grapes that turned bronze on the vine. Mama liked to say scuppernong grapes were the first signal of fall. Heyward was especially good at finding cooter eggs, but Tripp, being tenderhearted, cried if anyone attempted to bring a turtle to the kitchen. Clementine welcomed our bounty and made jams and pies and delicious soups. She often shook her head while cooking and professed aloud how with all the ducks and turkeys and deer in the woods, and all the fish and crabs in the sea and rivers, and all the berries in the fields, a family could live like kings and queens at no expense.

Summer was a fecund season—the sheep had lambs, the cows had calves, and there were kittens to be found in the barns. I liked sheep well enough. They were sweet but dumb as dirt. Sometimes a ewe rejected her baby. That sent tenderhearted Tripp into tears for worrying about the lamb. But Daddy showed him how to take the orphan lamb in one hand and a different mama's lamb in the other, and gently rub them together. That way the smell of the good mama's lamb spread onto the orphan. Most times, that mama gave the orphan a sniff, thought it was one of hers, and she nursed it. Tripp had such joy in his eyes when the orphan was accepted, and after that, Daddy let Tripp work with the lambs. When he told Tripp he had the gift for working with animals, Tripp walked in high cotton for weeks.

For me, the highlight of that summer was returning to the tree hollow. Tripp was begging to see the big tree he'd heard so much about. I wasn't sure I could even find it again, but Covey led the way from her cottage through the woods to my tree.

The tree didn't look much different. Her limbs stretched far out over the clearing, so low some of them rested on the earth. There was a majesty about her that you just knew she was ancient. I approached the hollow slowly, my feet cutting a path in the soft grass.

Tripp slapped his forehead and muttered, "That there's the biggest tree I've ever seen."

It was true. Even when the three of us held hands, we couldn't reach clear around her trunk.

"I told you," I said.

"How do you reckon a tree could grow that big with a hole in its body like that?" he asked.

"A hole don't mean the tree is ailing," said Covey. "Wilton says a tree like this has lots of sap running through it, like our blood. When the innards decay, all the rot helps feed the tree as it grows."

With reverence, I reached out to touch the bark. The leaves of the fern that grew on the tree bark were now brittle and dry. "But the fern's all curled up, like it's burnt. It was all green when I last saw it."

Covey slowly ran her hand over the tree trunk, smiling as the fronds tickled her palm. "This here's resurrection fern. The leaves always look dead when they're dry. Only they ain't dead at all. When it rains, the fern comes back to life, all green again. That's how it got its name. Like the Lord's resurrection."

I looked at the thick layer of fern climbing up and cloaking the tree trunk and branches. "The fern doesn't hurt the tree, does it?"

Covey shook her head. "It's like a queen's fine cloak."

I smiled, liking that comparison a lot. I remembered the night I'd found the tree hollow. The rain was falling, and thunder rumbled. Then, the resurrection fern was indeed a bright green. I went to the hollow and scooted low to look inside the dark cavern. I remembered it was big enough to hold me, and maybe two or three more.

Tripp grabbed my arm, holding me back. "Careful, Eliza. Critters might be in there."

"And snakes," added Covey, her eyes wide.

"I don't remember any critters or snakes," I said, matter-of-fact, then stretched out my arms into the dark hollow and commenced clapping loudly, shouting, "Scoot! Scoot!" Behind me, Tripp and

Covey hooted and hollered at the top of their lungs. Then we stopped and listened, poised to run. If any animal or snake was in residence, I felt sure they'd have come out. When nothing stirred, I crawled in.

Once I was through the opening, the hollow opened up into a cavern. Teeny bits of light peered in through cracks in the wood, and dust motes that were stirred up by my crawling floated in the air. As my eyes acclimated to the dark, I gazed around in wonder. The hollow rose high up, almost high enough for me to stand, and the crevices created great arches that soared over my head and disappeared in the dark. The composted floor, mingled with patches of moss, was soft on my hands and knees, and the green grew along the inside of the tree like wallpaper.

Tripp and Covey crawled in, and we gathered in the center of the hollow. Together we sat in silence as we marveled at the towering inside of the cavern.

"Might could get Heyward in here too," I said in a hushed voice.

"Why are you whispering?" asked Covey.

I tried to explain how the hollow felt like sacred ground. There was so much history inside this moss-encrusted monument. Hundreds of years of different animals seeking shelter. Countless birds nested. Squirrels hid nuts. Maybe a slave hid here escaping bondage. Or an Indian passed a night here while hunting. Sitting inside this tree, I felt connected to something bigger than myself, and it mystified me. But how could I explain all that?

I shrugged. "Feels like I'm in church."

Covey giggled and bumped my shoulder. "You ain't never been to *my* church. It's too quiet in here for that."

"This is the best fort ever," Tripp said, his head turning from left to right. His eyes gleamed in the dim light, and he leaned forward with excitement. "Listen! We should make this our secret place. Just ours. We can have secret meetings and stuff. Maybe camp out in here."

"Uh-uh," Covey said in protest. "I ain't sleeping in here. Night's when the animals look for shelter."

"I'm not afraid of no skunk or raccoon," boasted Tripp, leaning back on his arms.

"Then I reckon you aren't bothered by those daddy longlegs over your head," I said.

With a yelp, Tripp sprang to my side of the hollow, knocking me flat against the wood. "Where? Where're the spiders?"

"Damnation, Tripp, get off me!" I hollered. "They're more afraid of you than you are of them."

Tripp gave his scalp a good scratching. "I wasn't scared."

"Well, don't fret." I brushed the dirt off my legs. "They're not spiders. They don't have venom. There's nothing in my tree hollow but harmless bugs and moss." I leaned back, grinning. "Feels right homey here, don't it? How come it took us this long to come back?" I asked Covey. "Tripp is right. This is a perfect hideaway."

"And we can't tell anyone about it," said Tripp.

"Except Heyward, of course," I said.

Tripp shook his head. "Not even Heyward. We have to pinky-swear." He stuck out his raised little finger.

Covey leaned in. "Okay. I swear."

I had to think on that a minute. No one wanted to include Lesesne. He couldn't be trusted. But it didn't feel right not to include Heyward. Then again, my older brother was making himself scarce this summer, acting all grown-up and too good to play with us kids. *Well, he deserves what he gets*, I thought.

"Okay," I conceded. "But if we're going to have a secret club, a pinky swear isn't good enough. We need to do something more powerful."

Tripp grew alert. "Like what?"

"A blood oath."

Covey looked at me with a frown. "That sounds like hoodoo. I don't fool with that."

"It's not hoodoo or conjuring. It's more like a sacred promise. Life or death. You'll see. Anyone got a safety pin?" I asked.

Covey went to the strap of her pinafore and unhooked a pin. The apron slumped down her chest. "Here's one."

I took the pin, then wiped my hands clean on my own muslin pinafore. Then, taking a breath, I stuck the tip of my index finger with the pin. A bead of blood instantly appeared. Covey and Tripp both gasped and shrank back.

"Come on, sissies," I cajoled. "I thought you said you wanted this to be a secret club. We have to be blood brothers."

"Sisters," Covey amended.

"Brother and sisters," Tripp corrected.

We kneeled close together. First, I held Covey's hand. She didn't flinch as I pricked the tip of her finger. I took my bloody fingertip and in the slow manner of ceremony, pressed it against Covey's pricked finger. We looked in each other's eyes and I felt a surge of affection for my best friend.

"I do solemnly swear to be your blood sister, loyal and true, for the rest of my life. Now you say it."

Covey licked her lips and spoke in a hushed voice as she repeated my words.

Next I faced Tripp. His eyes gleamed with anticipation mixed with fear. I admit, I was impressed he didn't whimper when I pricked his finger. Blood appeared and I pressed my fingertip to his and made the oath.

He grinned so wide he could barely speak. "I do solemnly swear to be your blood brother—and your husband—loyal and true, for the rest of my life."

I dropped my hand. "Aw Tripp, you're spoiling things. You can't say 'husband.' We aren't getting married, you dufus!"

"We are too."

"Not now we aren't!" I shook my head, frustrated with his claims. "Aw, go ahead now and swear to Covey."

The two completed the ceremony, swearing to be loyal and true.

"We should add *on pain of death*," said Tripp, holding up his index finger.

Covey and I lifted our pricked fingers and we all said in unison, "On pain of death."

Little did we know on that summer afternoon, when the sun shone bright overhead and the world was innocent, that those words would one day come back to haunt us.

Chapter Ten

BOBOLINKS (*Dolichonyx oryzivorus*) are small blackbirds dubbed ricebirds when rice production was a thriving industry in the southeastern United States. Huge flocks would descend upon the rice fields while on migration to fatten up for the remainder of the trip. Since they were capable of doing great damage to the crop, they were shot and killed by the hundreds of thousands.

1988

I paused my story, feeling the memories coming too hard and too fast. I exhaled slowly and looked around the table to see Savannah and Norah watching and listening with keen interest.

"I think it's time for a rest," I said. "Perhaps a sip of tea to wet my whistle."

Savannah briskly rose from her chair. "I'll get it."

She returned a short while later carrying a tray with tall, icy glasses. "I've got some sweet tea for us. And Mariama is here!"

A moment later, Mariama strode into the room like a breath of fresh air. "Hey, y'all," she called out, rolling in a cart filled with dishes. "I didn't want to interrupt the telling, but I thought you'd all be ready for some lunch. I brought lunch from the restaurant."

"Thank you," I said, catching the scents of shrimp, corn, okra, and andouille sausage. "That gumbo smells delicious."

Years ago Mariama had inherited Clementine's house, so she now lived just outside Mayfield. She often stopped by bringing gifts from her restaurant—a meal, corn bread, fresh produce. I knew it was her way of checking on me when I was alone in the big house.

Mariama set a large blue-and-white china soup tureen on the sideboard along with several bowls of the same pattern. Norah and Savannah got up to help serve the food.

"I want to hear more of those stories," Mariama said. "Clementine's my great-aunt, so I'm curious. I've always wanted to hear more about her."

"Then set yourself down. There's a lot more to tell."

I waited until everyone was seated before picking up my spoon and tasting the gumbo. "Clementine used to make her gumbo with alligator meat when she could get it." I smiled at Savannah's reaction.

"Your life back then sounds idyllic," said Norah. "Listening to you, I can picture my grandmother as a little girl."

"Our childhoods were far from idyllic. We had bad times to counter the good, same as we do now. Living life was harder. Labor was harder. Injustice was harder. Getting sick was harder. People died." I drew quiet, eating my gumbo as I scanned the mural with so many faces of the departed. Memories swirled, vivid and sharp. I set my spoon down as my hunger faded.

"Are you okay, Grandma?" asked Savannah, looking up from her plate.

"Oh yes. I'm just filled with memories. When I see the murals and tell the stories, the images come to mind so fresh."

"I'm astounded that you remember it all so clearly," said Savannah. "Like it all happened yesterday."

I reached for the corn bread, pleased to feel its warmth. As I spread butter I added, "Nostalgia is a peculiar thing. We tend to recall the sweeter moments that elicit a smile or make our hearts wax and wane . . . and forget the sad memories."

"I want to hear them all, good and bad. Daddy said they were boring, but they're not. Of course, I knew the names of the ancestors, but that's all they were. Names. Now I feel like they're real people who lived real lives—right here at Mayfield. Makes me wish I was alive back then. It all sounds somehow . . . better."

"That's what makes nostalgia a dangerous trap," I replied. "The happy memories shine brightest. They lure you into thinking the past was better than the present."

"Especially for people of color," said Norah. She shifted in her seat, looking at the murals. Her voice was low. "Covey and Wilton had to know—how did you put it?—their place."

I understood her uneasiness. "Yes, that was true for that time," I replied. "The bigotry and narrowness of the South, the nation, was deeply ingrained." I shifted my glance to the murals, struck by how many scenes of all of us—white and black—dotted the wall that told our intermingled stories.

"Norah, it's for you to decide how far we've come since then. I daresay, not far enough. But these are *my* memories, told true. Most every childhood is a time of innocence. Naïvete. And for us—me, Covey, and Tripp—they were the best times of our lives. Those early days formed the very foundation of who we were to become."

I dabbed my lips with my napkin, took a sip of sweet tea, and remembered back to those happy days. "The summers passed in much the same way, one after the other. We children prowled the boundaries of Mayfield, exploring, loving each clump of dirt. We learned the names of trees and birds and critters we came across. A found feather was a triumph. An animal was captured in pencil then added to our journals to be researched later in the library. Covey especially loved the plants. She taught us their names. Tripp loved animals." I paused. "I loved it all because all of it made up Mayfield."

Norah crossed her arms, her expression skeptical. "When did it change?"

My brows rose. "Say again?"

"When did the idyllic youth end and adulthood begin?"

I paused. We all knew that something happened to end the wide-eyed days of our childhood. But when? It was more a series of moments, of days, years.

I shifted my gaze to the murals and landed on a young man with a smile that lit up his face. He held a fishing rod in one hand, a rifle in the other.

"It began the summer of 1912," I began. "A life-changing summer."

Chapter Eleven

—◆—

CAROLINA GOLD (*Oryza glaberrima*) is the name given to rice cultivated in the Carolinas, particularly South Carolina. It was prized, known for its high quality and distinctive flavor. Carolina Gold was brought from western Africa during the colonial era and it thrived in the region's marshy landscape. Carolina Gold played a significant role in the economy and history of the region.

1912

Resilience is a remarkable thing. It requires strength, flexibility, and, what I've later learned, faith. It is defined by an individual's ability to be knocked down by fate, be tossed by uncertainty, and have one's fortunes taken away. Then pick oneself up from the dirt and try again.

That was Rawlins Rivers. The coast was still recovering from the hurricane of 1893 when two big storms hit in 1910 and 1911. Surges of fierce wind and black water came crashing along the Combahee River with such force the salt water wiped out Daddy's rice fields and those of all the rice farms along the coast. We heard news of boats even as far as Charleston pushed onto the city streets from the force of it. To lose one's crop so close to harvest hurts the soul. That year was the first time I saw Daddy weep. Mama said it was the death knell for rice planting in South Carolina.

The following season, when other farmers gave up planting rice and, worse, sold their land, my daddy planted Carolina Gold again.

He declared it was his duty. Mama called it his folly. They had arguments about it. Mama was all for abandoning Mayfield and moving to Charleston. Her parents offered Daddy opportunities for work in the city, but that just sparked more fights as Daddy claimed they shamed him. He believed in Mayfield, felt the weight of continuing the family legacy, and searched for other ways to bring in money.

Daddy could be convincing, and Mama, again, stayed by his side. She was frugal and did the family sewing, including making us our new clothes. She ran the household and assisted in the chores. But she refused to lower the standard of living, in particular for her children. Thankfully, her parents stepped in. The Bissettes helped their only child by helping her husband, which meant keeping Mayfield afloat.

The summer of 1912, the farm was aflutter with the news that Daddy bought himself a new horse. Not just any horse. A fancy Marsh Tacky stallion with a fine lineage that Daddy had his eye on since it was a foal. This horse, he claimed, was his hope for the future.

Daddy wouldn't have any other kind of horse than a Marsh Tacky. He said the South needed tough horses that could thrive in our swampy, mucky soil. Marsh Tackies had been used to plow the fields, plant the crops, bring in the hay crop, pull wagons, and haul manure for generations. Some horses were just for transportation. Every one of them had a job to do and did them well. Truth be told, Daddy couldn't run the farm without them. No machine could run in the low-lying coastal terrain of the rice fields. The soft, muddy soil swamped the machinery. The Marsh Tacky was *the* horse to get the job done.

On the day the Marsh Tacky was to arrive, the excitement was so intense we couldn't think of anything else. Covey, Tripp, and I were gathered at the river dock, on the lookout for a sign of the boat coming. Heat shimmered on the water and gnats fluttered in the haze. Daddy and Wilton had left at dawn to bring the great horse to Mayfield by the river and were due soon. Tripp and Covey eagerly put a cane pole in the water and a short while later commenced dancing because they'd already caught a fine flounder. While the two of them fished, I sat on the dock, dangling my feet in the water, and daydreamed of riding the new stallion, cantering in the fields so fast my hair streamed behind me.

I was leaning on a piling at the end of the dock when I heard heavy footfall reverberating on the wood. I looked lazily over my shoulder and caught sight of Heyward coming my way. My heart sang at seeing him home again. I missed him terribly when he went off to high school in Charleston. At fifteen, my brother's body was changing as fast as his voice. He had a young man's shoulders that tapered down to pants that had to be belted to stay up. No matter what Clementine fed him, he stayed slim. His white shirt was rolled up at the sleeves under his overalls, and a long piece of grass dangled between his teeth.

He had another one of his new friends in tow. Heyward gathered friends like a bee did pollen. I'd never seen this one. He was equal to Heyward's height and width, with his same blond hair and suntanned skin. In fact, they looked more like brothers than Heyward and Lesesne did. The shirttails of his unbuttoned chambray shirt flapped and swayed as he walked with the confident stride of a boy who knew the world was his oyster.

I scrambled to my feet. Closer, I saw the boy's features were softer than Heyward's chiseled ones. Even pretty. He laughed at something my brother said and it seemed his entire face lit up with his smile. In that moment my heart skipped a beat.

"Hey," Heyward called out with a short wave.

"Hey back at you."

The boys reached my side, and though I didn't deign to look at him, I could feel the stranger's eyes on me, assessing. Annoyed, I turned to give him a sharp look, the kind that told him to quit it, but when I faced him, I was caught by eyes so blue I felt like I was burned. I sucked in my breath and simply stared back at eyes all the brighter for the tan of his face. As if he figured out my feelings, he looked up at the sky.

Heyward pulled the grass from his mouth. "Lizzie, meet my friend, Hugh."

My cheeks burned as I stammered out hello.

Hugh looked at me again, this time with the look of amusement I'd seen on a cat that played with its catch. "Hey, there," he drawled.

"Hugh is our neighbor. He's one of the Rhodeses from the Magnolia Bluff Plantation down yonder. They took over from the MacDonalds last winter."

I remembered Mama talking about the Rhodes family at dinner one night. She'd gone over to greet Mrs. Rhodes with a pie and declared her to be "a darling." Mama added how Mrs. Rhodes was a Barnwell from Beaufort, and thus had local ties. Mr. Gerald Rhodes hailed from Charleston. She leaned in to indicate importance. "He's a Pringle. And that," she said, putting the cherry on top, "means he's a member of society." She went on to tell me the Rhodes family had three fine-looking sons. Heyward and Hugh being the same age, Mama was pleased to see Heyward befriend him. She gave me a knowing look and told me that the second son was the same age as I was, so I could have my pick. The memory of this caused the pink of my cheeks to deepen.

"No sign of Daddy yet?" asked Heyward.

I shook my head and turned to the river, feigning great interest in searching for the boat. Hugh's presence annoyed me no end on this special day. "Mama didn't come down," I said with meaning. Mama was making a point of not showing up. We could tell from her comments that the cost of this horse was putting Mayfield at risk.

"Reckon she's still put off with the idea of a new horse," said Heyward. "But Daddy knows what he's doing."

I could only nod my head and share his belief. If both Daddy and

Wilton believed in the horse—they knew more about horses than anyone else in the entire world—then what more proof did I need?

Covey and Tripp joined us from the landing and Heyward made the introductions.

"What'd you catch?" asked Hugh amiably, pointing at Tripp's fishing creel basket.

Tripp's face was already getting sunburned, making his freckles come out in force. He eagerly opened his basket, pulling out a large flounder with pride. "Isn't he fine? Makes my mouth water just looking at him."

"What'd you use?"

"Just some mud minnows." Tripp put the flounder back in the basket and drew out a trout. "This here's the prize. I had to keep moving to catch this speck," he said, placing the fish on the wet grass in the basket.

"Mind if I join you sometime?" asked Hugh.

Tripp cast a worried glance at me and Covey. I knew he was thinking of the pact we'd made, how we couldn't invite anyone else to join our sacred triumvirate.

"I reckon you can join us," I told Hugh in an offhanded manner. "Long as you bring your own bait."

Hugh netted me in his gaze again. "*You* fish?"

I felt the familiar fury bubble up whenever someone questioned my ability just because I was a girl. "I expect I'm a damn sight better than you."

A short laugh burst from Hugh's lips.

"Don't challenge her," warned Heyward. "She'll put her mind to it and there'll be no peace until she wins."

"Eliza's the best fisherman among us," Tripp declared in my defense. "She's good at whatever she tries."

Hugh's blue eyes lit with amusement at Tripp's strident defense. "You her beau or something?"

Tripp flipped the top of his basket closed and said with a smug smile, "Or something." He met Hugh's gaze. "We're going to be married."

I closed my eyes and silently groaned.

Hugh's brows rose. "Is that so?" he drawled as he wiped his hand over his smile. "I hope you'll invite me to the wedding."

Heyward laughed. "He's always saying that. Don't pay him no mind."

Just then, Covey yelped and pointed downriver. "I see them coming!"

Our attention shifted to the barge coming upriver. The engine churned loudly, and steam poured from the narrow stack. Daddy stood at the bow, hat in hand, a wide grin stretched across his face. He waved exuberantly. I wanted to hold the memory of his face at that moment forever in my heart. It was as I imagined the face of some ancient man might've been like when he brought back fire to the tribe. Hope, happiness, and something more powerful shone in that smile. Something akin to being a hero.

The covered barge had seen better days. The paint of the hold was chipped. Beneath, dozens of wooden barrels and boxes were stored for delivery. The front of the ship held not one but three horses. The stallion was dancing nervously. The mares were taking in the scenery. The boat slowly eased close to the dock then weighed anchor. We kids were shooed off the dock to give room for the grooms to unload.

The ramp was lowered, clanging loudly against the dock, and Daddy climbed down. He waited impatiently as the groomsmen grappled with an anxious horse.

Suddenly a horse's large head appeared from the enclosure. His ears were flattened, and his eyes were wide and wild. My heart went out to the great beast. He trembled and glared then shook his head imperiously. When the groomsman jerked the lead, the horse half reared then pawed the deck. *Don't rush him*, I thought to myself. It was a dangerous moment for horse and man alike.

"Take it slow," Daddy yelled to the groomsmen. "The trouble we had loading him still has him spooked."

"Ain't none of the horses like the boat or the water," called back the groomsman. "We know our job. Let us do it. He'll either come down the ramp or jump in the water. I'm hoping he don't jump, but it's his choice."

Daddy tightened his lips and planted his fists on his hips, but waited at the end of the ramp, ready to assist when called. We kids held our breaths and watched as the stallion slowly began moving down the ramp, high-stepping and cautious.

I felt my heart expand, almost too big for my chest as my mouth opened and my breath came short. The stallion was a rich bay color with no white save for the star on his forehead. He was a big boy with strong muscles rippling as he walked. When they reached terra firma, the stallion paused and stood stock-still to gaze around, taking it all in. Sunlight glistened on his sweat and despite his seeming confidence, I could see the fear in his eyes.

Daddy came to our sides as we watched the horse prance and paw. "Meet Capitano," Daddy said, his gaze sweeping over the majesty of his horse.

"He's bigger than most," Heyward said.

"He's fourteen point three hands," Daddy said with pride.

Hugh whistled at that. "Good sized for a Marsh Tacky."

Daddy wiped his brow and shook his head. "He's had a tough time today. And he gave us one too." He took a breath and rubbed his jaw, harbingers that he was rolling into one of his stories. I leaned forward eagerly.

"So, it went like this," he began with a drawl. "Admittedly, I don't know of a horse that willingly jumps onto a barge. I was expecting some upset, especially from a stallion. Sure enough, Capitano balked the minute hoof met ramp of the barge. I tell you, he wouldn't budge. When we pulled, he started pulling the other way. When he reached the end of the lead line, well sir, that's when he began to rear. He backed off the ramp and only then did they get him calmed down some. Next we tried putting a rope across his hindquarters to pull him onto the barge. But he's a clever one and he slipped out of it. He's snorting and pawing and daring us to approach like some demon."

Daddy put out his hands. "It was then I noticed he kept looking back at the mares. So, I had a plan. I told the groom to just walk him a bit while we load the mares first. Those sweet girls loaded easily. Capitano watched it all and I reckon he figured if they could do it, so could he. And he didn't want to be left behind. The groomsman walked him slowly in a zigzag pattern back to the ramp. Capitano's breath came quick, and we girded ourselves for a battle. But then, like a sweet siren, one of the mares called out to him. That stallion lifted his head and stepped onto the ramp. He stopped. I held my breath. Then suddenly he took a single big leap and next thing you know, his front hooves are on the boat." Daddy laughed and slapped his hands. "It was noisy, and the clanging scared him a bit, but he was on board. We slammed the ramp closed and breathed a sigh of relief."

"No wonder he's spooked," Heyward said. "Poor guy."

"Yeah, he's young and all of this is new to him." Daddy pointed a finger at us. "Still, y'all be mindful of my words and don't go near him. That horse will kick you as soon as look at you."

"When can I ride him?" asked Heyward.

I looked at my brother like he'd grown another nose. "Didn't you hear what Daddy just said?"

"There ain't a horse I can't ride," Heyward boasted.

"You may have met the first one," Hugh chided.

"We'll wait on that," Daddy said then skewered Heyward with a pointed look. "Don't go near him."

My attention was diverted to the pretty mares coming down the ramp. One a smooth, red dun and the other a beautiful grulla, both with thick, dark lines that appeared to be painted down the ridges of their backs to the slopes of their tails.

"Excuse me while I tend to my ladies," Daddy said.

"They're coming too?" I asked in surprise.

"Sure are," said Daddy with a wink.

Covey leaned close to me. "Your daddy must've been like a kid in a candy store. He's done gone and buyed himself two more."

Daddy overheard and reached over to pat the top of Covey's head. "True enough. Those mares," he said pointing, "will bear the future of Mayfield."

All I could think about was what Mama was going to say.

When she learned about Daddy's new "investment," Mama had a hissy fit. It wasn't until several days—and brandy-fueled nights— later that Daddy convinced her to at least come to the barn and look at the stallion.

I stood in the barn shadows with Heyward and Lesesne as Mama approached the stall. Her long skirt rustled as Daddy walked beside her crooning out all Capitano's attributes—his pedigree, strength, size—and boasting how this horse would win all the blue ribbons and put the Marsh Tacky on the map. Before long, he extolled, there would be Marsh Tacky horses pulling carriages and plows all up and down the coast. "Just wait," he told her. "Capitano will make us our fortune."

Mama stood in front of Capitano's stall and watched with an imperious air. In the pensive silence, the stallion drew near and the two of them locked gazes through the metal bars. I clutched Heyward's arm and said a quick prayer. Capitano's head bolted up arrogantly. He snorted, turned and strode to the rear of the stall, showing her his backside before releasing a loud fart. Heyward guffawed and I slapped my hand over my mouth. Mama swung her head to look at Daddy with narrowed eyes. "Looks like you bet on the wrong horse. Again." Without another glance at the horse, she strode out.

By the end of the first week, Daddy's smile had slipped into a frown. The second week, Daddy and Wilton were at their wits' end with the stallion. They stood in front of Capitano's stall in conference. Tripp and I had finished feeding and watering the horses and went to stand beside Heyward and Hugh at Capitano's stall at the opposite side of the stable from the mares. Hugh turned and acknowledged my presence with a nod before fixing his attention back on Capitano. The stallion was warily eyeing Daddy and Wilton, his nose up and showing the whites of his eyes.

"What's going on?" I asked Heyward. It pained me to see the stallion so frightened.

My brother's eyes were bright with enjoyment, like he was at the picture show. "It's a standoff." He chuckled. "I'm betting on the stallion."

In the past weeks the two mares had settled in well enough. The sound of their munching oats could be heard throughout the stable. But Capitano didn't like anyone or anything. He glared and kicked the stable walls, stomped and snorted threateningly whenever Wilton or Daddy came to feed and water him.

"This isn't working," Daddy grumbled to Wilton. "That horse has to eat."

"He's eating. Some," Wilton replied quietly. "Some."

Daddy crossed his arms in frustration. "What'd they sell me, anyway?" he muttered to Wilton. "A devil's seed? It's like he's never been broke. He kicks and is aggressive. He won't let us near him, much less put a saddle on him. I never saw a horse that didn't gentle with you. God's truth, I'm worried. I bet a lot on that horse."

Wilton scratched his jaw. "He was settled when you bought him. Had his mama and familiars around him. This here's a high-spirited stallion, not some gelding or mare. You wanted him because he has a fire in his belly."

"I didn't think he was mad."

"He ain't. He just needs time to find the one person or animal he can trust." He rocked on his heels then said, "You know, maybe I could bring in one of Clementine's cats."

"Say what?"

"I've known a barn cat to calm a horse. Maybe a goat. Or I reckon we could bring close one of the mares he come with. They're his pasture mates. He knows them and they smell of home. Those girls have to find their place in the pecking order here. But he already knows he's the king."

Daddy glanced at Wilton. "Be careful of yourself. I can't lose you." As though on cue, Capitano kicked the stall. Daddy grimaced. "And don't let the children near him."

"That'll be hard." Wilton glanced over his shoulder toward the pack of us leaning on stalls and sitting on hay bales. At his glance, Heyward stood up to come forward. Wilton gave him a subtle shake of his head. Heyward's face fell and he stepped back.

"Heyward's eager. And Eliza . . ." Wilton chuckled softly. "That one is here most every day when the sun goes down. She slinks in like a barn cat when she thinks no one is here."

Daddy's face sharpened. "What's she doing in here?"

"Singing."

"What?" Daddy paused and cocked his ear like he didn't hear right. "You say she's singing? What the . . . I don't like her in here alone with this horse."

"She doesn't go in the stall. I'm watching her and wouldn't allow that. She just stands by his stall and sings to him. Real sweet like. Truth be told, the only time I see that horse settle is when she sings to him."

Daddy squinted his eyes in thought then turned his head to look at me. Feeling his gaze, I sat up straight. I saw something shift in his eyes when he studied me. A kind of wonder and, dare I think it, respect.

"Lizzie, come here a minute."

My eyes widened and I rose from the bale of hay, aware that all the kids were watching me, the whites of their eyes showing just like Capitano's. I walked slowly and confidently, careful not to startle the horse. Capitano snorted and shook his head when I approached. I glanced up and met his big eyes, then looked at my daddy. "Yes sir?"

"I hear tell you've been sneaking in here at night," Daddy said.

My stomach fell as I prepared to meet my doom. "Yes sir."

"You sing to Capitano?"

I swallowed. "Yes sir."

"What do you sing?"

I was flummoxed and my head spun. I scratched my head in thought. "Well, sir, I don't rightly know. I sing whatever comes to mind. But . . ." I paused, not wanting to sound like a silly girl.

"But what?"

I rubbed my nose and muttered, "I think he likes 'Camptown Races.'"

A short laugh escaped Daddy's lips. "Say again?" He turned to Wilton and was greeted with a wide grin. Daddy shook his head and said, "Well, go on. Let me hear it."

"Now?" I glanced over my shoulder to see Hugh watching me with curiosity shining in his eyes. Heyward was watching me too, only his expression was stunned.

I blew out air, nodded, then turned to face Capitano. The horse's eyes were on me, liquid and curious. I didn't see any changes that meant he'd rear, bite, or kick. Emboldened, I strode up to his stall and grabbed hold of the metal bars, pressing my face closer. Capitano took a step toward me. I could feel his warm breath on my face.

"Careful now," Daddy said softly.

I wasn't the least bit afraid of Capitano. When that horse looked into my eyes, I saw clear as day that he didn't have a mean bone in his body. He was frightened and lonely, was all. Capitano was the only stallion in a barn with geldings and mares. Daddy kept him separate from the others. Treated him differently. Had high expectations for him too. Those nights I visited him, I stood close in the dim light and spoke in a low, soothing voice as I told him I felt the same way. I was the only girl in my house among my brothers. My family had expectations of me too. I didn't comprehend what they wanted, not really, and I was sometimes afraid. No one asked if we wanted the burden. But we knew we had to carry it. I told Capitano I would be his friend. He didn't have anything to prove to me.

"How are you doing, Captain?" I asked in a soothing voice. I understood why they gave the stallion a Spanish name. It was on account of the Carolina Marsh Tacky being developed from Spanish horses brought to the island and coastal areas of South Carolina by Spanish explorers and settlers as early as the sixteenth century. But I didn't speak no Spanish, and *Captain* felt right on my tongue. I figured the horse liked it too. When I called him Captain, he nickered.

I cleared my throat and began to sing in a soft voice:

De Camptown ladies sing dis song—doodah. Doodah.
De Camptown race track's five miles long—oh doo dah day.
Gwine to run all night
Gwine to run all day,
I'll bet my money on de bobtail nag
Somebody bet on de bay.

When I finished, Captain nickered again and shook his head. The taut rippling of his muscles stopped. He strolled over to the other side of the stall and commenced to pee a river.

Daddy whooped and slapped Wilton on the shoulder. "I'll be damned. Looks like Capitano's found his familiar."

Wilton rubbed the back of his head and acknowledged the truth of it with a slow nod. "I have to admit, this is the first time someone stole my rodeo. But if that horse can be gentled by a small girl, I'll take it."

I beamed at Daddy and Wilton, proud to have been found worthy in the barn. From my peripheral vision I watched Heyward cross his arms and frown. It served to make my grin bigger.

Daddy pointed a finger at me. "Still," he said in a firm voice, "I don't want you going into that stall alone, hear? I still don't trust him. Not till I give you the go-ahead. But you can accompany me and Wilton when we do the feeding and watering. We'll take it one day at a time."

"And I can still come in and sing to him?"

Daddy reached out to rustle the hair atop my head. "I'd appreciate it if you would."

Chapter Twelve

FOREST TRAILS traverse the ecologically rich area encompassing the water-
sheds of the Ashepoo, Combahee, and Edisto rivers. The trails are made up of
organic matter, including fallen leaves, twigs, and decomposing plant material.
Over time, these organic materials break down and contribute to the nutrient-
rich soil along the trail.

1912

June became July, then the dog days of August approached. We were
seeking shade like black dogs in a heat wave.

I rose early each morning to spend time with Capitano in the
cooler morning air. He expected my presence in the stable, even
demanded it. He settled on me to feed him and let me, and only me,
brush him and stroke his velvety nose. It was in these everyday
routines that trust between us was built and we became friends.

Mama came to accept the horse's affection for me. I venture to
think she maybe even took pride in the fact that I—being a girl—was
the chosen one. Not that we discussed it, or she ever openly praised
me. It was more she looked the other way when I went to the barn.
And there was one morning that I awoke to find a new pair of tall
riding boots and gloves by my bed.

As much as I enjoyed my time with Capitano, I had less time with
my other friends, Covey and Tripp. As we grew older, we took on
more responsibilities at Mayfield. Tripp loved helping at the animal
barn. Covey assisted Clementine in the house. Still, we gathered in

the tree hollow most afternoons with sugar cookies to talk about our days and just be together.

When at last came the day Daddy let me saddle Captain for our first ride, I felt the first indefinable something in the air that hinted at a change in the seasons. The horses felt it too. The sky was clear, the air cooler, and the mosquitoes were at bay. When I nodded that I was ready to mount, Daddy's hands trembled when he gave me a lift up. I knew he was afraid I'd be hurt, but I wasn't scared in the least. I couldn't wait to ride Captain. I put my boot heel in his hands and in a single hoist, I was astride my horse. Captain shifted his weight, testing my weight on his back.

"Don't do anything rash," Daddy said as he shortened the leather stirrups. "Just take him around the pen a few times. Keep it slow and easy."

"I know what to do." I looked to the fence and saw Heyward and Hugh perched and eagle-eyed. I shook off their gazes like Captain shook off the pesky flies.

Cap began walking at the mere pressure of my leg and a click of my tongue. I walked and trotted him around the pen, me learning his cues and he learning mine. At the completion of each circle, Captain veered toward the gate like a magnet. I guided him away, but I knew what he was asking for. He was a smart horse and bored with the pen. He sensed the wide world outside the gate. After a short workout, I slowed to a stop. Captain lifted his head as high and curved as a Persian painting.

"You're not going out," Daddy called back from the fence.

"What are we waiting for? He's not happy stuck in here. He's ready to go out on the trails. I can handle him. I promise."

Daddy looked at his boots, then lifted his head to Wilton. He met Daddy's gaze and nodded his head.

"I'm going with you," Daddy declared, straightening.

"Me too!" called Heyward, leaping from the fence. Hugh was right behind him. They sprinted to the stable to mount up.

I grinned as I took a few more rounds of the pen. Finishing the third, I spotted Daddy, Heyward, and Hugh saddled and ready.

I sensed Cap's eagerness in the tautness of his muscles and how he held his head high and his neck outstretched. I bent to pat his neck. "This is our moment, Cap," I said. "You trust me, and I'll trust you."

The gate opened and I was proud that Cap didn't charge out. "Good boy," I murmured, then nudged him with my leg. His ears communicated his emotions. They were pricked forward as we left the fenced area and walked single file along the gravel path that led to the woodland trail. I felt the tension flow from Captain as we ambled along the shaded forest trails. His ears were erect and his tail high as he took in his surroundings. It seemed all of nature was smiling on us this morning. The sun shone on the dark, green pines and there were just enough clouds to provide passing shade.

Hugh trotted up to ride beside me. The dun mare and the stallion, being pasture mates, walked in easy camaraderie. "You're good on that stallion," he said.

I turned to look at him, feeling saucy. I knew I was doing well, but it was nice to hear. He had a straw cowboy hat on his head, and his blue eyes appraised me beneath the rim.

"I think you're riding the tough one."

"She's a good girl," Hugh said, reaching out to pat the dun. "She was just checking me out." We walked a few paces. "Like you did when we first met."

I gave a snort of disbelief. "I most certainly did not."

"If you say so."

"I don't have time for silly talk," I said and gave Captain a nudge, sending him into a trot. Hugh clicked and the dun came trotting up once more to our side.

"Hello again."

I glanced at him with disdain, then with pressure from my legs, sent Cap into a canter. I heard Hugh laugh behind me.

"Hey, slow down!" came a shout from Daddy.

I laughed to myself, knowing I wasn't going to slow down. Captain and I were having too much fun. Up ahead the trail opened to a field of soft grass. My heart expanded. I knew where I was.

"Let's show them how it's done," I said and loosened the reigns. The Captain lifted his big head, tasting freedom, and he pushed himself faster over the grass. I heard Hugh galloping behind me. I bent low against Cap's neck and tucked in. Cap's ears went back, and he pushed himself faster. My hair was a flag waving behind me. Ahead was my glorious live oak tree. Her dark, mysterious hollow draped in curling ferns, her limbs stretched far out in welcome.

After rounding the tree, I spotted Hugh and Daddy entering the field at a canter with dust at the hooves. "Whoa, boy," I said. Hugh caught up to our side, a grin stretched across his face. Together we slowed to a walk and let the horses cool.

"You're something else," he said, squinting at me in the sunlight.

"Where's your hat?"

"Blew off somewhere in this field," he said with a short laugh. Then, indicating Captain with a lift of his chin, he said, "That's one fast horse."

"The fastest I've ever ridden." I glanced up to see Daddy cutting across the field toward us, Heyward behind him. My gut tightened and I worried that I'd be yelled at in front of Hugh. But what did I expect? I'd disobeyed his order. Captain stood as noble as the prince he was, his body glistening in the sunlight. His head was up and he whinnied when Daddy and Hugh drew to a halt before us. I sat behind his raised neck, proud of my horse, and held firm the reins. I'd get no less than I deserved.

Daddy's eyes were bright and focused on the stallion. He took a breath. "You call that going slow?" His tone was accusing.

"No, sir."

He shook his head and muttered something I couldn't hear.

Hugh spoke up. "It's my fault, sir. I challenged her to a race."

Daddy's eyes were thunderous when he turned on Hugh. "You're a damn fool."

"Yes sir. Sorry, sir."

I held my breath.

"Did you see how fast Capitano was?" asked Heyward, diverting Daddy's attention.

Daddy curtly nodded and looked out over the field. He fought a smile. "It was a sight to see."

"He's got more in him," I said. "He loves to run. I didn't have to urge him. Not at all. He's got heart." There wasn't nothing that Daddy loved more in a horse than heart.

Daddy's eyes gleamed as he listened, and his gaze swept the beautiful bay stallion. I knew this was what he'd hoped for, and it was a joy to be able to show him his worries were for naught.

"He's still young," Daddy said in a gruff voice. "And he needs training. You rode him well, Lizzie." Then, almost begrudgingly, "You're a natural."

I beamed in the saddle.

Daddy turned to Heyward. "I want you to start riding him. Put him through his paces. He's ready to train."

Hurt stung deep. "But he's my horse," I blurted out. "He runs for me."

Daddy turned to look at me kindly and smiled in a condescending way. "That he does, darlin'. And you've done good with him. Real good." He paused to adjust his seat. When he looked at me again, his smile was gone. "But he's not your horse. He's my horse. And your brother is the one who will be riding him in the races."

"But Daddy—"

"Capitano has to win. Plain and simple. That's his job, hear? To show the world how great he—a Marsh Tacky—is. He must if he's going to bring in a stud fee worthy of him."

I opened my mouth to speak, but Heyward gave a subtle shake of his head to indicate I shouldn't. My shoulders slumped and I tightened the reins in my hands. "Yes sir. I'll walk him back." I guided Captain toward the trails home, leaving all my triumph on the field behind me.

Once on the woodland trail the shade was cool, and the loamy smell of compost filled the air. It was a comforting scent. I felt the strain of the morning ease from my shoulders as I rocked in the saddle. The tears that filled my eyes shamed me. I told myself I was being foolish. What was important was Captain had his chance to escape the pen and run free. I helped him show Daddy what he was capable of. Maybe I couldn't ride him in the races, being a girl. But I could give Captain the confidence he needed to win. I could do that for him. For Daddy. For Mayfield.

Hugh rode the dun up beside me and we walked in tandem for a while, the wide hooves making soft thud noises on the earth. In a nearby pine a mockingbird was singing its heart out in a long repertoire. I listened to his song, thinking he didn't ask for any thanks for his soul-piercing effort. He sang for the joy of it. There was a lesson there.

Hugh finally spoke. "Ain't nobody ever going to ride that horse as well as you can."

I looked over and saw the violence of his emotions in his heavy-lidded eyes. I was confused by it and could only mutter, "Thank you." And then loyalty to my brother won out. "Heyward's the best rider."

"He's good. I'll give him that." Then Hugh smiled. "But not as good as me."

Now it was my turn to laugh. There was a friendly camaraderie in his glance.

"And not as good as you," Hugh added. "Least, not on that horse."

"We'll have to see," I said, accepting my fate.

"I've seen you fish, and I've seen you ride. Boy or girl, you're the one to beat, in my book."

My mind swirled as I looked ahead at the trees and leaves, not see-ing anything. Cap set one foot before the other as I rocked in silence. But my heart was beating fast. I didn't care if Hugh ever called me beautiful or wrote poetry in my honor. Nothing else Hugh Rhodes could have said to me would have sounded so sweet on my ears.

Chapter Thirteen

GREAT HORNED OWLS (*Bubo virginianus*) are common owls in North America. Named for the tufts of feathers that sit on top of its head, they have big eyes that don't move in their sockets. Large birds of prey with a wingspan up to 4.5 feet, owls are monogamous, very territorial, and often remain on the same territory year-round.

1914

We plowed through the fall and winter seasons like oxen through hard, clumped soil. Heyward and Hugh—our golden boys—had left for high school in Charleston and Mr. Coxwold mourned his prize pupil's absence from the schoolroom. During the chill of winter Covey often stayed the night at Mayfield. We'd while away our free time talking about everything and nothing while sitting in front of a warm fire or cuddled near the warmth of the iron stove with Clementine in the kitchen. We moved from merely reading books to writing our own. Our imaginations knew no bounds as we created stories of lost princesses, being shipwrecked on uninhabited islands, or fairies in the forest. Covey and I became more than friends. We were soulmates. I could tell Covey anything and know she'd keep my confessions secret.

Yet, no matter how much I chatted on about my life and problems, it was rare for Covey to share with me her inner thoughts. She listened, asked me questions, had advice to offer, as any friend would.

But I sometimes wondered if she did not have problems, or if she simply preferred not to tell me her secrets.

March heralded spring. Covey and I were in the library, eagerly anticipating the end of the school year when the doors would be thrown open and we'd be free to explore the outdoors. We pulled out our journals to ready them for our summer wanderings. I gingerly turned the worn pages filled with years of my notes, drawings of birds and insects, and littered with dried leaves, wildflowers, and a few bird feathers.

"What's this bird?" I asked Covey, pointing to my drawing of a black-and-white bird with pointy wings.

Covey leaned over and snickered. "I've never seen a bird with legs so long and feet so big."

I slapped my hand over my childlike drawing. "Aw, be nice."

"That's a kite," she replied with a giggle. Covey opened her journal to the page depicting her own rendition. Covey's drawings were things of wonder. Where my drawing looked like a stick figure, hers were exquisitely detailed, with beautiful color. She even painted in a backdrop of bright green loblolly pines with their scaled tree trunks.

"How'd you learn to draw so fine?" I asked, feeling only admiration. "I swear, I feel like I'm looking at the real bird."

Covey smiled, pleased. "I don't know how I do it. I just do it."

My mother entered the room carrying two steaming mugs of tea. We welcomed the tea with thanks, holding the warm mugs in our cold fingers.

Mama bent over to look at our journals. "What are you working on there?"

"Oh, nothing," I said, moving to close my journal. I didn't want her comparing my drawing to Covey's for surely it would be found wanting.

Mama's hand was quicker. She stopped me, spreading open the

book. "You're identifying birds?" she asked us. I wasn't sure how I felt about the hint of incredulousness in her voice.

"Yes'm," replied Covey. "And not just birds. But all the critters and plants we find outdoors. Every summer, it's like a game for us."

Mama moved so close I smelled roses. "Your drawing is good," Mama told Covey. "Can I look?"

Covey handed my mother her journal. I saw Covey wring her hands as Mama studied page after page.

"You have talent," Mama said at length, her eyes appraising Covey. "I'm glad you're in school with Eliza. You are a good influence on her." She gently put her hand on my head then leaned over to look at my journal. I was glad to see how Mama had taken a liking toward Covey over the years, though I still writhed in discomfort under her critical gaze. I sighed, slouched back in my chair.

"Mine looks like a three-year-old drew it," I admitted, grimacing in embarrassment.

"True. But look at all you wrote to describe the bird," Mama said. "Your details are excellent. And . . ." She paused and surprise entered her voice. "What's this?"

I opened my eyes to see she was pointing at a verse of poetry I'd written. I silently groaned to myself. Now I was really going to be mocked. My mother not only wrote poetry, she read in her books of poetry every day like a nun did a prayer book. "Oh, don't look," I said, leaning forward to cover the words with my hand. "It's nothing."

Mama slipped the journal from my hand and read aloud my poem on the swallow-tailed kite.

A graceful bird of black and white
Darted swiftly into sight.
On pointed wings, with dips and curves
In forked tail spirals and snowy whirls.

Oh swallow from the gods up high
I stand quiet for a reply
to the prayers of a lonely soul.
Will you make a splintered soul whole?

Do you signal that winter remains,
a time of cold, hunger and pain?
Or are you a harbinger of spring
when the sun shines and weary hearts sing?

Mama's dark eyes studied me with the same intensity she'd read the journals, as though searching for something important. "Did you write this?"

My hands curled tight. "Yes'm."

Mama's face stilled, then she slipped the book down to the table. "It's a sweet enough ditty. A bit mawkish," she said in a manner of pronouncement. "But your metaphors are wrong. Kites are not messengers from God. That would be ravens and crows. Perhaps eagles. Or doves. Noah, you recall . . ." She pinned me with her gaze. "Do you have any other poetry you've written?"

I shrank in my seat and lied. I did write poetry. Though she never taught me, like she did Lesesne. When I felt the urge the words just flowed out of my heart, not my head. I was sure they were all as silly as the one Mama just criticized. Hearing her say it, however, my soul felt bruised. My mother was the last person I wanted to show anything I wrote.

"No," I replied.

Mama's brow rose. "Really? You wrote only one poem?" She waited for me to say something, as if she knew I was lying. I felt like a small bird in the trance of a cat.

Suddenly, Covey spoke. "Excuse me, ma'am. I don't mean to be rude. But in truth, the kite *is* thought to be a messenger by some tribes of the Indians. Wilton told me."

Mama shifted her gaze back to Covey. "Did he?"

It sounded more like a challenge than a question. I held my breath.

Covey did not look away. "Yes'm."

Mama moved closer to Covey and looked again at her journal. "I don't see that you've identified this bird."

"Oh, that's because I know what it is. It's a kite," Covey replied easily.

"Yes, but what kind of kite?"

Covey stared back at her, eyes wide. "What kind?"

"Girls, I took great pains to organize the library so it shouldn't be hard to locate reference books." Mama walked swiftly across the room to the shelves, her skirt swishing at her ankles. She raised one hand to indicate the shelves. "Pay attention. Starting from the left, this is the wildlife and nature section, where you'll find books to help you identify the animals in your journals." She continued walking along the bookshelves. "This is agriculture. South Carolina history. National and world history." She walked to another wall of the room. "This is fiction. Here, the books are in alphabetical order by author."

She eyed the wildlife and nature section then pulled out three books and set them on the table. Slapping dust from her hands she said, "You can start with these."

Covey and I gasped in awe when Mama carefully opened the pages of a book by Mark Catesby. It was very old; its leather bindings were dusty and curled. Mama was reverent as she revealed one page after another filled with gloriously colored birds.

"Girls, it pleases me that you are so diligent at your studies. I've spent many hours in this library." Her gaze flickered across the room with a proprietary air. "These books have been my dearest companions over the years. If I can be of any help to you in your research, please let me know." She put her finger on Covey's drawing of the kite. "That is a swallow-tailed kite."

With a perfunctory smile, she left the room.

I watched her straight-backed walk, elegant and sure, as she departed. There were times I'd wondered why my father married my mother. She could be volatile. Contrary. Opinionated. And yet, she was also intelligent and even kind. Like today. Mama seemed right eager to help us with our studies. Almost like she wanted to join us and study too. I scratched my head and thought there was still so much I did not know about her.

Covey leaned closer and asked in a quiet voice, "Why didn't you tell your mama about your poems?"

I turned my attention to my journal. "Why do you think?"

"She might like them. She's always going on about poetry. She might think better of you if she knew you were writing some."

"They're not good."

"I think they're good."

I smiled, embarrassed for the compliment. "You're my best friend. You have to say that."

Covey reached over to tap my hand. I looked up to meet her soft hazel eyes.

"Just don't throw them out. Give them to me. I like them. Promise?"

I snorted, but inside was pleased. "Aw, heck, Covey. Sure, I promise."

The following morning the rain stopped, and birds resumed their myriad calls from the trees. The kitchen was warm and redolent of the scents of sizzling bacon and perking coffee. Clementine was at the wood-burning stove, swiftly moving from pot to pan. Covey, Lesesne, and I sat at the scrubbed wood table shoveling in grits before the school bell rang. Clementine kept the kitchen door open on days the oven ran hot, but I could still feel the pressing heat pouring out. Suddenly Clementine let out a short yelp. I swallowed hard and swung my head around.

"Lord in heaven, what did you bring me this morning?" she cried as she slammed down the coffee pot and hurried to the door. At the threshold, Midnight, the feral black cat, stood with something in its mouth. Calmly, it dropped a small bird from its mouth then looked at Clementine with pride.

"Oh no!" cried Covey, rushing over to look closer. She shooed the cat away, and hovering over the small bird, her face fell. "Aw, it's a Carolina wren."

Midnight sauntered to the porch, sat, and watched our reaction with detached interest.

"Can you save it?" I asked, rushing to her side. The bird's eyes were closed and legs stiff.

Covey shook her head. "It's dead. Poor thing." She scowled at Midnight. "Bad cat." She hissed. Then said to Clementine, "You ought not to let that cat kill birds."

Clementine remained unflustered. "Child, you know that's just a cat's way." She fetched kitchen scraps from the table then went to the porch and tossed them to the waiting cat. Though Clementine clearly favored the animal, even named it, she never claimed it. "I don't see you frettin' when he brings us a mouse."

"It's wrong to kill such a sweet bird," Covey argued.

"A cat's got to make a livin' too," Clementine said. "You're eatin' bacon now, aren't you? You know where that came from."

We all kept our silence.

Lesesne drew close to pick up the dead bird. He held it in his palm, looking at it dispassionately while touching the stiff straight legs. I hurried to his side, sticking out my hand.

"Give it here, Les," I said. "I'll bury it."

He turned his shoulder. "I want to study it. I'll bury it when I'm done."

"Best to bury it now," Clementine said firmly and reached out for the corpse.

Lesesne frowned but handed it over, then looked out at the cat sitting on the porch, licking its paw. "That cat ought not to have done that."

Later that day when we returned to the kitchen for afternoon snacks, we found Clementine sitting in a chair crying softly. The black cat lay couched in her ample lap. Only it wasn't moving. Covey and I exchanged worried glances and gathered around her, slipping our arms around her shoulder.

"What's happened to Midnight?" I asked in a soft voice, knowing something was wrong.

"I don't rightly know," Clementine said. She sighed shakily and stroked the dark mass of fur that was Midnight. "I went out to carry lunch to Wilton at the barn, and I spied Midnight just lying on the ground. He was already gone."

"He seemed fine this morning," said Covey. It sounded pitifully inadequate.

I noticed a spot of blood on the cat's head, right over his eyes. Lowering to look closer I said, "Why lookee here. Something hit him. A small rock. Or maybe a pebble."

Clementine only shook her head and sniffed. "I reckon he just fell. You know how he liked to climb up on the stable roof."

Suspicion struck deep and I looked over to Lesesne. He sat alone at the table, gazing out the window, eating his corn bread, seemingly oblivious to what was being said. "Where's your slingshot?" I asked him. Daddy gave it to him for Christmas and told him never to shoot a living thing with it. But all that winter, Covey and I found dead birds and squirrels in the woods.

Lesesne remained staring impassively out the window. "You hear me?" I called out louder. This time my brother slowly turned his head and lifted his heavy-lidded gaze to mine. He opened his mouth as if to answer. I leaned forward. But instead of answering my question, he bit off another piece of corn bread and began to chew. His lips turned slightly to a faint smile before he looked away again.

My heart went cold. Shaken, I glanced over at Covey. Her eyes were as wide as mine. We shared a knowing glance.

Chapter Fourteen

❦

THE MARSH TACKY (*Equus caballus*) is a breed of horse native to the South Carolina low country. It is a small-to medium-size horse with a compact build and solid hooves known for its resilience, endurance, sure-footedness, and ability to navigate through marshes, swamps, and difficult landscapes of the region. The Marsh Tacky is South Carolina's official state heritage horse.

1914

The summer of 1914 I turned fourteen and was coming into womanhood. Mama and I had come to an uneasy peace. I agreed to take on assorted household duties and learned to sew, mend, and do needlework. Things Mama said were necessary skills for a young woman. In exchange for my docile domestication, I was allowed to assume Heyward's duties in the stable when he was at school in Charleston. I now helped train the horses and basked in Wilton's and my father's compliments.

The farm was surer-footed after the previous seasons' bountiful crops of cotton, corn, and sweet hay. The cucumbers did so well Daddy planted a bigger crop. "It's going to be a good year," he predicted, slapping his hands like a man before a feast. It was fine to see Daddy feeling hopeful again. Though Mama was concerned about Daddy's strutting ways. "Don't count your chickens before they hatch," she warned him. Clementine shook her head and chuckled, "I hope you like cucumbers."

Though our farm provided plenty, Covey and I rode every week with Wilton in the horse and cart to the farmers' market for fresh butter and cheese, and other fixings when our supply ran out. Wilton traded mutton, pork, and duck for beef, a welcome change of diet at Mayfield.

Though our world felt insular, a war had started overseas. War was good business for Beaufort, however. The U.S. Marine Corps started a training program right here in Beaufort at Parris Island. It brought jobs and much needed income to our coastal city. The streets were abuzz with news of German submarines attacking merchant and passenger ships, though President Wilson declared we would not enter the fray. Heyward and my daddy were all fired up about it, that was for certain.

Nineteen fourteen was important to me, because it was the year Daddy declared Capitano was ready to race.

Heyward was returning from Charleston for the big race. The house was brimming with excitement. The Easter holiday had Mama and Clementine busy in the kitchen boiling eggs and baking cakes.

I was out breezing Captain through his workout. As I dismounted, Wilton came forward and took the reins. My face was red from exertion.

"The race will be run on the sandy beach at Edisto," he said, then reached up to stroke Captain's neck. "He's fast here, sure 'nuff. But I'm not sure how he'll run on that track."

"He's a Marsh Tacky. They love the sand," Daddy said with confidence.

"Captain will do fine on any track," I said.

Wilton chuckled and shook his head. "You're mighty confident in that horse, aren't you?"

It was my turn to stroke Captain's long neck. He was still moist from his workout. "Mr. Coxwold read us a book by Washington Allston. Mama said we were distantly related to him," I added, knowing that would impress Daddy. "He wrote, 'Confidence is the soul of genius.' Well, sir. I figure we just need to give Captain the confidence he needs to win the gymkhana."

"And just how do you propose we do that?" Daddy asked, amused.

"Tell him he's going to win," I replied, looking into the horse's watery brown eyes. "And believe it."

The gymkhana was held every spring at Edisto Beach. It was a sprint race open to any breed of horse. The race brought no prize other than bragging rights, but for a breeder, it was a major opportunity to showcase one's stock. Daddy had raced Marsh Tackies before, and they did tolerably well. But this year he was crowing that Capitano would win it all. I worried that if Captain failed, then somehow I would fail as well.

After Daddy and Wilton left the barn, I relished a few minutes alone with Captain. His ears flickered when I drew close, and he came to nuzzle my pocket.

"I spoil you. You know that, right?" I scolded as I reached into my barn pinafore pocket to retrieve a bit of apple. I reached up to pat his neck, scratch behind his ears, then let my palm slide down his velvety nose. It was a pattern we both knew well. Captain thrived on routine. As long as he kept to his schedule, he was in good spirits. Change it, and he grew obstinate. I cleaned his hooves then changed his water. When I was done, I leaned against his neck and spoke softly.

"Cap, you remember Heyward. He's ridden you plenty of times. You get along fine. Heyward's a good rider, gentle with his hands. Today, he's going to start riding you for a while. For that race I've been telling you about. When he takes you to the meadow, he's going to let you run free. When he does, I want you to show him what you've got. Okay?"

I heard the barn door open. Covey came running in, eyes blazing.

"He's arriving!" she cried. "Heyward's coming!"

I felt a surge of joy. I moved quickly to return my brushes and close the stall. Captain snorted, aware of the excitement. I patted his neck then galloped after Covey to the front of the house, arriving just as the gleaming black open carriage, streaked now with dirt from the roads, came to a stop before the house. Panting, Covey and I beamed when we spotted the two young men in travel clothes sitting under the awning in back. Mama and Daddy made their way down the front stairs, and Mama's gaze took in the Rhodeses' fine carriage.

Hugh was the first to stand. He swung open the carriage door and jumped to the marble mounting block, then offered his hand to Heyward. When my brother rose, we all gasped to see his arm in a sling. I ran up, refraining from springing into my brother's arms. I stopped abruptly, my cheeks hot, and brushed the hair from my face.

"You're home!" I cried, then blurted, "What happened to your arm?"

Heyward made a face and shrugged. "I broke it."

"You *what?*" boomed Daddy.

I swung my head to see Mama and Daddy approach. Mother's face was all concern. Daddy's face was thunderous.

"Heyward!" Mama cried, rushing to his side. Her hands fluttered about the cast, not daring to touch it. "Tell me what happened?"

Heyward's glance moved uneasily to Daddy. His smile grew forced as his brows gathered. "It was a football accident. It's a small break. Nothing to worry about."

"Football!" Daddy exploded. "You broke your arm playing a *game* when you knew the Edisto races were coming? How could you be so reckless?"

Mother glared at him. "He didn't break his arm deliberately, Rawlins. Now hush, or it'll be your neck that breaks next."

Daddy clamped his lips tight then stormed up the stairs into the house. Heyward exhaled and met Hugh's gaze with a crooked smile. In the resulting silence, muffled sobs could be heard.

Heyward turned to Covey. "Why are you crying?"

Covey moved her hands from her tear-stained face. "I'm not sure," she choked out. "Part of me is crying because I'm happy you're home. Part of me is crying because I'm sad you're hurt."

Heyward's face softened. "Be happy. It's much better than being sad."

"You all go inside," Mama said, shuffling them off. Then to Hugh, "Will you be joining us for dinner?"

Hugh shook his head. "Thank you, but no ma'am. My parents are expecting me. I'll come by tomorrow to check on the patient, if that's all right."

"It'll be our pleasure. Thank you again for bringing Heyward home in your fine carriage. You're a good friend. Please send my best to your parents. I expect we'll see them at the races?"

"Yes ma'am. They wouldn't miss it. They're bringing out a few maidens."

"Very good then."

Hugh's gaze shifted to me and swept over the riding britches under my skirt and the soiled barn pinafore. Catching my eye, his smile widened, and he tipped his cap. "Miss Rivers."

My cheeks flushed the color of the azaleas as I watched the carriage drive off.

A chill was felt in the house that had nothing to do with the weather. Daddy was drinking in his barn office. Mama's smile was forced at the dinner table. We struggled through a meal of roast lamb and potatoes, after which we ducked off to our rooms. That night we heard our parents fighting and hollering up a storm. The raucous across the hall made sleep impossible so I retreated upstairs to sleep in Heyward's attic room on the spare bed, feeling grateful Tripp hadn't yet arrived to witness the spectacle.

The moon was bright outside the window, casting the room in a silvery light. I lay for a while listening to the tree frogs serenading in the damp night. I couldn't see my brother across the room, but I knew he wasn't asleep.

"Does it hurt?" I asked about his arm.

"More an ache."

"I'm sorry you got hurt."

"I'm sorry too." He groaned loudly. "I didn't figure Daddy would be so blistered. I feel bad about it. He won't even talk to me."

"He will. He's just got a lot of pride riding on that race."

Heyward didn't reply.

"Well, you didn't do it on purpose," I said to make him feel better.

When Heyward didn't reply again I knew he'd fallen into one of his quiet spells. I rolled over to my side and mumbled, "Good night."

<hr />

The following afternoon Hugh returned to Mayfield as promised. Entering the house, he whispered gravely that he had news to share and instructed us to gather at the gazebo. The white wooden structure was tucked in the trees by the river, out of sight and sound from the house.

The yellow powder of pollen coated the earth and the gazebo benches and clung to our boots as we tramped over the grass. Even the river was a swirling slate blue and yellow like a Van Gogh painting. Lesesne's nose was running, and his eyes were the color of poppies. Hugh took a rag and wiped the pollen off the white bench for Covey and me to sit. We huddled close as Hugh bent forward, arms on his thighs. He spoke in the low tones of secrecy.

"I found out that your father and my father made a bet on the race. That's why your father is so upset you're not riding."

"A bet?" Heyward's features sharpened. "What did he wager?"

Hugh hesitated. "You recall how your daddy's been after our pond that abuts our properties?"

Heyward's chin jutted out. "*Your* pond? Sweetwater Pond has always been Mayfield property. It shouldn't never have been sold."

Sweetwater Pond had been sold decades ago in a desperate moment by Rawlins's father when the rice plantation failed. Our grandfather had bills to pay and hungry mouths to feed. Likewise, Daddy didn't have the money to buy it back. It was all he could manage, with Mama's support, to keep Mayfield afloat. But the dream of bringing Sweetwater Pond back to Mayfield was always in our hearts.

Covey gently touched Heyward's arm.

Heyward met her gaze, nodded, and mumbled an apology to Hugh.

I watched the exchange and wondered about Covey's influence over my brother.

Hugh spread out his palms with equanimity. "The deed was done long ago. It was part of our property when we bought it. My father doesn't hold any special attachments to the pond, truth be told. But he's grown partial to Marsh Tackies. Do you recall he came by to look at the horses a while back?"

We nodded.

Hugh cast a wary glance my way. "Well, Daddy saw Captain run. And he's been yearning for that horse ever since."

I bolted to my feet. "Well, he can't have him!"

"Ain't no way Mr. Rivers will ever sell that horse," said Covey.

Hugh put his hands up in defense. "I know, I know. So does my daddy. He knows your father loves that horse. And he knows he loves Sweetwater Pond too." He slapped his palms on his thighs in summation. "Thus, the bet."

Heyward sat straight, his face pale. "You mean, Daddy bet the horse against Sweetwater Pond?"

Hugh nodded. "If your dad wins, he gets Sweetwater Pond. And if he loses—"

"—your father would get Captain." My voice choked.

Hugh nodded again, his face grim.

There was a pained silence as we all considered the possibilities.

"Shit," said Heyward as he leaned back against the railing. He put his hand to his forehead and groaned.

I couldn't speak. I couldn't imagine losing Cap. I slumped back to the bench and felt Covey's hand over mine.

Heyward sat bolt upright. "Wait. If Capitano doesn't race, the bet is off."

Hugh shook his head. "If he doesn't race, your father forfeits."

"But that's not fair. Not if there isn't a race!" I yelled, directing my anger at Hugh. After all, he was in the enemy camp. "You can't just take our horse."

Hugh looked stricken. "Lizzie, don't be mad at me. *I* didn't make the bet."

"You're a Rhodes, aren't you?" I said accusingly.

"I'm on your side. I came here to help."

For a moment, we eyed each other, tongue-tied.

"Don't kill the messenger," Heyward said sullenly. "We're in this mess because of me."

"What can we do?" I put my hands to my face.

"I thought about it, and I have an idea," said Hugh.

All heads turned toward him.

"Eliza has to ride Captain," said Hugh.

My mouth slipped open as I stared back at him.

"She can't," snapped Heyward. He looked at me apologetically. "I wish she could," he hurried to add. "She'd win it over me. But she's a girl."

Everyone waited for me to explode, but I couldn't argue the fact.

Hugh looked at Heyward, eyes flashing. "I found a copy of the rules," he said. "Nowhere does it state that a girl cannot ride. The race is open to all horses, and it doesn't state the rider has to be a male or a female, child or adult. It's merely a social custom." He grinned victoriously. "Officially, Eliza could ride and win."

I held my breath and looked at Heyward, waiting for his response. Could it be possible?

Heyward's brow furrowed and he scratched behind his ear as he pondered. Then he dropped his hand in a desultory way. "You know as well as I do if Lizzie shows up on the horse, they'll never let her ride. Hell," he swore. "The women will be up in arms same as the men. Maybe worse. They'll stop her."

"Not if they don't figure out that it's her," said Hugh.

"What do you mean?" asked Covey.

Hugh turned to Heyward. "Who knows about your broken arm, besides us?"

"No one outside of Mayfield," replied Heyward slowly. He looked at Hugh with a glint in his eye, catching on.

"Exactly," he said, grinning back. "The race is in a few days. No one has to know it's not you riding Capitano." He spoke quickly as he relayed his plan. "You go to the race but you hide the cast."

"How is he going to do that?" asked Lesesne.

Hugh waved the question aside. "We'll figure out something. When it's time for the race, Eliza slips in wearing the same outfit Heyward was wearing. In all the rush and excitement, they'll assume Heyward is riding. Why would they think differently?"

"That's a pretty big assumption," said Heyward. He turned his head my way. "I mean, look at her. She's too small. And her hair is dark."

Hugh's face tilted in study. "She's a mite, that's true. But she's flat as a pancake. If she wears a cap with a low bill to cover her hair, and keeps her head down, she could pass for a boy."

My cheeks flamed at his description. Lesesne snickered and Covey squeezed my hand.

"Might could work," said Heyward doubtfully. He crossed his arms in thought. "Here's another idea. Why don't *you* ride Captain?" he asked Hugh. "He likes you well enough."

Hugh shook his head. "Can't. I have to ride for Magnolia Bluff."

"You'd be riding against me?" I sputtered.

Hugh nodded somberly. "And I'll race to win."

We looked at each other, neither of us speaking. I hated Hugh at that moment. My heart broke and I felt betrayed. How could he run against me when he knew the risks I'd be taking? When he knew Captain was at stake?

Hugh looked back at me, equally pained. "I'm sorry, Lizzie. If I hold back, my father will know. The race would be questioned. And so would my honor. The plan would be revealed, and all would be lost anyway."

"But—" I stammered, pursing the subject. He made a good case, but I couldn't let it go.

"But." Hugh's gaze held mine. "Lizzie, I still think you'll win," he said earnestly. "I wouldn't suggest you do this if I didn't believe it. You're a better rider than I am. And you've got a better horse. Eliza, the race is yours to win." He crossed his arm against his chest. "But if you don't want to do it, I'd understand. After all, this risks your reputation as a lady."

I scoffed. "I don't care about that."

"You should." His face was serious.

I tightened my lips, unsure of what to say.

"Mama will have your hide if you race," Lesesne said casually.

"You won't tell her?" challenged Heyward, leaning forward menacingly.

Lesesne smirked. "Of course not. I'm just saying. You know I'm right."

"I don't care about that either," I said mutinously. "She's never happy with what I do anyway."

There was a pause while everyone waited for someone else to make a suggestion.

"It won't work," said Heyward in a defeated tone. "Think it through. Daddy is the one registering for the race and he's the one taking the horse to the starting point. We can't fool him, and he'll never agree to our plan."

Hugh sighed and leaned back against the railing, slump shouldered. "Well, it was an idea."

Lesesne spoke up. "I'll ride Captain."

We all swung our heads to look at him. It took us a moment to digest that he would volunteer to help. Then, his suggestion took root.

"You'd do that?" I asked. "For me?"

"Daddy will have Eliza's *and* your arses," warned Heyward.

"Only if we lose that bet," Lesesne replied urbanely. Then his expression grew serious. "Sweetwater Pond should belong to Mayfield."

"Thanks for offering, little brother, but *you* ride Capitano?" Heyward shook his head. "All that will happen is we'll both have broken bones. And we will still lose that race."

"I have no intention of riding that hellion," Lesesne said with a smirk. "All I have to do is *tell Daddy* I'll ride Captain." He glanced my way. "We are closer in size, so she won't raise alarms. Eliza will ride Capitano. To win."

Chapter Fifteen

A GYMKHANA is an equestrian event involving various timed races or games that showcase the teamwork between the horse and rider. It typically consists of a series of obstacles that test the horsemanship skills of the riders and the agility, speed, and responsiveness of the horses.

1914

The morning of the gymkhana, our family, Wilton, and Covey traveled together by boat to the race site. It was an easy journey cruising past great houses that faced the water and a blur of pink and white azaleas. I led Capitano directly to the horse stalls erected for the race. A crowd was already gathering, and the air was festive.

Once Wilton settled Capitano, he and Daddy left the stalls to make arrangements for the race, and Heyward and Mama made their way to the spectator area. Lesesne, Covey, and I immediately snuck into the back of the horse's stall like barn rats. As Lesesne unbuttoned his blue flannel shirt, Covey knelt to open her large basket. She pulled out a fresh shirt for Lesesne and a pair of trousers for me. When she stood, she had a pair of shears in her hand.

"Are you sure you want to do this?" she asked me.

I finished buttoning Lesesne's shirt and pulled my hair out from the braid. It fell over my shoulders in riotous curls. "Just do it before I change my mind."

"What? You're going to cut your hair?" Lesesne looked ill.

"I have to, if I'm going to look like a boy. Besides, my hair's too thick to fit under a cap."

I sat resolutely on a bale of hay and Covey began sawing at my thick dark hair. I closed my eyes and visualized the race.

"That's as good as it gets," Covey said, stepping back to admire her handiwork. "I don't have a mirror, so you'll have to take my word for it."

I looked at Lesesne. I knew if it looked funny, he'd laugh. Lesesne's long face was thoughtful, but I saw approval in his eyes.

Covey hid the long shank of dark hair in her basket while I tightened the trousers around my waist with Lesesne's belt. My brown boots were good enough to pass scrutiny. When done, I looked up to see Captain eyeing me with uncertainty. He whinnied and shook his head.

"I don't look the same," I said. "Oh, that's not good."

"He'll be fine," Covey said with authority. "But we're missing one important piece of our disguise." She lowered to pull out a boy's cap from the basket and slapped it on my head. Then she walked around me, tucking in wayward hairs, tugging down the cap, straightening my collar. Then she covered her mouth and laughed. "Actually, you make a pretty cute boy."

"Thanks a lot," I scowled while Lesesne hooted.

As the other riders came into the stalls to saddle their horses, Hugh found Captain and our stall. He was dressed for the race in riding breeches and boots. He squinted and peered in. "There you are."

I came closer, staying out of sight of the others. I smoothed the plaid shirt and asked, "How do I look?"

His eyes crinkled. "Like a girl in boys' clothes." After a laugh he said, "No one will think you're not Lesesne. Well done." He looked over his shoulder. "Now hurry. I've come to help you get saddled up."

He easily lifted the saddle onto Captain's back and quickly tightened the girth. He handed me the reins. Captain snorted and stepped back.

"Whoa," Hugh said, giving me a surprised look. "What's spooked Cap?"

Was it my fear he sensed? Or because I looked different? I removed the cap from my head, and stepping closer, let him sniff me. "Hey, boy. It's me," I cooed.

"What did you do to your hair?" Hugh asked, staring at me with eyes wide.

"Shh . . ." I whispered, looking over my shoulder. My hand darted up to the shorn hair at my neck. "Covey cut it. It wouldn't fit in the cap." Seeing his distress I blurted, "I had to do it!"

"Yeah, okay," Hugh said, clearly shaken and trying to recoup his composure. "Captain seems fine now. We should get you up."

I replaced my cap and led Captain to the threshold. Hugh bent with his hands joined. I set my boot in his hands and swung my leg over the saddle. Hugh adjusted the stirrups, his hands taking firm hold of my boot. At knee level, his hair was so blond it looked white. I wanted to reach out and run my fingers through it, to tousle it like Daddy used to do with Heyward. But Hugh wasn't a little boy. Definitely he was not.

"Why do you root for me?" I asked him. "Not even my mother roots for me."

Hugh's fingers paused and he looked up at me. His blue eyes radiated sincerity.

"When you do well, it makes me want to do well." He took a breath. "I believe in you."

My mouth dropped in astonishment. I could only look back at him in wonder.

Hugh swung his head at the sound of approaching horses. The moment was broken.

"Now you hurry," I said, "or you'll miss the race."

Hugh laughed. "No way I'll miss the chance to see you race." He turned and hurried off to his stall.

Lesesne appeared at the stall entrance and gave the okay sign.

Covey approached, her face raised and her palm on my boot. "You can do this," she said earnestly. "There's no one who can ride like you. And there's no better horse out there than Capitano."

I nodded. I knew Captain would take his confidence from me, and I'd take my courage from him. Together, we'd give this race our best.

The sun was merciless yet as many as one hundred people lined both sides of the beach from pole to pole dressed in light colors and straw hats, the women holding parasols. I kept my head down as we walked to where a portly man stood sweating in the sun holding a large red kerchief. Captain was young and inexperienced, full of himself as he pranced and pawed aggressively. I struggled to keep him in line. The stallions eyed each other, snorting, challenging, eager to bite. The riders clenched the reins tightly to hold them steady as the seconds seemed to tick by like minutes.

Hugh leaned closer, keeping his stallion in check. "Good luck."

"Good luck," I replied. I squeezed the reins and lowered my cheek to rest against the fur of Capitano's neck. I could feel my blood racing as I breathed in his scent. "It's you and me, Cap. Let's run for the fun of it, same as always." I stroked his neck, feeling the muscle ripple, then straightened and took a deep breath.

The heavy-set man came to stand in front of the waving line of horses. He raised his arms. In one hand was the red kerchief. I felt Captain's muscles pulling tight beneath me, like a giant coil about to spring.

His arms came down. A cheer went up. Captain sprang forward, pushed by the power of his hind quarters. The stretch of beach glared in the sunlight, but in my mind I was in the meadow, heading to my tree with her outstretched limbs.

When we reached the pole we were a length ahead of the other horses, but I made a dreadful mistake and overshot the turn, losing critical time. Captain wanted to keep running straight ahead so I pulled him in firmly and gently. As we made the turn my heart sank seeing the three other horses galloping far ahead. I bent low to his neck, buried my hands in his thick mane, and tucked up my knees. "Go, Cap. Run for us!"

Captain didn't like to see the rears of other horses. As he stretched out his legs, sand flew up in clumps from his hooves, and he handily passed the palomino, then the black-and-white Walker. We reached Hugh and matched each other stride for stride. I turned my head to glance at him. That was my second mistake. My cap flew off and I felt the air rush through my short curls. *Too late now*, I thought, and focused again on the race I had yet to win.

Captain found another reserve and I felt his energy surge beneath me, even faster, as he pushed forward. I cried out with joy as we passed the finish line first by a head and heard the roar of the crowd.

Captain didn't just win, he won with a flourish.

Hugh caught up to me on his stallion, finishing second. "You did it!" he shouted, beaming in a way unsuitable for someone who'd just lost the race. I loved him for it.

I ran my hand through my hair and shook my head, laughing with pure release and joy. Together we trotted back to the starting point where a small group of men gathered. My father was the tallest one in the group, and he stood wide legged with his arms open in welcome. As I neared, his face shifted from joy to shock of recognition. Beside him, Wilton's eyes flickered from my face to my father with worry. Heyward could not contain his joy. He fist pumped the air as Captain came to a halt.

A crowd gathered quickly around us, and I heard repeatedly the exclamation, "It's a girl!"

Daddy came to Captain's side and let his hand glide along the horse's strong neck. Then he looked up at me. His eyes searched mine.

"Lizzie, are you hurt anywhere? Are you okay?"

I shook my head, my curls free. "I'm fine." He reached up for me and I slid off the horse into his arms. My legs felt so watery I could barely stand. Daddy held me tight for a moment, then released me.

After a quick swipe at his eyes, he took the reins from me and handed them to Wilton.

"That was a fine ride, Miss," Wilton said.

"The Captain takes all the credit," I replied. "He'll need a hearty rub."

"I'll take good care of our champion," Wilton said, then led a tired and compliant horse to the stalls.

The conundrum began as word spread from lips to lips that a girl had ridden the race—and won! The stout man with the red kerchief called for the panel of judges to convene. Heyward fought his way to my side and put a protective arm around me. I could see the other horses being led from the beach to the stalls by groomsmen and looked for Hugh, but I couldn't find him.

"Watch her," Daddy told Heyward and pushed his way close to the panel of judges. Mr. Rhodes was already there, and beside him I spotted Hugh. Everyone was shouting and I couldn't make heads or tails of gibberish.

A short while later, Daddy returned with a coterie of men. His face was solemn. Heyward dropped his arm from my shoulder but remained at my side.

A short, slender man in a gray suit and striped waistcoat lifted a clipboard. Poising his pen, he asked, "What's your name, young lady?"

I cleared my throat. "Eliza Pinckney Rivers. Sir."

He looked at me through narrowed eyes. "That's an important name. Not one to shame."

"No sir."

"Your age?"

"Fourteen. Almost fifteen."

"Are you the owner of the stallion you rode?"

"No, sir. My father is the owner. Mr. Rawlins Heyward Rivers."

The man wrote all this down. "Did he know you were the rider of this race?"

"No sir."

"Why did you ride in the race?"

"To win," I replied honestly.

A wave of laughter followed my reply. The official didn't appreciate my answer. "I mean to say, did you realize you were breaking the rules?"

"But I wasn't," I replied. "Respectfully, sir, nowhere in the rules does it state that a girl—or rather, a female—cannot ride in the race."

Somewhat flustered, the official rifled through the papers. "Says right here in your registration that a Mr. Heyward Rivers was to ride in the race."

Heyward stepped up and answered in a clear voice. "Yes sir. I'd intended to. But I broke my arm." He indicated his cast. "Eliza, my sister, filled in for me. No harm intended. Sir."

The official looked at the cast and scratched his jaw in consternation. He turned and walked away, signaling to his fellow judges to follow.

A moment later, the panel of judges returned to the center of the raceway. The stout man waved his red kerchief and shouted, "Quiet! Attention!" The crowd gradually silenced.

"The winner of the stallion race is Mayfield's Capitano."

Daddy hooted, picked me up, and swirled me around while a great cheer rose. On the wind was the cry "A girl won the race!" My head and heart were swirling as Heyward took his turn hugging me, then Lesesne, who must've heard the commotion from the horse stalls and came running. Last was Hugh. He squeezed me with jubilation. I felt like a candle was glowing inside of me, bright and incandescent. I couldn't stop smiling. I won the race for Captain. For Daddy. For Mayfield. Pride made me confess, at least in my head, I had won the race for myself as well, and for girls everywhere.

The crush of spectators surrounded us. Many were looking at me with curious eyes, turning to one another and speaking behind palms. Some were smiling. But there were also some delivering hateful looks. I felt more like a creature in a freak show than a victor of a race.

"Eliza!"

My mother's voice rang out above the clamor. I spun around to see her bearing down on me, three women at her side. They all were stylish in snug-fitting spring frocks and broad-rim straw hats embellished with flowers and feathers. Mama looked regal in a dress of white lace, her dark hair upswept under a dramatic hat. But her face was thunderous.

I felt Hugh's grip tighten on my shoulder before he dropped his hand.

Mama stopped before me and tightened her lips. She knew she had to hold her temper in front of her friends, who were listening intently for the exchange that would serve as fodder for gossip for weeks. I felt their critical gazes sweep over my britches, my shorn hair and shivering. I might not have broken the race's rules, but I saw clearly that I was guilty and condemned for breaking a significant rule of conduct for women. Mama's worst fear had been realized.

Suddenly Mama released a high-pitched laugh and threw up her hands with dramatic flair. "Lord, help me, look at my girl. Isn't she a spitfire?" she exclaimed as she took a step toward me. She reached out with her lace handkerchief and began to dab away the bits of sand and dirt from my face. Then bent close, her dark eyes seethed as she reached out to touch the short curls. Quietly, so only I could hear, she whispered, "Eliza, I swear you were born to shame me."

The words struck true. I shrank within myself, the joy of my success withering in my heart. I watched, silent, as Mama returned to her friends exclaiming with exaggeration, "I swanny, what's a mother to do?" They walked off, chattering like a flock of birds.

⇒

We remembered that night as the night of the banshee. Mama was once again in her cups, which sparked another row with Daddy. Even for them, this one could wake snakes. Mama wailed and shocked us using a vocabulary that Heyward derisively called, "no better than a fishmonger's." We each found our escape route. Heyward left to go to some friend's house. Lesesne remained in his room behind a closed door. I pictured him lying in his bed, quivering with a pillow over his head. I fled to the stable.

The late night's damp chill went straight to my bones as I made my way to the barn. A great horned owl pierced the quiet, hooting its melancholy call from somewhere high in the trees. A heartbeat later, softer hoots replied from the juveniles, ready to fledge. I tightened my white flannel robe over my nightgown that appeared slightly bluish in the moonlight. I thought how we Rivers children were like those owl fledglings. Tonight, we were all flying from the nest. Which of us would succeed on the wing? I wondered. Which of us would fall to the earth?

Inside the barn it was dark, and heat from the horses warmed the air. Soft knickers sounded from the dark as I passed by with my lantern. The Captain stood in his stall, his liquid brown eyes alert.

"Hey there. Surprised to see me at this hour?" When he gave a soft whinny and shook his head, I laughed. "So, you hear the war being waged up the hill, huh?" I reached up to stroke his nose. "Don't be bothered by it. They'll be lovey-dovey by morning. I brought your favorite." I pulled an apple from my robe pocket. He took it greedily.

A figure stepped out from the shadows. I gasped as I jumped back, nearly dropping my lantern. The tall height and blond hair were a welcome sight.

"Heyward, you scared me," I said, putting a hand to my breast.

The boy stepped closer into the lantern's light. His features were not chiseled but soft. The smile not thin lipped, but full. The blue eyes hesitant.

"Hugh!"

"I . . . I had to see you," he said haltingly.

I stared back and licked my lips, awash with confusion that he would be here, in our barn, at this time of night. To see me. "Why?"

Hugh tilted his head and searched the barn ceiling, as if to find his answer in the rafters.

I spoke again, collecting my wits. "How'd you know I was here in the barn? At this time of night?"

"Well," he said with a shy grin, "I, uh, went to your window first. Thought I'd throw a pebble or something like that. I'd heard somewhere that was a way to get a girl's attention. I tried, and my aim was true. But you didn't appear. When I heard the—" he paused "—commotion, I thought you might be in the barn." He smiled sheepishly. "And here you are."

"I'm sorry you had to hear that."

"Aw, don't be. Do you think you are the only one whose parents argue?"

I moved to sit on the hay bale outside of Captain's stall. "There's an argument, and then there's *that*," I said, indicating the direction of my house with a jerk of my chin. I set the lantern on an adjoining hay bale and leaned back against the wood stall. "It's bad tonight," I said in a soft voice. "Worse than usual." I plucked some hay from the bale and tossed pieces to the floor. "It's my fault." I shivered and wrapped my arms around myself.

Hugh grabbed his jacket and draped it over my shoulders.

"Thank you."

He rocked on his heels and stuck his hands in his pockets.

I scooted over. "There's room for two."

Hugh slid on the hay bale beside me, so close his thigh rested against mine. He seemed nervous and looked at the stalls rather than at me. I felt every nerve ending in my leg tingle where it touched him. Only then did I realize I was alone with a boy in the barn at night—in my nightclothes. If the banshee were to find out, she'd howl even louder.

"You didn't answer my question," I said in a small voice. When he looked at me, I asked, "Why did you have to see me?"

Hugh released a sigh, and he leaned forward to rest his forearms on his thighs. I felt the pressure against my thighs increase and swallowed.

"I . . . I didn't get to talk to you after the race." He shook his head with a snort. "It was crazy."

"Yeah." Memories rushed back.

"I wanted to tell you . . ."

"Oh Hugh, wasn't it wonderful?" I gushed, interrupting him. I sat straighter and my words flowed out. "Your plan was genius! No one suspected it wasn't Lesesne on Captain. I waltzed right up to the starting line. What a moment that was. I could feel Cap's will to run. When that flag dropped . . . Did you see him? Of course you couldn't . . . He leaped forward and ran his heart out. I just held on for the ride."

"I didn't see much but the curve of his behind smack in front of me," Hugh said with a chuckle. "And you tucked in like some professional jockey. Where'd you learn to ride like that?"

I shrugged. "I just do what comes natural and pay attention to what Captain tells me he wants. And he told me he wanted to run. Once the race started," I said, stretching out my arms like I was holding the reins, "I was both holding on tight and at the same time, inside, I was letting go. It's like I was flying."

I turned my head to see him watching me, a quizzical look on his face. I felt my cheeks flame and let my arms drop. Looking down I said, "You're probably laughing at me."

Hugh shook his head and said in a serious tone, "I'd never laugh at you, Eliza. I think . . . well . . ."

I tilted my head to glance at him. His blue eyes bore into mine and he was struggling with his words. This time I did not interrupt him.

"I . . . think you're wonderful," Hugh blurted out, then quickly looked away.

I put my hands to my cheeks, feeling their heat. No one had ever said such a thing to me before.

"And you're brave," Hugh continued. "I don't know any other girl who would have done what you did. Or could have." Hugh faced me again and I saw his gaze move to my hair. A small smile appeared as he reached up to tug gently at a small curl at my temple. "Even this."

My hand flew to the short hairs at the nape of my neck. "Oh, my hair," I cried feeling shame and sorrow.

"I like it," he said. "It's . . ." He averted his gaze. "It suits you."

I felt his eyes on me again as he studied my curls.

"In school, we read a book called *Red Badge of Courage*," he said. "In it, this young soldier sees the bloody wounds of other soldiers as badges of courage. I see your shorn hair as your badge of courage. You went to battle too. And you came out a victor." He lowered his head.

"Cutting my hair is nothing for me to boast about." I reached up to brush locks from my forehead. "Why, I only did what I had to so I could win the race."

"And that's the definition of *courage*."

I dropped my hand and looked into his eyes and the admiration I saw there. And something more. My heart quickened.

"Ignore all those who mock you or criticize your hair. They don't appreciate what you accomplished today. You are the first girl . . . the first female who raced in—and won—the gymkhana. And on a Marsh Tacky to boot!" Hugh shook his head with a grin. "You gave your daddy bragging rights for the rest of his life. And won the pond back to boot. And my daddy's already ponying up with stud fees in hand. I'm sure others will too."

A short laugh escaped my lips. "Is he? He's not mad? About me, a girl, besting his son?"

Hugh scratched his head ruefully. "That you did."

"I thought he might challenge the result."

"Nah, he's not happy but he's a fair man. He even said you were the best rider in these parts. For a girl."

"I reckon that's true enough," I said, then added, "Boy or girl." I reached up again to rake my mop of curls. "But my hair . . ." I moaned. I felt as shorn as a sheep. "Mama says it was my best feature."

"No. Your eyes are," Hugh said. "They're right pretty. You can get lost in them."

I looked up, astonished.

"Your hair will grow back," he continued. "You're still *you*."

He took my breath away. I sat motionless, speechless. Hugh turned his shoulder from me then reached into his pocket. Facing me again, he put his two closed palms in front of me. "Pick one."

I loved this child's game and smiled eagerly. After pondering a minute, I tapped his left hand. Opening it, the palm was empty. I clicked my tongue and sat back, crossing my arms.

Hugh laughed and opened his right hand. A long blue ribbon sat coiled in his palm. "I figured your daddy would keep the blue ribbon from the race. I bought this to give you after the race. To wear in your hair." He looked again at my short curls and held back another laugh. "That was before you cut your hair."

I snatched the ribbon and held it dangling between my two fingers. I gazed at the slender silk with wonder. Hugh bought me a blue ribbon. "I love it," I gushed. "It's beautiful."

His smile spread across his face. "Maybe you can wear it when your hair grows back."

"I have a better idea." I gave him the ribbon then stuck my arm out and pushed back my robe sleeve. "Tie it on my wrist. Please. That way, I'll be able to see it all day long."

He clumsily tied the ribbon, both of us chortling at his failed attempts. When at last he succeeded, he held my wrist with a proprietary air. He lifted his face so close to mine I could feel his breath on my cheeks. The air thickened between us, and my breath came quick. Then, slowly, he tilted his head, and his face drew even closer to mine. I measured his progress in breaths till his lips hovered over mine.

That was a leap too far for me. I pushed back the jacket and sprang to my feet. "I best get back," I blurted, then grabbed my lantern and ran back to the house. I could face the mayhem within those walls better than the turmoil going on in my heart.

Chapter Sixteen

⟞⬥⟝

THE CAROLINA WREN (*Thryothorus ludovicianus*) is a small bird native to the eastern and southeastern regions of the United States. It has reddish brown on the upperparts and pale underparts, and an off-white eyebrow stripe above its eyes. It is highly active and known for its upright tails and cheerful, melodious songs. It is the state bird of South Carolina.

1914

The sun rises even after the worst of nights. Every bone in my body ached from the exertion of the race, and my breathing still skipped a beat as I remembered my conversation with Hugh in the barn. I lay in bed, listening to the birds chattering and wondering why the house was quieter than usual. No shouts ricocheted from Lesesne and Heyward, no pots and pans were clanging in the kitchen. It seemed everyone had abandoned ship after the night of the banshee. I rose and quickly dressed, taking care to select a clean and pressed pinafore. In the bathroom I scrubbed my face, but looking in the mirror I moaned with dismay at my reflection. My skin was pinkened from the race on the beach, and there was nothing I could do about the cropped mop of curls.

I tiptoed down the hall, pausing at Mama's bedroom door. It was still closed and silent within. Downstairs, the kitchen was empty. Only the smell of coffee lingered. Hearing women's chatter, I peered out the kitchen door. Clementine was in the yard helping the two women hired to do our laundry. My stomach rumbling, I scrounged the larder and found an apple. I idly chewed, waiting for the inevitable summons from my mother.

It came a short time later. Lesesne entered the kitchen looking as tired as me. An unspoken truce floated between us following our joint effort at the gymkhana. I picked up no trace of his usual teasing rancor when he said, "Mama wants to see you. She's in the living room."

Les didn't have to tell me I was in trouble. I smoothed my pinafore, tucked my unruly hair behind my ears, then walked down the center hall to the living room.

Mother sat on the pale blue silk sofa. She was neatly groomed in a navy skirt and white cotton blouse. She appeared tidy, but as pale as last night's moon. I stood meekly before her, grateful for my care for my appearance.

Mama looked up when I entered. She lowered her cup and saucer on the side table then set her gaze to capture mine. Her eyes appeared tired, not angry. Maybe defeated too. Like she'd lost the race.

She took a breath then said, "Eliza, it's decided. You'll be leaving Mayfield and attending school in Charleston."

I blinked, unsure if I'd heard correctly. "Beg your pardon?"

"You heard me. I don't see why you're surprised. Your . . . performance . . . yesterday at the race was the last straw. It's clear you are out of control. What did I hear someone say?" She put her fingertips to her temple. "Ah yes. *Your daughter is running wild.*" She lifted her gaze to my hair and sighed. "I've done the best I can, but clearly, I've failed. You are approaching womanhood, and since you are ready to begin higher learning, you'll do so in Charleston. There are excellent schools there, culture, and the right society."

"But . . . I don't want to go to Charleston," I stammered. "I want to stay here. At Mayfield."

She ignored me. "I will move to Charleston with you to my parents' house. Lesesne will join us as well."

"And Daddy?"

"He'll stay at Mayfield, of course."

My face was mutinous. "Then I'll stay with him."

"Don't be ridiculous."

"I don't want to go to school in Charleston." I cried, my throat thickening. "I'm meant to go to Beaufort. It's all arranged."

"Not any longer."

My fists clenched. "I won't go! I am not leaving Mayfield."

"Please don't raise your voice. I have a headache." Mama waved her hand in dismissal.

My breath quickened. This couldn't be happening. I expected some kind of punishment . . . but leaving Mayfield? "Mama, what about winning the race?"

"You dare mention that race?"

"We got back Sweetwater Pond!"

Mama's dark eyes flashed. "Do you think because you've won a horse race that I should praise you?" She laughed bitterly. "*Please.* Your win was my failure. A young lady should know how to ride, yes. For pleasure. To get from A to B. To join a hunt. But racing . . . as a boy . . . in britches?" Her voice rose, emphasizing each point.

I stood erect, even defiant. I would not be ashamed of my race.

Mama composed herself and lowered her voice. "Eliza, you're fourteen. We must face facts. You have no appreciable skills, no exceptional talents for a young lady. You have only your face and figure to secure your fortune and . . ." She raised her hand to indicate my hair. "But now, well . . ." She shook her head, not needing to finish the sentence. "Your greatest asset is your pedigree. You are Eliza Pinckney Rivers. Yesterday, you threatened your reputation. I cannot allow it. No more."

Her gaze wandered to the window to look at her beloved rose garden. The sunshine came in slants from the mullioned panes, barely reaching the Persian rug. When she turned toward me, her face was implacable.

"I've selected a college preparatory school for girls. Mr. Coxwold informs me that you are exceptionally bright."

That old prune face never hinted at that with his rude treatment of me and Covey.

"Eliza, you are my daughter and I want what is best for you. I know you love Mayfield. But remember. Someday, you will have to leave and create your own home with your husband."

"I won't marry if it means I have to leave Mayfield. I'll stay here and help Heyward. He won't even have to pay me."

Mama laughed softly, but it was a sad laugh. "You are still so young," she said. "Do not fret. It is only for the school year, like Heyward. You'll have summers here," she tossed in to sweeten the offer.

It astonished me that she was trying to make me soften toward the idea, but I refused to yield. I crossed my arms across my chest, glowering.

"I know you're angry. You always seem to be angry at me," she added, shifting her weight on the sofa. Then with resignation she said, "Someday I hope you will come to understand I'm doing this for your sake. There is a great deal that awaits you in Charleston that is not available in this"—she waved her hand—"wilderness."

"You aren't doing it for my sake," I shouted, angry enough to speak the truth. "You're the one who wants to leave. Go! But I'm not going. You can't make me!" I covered my face with my palms and began to sob hysterically. My fatigue was my undoing.

Mama's brows furrowed and, wincing in pain, she said sharply, "That's enough." When I didn't stop she said, "Go outside and help Clementine finish the washing. I don't have the strength for it today." When I didn't move, Mama put her hand over her eyes. "Go *now*."

I lifted my tear-stained face. "Where's Daddy?" My tone challenged her.

Mama dropped her hand and said with a disparaging huff, "I know what you're thinking, and it won't work. Not this time. It's decided."

A sanctuary is a haven of refuge. People tend to find such places in time of need, and I found mine at my tree hollow, or riding Captain, or in the cottage with Covey. I needed my best friend now and raced along the well-worn path to her. The pine needles were soft under my feet, sounding lonely, one foot after the other. I took the river path. Here and there a dogwood bloomed white or pink and a redbud offered a pop of color. A late flock of hungry robins foraged along the river's edge, searching for worms. From the trees, I heard the cardinal's *cheer cheer.* By the time I spotted the white cottage, my hot anger had morphed into simmering sorrow. Covey stood on tiptoe hanging sheets on the line. When I called, she turned and waved with joy.

I sprinted the short distance to her side, arms extended, and though I'd meant to be calm, tears gushed out with my words. Her arm slipped around me, and we walked arm in arm to the front porch to settle on the wooden chairs. Covey brought out mason jars of sweet tea, which I drank thirstily. My story spilled out as we sat knee to knee.

Covey sat back in her chair, taking in the news. She blew out a stream of air, shaking her head in disbelief. "We knew your mama was gonna stir the mud after the race . . . but leave Mayfield?"

"I won't leave," I said, shaking my head mutinously. But even as I spoke, I knew my words were meaningless. What choice would I have?

"Remember the very first time you came here and asked if you could live here?" Covey asked. "We were only eight years old then. Some days it feels long ago. Some days it feels like yesterday. But we're fourteen now. We know better." Covey reached out to take my hands. "Eliza, if your mama goes to Charleston, I still say you can always live here. With me and Wilton. Forever."

She was smiling and her words touched me deeply. I wanted nothing more. But she was right. We were older now, old enough to see the folly of that dream.

"Someday, when Heyward gets married and his bride tosses me

out of the house—" I offered a sad laugh "—that's what we'll do. But now . . . You know that my mama . . . and even Wilton . . . won't let that happen." My words rushed out in a wail. "Oh Covey, I know they're going to force me to go to Charleston. Mama and Daddy are for it. I can't fight both of them."

Covey's face crumpled. "Eliza, you're my best friend. My only friend. I can't bear the thought."

She and I hugged, holding tight, as though we could somehow physically hold our friendship together.

Pulling back, I searched the face before me. Covey's eyes were tear filled, like mine. What would happen to her, alone at Mayfield? Where would she go to school? That meant so much to her. Suddenly, an idea sprang to mind. It seemed too easy . . . too possible. Wiping my eyes, I almost shouted, "What if you went with me?"

Covey jerked back. "*To Charleston?*"

I hurried to explain. "Mama's house in Charleston is bigger than Mayfield. There's a lot of room. You can live with us there."

Covey looked at me like I'd grown two heads. "I can't be no guest in a white folk house *there*. Charleston's not Mayfield."

"Well, I know," I stammered. "But . . ." I paused, ashamed of the words I was to say. "There are . . . rooms you can stay in."

"Servant's quarters."

I swallowed hard, ashamed. In Charleston there were strict laws enforcing where Negroes could not go—restaurants, schools, parks, churches, restrooms, transportation, even what door they could use entering a house. Nearly every facet of life. But Covey was not a servant, and I never thought of her as one. Yet we both knew the constraints of society.

Covey straightened in her chair and tightened her lips. "I don't think so . . ."

"Covey, think about school. I know how important learning is to you. When Lesesne and I leave for Charleston, Mr. Coxwold will no longer be our tutor. Where will you go to school?"

Covey's brows gathered as she became agitated. "I . . . I don't know. I haven't thought . . ." She put her fingers to her temple. "I suppose I could go to the Robert Smalls School in Beaufort. Or maybe the Penn School in St. Helena."

"That's twenty-five or thirty miles away. Too far to ride a horse every day. Even a carriage." I looked down. We both knew that there would be no carriage.

Worry flooded her face and she let go of my hands and rose. Covey began pacing the porch.

I pressed on. "If you were in Charleston, you could go to a Negro school. And we could stay together. I know it will be hard, but Covey, think of your future. You don't want to be stuck here. You want to become a teacher."

Covey stopped abruptly and looked out over the field. "You don't need to worry about me. I'm not your responsibility."

"Covey . . ."

She shook her head. "Wilton would be alone . . ." Her voice was almost a whisper.

"No different than Daddy. We'd come home for the holidays and summer."

Covey slipped back down on the chair. I watched her long, delicate fingers dig at her nailbeds.

"I believe Wilton would want you to continue school," I said softly.

"I don't know," she replied with a shake of her head.

"At least say you'll think about it."

Her gaze met mine. "Would your mother even allow it?" Covey asked dubiously.

In my heart, I knew Mama wanted to go to Charleston more than she wanted me to go to school there. She was using my circumstances as a convenient excuse to move back to her parents' house. Knowing this provided me with a position of power.

"If I come quietly, obligingly . . . I believe she would. And Daddy will support it, for certain. You know he'd do anything for you and Wilton."

"What about Heyward?"

I scrunched my face in indignation. "It doesn't matter what he thinks. He won't even be at the house. He boards at Porter." My voice softened. "But Covey, you know he supports you. He's your friend."

Covey had her head in her hand. "This is dangerous. I've heard talk among my folks about the Jim Crow laws in Charleston, and I'm scared about what would happen to me in a place like that." She dropped her hand and looked at me, eyes blazing. "Eliza, in Charleston I cannot be your friend. Except in secret. It's too risky for me. Even if I went . . . it's not going to be easy. Our friendship . . . could change."

"Never."

She paused, then looked at me, eyes appealing. "But you're right about one thing. I want more than what's available for me living here at Mayfield." After a breath she asked, "Do you really think we could do it?"

"I do. Yes, it will be hard for—both of us. But we can do it."

Covey licked her lips in thought, then leaned back in her chair. "If Wilton agrees . . . and your mama allows it . . ." Her face released a smile of hope, and she nodded in agreement. "I . . . I will go to Charleston with you."

Chapter Seventeen

⟨⟩

JIM CROW LAWS were state and local laws introduced in the Southern United States in the late nineteenth and early twentieth centuries that enforced racial segregation. The racist laws remained on the books until 1965.

1988

My water glass was empty. The food was congealing on the plates. I looked at the women sitting at the table and saw they were, amazingly, patient. Still wide-eyed and attentive.

Norah leaned forward, her brows furrowed in thought. "Your story takes place around 1915, right?" When I nodded, she continued. "You were either very brave or very naïve. Was a friendship between a white girl and a Black girl at that time, well . . . even legal?"

"You're quite right," I replied. "This all happened so long ago, I forget how hideous Jim Crow laws were during that time. Interracial friendships were very rare and definitely frowned upon, even openly scorned. Discrimination and segregation were deeply ingrained in us all. No, we were not naïve. Especially not my mother. Covey and I accepted new parameters around our relationship. Covey had to live in the servants' quarters. We couldn't go out of the house together as friends. Or even behave as such in front of the other servants. It would be hard for me. Harder yet for her. But we both understood what was at stake."

"Where did Granny Covey go to school? She couldn't go to the school you went to."

"No, of course not," I conceded. "Schools for Black students were limited at that time, true, but Covey was accepted into the Avery Normal Institute, one of the most prominent schools in Charleston." I smiled, remembering Covey's joy at the news. "She loved that school. It provided her with an excellent education, cultural events, and an introduction to Black society in the city. Most of all, she could continue her dream of becoming a teacher."

"That all makes sense now. Grandma used to tell me how schools such as Avery made all the difference for young Black students, like her, during that time. But honestly, this is the first time I've heard how it all happened. How she got there and where she lived. How she made her dreams come true." Norah pursed her lips. "It seems you were both very brave."

"Truth be told, Covey saved *me* every bit as much as I saved her." I smiled. "Isn't that what best friends do?"

———◆———

I returned to the dining room a few hours later. The crystal chandelier created a prism of color on the walls as the sun set. I smiled to see the table set with the family china and silver. Red and white roses from the garden clustered in crystal vases. The mouthwatering scents of garlic and rosemary emanated from the platter of roast lamb and potatoes and filled the room. Savannah and Norah had been busy, I thought, pleased to see them getting along so well. Savannah's youth was evident in the jeans and white T-shirt, and her long hair was pulled back into a ponytail as she placed thick damask napkins at each setting. Norah had changed into casual white linen pants and a flowing shirt. A small diamond sparkled at her neckline. Their chatter and laughter brought back, with stirring clarity, memories of other dinners at this table. Other voices . . . other years.

"Here we all are," I exclaimed, entering.

Norah hurried to the side table to grasp the bottle of red wine. "Would you like a glass?"

"Yes, please," I replied, settling into my chair.

Norah poured the wine and we all sat to enjoy the delicious lamb, a crisp salad, fruit, and cheese.

"Now, where did I leave off?" I asked.

Norah answered, "Covey said she'd go to Charleston with you."

"Ah, yes," I said, looking up at the mural. "Look there, just to the right of the window." I pointed to a mural depicting a large carriage riding along the allée of oaks. "Do you see the scene of the carriage?"

"The one with all the people in it?" asked Norah.

"Yes, that's it. If you look closely you'll see the people inside are Mama, Lesesne, Covey, and me."

Savannah rose and walked closer, then bent to peer at the scene. "It is! All these years I've seen these murals, and I never knew they were stories of us." She leaned forward, squinting at a scene. "But . . . what happened to Uncle Heyward? I don't see him there. Didn't he go to Charleston too? And Hugh?"

"Heyward and Hugh went separately to Porter. By train." Memories flooded my mind and once again I saw their faces: Covey's so beautiful, Heyward's chiseled features, Lesesne's urbane smile, Tripp's freckled sincerity, and Hugh's brilliant blue eyes.

"The mass exodus from Mayfield to Charleston was scheduled for August tenth," I began.

Part Three

THE CHARLESTON YEARS

A door just opened on a street—
I, lost, was passing by—
An instant's width of warmth disclosed,
And wealth, and company.

The door as sudden shut, and I,
I, lost, was passing by,—
Lost doubly, but by contrast most,
Informing misery.

—EMILY DICKINSON

Chapter Eighteen

—◆—

FRESHWATER PONDS within the ACE Basin play an important role in the overall ecosystem. While the ACE Basin is known for its rice fields, expansive salt marshes, and tidal systems, small freshwater ponds contribute to the region's biodiversity and provide a valuable water source for wildlife and plants.

1914

Our summer days were winding down as my mother's threat of us leaving Mayfield for Charleston schools became a reality. It wasn't love but school that was breaking up that old gang of mine.

Heyward and Hugh were returning to the Porter Military Academy. Lesesne was registered at the Gaud School for Boys. Many arguments ensued between my parents about Covey joining us in Charleston, but ultimately they reached a compromise and agreed that Covey could join me in Charleston in exchange for our promise to follow Mama's instructions and for me to willingly comport myself as a lady. Covey was enrolled in the Avery Normal Institute. And I would attend Ashley Hall School for Girls. Tripp was traveling the farthest, all the way to Massachusetts. Our troop would be physically divided, but geography was never what bound us.

During those final dog day afternoons, Sweetwater Pond became our daily destination to swim, picnic, and lollygag. On our last day, the air smelled sweeter, the water felt more refreshing, the sun shone brighter, and being at Mayfield with my friends was all the more precious.

As we approached the acre-wide pond on horseback, the deep green of summer leaves on surrounding trees reflected in the water to make it appear a shimmering emerald. I shared my father's desire— no, his visceral need—to keep hold of Sweetwater Pond. I was proud of my role in bringing it back to Mayfield. I wanted to hold tight to every precious acre. I brought my horse to a stop. The Captain whin- nied and shook his head, feeling tension.

As I peered over Sweetwater Pond, I wondered how all this land, this wilderness, could truly *belong* to my father. Or Heyward, or even me. Did owning a piece of land mean I owned the animals who lived on it? That didn't seem right. Does the snake bend to my wishes? Of course not. The Bible said God gave humans dominion over animals, but I believed that meant we should have reverence for all life.

What I wanted to do was not rule over the wild creatures of the land, or the fish in the water, or the birds in the sky. I wanted to de- fend and protect this pond, this land, and all the animals that lived on it. I felt within me the same ferocity of territorialism that any bird or animal in the wild did. This was my home. Mama might be able to move me to Charleston, but she could never tear me away from my feelings for this land.

"Lizzie!" called Heyward. "What're you doing back there? Giddyup!"

I saw the troop had dismounted and were already setting up camp. I clucked my tongue. The Captain was eager to join the others.

We unpacked a picnic of ripe tomato and cucumber sandwiches, cold chicken, and watermelon. We put our stone jugs into the pond so we'd have refreshing, chilled water on such a steamy day.

After everything was unpacked, Covey and I removed our skirts and waded into the pond in our britches and shirts, like the boys did. While the boys roughhoused, Covey and I swam across the pond and back, matching strokes like synchronized swimmers. I loved the freedom of kicking and stretching without fighting the current of the rivers or, hopefully, alligators. When we finished we climbed ashore, panting from the exertion, and lay on the shorn, soft grass to dry off.

The intense heat dried my skin and hair in no time. Scandalous as it was, I loved my hair being short. I could rake my hands through the curls and be done with it. No more rat's nest or itchy hair down my back.

I was just sliding into sleep when I felt a shower of cold droplets. I shrieked and opened my eyes to see Hugh shaking his head over me, laughing.

"You are a dog," I cried, pushing him away. "That's mean. I was just drifting off."

He stretched out beside me on the blanket, radiating cool from the pond. Lifting my palm to shade my eyes from the sun, I peered at him. He leaned over me, his face damp and tanned, his eyes as blue as the sky over his head. I wanted to touch his face, so close, and as though sensing my thoughts, Hugh reached out and pulled on a short dark curl, then let it spring back. The touch sparked my heart and I saw something shift in his eyes, from amusement to a smolder I felt myself.

"Hey, you two," shouted Tripp, trotting up to us. "Want something to eat?" He plopped himself down on the quilt at my bare feet and began to tickle them.

I pulled my legs up, swiftly maneuvering to sit. "Stop!" I moaned. "You know I hate being tickled."

"You let him tickle you?" asked Hugh, also shifting to a cross-legged sit. His smile shifted to a frown.

"All the time," I said, annoyed, and delivered a quick kick to Tripp's leg that only made Tripp laugh again. "Quit it."

"Aw, you love it," said Tripp, grabbing for my feet again.

Hugh stretched over to grab Tripp's hand and hold it. "She's getting pretty old for tickling, don't you think?" he said, a tone of warning in his voice.

Tripp nonchalantly brushed his hand away. "Oh, it's been ages since I tickled her." He snorted a laugh. "Or she let me."

Covey and Heyward joined us with the picnic basket. Heyward gave Tripp a loaded glance as he passed him a sandwich. "She's too old now," he said with finality.

My brother settled on the blanket beside Covey, and they commenced passing out lunch—sandwiches, apples, carrots. I watched Tripp sitting cross-legged, eating, a bemused expression on his sunburned face. I smiled at his childlike joy. I loved Tripp like a brother. I never thought that his tickling or shoving or boyish gestures as anything other than brotherly fun. Tripp was still slight of build, and his pale skin was freckled rather than tanned. He'd started wearing glasses—round wire rims that encircled his large eyes with eyelashes so pale they were barely visible. They gave him the appearance of an owl.

I glanced back at Hugh. In contrast, he was chewing moodily, studying Tripp with a strange intensity. I knew I'd react very differently if Hugh tickled me. My heart fluttered. I definitely did not think of Hugh as a brother.

"Make room!" called out Lesesne as he clumsily planted himself on a blanket beside Tripp. Dripping, he swiped his hair from his face then leaned back on his arms to catch the sun. Drops of water clung to his long lashes. My younger brother was filling out, becoming a handsome young man. He'd lost his boyish softness to the chiseled cheekbones and jawline that both my brothers inherited from Daddy.

"Hey Tripp," Lesesne said, grabbing Tripp's foot. "Want me to tickle you?"

Tripp kicked his foot away, laughing. Instead, he reached over to hand Lesesne a sandwich. They exchanged smiles.

As he chewed, Lesesne's gaze was fixed on Tripp, who was busy talking with Covey.

"Les," I called out. "Are you all packed up for school?"

Lesesne turned my way and offered a shrug of indifference. "Mama's just going to repack it all anyway, so I'm leaving it to her."

Typical, I thought of my lazy brother. But I couldn't argue. Mama would likely go through my suitcases as well. I lifted my chin and moaned loudly, with frustration. "I can't believe this is our last day."

"Stop whining," said Heyward. "I've gone to Charleston for the last two years and believe me, time goes by fast. Mama will make sure you're busy every minute." He smirked. "I'm sure she's filling your dance cards even now. Her obvious goal is to find you a suitable husband," he added teasingly.

Tripp forced air thorough his nose and pushed back his eyeglasses. "Makes me mad that I have to be stuck in Massachusetts when you finally come to Charleston, Lizzie. It's not fair. I'd take those dance cards and put my name in every slot."

"That's kind of you," I said, amused. I couldn't imagine going to dances.

"Don't you worry none," Hugh said, stretching back on his arms and crossing his legs at his ankles. "I'll make sure Miss Rivers's dance card is filled."

Tripp swallowed hard and wiped his mouth with his hand. "As long as you know that I'll be escorting her to the St. Cecilia Ball."

"Oh really?" Hugh drawled. "Is that arranged too, by your mothers?"

"As a matter of fact, it was," said Tripp, coloring. "Eliza and I are to be married."

"Tripp, stop," I said with an annoyed laugh.

"We are," Tripp declared, and there was no humor in his voice.

This was met by a strained silence. It was a family joke that Tripp and I were to be married. Something we played at as truth when we were little. But I was now fourteen, with Hugh sitting beside me, and the joke was no longer funny. I looked at Tripp's face, flushed and adamant, and felt a fissure of worry that Tripp actually believed it.

Lesesne moved to lie on his side and tossed some wild grass toward Tripp. "You're plumb crazy if you believe that. Your daddy's a second son, like I am. He hasn't got one dime to rub against the other. No way you can win Mama's approval when other offers come in."

"Les, that's a horrible thing to say," I said.

"It's true," Tripp replied without remorse. Then he sat up straight. "But I've got it all planned out. I'm going to Amherst, and it being a top-rated high school, I should get into a first-rate college to study veterinarian science. Then I'll open a practice in Charleston. I'll be able to take care of Eliza comfortably." His face appeared almost smug.

I was struck speechless that he'd planned out our future. That he was serious about us getting married.

Les hooted aloud, causing Tripp's cheeks to flush.

Hugh intervened. "Seems to me you forgot an important step."

Tripp tilted his head. "What?"

"Well, sir," Hugh said as he moved to an upright position. "Seems to me what's most important is asking the woman if she *wants* to marry you, rather than assuming she will because her mama mandates it. I mean, we're living in the twentieth century!"

Heyward laughed and muttered, "Hear hear."

"Right," said Covey, surprising us with her voice. "We women want to determine our own destiny. We want the right to education. We want the right to vote without prejudice due to our sex or the color of our skin. And most certainly we want the ability to choose our own husbands." She paused to take a breath. Then, plucking bits of grass, she added, "I may never be able to marry the man I love. But I won't settle." Looking back at Tripp, she said, "If it's not for love, I won't marry. I'll take care of myself, thank you very much."

I listened to Covey's rare outburst with wonder. Where did such a declaration of passion come from? Everyone seemed moved by her confession. Tripp's lips were tight, perhaps from embarrassment. Heyward looked out at the pond. Hugh studied his sandwich like it held the secrets of the universe. Lesesne looked at Heyward, then at Covey with a fixed gaze.

Hugh turned to me with a question burning in his eyes. "What about you, Miss Rivers? What is your view on marriage?"

"I think all this talk about marriage is making me itch," I said, slapping a mosquito from my arm. I glanced at Tripp and my heart ached to see that he was hurting. "I'm getting eaten alive. Come on, Tripp. Let's pack up and go home."

His eyes filled with gratitude, and he immediately began returning food to the picnic basket. "Lead the way," he called out, "and I'll follow."

That night a strange rapping sound at my window awoke me from my sleep. I slipped from my bed to push back the lace. The window was wide open to catch the night's coolness. I looked out, seeing a full moon that lit up the earth like a theater.

"Hey, Eliza Rivers. You asleep?"

I looked down to see Hugh standing below my window, a shadowed figure in the moonlight, looking up.

I called back in a loud whisper, "What do you think?" I saw the whites of his teeth when he grinned. "What are you doing here at this time of night?"

He put his finger to his lips then waved that I should come down. Filled with expectation, I shrugged on my eyelet robe and hurried barefoot down the stairs. At the door I slipped into my muck boots and stepped outside. The night air was balmy, and I stood for a moment, letting my eyesight acclimate to the night. The song of the cicadas swelled in the gray moonlight as I searched for Hugh. I saw his silhouette in the dusky light. He waved and walked quickly to my side. The whites of his eyes shone like beacons in the night. My heart skipped a beat in anticipation when he took my hand.

"Where are we going?"

"Shhh . . ."

He interlaced his fingers with mine and we set off across the garden. The dewy grass dampened the hem of my nightgown as I walked with Hugh across the back lawn. A fog was rolling in, making the white of the gazebo appear ghostly in the moonlight. We stepped up onto the wooden platform, and, releasing my hand, Hugh spread his jacket over the damp bench for me to sit on. I sat, ankle to ankle, and clasped my hands on my white nightgown, uncertain of what was to come. The mist thickened around us, creating a gauzy curtain. Hugh stood looking at me, seemingly indecisive, and though I was inexperienced in the ways of love, every neuron in my body was aware something important was going to happen.

He cleared his throat then sat beside me. With deliberation he took my clasped hands in his. I felt the warmth of them clear to my heart. Hugh held one hand in each and, looking down, I saw how large his hands were compared to mine.

"Eliza."

Reluctantly, I looked up.

"I had to see you," he said. "There are things I want to say. Before you leave for Charleston."

I remained quiet, my breath held.

Hugh took a breath then blurted out, "I like you, Eliza."

I blinked, taking the words in.

"Not just like a friend. Though you are my friend. Not like a sister. God, no, not like a sister." He moved closer beside me on the bench. "I like you," he continued more forcefully. "And it makes me jealous when Tripp talks about how he's going to marry you and how he's taking you to the St. Cecilia Ball."

"Oh, that . . ."

"*I* want to take you to the St. Cecilia Ball for your debut," Hugh exclaimed. "When that day comes, will you allow me to be your escort?"

I felt his hands tighten around mine, saw the earnestness in his eyes, and it astonished me when I caught sight of worry that I might say no. I almost wanted to laugh. I'd never given the ball much thought. It was desperately important to my mother that I attend. After all, it was my father's invitation to the exclusive St. Cecilia Ball that secured her entrance into society. I'd always assumed I would go with Tripp because, well, our mothers had decided that at our infancy.

To see Hugh place such importance on not merely attending the important ball, but being my escort for my debut, took my breath away. Suddenly I saw the fancy ball with new perspective.

"Yes," I said, looking into his eyes. "I would be honored if you were my escort for my debut."

Hugh freed my hands as his winning smile bloomed across his face. He slapped a fist into his palm, still beaming. "I didn't think you were going to say yes," he said. Then he wrapped one arm around my shoulder, tilted his head, and pointed at the starlit sky.

"You know I made a wish on that star," he said.

I looked up at the countless stars and wondered which one was his. "There are so many," I said.

Hugh turned his head, smiled sheepishly, and said, "My wish came true."

I held my breath. He was so close I was sure he would kiss me. Then his expression shifted, and I felt his arm slip off my shoulder. "Eliza, I'm sorry about Tripp," he said. "I know you were meant to go to the St. Cecilia Ball with him."

"To be honest, he never asked me. He just assumed."

"Right?" Hugh said, encouraged. "I mean, it was your mothers that arranged it, so it's not like I'm stealing his date." Talking more to himself, he paced a few steps as he rationalized his decision. "Tripp's a nice enough fellow. I like him and all." He stopped and looked at me intently. "But all is fair in love and war."

"Hugh . . ."

His gaze shifted to my lips and his eyes smoldered in a way I'd not seen before, triggering my heart to race and my lips to open slightly in a soft gasp. This time he did not hesitate. He held my shoulders, and ever so slowly, testing me in breaths, drew his lips to mine.

I was powerless against the magnetic power that drew me to him. Brain and heart were sending new sensations through my blood. I closed my eyes and, letting go, succumbed to the pull.

His lips touched mine. Gently. Two quivering, soft pillows that skimmed the skin before retreating. *Oh*, I thought. *More* . . . Then, in the space of a single, warm breath, Hugh's lips descended to mine again. This time his lips were hungry, urgent, as his arms encircled me. My breath caught in my throat, my head was dizzy.

I thought to myself, *My first kiss.*

Chapter Nineteen

—◆—

CLIMATE CHANGE refers to long-term shifts in temperatures and weather patterns globally over seasons, years, and decades. Since the 1800s, human activities have been the main driver of climate change, primarily due to the burning of fossil fuels (like coal, oil, and gas) which produce heat-trapping gases.

1988

I paused in my story, feeling the sweetness of the memory sweep through my body. The faces of Norah, Mariama, and Savannah were staring back at me in a dreamy fashion.

"Grandma Eliza, that's such a romantic story," said Savannah, slipping her chin in her palm and leaning against the dining table. "That Hugh sounds like such a babe."

I couldn't stop the laugh that came from my lips. "A babe? Well, yes, I suppose he was."

"Whatever happened to him?" Savannah continued. "I thought you two were perfect for each other."

"I thought we were too," I said softly.

"Did you love him?" asked Savannah.

Savannah seemed bent on digging out the details of the love story, as girls her age were prone to do. Norah's face was expectant, as well. In this moment, with the grace of time, thinking of Hugh did not cause the stab of pain it usually did, even after so many years. As I was telling this story, reliving the memories, surrounded by the support of these women, the days had returned to mind with a tenderness that softened my stone heart.

"Yes, I did love him," I replied. "He was my first love. I suppose I love him still." I readied myself for the question I knew was coming.

"Then why didn't you marry him?"

I exhaled, feeling the weight of my coming reply. "That, my dear, is another story." I put my palms on the table and moved to a slow stand. Every muscle felt weary from the stirring events of the day. "It's been a long day, and I need to turn in for the night. Let's meet here in the morning, shall we? Oh, and Savannah," I said. "Do be sure to call your parents and let them know where you are, hear? I suppose they have figured it out but best to get in touch with them so they know you're safe and sound."

"Yes ma'am."

The women bade me good evening, and I took the stairs to my room slowly, feeling my bones creak with the effort. The staircase was narrow and steep, not befitting a grand house. James and I had meant to change it, consulted architects, but the project would have demanded more major remodeling of the original house than I was prepared to do. So, it remained.

The sky was deepening, and my bedroom was cool and welcoming. All the windows were shuttered against the heat, casting lines of shadows across my four-poster bed. I slipped off my black Ferragamo flats. They were ancient but had served me well over many years. Still of some use. *Like myself,* I thought with a chuckle.

The day's events fluttered through my mind as I undid rows of buttons, a zipper on my skirt, undergarments. Filled with a strange lethargy, I tossed them to a nearby chair, feeling I was pitching away the memories of the morning's shareholders meeting along with them. *That horrid affair was only this morning,* I thought with wonder.

I walked to the adjoining bathroom. Over the sink hung a large ornate Venetian mirror, a gift from James that I'd always adored. I ran a brush through my thinning gray hair and idly looked at my aged reflection. How did I ever manage to reach eighty-eight years? *Tolerably pretty*, my mother had described me. I paused and a winsome smile bloomed. Hugh had called me beautiful.

Hugh. . . . I ran my fingertips over my lips and remembered again my first kiss. Over the years, important memories like that kiss had slipped from my mind. Or I'd deliberately tucked them away. But they were never forgotten. The memories lay dormant until an event, like today's telling of the story, ushered them forth again—vibrant, evocative, treasured—to release a renewed flood of sensations.

I moved my hand to my fluttering heart. What was the matter with me? I was awash in an odd languor from the stories.

"Hello, you," I said, looking into the mirror and feeling a sudden affection for the heavily lined, sagging face. It was the face of a daughter, a wife, a mother, a widow, a CEO, a matriarch. It was the face of a young girl who loved to sleep in the hollow of a tree.

The following morning, chatty birds outside my window woke me up. I'd slept blissfully as the evening breezes washed over me from the open window. I found Savannah and Norah already in the dining room eating breakfast. I gazed at my granddaughter. Savannah had always been a go-getter, a bit of a nonconformist. In that way, she was a bit like me, I thought, pleased at the notion. Her decision to buck her parents and come to Mayfield not only caught me by surprise but presented me with an opportunity.

I'd not been the best grandmother. I loved my granddaughters— gave gifts at appropriate times, included them generously in my will. Yet, all these years I'd put my work first and missed graduations and birthdays and celebrations. I had a strong work ethic and was compelled to succeed to protect my family and Mayfield by earning money. All noble, I supposed. But now, an old woman, I at last understood how time was my most precious commodity. And one that I had precious little of. Now was the time for me to let Savannah in.

I hardly remembered my own grandmother Bissette. She was an elegant though distant woman we visited from time to time. I knew she cared about me, as she did all Sloane's children. But she could be quite judgmental and harsh—and she was not affectionate. I couldn't remember her saying *I love you* or giving a compliment. I didn't want that to be how Savannah remembered me.

I joined the young women at the table. "Did you sleep well?"

"I did, thank you," replied Norah. "It's so peaceful here. I live in Philadelphia, so I'm accustomed to city noises. But I visit my parents in Cheyney as often as I can. It's a small town, pretty rural with farmland and rolling hills."

"That's where Cheyney University is?" I asked. "Isn't your father a professor there?"

"He is, though he's about to retire. He wants to raise vegetables and tend chickens," Norah said with a fond laugh.

"Well, he's Covey's son, after all." Then to Savannah I said, "Cheyney University is the oldest Black university in the United States. Covey was very proud that her son taught there." I looked again at Norah. "She must have been very proud of you."

"I like to think she was. I spent a lot of time with my grandmother coming up. It was Granny Covey who inspired me to study environmental science. She used to show me interesting plants in the garden and teach me about them and asked me to draw them. She insisted I learn both Latin and the common names. Did you know she taught master gardening classes after she retired?"

I nodded. "Covey always loved plants and trees. She was always sketching them. She was really quite a proficient artist. When we were children, we used to play school. Covey was always the teacher. She could be bossy."

"Yes!" Norah laughed. "We always knew where we stood with

Granny. But as demanding as she was, she was even more encouraging. She always told us that we could be anything we wanted to be. My grandmother was my role model. I wanted to be like her."

"You seem very much like her." I pointed to her intriguing eye color. "For one thing, you have her eyes."

"I've always been proud to have her eye color."

I turned to Savannah. "And you have your grandfather's eyes."

She bobbed her head up. "I do?"

I looked at Savannah's round blue orbs fringed with eyelashes so pale that without mascara, they were almost invisible behind her eyeglasses. "I look at you and see Tripp," I replied. "And that's a compliment."

Then I turned back to Norah. I was curious about the grand-niece I'd never met before. "But you didn't want to be a teacher like Covey . . . and your father?"

Norah shook her head. "Nope. The classroom was never for me. My passion is the environment."

"You mean climate change?" asked Savannah.

"Yes. These are important times, and frankly, I know too much about things like water issues, ecosystems, habitat protection, land management, conservation, not to be worried about what will happen to all this," she said, her hand indicating the land outside the window. "After I received my PhD in environmental engineering, sustainability, and science, I was offered a position at the Nature Conservancy in Pennsylvania."

"And now, here you are," I said. "Back where it all began. Full circle."

"Is it?" Norah pursed her lips. "To be honest, Aunt Eliza, as pretty as the landscape is, my family history here isn't all that great. I . . . I wasn't sure I wanted to come. My father . . . He won't."

"I don't blame him," I said, feeling the sting of shame.

"Still, when I heard about the creation of the ACE Basin Project and your part in it . . ." Norah shook her head with disbelief. "We're all watching in awe at what you're trying to achieve here. It's galvanizing to see individual landowners come together to put this ecologically important land into conservation. When my father told me about the shareholders meeting, I knew I'd have a chance to meet you. I had to come."

My heart filled with affection for the woman. I reached out to put my hand on hers. "I'm glad you did."

"I had to come too," piped in Savannah.

I looked at her, unsure of what she meant.

"I kind of wanted to come to Mayfield, because you asked me, but you know how Daddy reacted so I just . . ." Savannah raised her brows, whether indicating indifference or resignation, I wasn't sure which. ". . . I caved. But that was my first shareholders meeting, now that I'm legally an adult. I've only ever seen you as my grandmother. Someone I loved though was a little afraid of. But in that meeting . . . I didn't know that fierce woman. It made me want to get to know you better."

I looked at the two young faces, awash with gratitude. "And I'm very glad you came too. You both make me optimistic about the future. And it's my hope that in hearing these stories of the past, you'll be inspired to preserve and protect all that I love about this place."

I took a sip of my coffee then leaned back in my chair. "Now, about those stories. If I recall, we left off with us heading to Charleston for my high school years. When I changed from a country mouse to a city mouse." I took a deep breath. "When I grew up. Despite all my fears and worries, they were surprisingly happy years, especially given how adamant I was about wanting to stay at Mayfield," I said. "I was young and in love. Mama was in her element and so much more cheerful and obliging. In Charleston, I began to understand how hard it had been for her to live so far away from a city she loved. Those years in Charleston were easier in many ways. My grandparents had installed electricity in the house and indoor plumbing, which for us was a wonder. One click, and a room was filled with light! And we never had to carry buckets of water from the well to bathe." I shook my head in memory. "Such a luxury."

"Were you homesick for Mayfield?" asked Savannah.

"I missed Capitano very much. I longed to return to Mayfield, especially at the beginning. Yet my family and friends were with me and life was busy. The young can be quite good at adapting to change, don't you think?"

"I suppose," Savannah replied with a wisp of a grin.

Though the golden boys lived at the Porter Military Academy, they were frequent visitors at East Bay Street. Hugh was accepted as a suitor by my mother and was granted, even encouraged, to call at the house. I thrived at Ashley Hall. It was a far cry from the stifling schoolroom of Mr. Coxwold. An all-girls school shaped not only my academics but also my confidence. We were challenged as women and individuals. Such a concept! I was encouraged to make my own decisions rather than depend on male influence. Remember, women couldn't vote yet. At this point in history, women began challenging the social norms. It was an exciting time to be in Charleston. For someone like me, it was like lighting a flame to tinder.

"I was at the top of my class," I added proudly. "Not that it was enough for Mama. I was her pet project. She had me signed up for every class imaginable that might refine her wild child." I lifted my hand and began counting off. "Cotillion, etiquette, and the social graces. There was fashion, fine arts, French, and, of course, domestic skills. To be fair, I don't think she ever got over that horse race. Or what she liked to call our *public humiliation*."

"What about Granny Covey?" asked Norah.

"Oh goodness, Covey was a cyclone between her school activities and social work in the city. She was rarely at home. I remember how she'd breeze in for meals and a harried discussion of what she'd been involved in. I'd never seen her so engaged. Though of course I was happy for her, I admit I missed her company."

I dabbed my mouth with my napkin and adjusted my seat in my chair. What was coming next would shift the mood from the cheery days of childhood to the approaching darkness that came from overseas. The repercussions of the sequence of events I was about to tell had rocked the foundations of the Rivers family.

Chapter Twenty

THE OLD SLAVE MART MUSEUM, located at 6 Chalmers Street in Charleston, is the last building still in existence that was used as a slave auction site in South Carolina, and the first African American slave museum.

1917

I raced from my bedroom on the second floor to the servants' quarters on the third floor. It was a cold morning in the East Bay house, and the fireplaces had not yet been lit. I could see my breath in the air as I hurried up the back stairs. I pushed open the door to Covey's small bedroom. I found her nestled in her black iron bed, her head peeking out from a pile of patchwork quilts. I jumped into her bed and slipped under the covers.

"Your feet are freezing!" Covey exclaimed, laughing.

"Everything is freezing," I said, my teeth chattering.

"Why didn't you add more coal?"

Her stove was smaller than the ones in the main living areas and less efficient. I cuddled closer to her, rubbing my feet together under the covers. "Brrrr . . . I had to get warm first. Is it my imagination, but is it colder here in Charleston than at Mayfield?"

"Cold is cold, wherever you are," Covey replied, raising the covers to our chins. She didn't like winter, and this February was unusually frigid.

In the previous two years, Covey and I usually met early in the morning to share our schedules and talk about what was happening in our separate lives. It was one of the few times of day we could be together as friends. I missed our wanderings in the fields at Mayfield, talking after school in the library, and more, the ease in which we could walk together . . . anywhere. In Charleston we had to abide by the strict rules of segregation, never going out together, not allowing our friendship to slip out in words or deeds.

I jumped up and hurriedly lay more coal in the stove, stoking the flame. Then I scurried back to the bed and lay shoulder to shoulder with Covey. Faint plumes of our breaths hung in the icy air as I let my gaze sweep over the room. The servant's quarters comprised three rooms in the attic. The gabled windows provided glorious views of the harbor, the best view in the house, Covey said. But those windows let the wind seep through in winter. It was spare with minimal furnishings and the amenities were basic. But no other servants lived in, so Covey had the floor to herself. She used one room for her bedroom and another to house her art supplies. She was resourceful, making the most of every bit of material at her disposal, repurposing them and finding innovative ways to create art.

The walls of the rooms were a wonder. Art was everywhere—on old cotton sacks she'd stretched like canvas, wood boards, paper— revealing the trees, plants of Mayfield in glorious detail and color. When I walked into Covey's room, I felt I was stepping back home.

"It seems forever since we've been home," I said dreamily, looking at the paintings. "I can't wait to be back at Mayfield, where we don't have to be secretive. I hate having to sneak up here just to talk with you."

"Me too. Christmas there was really nice. I miss Wilton something fierce. We won't have another break until Easter," she said with a sigh.

I smiled, remembering the family gathering at Mayfield to celebrate the holiday. I rode Captain every day; Covey and I gathered holly, magnolia leaves, and Spanish moss and draped the mantels. I had been invited to Hugh's home for a holiday party, my first as

Hugh's guest. He had received plenty of teasing from his brothers, but they treated me with utmost respect.

"Hugh is coming over this afternoon," I said.

"Oh? Will Heyward be with him?"

"Of course." Hugh and I were not formally courting, so Heyward was his excuse to visit.

"I thought your mother didn't approve of him."

I turned my head. "What makes you say that?"

"She keeps sending other eligible men your way. There's that one young man . . . what's his name? The one with the dark hair. He seems taken with you."

"Oh, John Drayton. He's nice enough, I suppose. But Mama *does* accept Hugh as a suitor." I felt I had to make that clear. "She just doesn't want me to set my cap."

"And you haven't?"

I tapped my fingertips, blushing. "There's only Hugh for me. What about you?"

Covey made a snorting noise. "I don't have the time for romance. I'm too busy with school and art and my clubs. There's such an active social community for Negroes in Charleston that I didn't imagine existed. I feel like a sponge, soaking it all in." She drew the covers higher to her nose. "Besides, even if I did fall in love, I couldn't invite a gentleman caller here."

"You could meet for coffee . . ."

"Who says I don't?"

I giggled, happy for her. The heat from the stove was slowly warming the room and for a moment we were lost in our thoughts. "Oh, speaking of which," I said, turning to face her. "Will you join us for tea this afternoon when Hugh and Heyward come?"

Covey thought about that. "Will anyone else be there?"

"No. It's housekeeper's day off. It will just be us."

"Then I'd like that. Though I may be a bit late. I have a club meeting after school."

Later that afternoon I stood at the living room window looking out over East Bay Street, peeking behind the lace for the arrival of Hugh and Heyward. Light flowed into the great room through frost-tipped glass. The centerpiece of the living room was the elaborate fireplace, its mantel adorned with Oriental porcelain and a formidable painting of Charleston. In one corner of the room a grand piano invited one to play on the polished keys. I feared and despised that instrument, praying no one would ask me to exhibit my poor skills and mediocre voice that cracked in nervousness. Why couldn't I bring a horse into the parlor and show off my skills there?

Mama had the fire burning, the tea table set with pastries, and me presented in full dress. My mother was more interested in my practicing etiquette than setting my cap for Hugh Rhodes. Of course, he was from a good family, and they were neighbors in the small town of Yemassee, where everyone knew everyone's business. I suspect her only reservation about Hugh was geography. Though she never said so directly, she didn't want me to be stuck in the boondocks like she had been.

When I heard Heyward enter and call out his boisterous "Hello!" I hurried to sit by the fire in a relaxed, elegant pose, as instructed. My mother greeted them, their low voices punctuated by her high one.

Coats were removed, a few laughs shared, and suddenly Hugh's face was before me. He was handsome in his woolen school military uniform, taller and mature. His shaggy blond hair had been shorn. His cheeks were red from the cold. He searched the room on entering. When he saw me, his smile informed me that he'd walked all this way across town on this frosty day to see me.

"Heyward, how nice to see you. And Hugh, so good of you to call," I said in a pleasant voice that countered my wanting to leap up and hug Hugh.

Mother looked at our friendly group with satisfaction. "I hope the tea is to your liking, gentlemen," she said, her voice a melody. "Do let me know if you require anything else."

Heyward offered a grateful smile. "Everything is perfect, Mother. Thank you." After she left, he turned to me and said, "Is Covey here?"

I shook my head. "She hasn't returned from school as yet."

"It's been a long time since we've seen our friend," Heyward said.

As the men settled by the table, I took a breath and, with practiced grace, prepared the tea. I'd spent countless hours the past months studying the art of tea preparation—the proper measurements, water temperature, steeping times, and the use of tea infusers. I poured the tea, and when Hugh reached out to take his cup, his eyes met mine and a spark passed between us.

The men's conversation centered mostly around the war in Europe. It seemed no one could talk of anything else. I relished the chance to let my gaze linger on Hugh's thoughtful expression and the way his eyes seemed to hold a depth of understanding beyond his years.

"Hugh, do you believe war is inevitable?" I asked. Like most people in Charleston, and the United States, we were worried we would be dragged into the conflict.

"I do," Hugh replied. "The unrestricted submarine warfare is causing havoc on our ships. Charleston being a port city, merchants are up in arms. I fear the die is cast."

"Not much time, I'll wager," said Heyward, leaning forward with his arms on his knees. "Sinking the *Lusitania* was the last straw."

"We're ready to go and settle the score," said Hugh with determination.

I wondered at their enthusiasm. Who wanted to go to war? I abhorred the very idea of the two men I cared for most in the world thrust into danger. "Amidst the uncertainty," I said, gazing at Hugh, "I find solace in your presence here today. You bring a sense of calm that I cherish."

Hugh's breath caught. Beside him, Heyward's lips twisted in mirth as he looked at the ceiling.

"Eliza, your spirit and intelligence inspire me," said Hugh earnestly. "In these troubled times, you shine like a beacon of hope."

We spoke in polite code as our feelings hung in the air between us, palpable, begging to be explored.

The doorbell rang, and Heywood rose quickly, eyes trained to the door.

"Oh, that must be Covey." I tilted my head to hear the door open and a voice I recognized. Not Covey, but Barbara, a friend from school. I liked her well enough but had not invited her. I felt my body coil in nervousness. What would I do when Covey arrived for the tea?

Barbara entered the living room with her usual vivacity and confidence. Auburn curls framed her face, and her ample hips swayed as she crossed the room. Hugh joined Heyward on his feet, and I could see Barbara's surprise—and delight—at seeing the two young men.

"Forgive me for just stopping by. I didn't know you had visitors, Eliza," Barbara said with polite hesitancy.

"You know my brother Heywood," I said, gathering my composure and rising. "And Hugh Rhodes."

Barbara's color heightened. "I most certainly do. Why Heyward, I do believe you promised to call on me?"

"My apologies," Heyward replied, escorting Barbara toward the tea. "We've been hard at it at Porter."

"Barbara, please sit beside the fire and warm up," I said and began preparing a fresh cup of tea. I sent a meaningful glance at Heyward. He shared a look of concern that it would be difficult when Covey arrived. "We were just discussing the war in Europe."

"Oh, let's not talk about that boring old thing," Barbara said lightly. "It's just too nasty outdoors to talk about something so chilling." She accepted the cup gracefully and took a small sip. "I'll be coming out next year," she added, fiddling with the lace at her wrist. She slowly raised her eyes to Heyward. "I hope by then we might be good friends."

My eyes widened at Barbara's brazen suggestion. Hugh was tightening his lips to stop from smiling and I could see Heyward was caught off guard. He offered a polite smile in reply.

Barbara skillfully deflected the attention from her to me by saying, "You'll be coming out next season too, won't you Eliza? Arthur Middleton has declared to anyone who would listen that he'll be your escort."

My gaze darted to Hugh, whose face was coloring.

Hugh put down his teacup and leaned toward me. "Actually, *I* will have the honor of escorting Miss Eliza Rivers to the St. Cecilia Ball."

I saw Barbara's hand cover her open mouth. I turned to look at my older brother and saw approval in his face. It was well known that the St. Cecilia Ball held special significance to our families. It would mark the turning point of our relationship.

As though on cue, the hall door swung open, and Covey walked in, her cheeks pinkened by the cold. She radiated energy and grace. Her smile brightened at seeing Heywood and Hugh.

Heyward sprang to his feet. "Thank goodness you're here. I . . . we were afraid we would miss seeing you this visit."

"I hurried home from classes," Covey replied, then looking across the room, exclaimed, "Hugh! I've missed you both. You're well, I hope? No frostbite?"

As they chuckled, Covey came to my side, and we kissed cheeks warmly. Then turning, Covey abruptly paused, seeing Barbara sitting with her back to the fire. Knowing her as well as I did, I immediately sensed her tension. Despite the roaring fire, the air in the room felt chilled.

I took a breath, fully aware that formally welcoming a Negro in our parlor as an equal was scandalous. Mama made us promise to adjust our behavior to suit the expectations of society, and we had just crossed that line.

Barbara sat stiffly in her chair, her face solemn. I forced a smile and with practiced ease said, "Barbara, let me introduce Miss Covey Wilton. She's attending the Avery Institute here in Charleston."

Covey smiled and offered, "Nice to meet you."

Barbara coolly regarded Covey then replied in a clipped voice, "How do you do."

"We all grew up together at Mayfield," I explained.

"I see," Barbara said frostily.

"Forgive me for interrupting your visit," Covey said quickly. "I just stepped in to say hello."

"She lives here?" Barbara asked me.

"Why, yes," I replied after a moment's hesitation.

"I am under Mrs. Rivers's employ," Covey replied smoothly. Then she looked up at Heyward. "Again, it was a pleasure to see you. Now if you'll excuse me. Goodbye."

"You must stay," said Heyward, stepping forward in a rush. "You only just arrived."

Covey looked over her shoulder at the door then drew her shoulders back, a stance I knew meant her mind was made up.

"I'm sorry, truly I am," Covey said to Heyward. "I just hurried over to say hello. And now I have." She smiled brightly. "I hope to see you next time you visit."

With a quick farewell and a meaningful glance toward me, Covey left the room with unhurried grace.

Heyward's smile fell as he watched her leave. He abruptly looked at his watch and turned to Hugh. "Sorry, old boy. We best be off as well. The trolleys are running slow with the frost."

Hugh's brows gathered and he tilted his head in question, as if in protest. But Heyward appeared resolved to go. Hugh sighed then came to my side and took my hand. "Thank you for tea. I hope to be able to visit you . . . and the family . . . again before too long."

"I hope you will," I said, disappointed at his leaving so soon. I wanted to kick my brother in the shins but could only assist them with their coats. They bid Barbara and I a polite farewell and stepped out into the icy night.

Barbara and I returned to our seats by the warmth of the fire. I enjoyed the heat against my back and could relax now that the tension had passed. I thought Covey had handled the awkwardness with great presence of mind and grace.

"That was one rather uppity Negro," Barbara said before taking a sip of tea.

"I beg your pardon?"

"Well," she said, putting down her cup. "I mean, she practically invited the young men to return. To *your* house. A maid!"

"She is not my maid," I replied sharply, my patience strained. "She's my friend."

"Oh. But," Barbara stuttered, confused. "Goodness, I just . . . I mean, she's in your employ."

I took a breath, forcing myself to gain control of my frustration. I had to maintain the façade we had carefully created. Yet, in my own home, at least, I wanted to be honest. "Yes, she is," I replied. "Covey is my mother's secretary while she attends Avery." I set my cup on the table as well and gathered my hands in my lap. "The warmth you saw was due to our childhood association at Mayfield. Covey is very dear to me."

"I see. Of course. Well," Barbara rose abruptly. "I really must be going. My parents don't appreciate me walking the streets when the sun sets."

After I escorted her to the door, we shared farewells as chilly as the outdoors. I returned to sit alone in the living room. The fire smoldered and cast shadows in the darkening room. Would I hear gossip tomorrow about my friendship with the uppity Negro woman living in our house? Barbara was a friend, and a fair-minded, kind woman. I hoped she would not make trouble for me.

All these weeks, Covey and I had been so careful, making a point to never go out in public together where people might observe our friendship. If Mama heard about this . . . I marshalled my flying thoughts and calmly evaluated what had just happened. Barbara's response to Covey stung. I'd been flustered, but Covey had handled the situation with a finesse that I realized now came from a far better understanding of racism in the world we lived in. I was frustrated and angered by it. And all the more determined not to allow hate to separate us.

Chapter Twenty-One

———◆———

MIGRATION describes periodic, large-scale movements of populations. For example, birds migrate from areas of low or decreasing resources to areas of high or increasing resources, usually for food and nesting locations. The ACE Basin is a summer sanctuary for many migrating songbirds.

1917

The school year had ended, and at last it was time for Mama, Lesesne, Covey, and I to pack up for the journey back to Mayfield. Mama's parents had gifted her a new Model T town car, and this would mark our first long-distance trip in the automobile. I wondered at the sleek curves and polished exterior but knew the horseless carriage was yet another sign that our world was evolving. When I arrived in Charleston for school, there were more horse-driven carriages than automobiles on the streets. In only three years the number of autos had more than doubled. It seemed the horse-driven carriage was an anomaly. The impact of this reality on my father's dream for the Marsh Tacky horses did not escape me. Like in so many other ways, my father clung to the past, ignoring the changes inherent in the future.

The trip to Mayfield in an automobile would take several long and arduous hours on uneven, dusty roads. I imagined the rhythmic clickety-clack of the railroad cars Heyward and Hugh were enjoying whenever we jolted on the numerous potholes and ruts. Thank heavens Mama had hired a driver who knew the way because there were no road signs once we exited the city limits. We passed miles of pine

forests and saw few shops and homes. The long stretches of road offered no place for a car to break down. It showed foresight for Mama
to carry her own additional gasoline.

Every time we came upon a horse-drawn carriage, we had to slow
down lest we spook the horses. We pretended not to hear the mumbled
slurs and nasty looks as we passed. Here and there we spotted migrating birds overhead or roosting in trees. Purple martins, swallow-tailed
kites, prothonotary warblers, summer tanagers—they were all like us,
intrepid travelers returning from our wintering grounds.

My heart swelled with relief and pride when at last I spotted
Mayfield through the dense foliage. Covey and I clutched hands
in excitement as we drove up the beloved allée of oaks, which were
bowed as though in greeting. The automobile's engine shattered the
pastoral quiet as it roared up the driveway and came to a creaking,
belching stop.

The front door swung open, and Daddy came bounding out.
His face was freshly shaven, his silver and blond hair neatly combed,
clearly excited at our—or rather, Mama's—return.

"Welcome home!" he called, rushing down the stone stairs of the
entrance.

The driver hurried to open our door. Covey and I scrambled out,
eager to be free of the noisy contraption and to set foot on Mayfield's
soil. I smoothed out my traveling outfit, wanting to appear my best
for my father. It had been months since I'd seen him, and I hoped
he would notice how grown-up I had become. "Daddy!" I called out.

He frowned as he took in the sight of the Model T.

Mama's gloved hand emerged from the auto to take hold of the
driver's. Her head appeared, hat in place, and she blinked in the sunlight before she gracefully descended.

"Hello, Rawlins," she said, smiling sweetly.

He lit up when he saw Mama. They shared a knowing look that
spoke of their connection, and something more I was too young to

understand. Then his expression changed. Daddy was never good at disguising his emotions. His eyes were fiery as he took in the mass of black steel.

"You bought an automobile?" His tone was incredulous.

Covey and I cowered near the trunk of the car and exchanged worried glances, while Lesesne leisurely climbed from the interior then stretched, his hands on his back, moaning audibly. He stopped and looked sharply up, hearing the tone of Daddy's voice.

Mama appeared unfazed. She shifted her hat. "Technically my parents bought it. But yes, it belongs to me." Mama looked up at him and smiled. "A birthday present."

"You know very well," Daddy said in a strangled voice, "that the damn horseless carriage is the death knell for my efforts with the Marsh Tackies. *Our* future."

Mama slowly shook her head as a pitying smile played at her lips. "Oh Rawlins. Leave it to you to always bet on the wrong horse."

Daddy's eyes flamed and seeing his hands bunch into fists at his thighs I thought, for an instant, he might strike her. He'd never gone that far, but Mama was deliberately taunting him.

Lesesne cast a sly glance at our parents and said in a low voice. "Does this mean we should all go to our rooms?" He scoffed, turned, and headed toward the house, ignoring Daddy.

I watched him casually walk off, stunned at this sign of how much Lesesne had matured in the past months. The withdrawn, unsociable boy was gone.

"Welcome home!" Wilton walked up with his long-legged gait. His rugged hand, lifted in a wave, was testament to his efforts as manager of the estate. He was dressed in his usual dark pants and white cotton shirt. I relaxed, knowing Wilton always had a calming effect on my father.

He stopped and crossed his arms while his gaze took in the automobile, its black metal now splatted with mud. He rubbed his jaw and shook his head slowly. "Looks like that horseless carriage was run hot and put up wet. Don't you worry, Missus. We'll see to getting it cleaned for you."

"Thank you, Wilton," Mama said, seeming pleased to see him. "You're looking well. But I won't delay you. I know I'm not the lady you're here for." At that, she turned to indicate Covey.

Wilton's weathered face broke into a wide grin when he spied his daughter. Covey ran across the gravel into his arms as we looked on. In truth, I felt a bit jealous of their obvious affection, in such sharp contrast to whatever was going on between my parents. My daddy hadn't even bothered to say hello to me before they started right in. Seeing me standing alone by the Model T, Wilton waved me over. I sprinted to his side, and he included me in his hug.

"I best take Covey home now," Wilton said "Give y'all some time to be together, after such a long absence. Nice for a family to be united." Turning to me he added, "Speaking of long absence . . . I know a certain horse that's been pining away to see you again."

"Captain! Where is he?"

Grinning, Wilton pointed to the barn. "Out in the paddock."

I surged forward.

"Eliza!" my mother called.

I stopped and turned.

"A young lady does not run off like that," she said in a voice of iron. "You will go inside and change into your riding outfit. And pay your respects to Clementine. Then you may visit your horse."

I reined in my enthusiasm. The hard-learned lessons of the past years in Charleston pulled like a harness. "Yes, ma'am." I waved farewell to Covey, then walked with as much grace as I could muster up the stairs to the threshold, aware of eyes on me.

I turned to look back, taking in the view of Mayfield. I breathed deep, feeling a material change take over me. Ladylike behavior be damned. I was home.

Chapter Twenty-Two

———◆———

THE AMERICAN BULLFROG (*Lithobates catesbeianus*) is a common amphibian found in lakes and ponds. It is an efficient hunter of beetles, grubs, cutworms, grasshoppers, snails, and slugs. The largest frog species in the United States, the bullfrog breeds from March to August. It has a very deep call, which resembles the mooing of a cow.

1917

I dashed up the stairs to my room and slammed the door. As my fingers hurriedly undid countless buttons, I felt released from the pressure of my mother's expectations. I swiftly changed into my old riding britches, savoring the softness of freedom. I would not be tamed here.

I raced in an unladylike fashion down the stairs and tore out the kitchen door, stopping only to give a surprised Clementine a hearty hug. As I galloped across the yard, the warm summer breeze tousling my hair, I heard my father's voice call out, "He's in the front field!" His words spurred me on.

The pastures were green with patches of clover over which bees hummed. I reached the rustic wooden fence and wasted no time climbing up on the bottom rung. I spotted Capitano across the field, his bay coat gleaming in the sun.

"Captain!" I called out, leaning far forward. "Cap!"

The stallion abruptly lifted his head, his majestic mane catching the breeze. Spotting me, his head jerked a bit higher. In a breath, he took off toward me with unrestrained grace. I watched in awe the power of his muscles as he galloped across the field and came to a sudden halt before me.

Capitano nuzzled his nose against me, emitting a joyful whinny and snorting playfully. I couldn't hold back my tears as I embraced his powerful neck. "Oh Cap, I missed you so." The connection between us was built on trust, and I worried that he didn't understand why I was gone so long. But he just seemed happy to see me now.

I climbed the fence and mounted Captain's back. The seat felt natural, and I knew memories were playing in his mind as his muscles rippled beneath me. "Let's go." Clutching his mane, we took off across the sprawling field.

After our run, we left the pasture and walked leisurely through the shaded woods, cooling down along a path that in our absence was overgrown, barely visible beneath the thick carpet of leaves and moss. But we knew our way. Before long we arrived at my private oasis, Sweetwater Pond. The heavy foliage was reflected in the water, which cast an emerald sheen on the stillness. I climbed down and wasted no time removing layer by layer of garments until I stood bare to the breeze. I slowly waded knee deep into the cool, clear water, and watched the sun-dappled surface shimmer and cast patterns upon the surrounding trees. I laughed out loud, hearing my voice echo in the stillness, then took a deep breath and plunged.

The water enveloped me, and I kicked my legs, propelling myself forward and slicing through the still water. I felt the dust and grime of the city slide off my body with each stroke.

Here I could escape the outside world, if only for a short while.

Emerging from the water, I sat on the soft grass, stretched out my legs, and let the Southern sun do its job of drying me. Dragonflies danced above the water, their iridescent wings glistening in the sunlight. Bullfrogs croaked in chorus against the occasional splash of a fish breaking the pond's surface.

It was in moments like these, immersed in Mayfield's wilderness, that I felt most alive. In the city I shut my senses down against the cacophony of horns blaring, shopkeepers calling out, and constant talk. This bit of quiet wilderness allowed me to find myself again.

I leaned back on my arms, faced the sun, and took a deep breath in my solitude. Then, I heard the sound of a horse approaching. Capitano raised his head and snorted. With a gasp I grabbed my clothes and dashed behind shrubs. Cursing like a fishmonger at the intrusion, I slipped my arms into my linen shirt as I peered through the branches. I was old enough now to realize the dangers of being alone in the wild. My heart raced at the sound of hooves getting close, the rustle of branches.

"Lizzie!"

I closed my eyes and exhaled. I knew that voice. Opening my eyes, I saw Hugh riding up to the pond. He was wearing a summer suit, sans jacket and tie. A straw hat tilted back on his head.

"You stay right where you are, Hugh Rhodes. I'm not decent." Crouching low, I clumsily thrust my legs into my britches, my damp skin making it difficult.

"I'll look the other way," Hugh called back, a laugh in his voice.

I heard his feet hit the earth in a soft thud as my fingers raced up the buttons. I combed my wet hair with my fingers, took a breath, then stepped from the cover of bushes, shyly pulling back my hair.

We faced each other across the high grass. Hugh stood in his loose linen shirt, his arms at his sides. It had been weeks since we'd seen each other, and I felt uncharacteristically nervous. Suddenly, Hugh rush-walked toward me. In a few strides he was at my side, wrapping me tightly in his arms. I felt his breath at my ear, heard him whisper my name, "Lizzie."

I pushed him back, mumbling, "I'm all wet."

"Oh," he said, awkwardly moving away. "Sorry." He swiftly turned his head so not to look at me. Still in his traveling clothes, he looked hot and miserable. A trail of sweat slid down his face.

"Why didn't you change your clothes?"

"I didn't want to wait. I came here straightaway from the station to see you. When I heard you'd gone for a ride, I just"—he shrugged—"figured you might be here."

I laughed at his folly. Of course he knew my favorite places. "Since you're here, why don't you take a swim? Cool off some. You look ready to expire."

Hugh turned and gazed at the pond. "Looks inviting."

"Well, go on, then."

He turned to look back at me. "You aren't coming in?"

"I've already been." I looked down at my damp blouse. "Can't you tell?"

He colored and swiftly looked away again. "Uh, yeah. . . . But, why not come back in?"

"I'm not bathing au naturel, if that's what you're thinking." I snorted in a most unladylike way.

His back still to me, I heard the tease in his voice. "Wish you would, but you can just go in your britches like you always do."

I turned to pluck at a shrub and said, "Well, I guess I could."

He turned and met my eyes, grinning victoriously. "Good. No more talking, hear? I'm sweltering." His fingers flew down the buttons of his shirt and he threw it to the ground, then he tore off his undershirt. I caught a glimpse of his broad shoulders and muscular chest covered now in pale hair that wasn't there the previous summer. His hands went to his belt, and it was my time to turn my back. I didn't face him again until I heard him hoot out a rebel yell. I swung around in time to see him running in his loose-fitting drawers into the pond and dive under the water.

Laughing, I followed at a leisurely pace and entered the cool water again. Hugh was already halfway across the pond, slicing through the water with strong strokes. I strolled in thigh deep and let my fingertip trace circles on the surface. Hugh reversed his direction and swam toward me. My hands went still, and I stood as still and straight as an egret watching him approach. He stopped a foot away, rising from the water to stand. Droplets fell from his hair, his eyelashes, his bare chest, and he was breathing heavily.

I felt a shift in the air; my heart quickened.

He stared at me, and I could see longing in his blue eyes. Indecision. Then, mumbling a curse, he suddenly reached out to pull me close against his chest. I gasped, my head tilted up. Lowering his head, he pressed his lips against mine. I was swimming in sensations. His lips were cool and wet as they slid across mine, like the pond. But I felt in him an earthbound sensation that was more feral. His lips trembled and his hand slid down to my buttocks to push me against his body. I gasped, feeling something hard against my leg. Wrapping my arms around his neck I pressed myself against him, hungry for more. I heard a soft moan escape my lips.

Suddenly, Hugh pulled away.

Confused, I protested. "Don't . . . don't stop."

"You don't know what you're saying." His voice sounded gruff, almost angry.

"I do," I argued. "I don't want you to stop kissing me."

Indecision flared in Hugh's eyes. He took another step back away from me. I felt the chill of my wet clothing against my skin.

"Do you even know what kissing leads to, Lizzie?" he asked, eyes blazing.

The shift of mood was so sudden, and he sounded so frustrated, I didn't understand.

"Leads to?"

Hugh looked skyward. "Hasn't your mama explained things to you yet?"

"About kissing?"

"About what happens *after* kissing."

Understanding dawned. "I grew up on a farm, Hugh. I've seen

plenty of animals mate, if that's what you're referring to." I crossed my arms, feeling desperately embarrassed. "Is that what you think we're doing here? Because I thought we were just kissing."

Truth be told, I didn't know much about mating between humans. I'd heard cries and sighs coming from my parents' bedroom at night, so I knew the *sounds* of coupling. But Mama and I never had a discussion. Mama was more concerned about how I looked and behaved in front of the opposite sex. She didn't seem the least worried about how I'd behave behind a closed door with a man. And yet . . . I was certain she would say this was not a subject a young lady should be discussing with a young man . . . alone . . . half dressed . . . in the wild. I turned and made my way toward shore.

Hugh strode after me, clutching my arm as I reached the grassy bank.

"Eliza . . ."

"Stop talking about such things, Hugh," I said, pulling my arm away. "You're embarrassing me."

"I'm sorry, Eliza. I don't mean to do that. It's just . . ." He raked his hair again with both hands. "You shouldn't be swimming out here alone." He reached out with both arms. "What if I was some stranger? Someone who is not to be trusted?"

"Hugh, I swim here all the time," I said, spreading my arms. "No one's ever surprised me."

"*I* came here, didn't I?"

I fell silent.

"I'm asking you, Lizzie," he said in a calmer voice. "Please be careful. You're not a little girl anymore. You're a—" his eyes fell to my chest "—a beautiful woman." He almost choked on the words.

Forgetting the scold, I tried not to smile. He'd called me beautiful. I nodded compliantly. "All right, Hugh. I won't."

Hugh, as though surprised by my meekness, took a deep breath and walked a few paces nervously. "I worry because I care about you. A great deal." He stopped again before me. "Lizzie, I . . ."

I held my breath.

"I love you."

I swallowed at his confession. It was like the world had stopped and all I knew, all I could take in, was that we were standing next to Sweetwater Pond and Hugh told me he loved me.

His voice grew tender. "You see, kissing . . . like this . . . with you . . ." he stretched out his hand and indicated my damp clothes ". . . smelling of sweet water and your clothes clinging to you in ways they shouldn't . . ."

With a self-conscious gasp I looked down to see my breasts outlined by my damp shirt. My pink nipples created peaks in the fabric. I swiftly turned my back to him and began flapping the shirt away from my body, mortified.

"I have feelings that I may lose control of," Hugh said in a choked voice. "I can't let that happen. Not until after we're married. Do you understand? It's not that I want to stop. It's that I like you too much *not to* stop."

I turned back to him, my gaze searching his. Did I hear that correctly? "After we're married?"

"This is not the time to talk about that," he said. He seemed to be mustering his courage. "I should go." He took a step toward the bank.

"Hugh!"

He stopped.

"I wonder . . . I mean . . . Well, if you think we might get married someday . . ." I looked down again and said in a small voice ". . . why do we have to stop?"

Hugh laughed shortly, incredulously, then took me once again into his arms. He pressed his lips to the top of my head. "Eliza," he said in a low voice. "Dear Eliza." I felt his arms tighten around me, then he released me to grip my shoulders, and drew his face close to mine.

"We must stop because it wouldn't be right. You're too young." He puffed out a plume of air and dropped his hands. "And your father would tan my hide if he knew I'd even seen you"—he waved his hand near my chest—"this way. Much less take advantage of you."

"Take advantage of me?" The notion prickled and I pushed him away. "I'm not about to let you or anyone else take advantage of me."

Hugh drew me into his arms once again. "Don't I know it. Not you. Not ever. Still," he said, looking into my face, "trust me, will you? We must wait."

"My grandmother was married at my age."

"That was a different time. Another era. You've not yet graduated from high school. Or come out into society." Hugh took my hands and spoke with deliberation. "When those things happen, when I'm able to properly take care of you. . . ." His expression grew serious. "When the time is right, we will do this proper. Until then, I don't want you swimming alone in the woods. Or walking around in wet clothes." He cleared his throat and let go of my hands. "I really should go. I haven't seen my parents yet."

"You won't come for dinner? We're celebrating Heyward's graduation."

"My parents are hosting their own graduation dinner. Can I see you tomorrow? Eliza, there are things I want to talk to you about."

I nodded, mute at the possible discussion.

The water rippled as we strode from the pond toward where the horses were grazing. Hugh kissed me again, softly this time. "I'll come by tomorrow after lunch. We can take a swim together." When he saw me smile, he laughed and added, "In our swim clothes. We'll bring Heyward. I don't trust myself alone with you here."

I watched him ride off the trail until he was enveloped in the foliage. I put my hands on my chest where my heart thumped wildly. *Hugh said we were getting married.*

The family had already gathered in the dining room when I entered. Daddy sat at the head of the table, his usually windblown hair slicked back, clean shaven, and in his dinner jacket. Mama was resplendent in white lace with her dark hair, graying at the temples, swept high on her head and adorned with pearls. My brothers were also wearing dinner jackets and looking grand. I entered wearing a blue silk frock with my hair fashioned in the new upswept style that Mama approved of. I basked in the compliments.

"My little sister has certainly grown up," Heyward said, raising his glass in my direction.

"Amazing what a little soap and water can do," quipped Lesesne. Daddy silenced him with a look. "You look lovely, my dear," he said.

"Where's your friend Tripp?" asked Lesesne. "I thought for sure he'd be tagging along with you for the party."

I didn't rise to the bait. "You take a particular interest in Tripp."

Lesesne's brows rose in surprise at my retort. Then he shook his head and waved me off, striding off to his seat at Mother's left.

Heywood thoughtfully pulled out my chair then took his seat at Mother's right. I smiled demurely and murmured my thanks as I slid gracefully into the chair. The long mahogany table was gleaming, the family silver was polished, and the candles were ablaze. An undefinable charm of being enveloped together as a family permeated the room. Tonight, I was not the only one being evaluated. Daddy wanted to show Mayfield at its best to Mama and prove that he could put out the finery if the occasion arose. Likewise, Mama was intent on proving to him how time in the city had civilized his children.

Clementine prepared a feast of soup, fish and meat dishes, and several desserts. Conversation was more polite chatter, the kind of trivialities I knew my father hated. The weather, the routines at school, Daddy's recitation of crops being planted, and Mama's droning on about the Poetry Society. At the meal's end, Daddy stood and raised his glass. We quieted, sensing the importance of the moment.

"Tonight," Daddy began, "we celebrate the graduation of my beloved son, Heyward. As I stand here, my heart is filled with immense pride, joy, and a touch of melancholy. For this day means not only an end, but also a new beginning." He paused to look directly at Heyward. "I believe it is fitting to mark this occasion with a gift that symbolizes the trust and faith I have in you, my eldest son. As a token of my—and your mother's—love and confidence, tonight, at the occasion of your graduation, I have formally and legally named you as the heir to Mayfield."

This was no surprise to any of us; nonetheless, we clapped with joy as a family to witness the continuity. Heyward, as the eldest, would by law of primogeniture inherit Mayfield. Heyward had often assured me I would always have a place at Mayfield, regardless of whether I chose to marry or not. I could only hope that I'd be given a small patch of this beloved land to call my own. I believed Heyward would make this happen. As long as I had a foothold on my beloved Mayfield, I'd be content.

"Such a surprise," Lesesne said, lifting his wineglass. It was filled with half a glass of champagne, a boon from my father despite his only being thirteen.

"That's enough, Lesesne," said Daddy with sharp disapproval.

Lesesne leaned back in his chair, staring at his glass. I knew he didn't want the farm, so I wondered at his surly reaction. He might look like my father, but he was all Mama's boy. It was well known that the house he had his eye on was East Bay. Neither house would ever be mine. As a daughter, a woman, it had always been made clear that I'd marry into the house I would someday call home.

"Thank you, Father. Mother," Heyward said with heart.

Daddy was beaming. I wasn't sure which of the two men was the happiest.

"Son, this gift carries a profound significance. It speaks to how I entrust you with the responsibility of the next generation to uphold the land that has sustained the Rivers family for over one hundred years. This land is steeped in generations of our family's toil and dedication. It holds not only the legacy of our ancestors but also the dreams and aspirations we have nurtured in its fertile soil. This land represents our heritage and the indomitable spirit that has defined us."

I listened, stirred to tears at his words. I may be a woman, but I was a Rivers. I took my father's words as Bible truth.

"I raise my glass to you." Daddy lifted his glass higher and looked at each of us. "Let us toast Heyward's accomplishments." He looked at my brother. "And the possibilities that await you. Congratulations, my son. May your life be as bountiful as the harvest reaped from Mayfield. Cheers!"

"Cheers!" we echoed as we clinked glasses and sipped our champagne. It was my first taste of the sweet bubbly beverage, and I immediately took to it. "More, please?"

Mama frowned. "Only a sip, my dear. We mustn't gulp."

Embarrassed, I set my glass down, feeling the bubbles reach my head.

"I'm so proud of you, son," Mama said to Heyward. "And to think, you're off to Princeton next. That is the cherry on top of your education." She was exceedingly pleased that Heyward was admitted to the prestigious university that her father had attended. Behind the scenes, letters had been written, contacts made on Heyward's behalf. Both he and Hugh were accepted.

Heyward's smile froze, and his expression had me lean forward in my seat. Something was amiss.

"I want to discuss that," Heyward said, his brow furrowed. He glanced at Daddy, and from the exchanged look I realized Daddy knew what was coming.

"You know there's a war on in Europe," Heyward began, rubbing his palms together.

"Please, let's not ruin our celebration with talk of the war," Mama said.

"Mama, it's not talk anymore," said Heyward. "We've declared war on Germany. The United States is no longer neutral. More to the point, the government has established a national conscription system."

Mother paled. "That's only rumor."

Heywood shook his head. "It's fact. It was authorized."

"What is conscription?" I asked.

Heywood folded his hands. "That, dear sister, is a lottery that will draft men into military service. We are at war. The United States is offering Europe more than our resources. We will fight."

"No." Mama's voice was a whisper.

"I've given this a great deal of thought," Heyward said, sounding by the minute more the man and less the boy. "We all knew this was coming. Wilson couldn't keep us out. The Porter Military School has prepared me for being an officer. So—" Heyward pressed his palms together "—I have enrolled in the Officer's Training Program at Parris Island. I will sign up with the Marines next week."

There was a stunned silence. I looked from face to face, searching for someone to speak out either in objection or approval.

"Did you know about this?" Mama asked Daddy in a sharp, accusing voice.

He met her gaze. "Heywood informed me before dinner."

Mama tossed her napkin on the table.

"Sloane," my father said, his voice urging her calm. "This is a good decision. He can go in as an officer."

"I don't want him to go at all!"

"No one wants war. But we have to face the writing on the wall. Listen to me, Sloane," he said gesturing with his hands. "We know Colonel Dunlap. He's an honorable fellow. I've invited him to dinner at Mayfield often, he and other officers. And I had Heyward talk with him, man to man. The colonel has taken our son under his guidance," he added with a hint of pride. "Under the colonel's leadership, the Marines have expanded their base in Beaufort. His efforts are a credit to him."

Mother reared back in her seat. "You entertained him? Here? With Heyward?"

"As I said."

Mama swung her head to face my brother. "Heyward, why didn't you tell me of these conversations? Or that you'd visited Mayfield?"

"I knew it would upset you," Heyward replied evenly.

"Yes, I'm upset. You've been accepted at Princeton. I worked hard to make sure that would happen. I'm no fool. Of course, I knew war was coming. Once at Princeton you could request a deferment. You could stay out of the war."

Heyward's face went still. "Mother. Do you think I would do that? Don't shame me. I want to serve our country."

"How does fighting in Europe save our country?" Mama returned. "We can give them money, food, resources." Her voice chilled. "But not our sons. Wilson promised he would keep us out of war."

"A promise he couldn't keep," Lesesne said, entering the fray. "Mama, the German U-boats are bombing our ships. We feel that right here in Charleston, being a port city. The war isn't just over there anymore." Seeing her shocked face at his outburst, Lesesne shrugged. "We can't let them do that."

Mama's eyes flashed. "Don't take their side. In a few years they'll call *you* to fight. Two sons at war?" She shook her head so fiercely her chandelier earrings swayed. "I won't have it."

"Don't worry. Once we get in the fight, it'll soon be over," Lesesne said with boyish confidence.

I was heartened by my brothers' certainty but kept quiet.

"Sloane, our son is a man now," Daddy said, his voice even. "This isn't up to us. Heyward must make his own decisions."

"And you support him in this decision?"

Daddy nodded. "I most certainly support his decision." His tone grew cajoling. "You're a woman, so I don't expect you to understand, but military service is part of a man's role. It is our duty and our obligation."

"Hasn't this family lost enough to war?" Mama said, tears flashing for the first time.

Daddy swallowed thickly. I saw a pall slide over his face.

His father had come home from the War Between the States a broken man. The crops had been raided and the land was fallow. He'd lost two sons in the war and his wife died soon after he'd returned. His father remarried and Daddy was born soon after. Thank heavens, or the Rivers family line might have ended then. After the Civil War, Grandfather was a changed man. Some said he went mad. Others said it was grief that did it. He hid in his room like a spooked dog whenever the sky thundered. He acted erratically, mistakenly calling Rawlins by the names of his dead half brothers, made irrational decisions, and spent hours wandering in the woods. No one dared say the truth that he got lost on his own property. He died in a hunting accident, or so the coroner declared. There was talk in the family he took his own life.

"We have, indeed," Daddy said in a low voice. Then, turning toward Heyward, he brightened. "But I have confidence Heyward will make his country proud. As he's made us proud all of his life." He looked at Lesesne. "Son, I pray you won't have to enter this war. But if you do, I know you'll do your duty, as well."

"What about his duty to the family?" Mother said, her voice rising. "What was all that talk about duty and responsibility to Mayfield?"

"It's one and the same," Daddy said, leaning back in his chair in the manner of pontificating. "His duty to defend and protect Mayfield is synonymous with his duty to defend and protect our country. To make a sacrifice for the greater good."

"Mama, can you ask me to turn my back on my honor?" Heyward asked. "I can't. And I won't."

"You're registered for Princeton. Your future is secured. You'd give that all up?"

Heyward's face softened. "I'm sorry, Mother. My decision is made. I report next week."

Mother's face crumpled and she turned her head abruptly, staring out as she fought for control. Lesesne watched, for once not making some quip. Heyward turned to me. A sad smile crossed his face.

"Hugh will be joining me at Parris Island."

My blood chilled. Hugh too? I shuddered as Hugh's words from the pond flashed in my mind. He had said he wanted to talk to me the next day. Of course . . . Heyward and Hugh were going to war. Together. One wouldn't go without the other. It felt, suddenly, that my entire world was shifting.

"Oh Heyward . . ."

"We'll be fine!" Heyward said, his voice enthusiastic. "Us dough-boys. We'll be back before Christmas, gathered around this very table."

Part Four

THE WAR YEARS

Over there, over there,

Send the word, send the word, over there,

That the Yanks are coming, the Yanks are coming,

The drum's rum-tumming everywhere.

So prepare, say a prayer,

Send the word, send the word, to beware,

We'll be over, we're coming over,

And we won't come back till it's over, over there.

—GEORGE M. COHAN, CHORUS TO
"OVER THERE"

Chapter Twenty-Three

AN ESTUARY is an area where a freshwater river or stream meets the ocean. Port Royal Sound is an estuary of the Atlantic Ocean, located in the southern region of South Carolina. It is fed by three small rivers that flow into Broad River, which becomes Port Royal Sound. It is the deepest natural harbor south of Chesapeake Bay and supports a variety of marine life and various bird species.

1918

Our golden boys entered the Marine Corps, and it was a long, lonely summer with them gone.

After the boys left for Parris Island, Mama immediately returned to East Bay with Lesesne in the unwelcome automobile. Lesesne couldn't wait to get back to the city. I chose to remain at Mayfield for the summer, this never being any debate in my mind.

Even Tripp didn't arrive for his summer sojourn. His father acquired a place in Highlands, North Carolina, and brought his son and new wife to the mountains. Tripp wrote daily missives, filled with a satire I had not known he possessed, of their futile attempts to family bond. He wrote how he longed for Mayfield, asking pages of questions about the horses, sheep, cows, and the bird hospital. Always closing with how much he missed me and asking, *Do you miss me at all?*

Covey and I were inseparable. We did our chores together, chatting like magpies as we swept, dusted, or folded sheets. In our free time, we rode horses to Sweetwater Pond to swim, braided our hair, weaving in strands of clover, and read book after book, devouring pages as we slapped away mosquitoes and sipped sweet tea.

Many days we stayed at Covey's cottage. We felt so grown up being alone, not under the watchful eyes of adults. Covey painted for hours. Her skills were growing more confident and deliberate. She'd moved on from painting and drawing in notebooks to any surface she could find or afford—paper, Masonite, rocks, and driftwood. The plain walls of their cottage now displayed her murals of landscapes filled with wildflowers, birds, and trees. Stepping inside was like entering a museum of color.

As for me, I wrote poetry. Pages and pages of verse. My heart was bursting with emotions that summer. I couldn't contain my love for Hugh, my worry for him, my dreams of what our lives together might be like. The only way I could purge those feelings was to write. That summer poetry flowed from me like a river flowed into the sea.

In August, Covey and I returned to Charleston and our formal education and careful lifestyle. The city was somber as the Great War became a reality. No longer was the action occurring somewhere in the European theater. Charleston's position on the southeastern coast made it a prime location for naval operations, bringing the war to our shores. It affected every facet of our lives. When I was young, I used to stand on the piazza of the East Bay house and looked out over the harbor, searching for dolphins. Now I hunted for U-boats.

Like most others, I felt a surge of patriotism that fall. Many of the women I knew were volunteering to support the war efforts or being allowed to fight. I wanted to do my part, especially with Hugh and Heyward waiting to ship out. Still being in school, we couldn't work full time, but we could join the Red Cross. Every day after school Covey and I helped raise funds for the war, knitted socks, made bandages, and created care packages.

Our streets were filled with sailors, soldiers, officers, and support staff. Restaurants were always crowded, trains were stuffed, and the ports were shipping out food, ammunition, and the frightening gas masks. The city's trophy was a captured German U-boat. The boat was set prominently out near the Navy Yard, inspiring us to redouble our efforts. Everyone was humming the popular George M. Cohan tune "Over There."

But always the worry of when Hugh and Heyward would be sent *over there* was in the backs of our minds. Hugh wrote me letters telling of the exhausting yet exciting training they were undergoing. He sounded upbeat, telling me how great his Marine mates were, describing in detail the rifles he was using and the routines of military life. I didn't catch a phrase or word indicating fear. Oddly, that omission made me all the more fearful.

It was on a Friday in February 1918 that we dressed in our Sunday best to bid farewell to Heyward and Hugh in Charleston. The Rhodes family joined us, Mrs. Rhodes flanked by Hugh's brothers. One could not see them and not realize the somber reality that at any time more Rhodes men would be following Hugh to board a ship and join the fray.

Their regiment was assembled at the Navy Yard where piers, docks, and warehouses, necessary for loading troops and supplies, lined the waterway beside nearby civilian port areas. It was mayhem as we jostled through the sea of marines, seamen, and soldiers gathering before a converted cruise liner adapted to ship out the United States military to France. We weren't the only ones holding in our tears. There were so many other families, loved ones, and friends, waving American flags and bedraggled flowers, gathered to send the boys off. Mama, Covey, and I jostled for space as an orchestra played patriotic tunes. The mood was forcibly upbeat.

Hugh and Heyward looked dashing in their khaki uniforms with high standing collars. The gold bar on their collars marked Hugh and Heyward as lieutenants.

Hugh stepped away from his parents and seemed nervous as he reached out for my hand. "I want to talk to you. Privately," he said.

I followed Hugh away from the family to stand in a shadowed corner beside a ticketing wall. We were far from alone, but when I looked into his eyes, so intent and focused, I felt like we were the only two people in the world.

"Lizzie," he said, holding my hands in his. "I hate goodbyes. I don't want to leave you. To go off and fight. But I must and I will," he said, as though encouraging himself. Then his eyes brightened. "But I'll be back. As soon as I can. So, let's not say goodbye."

I laughed. "Then what shall we say?"

He smiled. "Instead, we'll say . . . *I'll see you soon.*"

My eyes watered and, tightening my lips, I nodded. *Please don't do this*, I thought to myself. I'd been working so hard to be brave. Not to cry but smile. But if Hugh went down this path I'd lose control and the tears would gush out.

Hugh let go of my hands and bent his head to pull his signet ring from his finger. He looked again in my eyes, earnestly.

"Do you remember our conversation at Sweetwater Pond?"

I blushed and nodded. "Yes. Of course."

"That was my clumsy way of telling you that I want to marry you. I love you, Lizzie. I want you to be my wife. I'm not in a position to formally ask you that question. But when I return, I will. I've talked to my father. And my mother. They approve, of course. And . . . Magnolia Bluff will be put in my name when I get back." He took a step closer. "We can be married then."

He spoke so earnestly that his words danced in my heart. I was smiling, sharing his dream, nodding my head. "Yes, Hugh. Yes!"

Hugh grinned with relief and took my left hand to slip his signet ring on my ring finger. We laughed when the heavy gold slid around, much too big. He moved the ring to my middle finger, where it sat securely. I stared down at the handsome family crest—a lion with its claws up in a fierce display against a shield with four stars.

"Oh Hugh, it's beautiful. I'll treasure it."

"This ring carries my promise of our engagement. You *will* marry me, Lizzie?" His eyes shifted to worry.

As if there was any doubt. "Yes, Hugh, I will marry you."

He burst into a smile and lunged forward, clasping my head in his hands to kiss me. It was a joyous kiss, the kind that sparkles with giggles and tears and promise. Then we hugged, holding tight, as though if we held tight enough we assured that we would never let go of our promise of a future together. At that moment, on a crowded dock, under a cloudy sky, jostled between strangers, I committed my love to Hugh more than I could in any chapel.

The call to board the ship echoed through the air, breaking our embrace. Hugh reluctantly released me, but kept his hands on my cheeks, as if memorizing every detail of my face.

I clutched his jacket. "Don't go," I said in a choked voice.

He leaned in, our foreheads touching. Time stood still as we held on to each other, trying to etch the moment into our hearts.

"Hugh!"

We both turned our heads to see Heyward fighting his way against the path of the crowd to our sides. He waved urgently.

Hugh dropped his hands and looked at me. "I must go."

I felt our time together disappearing second by second. Panic gathered in my heart, but I nodded, and fighting back tears, I spoke with determination. "Stay safe, Hugh. Come back to me."

"I will. I promise."

Heyward reached us. "Okay, lovebirds," he joked, then he swept me in his arms for a brotherly hug. When he released me, his face turned serious. "I love you, sister mine. Take care of Mama and Daddy. And Lesesne. You're the strong one. We all know that. I'm counting on you to keep Mayfield going until I get back."

"I will. Take care of yourself. Please, no heroics."

Hugh drew me close again and kissed me one more time. This was a farewell kiss—tender, sad, filled with longing.

Heyward slapped Hugh's back. "Come on, Lieutenant. We don't want to miss the war!"

"Write to me," I cried.

"I will. Every day. I promise."

"You too, Heyward."

Hugh suddenly turned, his face distraught. He cupped his mouth and called out, "Lizzie! I'm sorry I won't be there for the St. Cecilia Ball!"

I shook my head, laughing, waving him off. I wanted to laugh. What did a ball matter now?

I found Mama and Daddy standing with Lesesne at the edge of the dock. Covey stood with the family, as well. She'd refused to be left behind. I went to her side and watched the military personnel in a solemn procession, marching up the ramp leading to the awaiting ship. Each step forward carried palpable emotion.

I madly searched the men's faces lining the railing of the ship waving farewell, their hands cutting the air like so many flags. I jumped up on tiptoes when at last I spotted the beloved faces of Heyward and Hugh.

"Over there," I said, pointing.

Mama peered out at the ship and mass of men, tears streaming down her face. "Where?"

"There, second level. Center. Heyward! Hugh!" I cried at the top of my lungs.

"I see them," called out Covey, jumping up. "Heyward!"

Hugh and Heyward spotted us and slapping each other's shoulders, waved back, their blue eyes shining, white teeth bright against their tans. They were both so full of life. Brothers of the heart. I thought to myself, *I'll hold on to this image forever.* I felt the significance of this moment: the departure of my loved ones into the unknown, the hope for a safe return, and the knowledge that the world I knew would never be the same.

Chapter Twenty-Four

⇐⟩⇒

HORSES, DONKEYS, AND MULES served two missions during World War I: in harness, pulling guns, supply wagons, and other vehicles; and as saddle horses and, rarely, as the mounts for cavalry soldiers. They were the true "horsepower" of the war effort.

1918

The next few months our lives circled around the delivery of mail. The winter air was crisp, the icy rain fell, but every day around three p.m. Mr. Deveraux, the mailman, came ambling along East Bay Street.

Heyward was true to his word and wrote regularly. He was typically thoughtful, making sure that everyone got an individual letter from him. Once we had them in hand, we all scurried off with our missives to read in private. Then later, usually before dinner, we gathered in the living room to share our letters, treasuring each word. Some of the lines were redacted, to keep location and other information private. Some lines or sections we chose to keep private. For the most part, however, we were eager to read them aloud. He wrote to each of us about different aspects of his life. To Mama, Heyward often wrote about the food.

Dearest Mama,

The food on the ship was surprisingly delicious. The officers were put into the first-class cabins and the food wasn't all that different from what I might expect from a transatlantic crossing. The usual cabin stewards and waiters were in attendance. I admit, I did enjoy those two weeks.

Once on land, however, military life reasserted itself. We usually have two meals a day as rations are quite limited. We get a lot of canned food, mostly meat and salmon. We eat this with hard bread, or beans, or potatoes. On occasion, we get canned tomatoes and powdered eggs. Ah yes, and corn syrup. Liberal amounts of corn syrup.

Heyward's letters to me were often about his whereabouts and what he saw. We grew accustomed to the deletions in the letters whenever whereabouts were mentioned.

My dear sister,
We arrived in France in the city of ▮▮▮▮▮▮▮▮ *on the western coast. The water in the port was partially frozen. Ice formed along the shoreline, piers, and on the ships, the port was crowded with American troops. From there we were promptly transported to training areas.*

In this arena, the powers that be learned of Hugh and my knowledge of horses, and we were assigned to the cavalry. Believe it or not, we get about 10,000 horses and mules a week, so you can see why our help is needed. They're great beasts. My heart goes out to them. They pull guns and supply wagons, even under fire. We'd be lost without them. They're the unsung heroes of the war. Some of them are shell-shocked and timid or wild when they come back to us, or just old, or blind in one eye. Hugh and I do our best. In truth, the horses are like us. We are all being prepared for what we will face on the Western Front.

To Covey he described the flora and fauna, which delighted her.

Dear Covey,
Hugh and I have been sent to a forested area outside of Paris, a place suitable to train in various aspects of warfare—infantry

tactics, marksmanship, physical fitness, and coordination. Eliza
would do well with her eagle eye shot!

One creature that never fails to grab our attention is the
European red deer. Majestic and proud, they roam the forest with
an air of regality, their antlers held high. It's a sight many hunters
at home would like to behold. Being in the forest reminds me of
the delicate balance between man and nature. In nature, life and
death, beauty and hideous, prey and hunter seem to find a balance.
Animals follow their instincts for survival, not power. Coexistence
and a kind of peace exists. I wonder why we humans cannot get
along as well as animals in the wild.

To Lesesne, Heyward gave brotherly advice.

Dear Brother,

You are the only son at home, Daddy's right hand. Be a pillar
of strength and support for our family. While I may not be there
physically, I know you have the capacity to be a source of comfort
and encouragement to those around you. Offer a listening ear, lend
a helping hand, and be there for our parents and sister. I depend on
you. And, remember little brother, I am proud of you. Keep shining
your light in the world. I eagerly await the day when we can be
reunited.

The letters from Hugh I did not share. They were meant for my
eyes only. Hugh had a poet's soul, observant and philosophical. He
could be quite tender at times, so much so that after reading a line I'd
bring the letter to my heart and hold it there, eyes closed, committing
the line to memory.

My darling Lizzie,

As I walk through the forest I am surrounded by the symphony
of birdsong. So many different species! From the melodious trills of

nightingales to the rhythmic tapping of woodpeckers, their presence provides a soothing backdrop to all the training.

Yesterday I spotted a red fox on our patrol. It moved with a stealth and agility I admired. I often smile, thinking how you would love it here, marveling at and identifying the different species. We are alike that way, finding solace in quiet moments, connecting with the natural world. Do you remember our many woodland rides together on horseback? Our time at Sweetwater Pond . . . I think of those days often. The memories sustain me. I hope I'll have the chance to share these sights with you, to walk together through Bois de Belleau hand in hand. Perhaps we should return after the war on our honeymoon?

Until then, I'll continue to write. Please know I treasure your letters and read them over and over.

You are always in my thoughts.

Hugh

Through the winter and early spring, the letters arrived in batches in a feast-or-famine manner. One day we'd receive a week's worth of letters. This was followed by a dry spell before they resumed.

Then in May, the letters stopped. We grew frantic as we waited for word. Our only source of daily updates, battlefront accounts, and, worst of all, casualty reports came in the daily *Charleston News and Courier* newspaper. Mr. Deveraux told us that it was likely Heyward and Hugh had been moved to the front and that mail delivery from there was exceedingly spotty. Sure enough, in late May, letters began again. We cried with relief when the mud-splattered, wrinkled post arrived. The boys had indeed arrived in the trenches. The tone of their letters had materially changed.

Dear Mother,

I'm alive and well and hoping you are too. At present, Hugh and I are in the trenches, grateful to be together. The weather!

Rain, rain, and more rain has plagued us. Day after day, night after night. I'm soaked through to the skin, clothes, boots, and all. Up to our knees in water. Trench foot is a serious problem, and the regiment is attentive. It's a laugh to see a line of men sitting with their feet in the air for inspection. Water, water, everywhere . . . but do not worry, Mother. I've always been a good swimmer!

Dear Eliza,

Good news. Lately the line has been quiet. Only now and then do we get a shelling. How to explain shelling? I suppose it would be like asking how to explain hell. When it begins the air is filled with a deafening cacophony of thunderous explosions and sharp whistling. Remember the last big hurricane when we huddled together all night and the wind howled high and fierce? It's like that only much worse. When the shells hit, the ground shakes violently, shattering our trenches. Mud, dirt and debris fall upon us like rain. Pity the poor fellow who gets hit with shrapnel. But we persevere. Our will is strong. Our faith in the outcome is unshakable.

I look at those words and laugh at my hubris. In truth, I don't feel such bravado. Instead, oddly, I am numb. I know my duty and will fight when called. God save us all.

Stay safe, little sister, and live a life that brings you joy, vitality, and fulfillment. Support our troops from afar, honor our fallen heroes, and pray that my name will not be among them. If fate declares it so, I trust you will strive to create a world where war is but a distant memory.

Dear Covey,

I thought you'd like to know we have canaries in the trenches. The sweet little birds are kept in small cages and positioned in strategic locations in the trench. They are clever, lively, and full of cheer. They remind me of you. And they are heroes.

They are our early warning system. Their sensitivity to fumes signals the presence of poison gas. If they flutter in agitation or gasp, it gives us a warning and time to quickly don our gas masks. I know your tender heart is worried about the wee birds. We take great care of our feathered friends, feed them well, and protect them as best we can. Their song provides much-needed joy in the trenches. I defy anyone not to smile when a canary sings.

Dear Lesesne,

I loathe to think of you being here, little brother. Do not share this with the ladies, but death is a constant companion. The trenches are a bleak and unforgiving place, where the air is thick with the stench of death and despair. The trenches are narrow and crawling with non-human occupants, mostly flies and rats. We cannot rid ourselves of them. How can we, as fallen bodies litter the field? There are some left too long, that have swollen and burst.

I have witnessed friends and comrades fall in battle, their lives cut short in an instant. These haunting memories will forever be etched in my mind. I share this with you not to scare you, but because I want to protect you from the horrors I've seen. I cannot bear the thought of you facing this heartache. I beg you not to add your name to the list of casualties. I may not make it back, and as the second son it will be up to you to assume the mantle of family and Mayfield.

Stay safe, little brother.

Hugh's words were introspective:

My darling Lizzie,

I've sat down to write so many times, but words have failed me. All that I want to say to you, words of love and commitment, poetry and romance—they feel so out of place in this arena of despair. One harsh day flows into another as we wait for relief. Too soon our break is over, and we return to the trenches. We do our best to keep

our home tidy. I've brought flowers in and take joy in seeing the
colors brighten the mud.

But tonight, the moon is full and the stars above shine faintly. I
think back to sitting with you in the gazebo, holding your hand as
you spoke of your dreams and hoped they would include me. Tonight,
I put pen to paper to write about my dreams.

I do believe the war will end soon and at long last I will leave
this wretched place, board the ship, and return home to you. Home to
the great rice fields, the winding rivers and creeks, the Marsh Tacky
horses, and to our families. We are bound by geography, friendship,
and soon, marriage.

In recent letters my father has assured me that upon my return
Magnolia Bluff Plantation will be deeded in my name so that I can
marry. Mother is thrilled at the prospect of a wedding, and dare I
say, grandchildren. Lizzie, I know you love Mayfield. My hope is
you will feel as much a connection to Magnolia Bluff when you are
the mistress and make our humble acres your home. I want to marry
you and begin our life together immediately upon my return. I've seen
how quickly life can be snuffed out and I do not want to waste a single
moment of our life as husband and wife. As I sit under this full moon
that shines over us both, I promise I will do everything in my power
to make certain you are happy when you are my wife, my soulmate—
Mrs. Hugh Rhodes.

My love is yours forever,
Hugh

In June, the letters stopped again. Covey and I graduated from
high school, but with the war on there was little fanfare. Our thoughts
were consumed with the war, always waiting for Mr. Deveraux to
deliver any missive from Europe. The only letters we received were
from Daddy, asking when we would return to Mayfield. Then, in
late June, Mother returned from shopping pale-faced and drawn. In
her hand, she carried a copy of the *Charleston News and Courier*.

JUNE 26, 1918,
BELLEAU WOOD,
BOIS DE BELLEAU, FRANCE

The Battle of Belleau Wood was part of the Allied offensive to push back German forces and regain control of the strategically important Bois de Belleau. Fierce fighting ensued, notable for the resilience and bravery displayed by the U.S. Marines who launched multiple assaults, often engaging in hand-to-hand combat. They fought against heavily fortified machine gun nests, artillery fire, and mustard gas attacks. Though victorious, it was to date the bloodiest and most ferocious battles in the war with over 9,000 American casualties, including more than 1,800 fatalities.

Chapter Twenty-Five

—◆—

ROSES belong to the *Rosaceae* family and are some of the most well-known and widely cultivated flower species in the world. Roses are native to various regions across the globe and have been cultivated for thousands of years for their aesthetic appeal and symbolic meaning. These perennial plants typically have thorny stems, bear flowers in a wide range of colors, and are known for their distinct and pleasing fragrance.

1918

It was an ordinary day. A Monday. The heat of July was bearing down on us. Clementine was in the backyard behind the kitchen doing the laundry, and I was in the rose garden with Mama, working meditatively.

The enclosed garden was Mama's sanctuary. It was a captivating blend of natural beauty and man-made elegance. Redbrick walls and camellias formed the backbone, and the pathways and patio were also made of intricately arranged red bricks. Dominating the wall opposite the house was a black wrought iron gate that led to a vast park of live oaks.

Roses were Mama's passion, and she had all kinds in her garden— climbing roses with blooms cascading over the edges of the wall, grandiflora, floribunda, polyantha, miniature, and the queens—the hybrid tea, all in hues of scarlet, crimson, yellow, and white. They painted a tapestry of color against the brick walls. Small songbirds chirped and hopped from bough to bough of the live oaks to the sun-loving roses. I watched a bee land on a rose and begin its work. The fine hairs on its legs were thickly covered with the golden pollen, yet still it worked, unaware or uncaring that I observed.

Mama and I wore wide-brimmed straw hats against the sun, garden gloves, and thick canvas aprons to protect our linen dresses from snagging thorns. Like the bee, we were tending the blossoms, removing the faded or spent flowers from the bushes. There is an art to deadheading that I learned at an early age. Once a bloom is spent, remove the entire flowering head by cutting the stem just above the first leaf with five leaflets. This encourages growth and repeat blooming. Mama used to make me laugh when I was young by ringing her shears to the bloom and calling, "Off with her head!" from *Alice in Wonderland*.

I was thinking of that when I heard a car drive up to the house. I lifted my head from a hybrid tea, its blooms the purest white, to peer through the pierced design in the brick wall. I saw that it was a Marine vehicle carrying two men. My hands stilled and my blood chilled despite the heat of the day. I watched the two men walk in a slow, somber fashion up the stone stairs to the front door. The driver was young. The other was older, his broad chest covered with medals. He looked familiar.

"Mama," I said in a flat, breathless voice.

My mother looked up from her floribunda and seeing my face, her expression changed. She quickly turned her head to peer out the pierced brick wall. I heard her breath intake.

"That's Colonel Dunlap," she said.

Colonel Dunlap. My father's friend. In command of Parris Island. The man who came to dinner with Heyward. All these tidbits clustered in my mind, unwelcome connections that kept me frozen to the spot. I did not go to the front door, nor did Mother. We stood as stone solid as the brick wall, unmovable, waiting. I heard the doorbell ring, then the rush of footfall, my father's voice calling out, "Hello, Colonel."

In time, the door to the garden opened and my father stepped out. He was wearing a white linen shirt, but his hair was messed, like he'd run his hands over his head. When he met my mother's eyes, his face told all. He was followed by Colonel Dunlap in full dress uniform, and the unknown driver whose hands held an envelope.

Colonel Dunlap walked directly to my mother. He was tall, yet his large shoulders slumped as one carrying a great sorrow. Thick, bushy brows dominated his heavily lined face.

"My dear Mrs. Rivers . . ." he said, extending his hand.

My mother stared at his hand in midair. She hesitated, and I knew she dreaded the touch that preceded the ominous message. But protocol clicked in and she took his hand, barely touching his fingertips.

"Won't you sit down?" Dunlap asked and looked for a chair.

"Here," my father said, indicating a black wrought iron bench framed by an arched trellis covered in blood red roses.

"Miss Rivers?" Dunlap said, indicating that I should sit next to my mother. I looked into his solemn eyes and knew without a shadow of a doubt what message he had come to deliver. I moved stiffly, unaware of feeling, following orders. My father stood beside Mother, his hand on her shoulder.

Once seated, Colonel Dunlap turned to the other man, who at this moment was unmemorable. He took the envelope and extended it to my father. When he spoke, it was in the manner of recitation.

"As commandant of the Marine Corps, I am entrusted to express the Corps' deep regret that your son, Heyward, was killed in action in Belleau Wood, France. We . . . I extend my deepest sympathy to you and your family in your loss."

Silence.

I felt nothing. It was as though I was shot with bullets but had not yet fallen.

Again, Colonel Dunlap turned to his assistant, to retrieve a small black box. Inside was a star-shaped medal made of bronze. He pulled it out by the light blue ribbon that contained thirteen white stars in a cluster just above the star.

"Your son, Heyward Rawlins Rivers, was awarded the Medal of Honor, the highest honor, in recognition of his exceptional courage and selflessness in battle. Heyward went above and beyond the call of duty to protect his fellow Marines."

I heard my mother's breath come in short, shallow gasps as she clung to the metal bench armrest for support.

My father reached out to take the medal. His hand was shaking as he looked at it. He cleared his throat then spoke, his voice choked. "What did he do?"

The colonel sighed heavily and put his hands behind his back. "The date was June twenty-fourth. The Marines had been fighting the whole of the month in a bitter battle against the Germans for control of Belleau Wood. A very strategic location for the Allies. During a significant siege, many of his comrades fell. Heyward hero-ically carried several fallen Marines back to the trench, one after the other. While returning with a Marine in tow, they met machine-gun fire. It was mercifully quick. Your son showed uncommon selfless-ness. He was a hero."

"A hero?" my mother shrieked. She let out a piercing, gut-wrenching scream that echoed in the garden. Tears streamed down her face as she rose to confront the colonel.

"What do I care about those false words. I curse you and your heroism and medals. My son is gone! My Heyward. My boy . . ." Mama collapsed onto the bench in tears, covering her face. My father went to her side.

"Don't touch me!" she cried, recoiling. "Don't ever touch me again." Her dark eyes flashed with venomous accusation. "It's *your* fault he's dead!"

"Sloane . . ." My father's face was anguished.

"You encouraged him to go," she spat out at him. "You and your talk about duty and valor. I despise you. And you too," she said, point-ing a finger at Colonel Dunlap. "I let you enter my home, entertained you." Her face contorted. "You are nothing more than spiders wooing young men to your web. To their death!"

Daddy covered his face with his hands.

Colonel Dunlap spoke in a low voice meant to console. "I understand the pain you're experiencing. It's a difficult reality to accept. Lieutenant Rivers's sacrifice will always be remembered. His bravery honored."

Mother shrieked again, covering her ears. "Nooooo."

Clementine rushed into the garden to Mother's side. She wrapped her strong arms around my mother's shaking shoulders as she collapsed. "Come with me, ma'am," she said in a crooning tone. "Let's go to your room. Out of this heat. That's right . . ."

As they left the garden and entered the house, I remained unmoving, feeling nothing. I knew I was alive. I heard my mother crying. I saw my father before me. Colonel Dunlap. I was sitting in the rose garden. But I wasn't. Everything was muted. It felt otherworldly. I couldn't possibly live in a world where Heyward did not. My dearest brother could not be gone from Mayfield for long. He belonged here. He was to inherit. *Not true*, my brain whispered.

"Forgive my wife. She . . ." Daddy said absently in a low voice to Colonel Dunlap.

Compassion was etched on Colonel Dunlap's face. He exhaled heavily. "No need. The fair sex often responds like this, overwhelmed by the immense sorrow they must endure."

My father nodded, again at a loss.

I sat ignored as any stone garden statue. Something dire played in my mind. Call it instinct, or a woman's intuition.

"And Hugh?" I asked.

Colonel Dunlap turned toward me, his expression a bit surprised that I was still there. "I beg your pardon?"

"Do you have news of Hugh Rhodes?"

Anguish flashed again in his eyes, and I knew the second bullet was coming.

"I'm sorry," he said. "Hugh Rhodes was a great friend of your brother's, was he not?" Understanding flashed in his eyes. "Perhaps your friend as well."

"Yes."

The colonel digested this information and rubbed his hands together in thought. He turned to face me directly. His long, lined face didn't move but in his eyes I saw compassion.

"Hugh Rhodes was with Heyward in the battlefield, bringing in the wounded, you see. Gallant work." He looked off at the trees. When he spoke again, his voice was low. "Hugh was felled by a bullet alongside Heyward."

"They died together?" My voice sounded hollow to my ears.

"Yes. I'm sorry." He straightened and said with pride, as though it would be solace, "Lieutenant Hugh Rhodes is also being awarded the Medal of Honor."

In the future, some distant day, the fact that my golden boys died together would bring me solace. But not on that morning. The news of my Hugh's death was a final, brutal onslaught. My body stiffened as the bullet hit true.

I felt excruciating pain pierce my heart, ripping apart that vital organ. It was intense, overwhelming, devastating. I couldn't catch my breath. I felt myself slide. My hand groped blindly, and finding the trellis, I clutched it to steady myself. Rose thorns stabbed my fingers, but I held tight. The sharp prick brought clarity and focus. I sat straighter and found my voice.

"Have you told his family?" I asked.

"No, not yet," Colonel Dunlap replied. Then with visible effort he said, "I intend to visit them next."

Visit, I thought. *What an odd word for such news.* "That's good," I said. "I'll pay my respects tomorrow."

"My dear," my father began.

I shook my head to silence him.

Colonel Dunlap said with compassion, "There is no harder news to bear. I know. But in time, the pain will fade. Life continues. Have faith."

I slowly lifted my chin to look at him. He was middle-aged, his uniform was crisp, his face clean shaven. His brow and upper lip dripped with perspiration. I looked away and said dispassionately, "Thank you for coming."

Taking a moment to collect himself, Colonel Dunlap adjusted his uniform, brushed off some nonexistent lint, then looked up and said some words about support for the family, when the deaths would be registered, something about funerals. He coughed then added, "If there is anything I can do during this trying time . . ."

My father escorted the colonel and his nameless assistant out. I stood motionless, trying to catch my breath in air thick with humidity. A faint breeze swept through the enclosed space, carrying the scent of roses, cloyingly sweet. My stomach turned and I slapped my hand to my mouth. To this day, I cannot abide the scent of roses. I released my hold on the trellis. Rose petals fell and thorns were stuck to my glove. I tugged it off and saw bright red blood across my palm.

Deadheading, I thought. Spent flowers removed from the vine.

Chapter Twenty-Six

RACCOONS (*Procyon lotor*) are found in forests, marshes, prairies, and cities. They are nocturnal foragers, using their dexterous front paws and long fingers to steal eggs and raid garbage cans in cities.

1918

Clutching my bleeding hand, I ran from the cloying scent of roses and raced toward the house. Wilton held open the door, a silent sentinel, his face mournful. Inside, Mother's howls echoed. When I reached the second floor, I saw my father standing outside Mama's bedroom door, head bent. He didn't look up, didn't seem to notice me as I slid past into my room.

I leaned against the door, closing my eyes, on the verge of collapse. From across the room, I heard crying, and looking toward the sound, saw Covey kneeling at my bed as though in prayer. Her face lay in her hands, her body wracked with sobs.

"Covey!" I cried, astonished.

She swung around and I saw her face, swollen with tears. "Eliza . . . Oh Eliza . . . Heyward . . ."

"I know," I said and rushed to her side, dropping to my knees beside her. We held each other tight, unwilling to let go as tears gushed anew. With Covey, I didn't have to be strong. "And Hugh," I cried.

Covey pulled back to stare into my face, horror-stricken. "What? No. Hugh is gone too?"

"They died together."

Covey shook her head. "No!" she cried in a wail. Her face crumbled in grief. "Oh, Eliza. I'm so sorry. I'm so, so sorry."

We clung together, our tears mingling, our cries merging into a symphony of sorrow. There was comfort in each other's arms, we who loved them both so dearly. I don't know how long we cried together, but when our tears were spent, at least for the present, we separated to slump on the floor, hearts weary, sniffing and wiping away our faces.

"I don't know what to do," I said. "I feel lost. Heyward and Hugh are both gone. They were our shining stars. The world feels so empty without him."

Covey nodded, her head bent low. "Yes . . ."

"And Hugh . . . Covey, my world is over now. He was everything to me. We were to be married. Now nothing. Never to hear his voice. Never to see his face. Never . . ." I choked and brought my hand to my eyes. "I loved him so much."

"Yes," Covey repeated, taking my hand. She sniffed and sighed wearily. "I understand. Truly." We sat quietly for a while, then Covey added, "I, too, feel lost without Heyward. I loved him with all my heart."

Her words sank in slowly. I took a shaky breath then turned to face her with a mixture of confusion and disbelief. "Covey, what did you say? You loved him?" I skipped a beat. "As a friend, right?"

Covey raised her tear-stained face. There was question in her eyes first, then her gaze intensified, and she blinked rapidly. She opened her mouth to speak, closed it again. She rose up to square her shoulders and when she spoke, her voice was measured.

"Eliza, I loved Heyward more than a friend. Much more. He was my love. And I was his." Seeing my expression of shock, her gaze challenged me. "How could you not have known?"

I was taken aback, struggling to process the revelation. "Covey, I *didn't* know," I sputtered. "How could I have known? He never said anything to me. *You* never told me."

"Tell you? How could I? We dared not speak of it. But Eliza, you're my best friend. You didn't see? Weren't you paying attention? The many times Heyward and I were away together, didn't you guess? The looks Heyward and I shared. The stolen touches. How could you, of all people, not see that we had fallen in love?"

I stared back, speechless. I had not seen it. A friendship, yes. Admiration, that too. But not love.

"Are you sure he loved you?"

Covey yanked her hand from mine, eyes burning with accusation. "Are you sure Hugh loved you?"

I swallowed. A vignette of scenes flashed before me. Hugh at the pond, telling me that he loved me. The fervent look in his eyes. His hand holding mine. There was no way that Covey could mistake that knowing.

"Yes, I am," I stammered. "And if you say it, I don't doubt Heyward loved you." I saw Covey's expression shift from anger to gratitude. "I'm sorry I didn't realize it on my own. Of course, I saw you both together. We were all friends," I attempted to explain. "But perhaps it was denial."

"Perhaps . . ." Covey looked away.

The sense of injustice hung in the air. My mind raced at the thought of Covey and Heyward . . . but couldn't grasp it. Friendship, yes. Love . . . "I mean, Covey . . ." I began, stammering. "What future do you and Heyward have? You could never marry. Not here. Not anywhere that I know of. I . . . I don't understand how. . . ."

Covey's anger cooled, replaced now with a look of sadness and despair that broke my heart. I didn't know how to console her.

"Of course, I know what you're saying. Why do you think we had to keep it a secret? Never speak of it to anyone. Not even you."

Even me . . . I felt the sting of betrayal. "Did *Hugh* know?"

Covey shook her head. "Not while living here. Heyward and I agreed. But who knows what was said in the trenches?" Her face softened. "I hope Heyward *did* talk to Hugh. It may have given him comfort." She looked up at me. "Eliza, we were in such despair. So much so that we tried not to be together. To deny our feelings. Truly we did. We knew our love was futile. Some would say wrong." She looked at her hands, bare of any ring. "But love will not be denied. It gives you false hope." She wiped her eyes. "When the war broke out, we dared to think . . . we hoped . . . things might change. We were fighting for a better world. For freedom."

She took a shaky breath. "Honestly," she said grimly, "I didn't believe it possible. But Heyward could be very convincing. He had all these plans."

"What kind of plans? Not . . ." I paused, clutching my hands tight at a thought. "Not leaving Mayfield. Heyward would never do that."

Covey's eyes flickered with anger again as her face twisted with dismay. "You and your precious Mayfield. There's a world outside this boundary, Eliza."

"Not for me. Not for Heyward."

Covey did not move for a moment, then she reached into her pocket and pulled out a letter. The envelope was well worn, and I recognized Heyward's handwriting instantly. She held it out to me. "This was his last letter to me. I'm sorry, I couldn't share it. But now . . . Read it," she said, moving the letter closer to me. "He can tell you his thoughts better than I can."

I took the letter from her hands, feeling both dread at reading my brother's final words and an eagerness to feel close to him again. The ink could be seen on both sides of the paper, so thin and fragile, like a spun web. I unfolded it carefully, glancing up to see Covey watching me like a wary cat. I smoothed the paper in my lap with the tips of my fingers, caressing his words, marks made by my beloved brother. Then I began to read.

My dearest Covey,

Tomorrow, I lead a group of men to battle once again. The odds are not in our favor, but they never have been. Our orders are to maintain the ground we gained in the past few weeks. We Marines are a tenacious bunch and refuse to yield. I've witnessed remarkable bravery as we've advanced and captured key German strongholds. The dense forest is both our ally and our enemy. We've had heavy casualties. Still, we push on.

I do not tell you this to garner your admiration. Quite the opposite. Tonight, I feel the need for your tender ear. I am, I admit, afraid.

So instead, I think of better times. Sitting with you at the river, your head on my shoulder, as I rambled on and on. You've always been so patient, listening to my hopes, my fears, my desperate dreams for the future.

My darling love, I am sitting in the mud wondering about our future together. Here in France, I have hope. I see a possibility of us living as husband and wife in this distant land. There is not the insidious discrimination of class and race as in the South. I am forced to consider if, when I return to Mayfield, will our small bit of the world have changed enough after this horrid war to accept us?

We face rejection by our families and friends, our entire community. Legal restrictions. Limited opportunities. Cultural barriers. Even physical threats. That battle, I fear, will be greater than the one I face tomorrow. My sweetheart, do you have the courage? The resilience? The determination to navigate the challenges? Do you love me enough?

If I have a shred of heroism in my body, it is for the battle we face together. Even if it means giving up Mayfield, family, friends—everything! I will find a place where we can be together. Perhaps even as far away as France. Say you'll come with me.

I'm fighting for us.

Heyward

Tears filled my eyes, blurring the words. I looked up at Covey. Her face glistened with the residual moisture of recent tears. Her cheeks were flushed. Her eyes puffy from crying. Her brows, usually arched and defined, were now knitted with the weight of sadness. Yet there was a triumph in her expression that made her beautiful.

"I'm so sorry," I said.

Covey nodded. "Thank you."

Pat phrases. But the simple words held all we wanted to say.

Covey stood and smoothed her pink cotton dress with clipped strokes, then she adjusted the bun gathered at the nape of her neck. Likewise, I rose to stand a few feet across from her while my fingers tucked wayward strands back into my own chignon. It was strange, this new awkwardness between us. I wondered if it was just after-shocks from the news or the vulnerability one always felt after sharing something profoundly personal or a secret. From her fidgeting, I knew Covey felt exposed. Did she regret telling me about Heyward? Did she doubt my good opinion of her? Or did she feel relief the truth was out? The secrecy she and Heyward had kept shielded our friendship from this challenge. But now that the words were spoken, there was no turning back.

We stood facing each other, emotionally spent. "I'm glad you could tell me the truth," I said in way of farewell.

"Eliza . . ." Covey licked her lips and hesitated. "There's something more."

I waited, steeling myself. What more could there be?

Covey rested her palm against her abdomen, a protective gesture. "I'm carrying Heyward's child."

My breath sucked in. A child! Heyward's child. I burst into a wide grin of happiness. "My Lord, Covey—a baby!"

Covey laughed shortly. Her smile could not be contained. "It's a lot to take in. I know."

"Did Heyward know?"

Covey shook her head. "I don't know. I don't believe so. I wrote to him the day before I received this letter. I . . . I can't imagine the letter reached him in time."

"Oh, Covey, that's so sad. I'm sorry. He would have been so happy."
She looked up, her eyes hopeful. "Do you think so?"

"Of course."

"Yes, of course," she said, reassuring herself. "Eliza, I know this is complicated, given our situation. But I want you to know that I loved your brother deeply and I will care for his child. Our child."

I reached out to take Covey's hand, seeking connection. "You're not alone. We'll navigate this together. As friends. And family."

Covey retrieved her hand, shaking her head. She crossed the room, stopping at the window. She turned to face me, and her voice was firm. "I don't want your family to know."

"But . . . but why? Covey, they must know. It's Heyward's child, after all. All they have left of him."

Vigorously, she shook her head no.

"Covey, think! You won't be able to keep this a secret for long. Let us help you."

Covey crossed her arms in front of her and swung her head to look out the window. "I have much to think about. I need time." She looked at me again, her dark eyes emphatic. "I told you—my best friend—and my father. No one else knows. I don't want anyone else to know. Eliza, I trust you to keep my secret."

Chapter Twenty-Seven

⟨⟩

SOUTH CAROLINA PEACHES have vibrant color and luscious, succulent flesh. They are valued for their exceptional flavor and balance of sweetness and acidity. The season for South Carolina peaches is May through August with its peak hitting in July.

1918

The news of Heyward's death was catastrophic, lethal as one of those bombs Heyward described in his letters, blowing us all to smithereens. We were scattered. Mama kept to her bedroom, refusing to allow Daddy in. In turn, Daddy retreated to his barn office with a bottle of bourbon. I rarely saw him except at nightfall when Wilton helped Daddy back to his room, stumbling, and mumbling unintelligible sentences about Heyward. Lesesne, as usual, disappeared. He was like a raccoon that snuck into the kitchen at night to forage for food and hid away in his room during the day.

On a hot July afternoon three days after we learned the news, I was desperately lonely, feeling excluded, ignored, sad. I sat on my bed, hugging a pillow, and realized that the only people I had ever shared my innermost self with were Covey and Tripp.

Tripp had recently graduated from Andover and was off on a vacation in Cape Cod with his father and new stepmother. He'd be heading to Harvard in the fall. We were still dear friends, but Tripp had kept a respectful distance since Hugh and I became a couple. Tripp never said anything outright. He was too good-natured and avoided confrontation. He just . . . wasn't around. Was I ignoring him as well? Being away at Andover and his family's new house in the Highlands made our separation seem natural. And yet, I thought with a pang of guilt, I'd rarely answer his letters. He was my blood brother. A best friend. And I missed him. I needed him.

I went directly to the Queen Anne desk in my room and from a narrow drawer pulled out a pen and a piece of my stationery—a cream velum paper with my name embossed in blue.

I wrote to Tripp about Hugh's and Heyward's deaths. Putting the words down on paper made it all seem so final. My tears dotted the vellum. I ended by writing how much I missed him and all but begged him to return to Mayfield. I sealed the envelope with wax. It was done. I felt better for sharing my feelings with him, as though a weight was lifted.

I stood and looked out the window, now thinking of Covey. She had been staying at her cottage, and I felt her absence keenly. It should not have been a surprise to me that she didn't tell me of her love affair with my brother. When I thought back to all the times, the years, we had spent talking shoulder to shoulder—at the pond, in the gazebo, at her cottage, in this room—it was always me who talked endlessly about my worries, my feelings, my problems, my love for Hugh. And it was Covey who listened, commenting, but rarely sharing any of her heart with me.

I returned to my bed and flopped down on my back, my arms splayed at my sides. Covey and Heyward . . . Tears of shame filled my eyes. Looking back, it was all so obvious. How could I not have realized that all those days and evenings when Heyward said that he was going off to see his friends, and Covey simply offered how she liked to wander off alone, that they were secretly meeting? How could I have been so blind? Was I so self-concerned? The possibility shamed me.

Yet, I didn't feel it was all because I was selfish. Covey was by nature private about *everything*. I'd always assumed it was due to the difference in our wealth, our race, or social standing. There were some topics we simply stayed clear of. I didn't want to be a terrier ferreting out stories or answers to my questions when she clearly didn't volunteer. I respected my friend enough to listen to what she chose to tell me. But now Covey accused me of not paying attention, and I was left to ponder the truth of it.

And now here she was pregnant! I couldn't imagine a greater shock. My best friend was having a baby. My brother's baby. I rose from my chair and began pacing the room. I wouldn't be selfish again. Covey needed my help, now more than ever.

A knock sounded on my door. "Yes?" I called out.

Lesesne appeared at the door, a tray in his hands. "Mama's refusing her food. Clementine's tried. I've tried. Will you bring a tray in?"

"Why do you think she'd take it from me?"

"I don't know. She probably won't. But you can try."

I hadn't seen her in days, but I dragged myself from my bed and collected the tray from Lesesne. Wordlessly, I walked to my mother's room.

I knocked on the door and waited. When there was no answer, I boldly entered. The bedroom was dimly lit from streams of light sneaking through the slats in the closed wooden shutters. It smelled of toast and apples and alcohol. Looking at the bed, I saw her form under the cover, unmoving.

"Mama? It's me. Eliza."

"What do you want?" Her voice was low and slurred. Her body lifeless.

"I want to see you." I walked closer. "How are you?"

Silence.

I walked to the bedside and set the tray on the bedside table. "Mama, please try to eat. Everyone is worried."

Silence.

I felt a frisson of frustration. "I know you're suffering. We all are. You're not alone."

After a few minutes Mama cried in a wail, "Yes, I am! He was my son. I lost my child. A mother should never outlive her child."

"I'm so sorry." I sat on the mattress beside her.

"I don't know if I can go on."

"I know," I crooned, smoothing back her hair. "I feel that way too."

Mama shifted on the bed to look at me. Her face was pale and puffy from crying, her long hair disheveled across the pillow. I saw a blue ribbon mingled in the strands, a sign that Clementine had been there and tried to brush it.

"You lost Hugh too," she said, sniffing.

I nodded, grateful for her acknowledgment of my pain. "Yes, I lost both my brother and my intended."

She sighed heavily, and I turned my nose from the smell of brandy on her breath. "I'm sorry. Such a loss. A waste."

"Mama, we should think about the funeral service."

She looked at me as a child would, her gaze wide with question and confusion.

"Funeral? No, I don't think I can." Her voice sounded afraid.

"Yes, you can. I'll help you. Maybe praying together as a family will help us heal."

Mama's voice hardened. "We don't even have his body."

I shuddered. Colonel Dunlop had mentioned in his long mono-logue something about the casualties of this war being unprece-dented. How soldiers were buried in communal graves, often near where they fell in action. Which would mean, I supposed, that Hugh and Heyward would be buried together. Dunlop assured us the Marines would register the burial location, which was some comfort. I thought of Heyward's letter to Covey, telling her that perhaps one day they would move to France to live together. It was impossible to imagine Heyward not at Mayfield, yet I mourned that he wouldn't live in France with Covey. It was heartbreaking to think that the best we could do now was to visit his mass grave there.

"He's gone," Mama cried out, bringing her palm to her face. "My boy is gone."

I was lost in grief, feeling helpless. Looking at my mother I saw a broken woman. I thought about what Covey revealed to me. Wouldn't news of the baby please Mama? I felt trapped with my secret, torn between wanting to save my mother and be true to my friend. It was impossible to not offer my mother the hope that a part of Heyward was still alive. I felt I couldn't be that cruel.

"Mama," I said hesitatingly. "I've news. Good news."

She ignored me, weeping.

"Mama, Heyward is not completely gone."

Mama waved her hand and cried, "Stop speaking nonsense. If you're spouting spiritual jabber about how he's in heaven, watching over me, you can just stop. That doesn't help."

"No, not that. Listen to me." I took a breath, suddenly cautious. Then the truth spilled out. "Mama, Covey is pregnant. With Heyward's child."

Mama's breath stilled. Then, she bolted upright, her eyes wild. "What did you say?"

"Covey is carrying Heyward's child. They loved one another."

Mama pushed the hair from her face, her dark eyes alert. She held her hands at her temples for a minute, lost in thought. It was as though the news had turned her on, like the electric lights in the East Bay house. In a rush she pushed back the covers. I rose in the flurry, stunned by her swift movements. Mama's white nightgown was wrinkled and spotted with spilled food. She was usually fastidious, so it was difficult to see her in this state. She reached for the water at her bedside and drank several sips. Putting down her glass, she turned to me, her eyes flashing.

"You're sure about this?"

I nodded.

"Send your father in," she ordered.

"Yes, all right . . . Mama, are you okay?"

"Ask Clementine to prepare a bath. Then tell Covey I want to see her. Immediately. Wait." She dragged her fingers through her hair. "I need to bathe and dress. Tell her to come in an hour."

I stood frozen, wondering at this quick turn of mood. And I was stabbed with worry that I'd done the right thing. Guilt swept over. It was out now. I couldn't take the words back. My mind whirled with rationalizations. Surely, Covey wasn't thinking clearly. The grief over Heyward's death was so fresh. Of course, Covey wouldn't keep this news of a baby to herself when it could help the family recover from anguish? Covey would need the support of our family to raise the child. My parents would send him or her to the best schools, give the child every opportunity. Why, Heyward's child, if a boy, could even inherit Mayfield. Of course, Covey would want that for him.

"What are you waiting for?" Mama asked sharply.

"Yes'm."

I was waiting in the kitchen for Covey. Wilton had heard the request, pondered it, then after giving me a long look, had gone to fetch his daughter. It was midafternoon, and the July heat made the kitchen hotter than Clementine's oven. All the windows and doors were open to keep the air moving but to little avail. I sat at the wood table, fanning myself with a wide palmetto fan. Upstairs, my father was talking with my mother behind closed doors.

From outdoors I heard voices. I swiped the sweat from my brow with a napkin and sprang to my feet. Wilton appeared first, his tall frame filling the doorway. He held the screen door open for Covey to walk through. Covey looked slender in her best white eyelet dress. Unwittingly my gaze went to her abdomen. She wasn't showing yet.

"Quick. Come with me," I said and grabbed her hand.

I led her to the living room where we could talk alone. The thick drapes were drawn against the heat of the sun and the carpets had been pulled up and put in storage. Still the air felt stifling as we faced each other in the dimly lit room. Her eyes were wide with anxiety when they met mine.

"What's this about?" Covey asked.

I scratched my arm nervously. I couldn't let her walk in there unprepared. This was all my doing. I took a breath and met her gaze. "I'm sorry, Covey. I told my mother your secret."

Covey skipped a beat in disbelief. "What?" She brought her hand to her cheek, appalled.

I heard the anger and shock in her voice and pushed on, wanting to convince her that all would be well, that I'd acted in her best interest. I began speaking rapidly. "Mama was in bed, not eating, not coming out of her room. Drinking. . . . You know how she gets when she's sad. I couldn't console her. She kept crying how she lost her boy. Her Heyward. It was so sad, Covey. I felt so helpless seeing her like that. And . . . it just spilled out. I . . . I told her that there was part of Heyward still alive. That you were having Heyward's baby. Covey, you should have seen her. Mama sprang to life. She took a bath, she dressed. And now she wants to see you. Daddy too. They'll tell you how happy they are. How we all are here to help you."

Covey stood listening to me, her arms rigid at her sides, her hands in fists, her face tightening in anger. When at last I finished talking, she took a menacing step toward me.

"How could you?" Her shaking voice was harsh and accusing.

"Covey, I—"

"You betrayed me!" she screamed.

I sucked in my breath. I'd never seen Covey so angry.

"You had no right!" she cried. "This was my secret to keep. Mine!" She turned away. "I trusted you."

"But Covey, why keep it a secret? The truth was going to come out eventually."

"Only if you told anyone. And you did."

"Can't you see that we're happy you're having Heyward's child. It's a miracle. We have a part of Heyward still living."

She spun around, eyes blazing. "Are you?"

I hesitated, confused. "What?"

"Tell me, Eliza. How do you know your mother is happy about this? Or your father? Did they say that?"

"Well . . ." I stuttered. "When I told Mama, she was energized. She and Daddy are talking now. Imagine that this is a lot to take in. But of course, they're happy. Why wouldn't they be?"

"Oh Eliza," Covey spat out with disdain. "You are so naïve. And stubborn. You've always seen the world as you wish it to be, not as it truly is. And you expect the world to follow suit."

Stung, I sputtered, "What do you mean by that?"

"You've always seen the world through your own particular lens. When you were little and only wanted to work in the barn, you wouldn't try to understand or even consider why your mother pushed for you to behave like a girl. You simply refused. It didn't fit your view of the world. Then remember how you insisted I attend the tutoring classes? Your mother didn't want me in there. She knew a Black girl could not go to school with white children. Nonetheless you fought tooth and nail to make it so, not caring one whit about scandal. Not until you went to Charleston did you begin to change your behavior . . . because it suited you to do so! And even there, you put me in difficult situations, refusing to acknowledge the strict segregation of our races." She looked away, pressing her lips tight.

"And I love you for it," she said, turning back, her eyes shining. "But you're not a child anymore! I am not merely your childhood friend. I am a Black woman and you are a white woman. We live in different worlds. You cannot be blind to the situation I find myself in now. Heyward—" She broke at the name and took a moment to collect herself. "My Heyward is gone, and I've lost my support. I am a Negro woman having a white man's child. This is not a happy situation. For me, my dreams have ended. For your family, it is a scandal!" she cried, her patience at an end.

Covey wasn't arguing her point any longer. This wasn't about right or wrong. She was telling me how it was.

"If word of this gets out, your family would be stigmatized. Do you think your mother would tolerate anything to harm the Rivers family? Would she allow anything or anyone . . . me . . . to stain her darling Heyward's reputation? Better he was dead! Heyward knew this. Why do you think we kept our love a secret? Why did he suggest we leave Mayfield? The country? He knew things wouldn't change." Covey clenched her fists and paced the room.

"Covey, I thought I was doing the right thing," I choked out.

"For who?"

I was taken aback. "For you!"

"Not for your family?"

"I admit, I was thrilled to learn you were pregnant with Heyward's child. I wanted some part of him to continue. And yes, for the family. Think what this means to us. Heyward's child . . ." I took a step closer. "Covey, I truly believe you need our help now. And we *will* help you. There's no reason to keep your baby a secret."

"It's more than a secret," Covey cried, stepping away. "We aren't talking about girlish tales here. This is my life. My decision. My privacy! Do you think I'm keeping quiet to avoid a scandal? What do I care about a scandal! I choose privacy to protect my dignity and my child. You have no concept of the risk you put me in that I might lose both."

"You won't lose your child."

"How do you know?" When I didn't answer she put her hand to her forehead. "Your parents are upstairs now seeking legal, social, and financial solutions to address this situation discreetly. To make this problem go away before my dirty little secret is exposed. I know them. They will manipulate me and my child to suit their needs."

I listened to her reasoning, horrified because I heard hints of the truth in it. "Go upstairs and at least talk with them. Hear what they have to say. You might be wrong. I pray you are. If not, I'll help you find another solution. But please, Covey, go talk to them."

Covey stared at me, an expression of defiance blazing in her dark eyes. "No, Eliza! I will not do their bidding. I won't allow the Rivers family to have anything to do with my child." She pounded her chest with her fist. "*My* child. Not theirs. Not yours. *Mine.*"

Covey strode from the room to the front hall. She moved toward the kitchen, then stopped. Instead, she turned around facing the front door. With her shoulders back, she walked straight to it and swung the door open.

I chased after her. "Covey, wait. Don't leave like this. You're my friend. Let's talk."

Covey turned her head to look over her shoulder. Her face was expressionless, but her cold gaze sent a dagger through my heart.

"You're no friend of mine, Eliza Rivers. I never want to see you again." Covey faced forward and walked out the front door. Out of my life.

The following day, there was hell to pay. Mama ordered Daddy to go directly to the cottage and forcibly bring Covey to the house. Of course, another row ensued. Daddy begrudgingly refused. Instead, he and Wilton went alone to the barn office to talk. It was a long, drawn-out afternoon. We all knew this incident put Wilton in an untenable position. He was the manager of the plantation and worked directly with my father. More, as a Black man he had no legal redress in the courts. Finally, he was Daddy's friend. But he was Covey's father first and by rights, Heyward did wrong by her.

Mama paced in the living room. Lesesne remained moody and true to form, stayed in his room. When I knocked on his door to

Where the Rivers Merge • 263

check on him, he looked wan and glassy eyed. The room reeked of cigarette smoke, and I smelled alcohol on his breath. I returned with a tray of food and a pitcher of water.

The house was a ship on rocky waters, like the mighty *Titanic* that had sunk a few years before. My lifeboat was the kitchen, a humble haven. The old stove was an iron behemoth, the heart of the sanctuary, its blackened surface a testament to the countless meals prepared over flickering flames.

I found Clementine sitting at the long table, seemingly immune to the heat, humming softly while removing stones from a bowl of blanched peaches. I sat beside her, stretched my arm across the table, and rested my head on it. I smelled the scent of her sweat mingled with talc and the sweetness of the peaches.

"Why won't Covey just come?" I asked. It was more of a moan. When I heard no reply, I looked over to her. She was cutting the peaches in half and removing the pits with a gentle twisting motion, then slicing the peach into even thin wedges. Her lips were tight, and her silent composure held secrets and thoughts close to her chest. Yet there was a sadness to the mask.

"I know I did wrong to tell Mama about the baby," I said in way of a confession. "I betrayed Covey's confidence. I'm so sorry."

Clementine worked on.

"Covey called me naïve, and I know now she was right. I see it all clearly now, what with the way Mama's acting. She's more worried about a scandal than she is about Covey or the baby." I put my cheek down against my arm. "Heyward's baby . . . I just wanted to help. And I've only made things worse."

Clementine did not respond as her hands worked.

"I don't know what I should do. I started off to the cottage to talk to Covey, but I came back. I don't think I'd be welcome. I never saw her so mad." I looked again at Clementine. "Do you think she'll forgive me?"

Clementine rested her hand on the rim of the large bowl and

looked at me. Her dark eyes held depths unfathomable. "Perhaps in time. All in good time."

I sat up. "How much time? Do you think I should go see her? Apologize again? Maybe I should." I pushed back my chair to rise and felt Clementine's hand on my arm.

"Stay put, Eliza. Have a little patience."

"But what good will waiting do?"

Clementine put her knife down and retrieved the cotton towel. She dried her hands, ruminating on the subject, then sat back and looked at me.

"You and Covey, though you be friends, are very different. You live in different worlds."

"I understand the laws. We abided by them in Charleston. But we're at Mayfield. It's different here. We aren't segregated like we are in the city."

"I'm not talking just about prejudice," replied Clementine. "You see the world differently than most folks, but you must try to understand how your friend is thinking and feeling right now. In her world. That's what a true friend does."

Chastised, I slid back onto the chair.

Clementine reached out to pick up a peach. "Let's say you and Covey both had a hankerin' for a peach. Now, *you* would march out to the orchard, find a tree covered with peaches, and pick out the peach you wanted. Likely the biggest and juiciest of the lot."

"Sounds like me," I said with a light laugh.

Clementine nodded. "You'd climb up that tree and pluck that peach. Or if you couldn't reach it, you'd find a stick and shake that branch till the peach fall. Then you'd bite into that peach on the spot and eat it all up lickety-split. That's who you are. You know what you want, go after it with all your heart, and you usually get it. You a force to be reckoned with."

I settled my chin in my palm. "And Covey?"

"Now Covey, she'd go to the orchard, wander around it a bit admiring the trees, then when she found a peach she wanted she'd sit beneath it and wait for it to fall. Maybe draw a picture of it."

I chuckled at that. "Yeah."

"When that peach finally falls, she'd study it, smell it, then take a bite. If it was sweet and ripe, she'd eat it there. But if it was not ripe, or even mushy, she'd hold her hunger and take it home and make a pie with it. Or jam. Fix the peach with some sugar. That's who Covey is. She takes things in, ruminates a bit, and if there's a problem she figures out how to fix it. When she makes a decision, she holds true to it. Nothing or no one will change her mind. And she won't be rushed."

"You're saying I should give Covey time to make up her own mind."

"I'm saying have patience. Covey will do what Covey wants to do." Clementine picked up a peach and handed it to me with a small paring knife.

For the next hour, I sat with Clementine slicing peaches. Neither of us had anything more to say as we pared the fruit, tossed them with sugar, and drizzled them with lemon juice. When we finished, we put them aside to macerate and create a delicious syrup for the pie filling.

We were washing our hands at the sink when I spotted Daddy and Wilton emerging from the barn. Daddy's face was solemn. Wilton was leading his horse. The two men shook hands. Then Wilton climbed upon his horse and trotted off.

"I think Wilton's gone to fetch Covey!"

Clementine was drying her hands on her apron when Daddy walked into the kitchen.

I rushed up to him. "Is Covey coming?"

Daddy put his hand on my shoulder and cast a glance at Clementine. She looked away, her eyes troubled. "No," he said with a shake of his head. "Covey isn't coming. Not ever again."

I blinked, not sure I'd heard right. "What do you mean?"

"Covey's gone. She packed up her things this morning and left Mayfield."

"What? Where did she go?" I turned to look at Clementine. Her face remained impassive.

"Wilton said she went to her aunt's house, somewhere up in the North. Her mother's sister, I believe." He glanced again at Clementine for confirmation.

"But she can't just leave," I cried. "Daddy, she needs us now, more than ever."

"Don't get yourself all worked up," he said. "This was Covey's decision. Wilton and I worked out how we could help her in a manner she would accept. Don't ask," he added firmly, holding up his hand when I tried to speak. "That part is none of your business. And in truth, it might all be for the best."

"What about the baby? Will we get to see it?"

Daddy's voice was low, exhausted. "I don't know."

I looked at Clementine. I knew she knew something as sure as I knew she would never tell.

"This isn't right!" I exclaimed. Turning to Clementine, I cried, "Covey can't be gone. She just can't."

Clementine looked away.

I rushed past Daddy and Clementine to the door, and once outdoors I began to run toward the barn. Covey couldn't be gone. It didn't make sense that she'd just up and leave. To where? She never spoke to me of an aunt in the North. That was just some message she had sent to my parents as an excuse.

I slowed to a walk as my mind worked furiously on these questions. She did that because she wanted to escape my parents. Mayfield. Me, I realized. Her final words rang in my head: *You're no friend of mine, Eliza Rivers. I never want to see you again.*

I stopped and buried my face in my palm. My heart felt like a dead weight in my body. Like the ship had sunk and I had already drowned.

Chapter Twenty-Eight

———

CAROLINA JASMINE (*Gelsemium sempervirens*) is a species of flowering vine native to the southeastern United States. Prized for its fragrant yellow trumpet-shaped flowers that bloom profusely in spring, it attracts pollinators like bees and butterflies. It is the state flower of South Carolina.

1988

I leaned back against the hard wood of the chair, closing my eyes. I felt like I'd been at a confessional. Opening my eyes again I saw the faces of Savannah and Norah sitting across from me. I would receive my judgment from them. Savannah's face was knitted with question. Norah's, however, was masked with grief.

"Grandma Eliza," said Savannah, breaking the silence. She looked at me incredulously. "You really told Covey's secret? I mean, how could you do that?"

The accusation hurt more than I'd expected. I cringed in shame and felt my heart flutter. I was telling my story with honesty, not mincing words or shading the truth. Not just for them, but for myself, as well. Peeling back the layers, I saw more clearly how we all had been reeling from the shock of Heyward's and Hugh's deaths. None of us were thinking clearly. Still, none of that washed away the guilt I felt for betraying my friend.

"I have had many years to ask myself that," I said. "I was young. Naïve, as Covey had said. Though we had been the same age and had grown up together, I did not fully comprehend why Covey kept her secrets to herself. How could I? Despite our friendship, Covey couldn't share her personal problems, or her love of my brother, or any issues with me, a white girl. The barriers of racism were too deeply ingrained in us.

"At that time, however, I blithely thought our love for one another would conquer all." I shook my head. "I see myself now as Covey must have—a privileged, naïve child. Color may not have been an issue between us, but it was certainly a cruel obstacle in the world we lived in. What Covey had to deal with every day as a young Black woman during the Jim Crow era—the fear, the threats, the humiliation—were not anything I could truly understand. I don't say this as an excuse. Just that at that time, I truly believed we, the Rivers family, could help Covey raise her child. I wanted us to be one big happy family again. I was a fool," I admitted. "I didn't appreciate the depth of bigotry in the South and the nation. Or the consequences of telling her secret."

"Your understanding of her situation has nothing to do with your betrayal," Norah said, her voice tinged with anger. "It doesn't matter what the secret is. When a friend confides in you, breaking that confidence is breaking the friendship. Race has nothing to do with that. She was right to leave."

I felt the blood coursing in my cheeks and my heart begin its uneven pace. "You're right. It was wrong of me to tell my friend's secret, no matter the context. It was a grave mistake. One I've always regretted. Deeply."

After a length of time, Norah said more evenly, "I never heard this story, not fully. It was one of those family secrets that was hushed up. Something Granny Covey never talked about. All I knew was she left Mayfield and would never return. For a long time, she didn't tell anyone who the father of her baby was. She forged her own life. Mayfield . . . and you . . . were not a part of it. The Rivers family never were part of any of our lives."

An awkward silence fell. Savannah's face was cloudy, and she looked at Norah, hurt.

"Aunt Eliza . . ."

"Yes, Norah?"

"You mentioned my grandmother's cottage. I would like to stay there, if that's okay."

I felt relief she hadn't asked to leave Mayfield. "Of course you may. I would take you there myself, but I feel very tired."

"I'll take you," offered Savannah. "I know the way."

At the door, Norah paused, then turned to me. "Aunt Eliza. I appreciate your honesty. That can't have been easy."

I nodded weakly.

"You and my grandmother . . . As you said, you were so young. So much had happened, so quickly." She took a step back into the room. "My grandmother left Mayfield for more reasons than the telling of a secret." Her voice gained the strength of conviction. "She had to leave. She couldn't—wouldn't—raise her child in the servants' quarters. She couldn't evolve as a woman, or fulfill her dreams, in the Jim Crow South. The baby gave her the courage to leave."

Norah and Savannah said good night. Once they'd left, my eyes filled with tears that I let flow down my cheeks, and I wept. Eventually I stood and made my way to the staircase. I wondered if I had the strength to make it to the top. *Old woman*, I thought. There wasn't a choice if I wanted to rest in my own bed. Grabbing hold of the railing I began taking the stairs one at a time, each step requiring a pause and a breath.

Reaching the landing, I put my hand to my heart trying to catch my breath. Once again, I had endured, I thought with some pride. But how much longer? Hana had pestered me for years to install an elevator in the house, and I'd stubbornly resisted, sure that I could manage. Getting old was a series of challenges and humiliations. Clearly it was time for another change.

I had experienced so many changes over the many years I'd lived. Phenomenal, actually. I'd witnessed shifts in the role and rights of women, civil rights, communication, and travel. With age came wisdom. I thought of Norah's comments. They'd stung but were spot-on. We had to reach the place where our wish to understand the other person was as great as our wish to be understood.

A plan was slowly formulating in my mind for the young women, and for Mayfield, born from hope, which could be the answer I'd been waiting for. Elusive still. It was too early to say. I needed to finish the history of Mayfield and see how the women responded. If they were inspired, it was my hope they would hear in the stories a call to action.

—

The following morning, we met again in the dining room for breakfast. The strain of the previous day had dissipated like a ghost at first light. We were all trying hard to be cheerful and upbeat. Pleasantries were exchanged, and I was relieved to find us all chatting amicably as we ate. I inquired with Norah about her night in the cottage.

"The house is lovely. Knowing it was my grandmother's makes it special. Last night I sat on the porch in a rocking chair and watched the fireflies. It was magical."

"Muggy loving bugs," I replied with a smile. "That sight never gets old."

"I don't think I've ever been inside the cottage," Savannah said.

"It's kept locked, so unless your father took you, I doubt you have." I lifted my brows. "Goodness, I can't recall the last time it'd been opened for a guest."

"Long time," Mariama said. "I stayed there from time to time back when I was a girl."

"Wouldn't it be fun for us all to gather there one afternoon?" I asked. "We could pack a picnic. That little cottage holds a lot of memories." I was thinking into the future, and it occurred to me that in all the rush of leaving Charleston, I hadn't asked the girls how long they could stay. "Norah, how long will you be here at Mayfield?"

"I was wondering that myself. I've taken a week's vacation from work for this trip. But last night, in the cottage, I realized I was just tapping the surface of my family history. I loved my grandmother, but she never talked about her life before she came to Pennsylvania. Except for these little comments she'd sometimes make. I don't know if anyone but me caught them. It was usually in the garden. She had a bed of azaleas and said how they rivaled Mayfield. And the dogwoods and crepe myrtles. She told me she planted them because they reminded her of home."

"She used that word?" I asked. "Home?" For Covey, plants would define home.

Norah nodded. "Yes. She missed her father. My great-grandfather is buried somewhere here, right?"

Mariama nodded. "He sure is. In the family plot. It's a right pretty place not far from your cottage. It's in the African style, you know. We keep things in a natural state. We don't use stones or other markers, in keeping with tradition. I'll take you there. It could be difficult to find on your own."

"I'd like that, thank you. And I'd like to stay a little longer . . . if that's all right."

"Stay as long as you like," I replied, delighted. "The cottage belongs to your family. It does my heart good having Covey's granddaughter there. I know she'd be so pleased."

"I need this time. My family never talked about the cottage," said Norah. "It was just some place down South where Granny Covey grew up. The thought of coming here to visit never crossed my mind. But now that I'm here, I don't know. I feel oddly like—" she paused, then smiled "—like I've come home."

"Really? That's extraordinary. I'm so happy you feel that way." I turned to Savannah. "How about you, dear girl? Have you talked with your parents?"

"I checked in with them yesterday," she replied, then rolled her eyes. "I received quite a scolding."

"Well, you did sneak out without telling them. I imagine they were cross."

"Not so much at me as you. Daddy was pretty mad that you didn't show up for the luncheon. People were worried you'd died or something."

I laughed at the thought. "Were they?"

"I think he's glad I'm keeping an eye on you."

"Like a spy?"

Savannah giggled. "He wishes. To be honest, I'm Team Grandma." Norah and I laughed.

"Really," Savannah continued. "I love being here with you all, hearing the stories about this place. It's like I'm seeing Mayfield for the first time. I know this property has been in my family for generations. I get that and it's cool. But I never felt attached to it." She glanced at Norah. "It's like Norah said. I'm starting to feel like I belong here."

My heart fluttered. This was a new dawn after a dark night. "How long can you stay?"

"Well, I'm on summer break, and I don't have any big plans until college starts in the fall."

"Splendid!" I clapped my hands. "You're free as a bird. Like me. Stay the summer."

Savannah giggled.

"Well then," I said scanning the mural for another scene to prompt my next story. "Now that that's settled, shall I continue?"

The women nodded.

"Please, tell us more about what happened after your brother died," Savannah urged.

I found the scene in the mural of the family plot high on grassy Prospect Hill. The gravestones dotting the slope. *Heyward* . . .

"Simply put, the Rivers family fell apart after Heyward's death. We never recovered, not really. My mother could never forgive my father. She blamed him for getting Heyward involved with the

Marines and encouraging him to go. It was unfair, but for her the last straw. She resolved to return to Charleston. Lesesne would return with Mama to finish high school."

"And you?" asked Savannah. "Did you go to college?"

I shook my head. "No. I became a truck farmer."

Chapter Twenty-Nine

THE CICADA is a large insect with long, transparent wings. Since ancient times, the cicada has been seen as a symbol of resurrection, an association that owes to its life cycle.

1918

The bodies of Heyward and Hugh were never recovered. Thus, the caskets were empty at the memorial services for the Rhodes and Rivers families. I stood quietly dressed in black and looked at the caskets dully. I thought they were as empty and void of life as the discarded shells of the countless cicadas that hung on the tree barks.

Well-meaning people uttered worn-out phrases like *They are in a better place*, and *They will be greatly missed*, and *Life is for the living*. The trouble for me was, living held little meaning for me. I couldn't face the Rhodes family and mutter those meaningless words. Instead, I retreated to the barn, my usual sanctuary, where the scents of horses and hay comforted me. I brushed Captain over and over in a monotonous pattern, and when tired, slumped to the hay, my head against the wood, staring out at dust motes floating in the dimly lit stalls.

After several days in a stupor, my mother dragged me from the barn and set me in a bath of perfumed water. She and Clementine washed me and dressed me like a china doll. My clothes hung from my thin frame as though from a mannequin. Clementine combed my unruly hair while Mama fed me a few bites of egg. I had no appetite. Swallowing was a chore.

Only Tripp, who had come to Mayfield for the funeral, was able to lure me from my room. One morning he knocked on my door.

"We're going fishing," he declared. "I won't take no for an answer. You're pale and thin, holed up in the house. This isn't you. Hurry up. Get your britches and boots."

He wouldn't take no for an answer. Tripp loaded up the gear and a picnic while I slowly dressed. We hiked to a favorite spot on the Combahee River as the sun began its slow descent in the western sky. I stood on the grassy bank, my boots digging into the soft mud, as Tripp set the lures. He'd taken to fly-fishing during his years out east and was determined I should learn.

I wore my usual cotton riding britches, a wide-brimmed hat, and a long-sleeved shirt. Tripp, though, was fully outfitted with waders over a shirt the color of grass and a wide-brimmed straw hat that was rimmed with a band upon which he'd attached colorful feathered fishing flies.

I leaned against a poplar tree and watched as he fussed over his gear. He checked his fishing creel and patted the multiple pockets of his vest, each bulging with an array of supplies.

I laughed and called out, "I think you like the accessories more than the sport."

He made a face. "The match is the hatch," he said, bent over a small case filled with flies. "I have to choose the fly that closely resembles the insects currently hatching on the water. This increases the chances of enticing a fish to bite." He looked over his shoulder at the water. "Midges," he said decisively.

He led me to what he declared was the perfect spot on the riverside. He went on and on about the fine points of casting, but in truth I understood little of it. At length, Tripp gently placed the long fly-fishing rod into my hands for my first cast. He stood behind me to place his hands over mine on the fly rod. He was not a tall man, just a few inches taller than me, but his shoulders had broadened, and his arms encircled mine.

"Now relax and follow my lead."

As one, we raised the rod tip in a sweep backward. After a second's pause he said, "Now push." Together we propelled the fly forward, sending it sailing over the water to delicately land on the surface.

"We did it," I said, delighted and more than a little surprised.

"Again."

Together, we repeated the casting motion, over and over, allowing me to get the feel of the back-and-forth movement.

"Don't rush it," he said, close to my ear. "Feel the rhythm. It's a dance."

I became increasingly aware that his arms were around me, and that we were no longer children. Sensations flooded me and an image of Hugh flared in my mind. I suddenly felt uncomfortable with Tripp's closeness.

"I think I can do it by myself now," I said.

Tripp released me and stepped back, seemingly unaware of my discomfort. "Give it a go," he told me, placing the rod back into my hands. He put his hands on his hips and watched.

I thrust the rod forward and watched my line flail in the air before landing in the leaves of nearby shrubs.

"Oh no . . ."

"Don't fret," Tripp said, covering his smile with his palm. "It's more common to catch leaves than fish when you begin." He walked across the shallows to untangle the line from the shrub while I watched, embarrassed. Tripp called back good-naturedly, "It's the dance with the fish that I enjoy the most. Whether I catch one doesn't matter." He slowly made his way through the water back to my side. "Try again?"

I shook my head. "I think I've done enough damage for one day."

He laughed and reset his line. "It just takes practice. Someday I'll take you to our place in the Highlands, Eliza. There's great fishing there."

In the final hour of light, I watched him fish the river. Once he found his spot on the bank, Tripp raised his rod into the air and began masterful casts that fell into a natural rhythm, back and forth, allowing the line to unfurl longer and longer in a ballet of tight loops. I couldn't help but marvel at how the fly rod seemed to be an extension of his body and arms. I'd never seen him in this way before. Tripp had been the clumsy one in sports. The boy who didn't like to pick up a bat for baseball, or the pigskin for football. I was delighted at seeing him excel in the sport of his choosing.

He continued deftly making the fly skip in the riffles, teasing, until a fish rose up. He swung his face toward me, beaming. "Lizzie!" he called out victoriously.

"Tripp, you're wonderful!"

I understood the metaphor of a dance as he brought the fish to the net. Once in range, Tripp scooped the fish. "Got it!" Bending low, his long, slender fingers deftly removed the hook from the mouth of the fish. Then, he gently opened his hands. In a flash, the fish darted away.

"You let it go?" I asked, surprised.

He looked out over the water. "There's been enough death."

We fell into silence. It was twilight, that otherworldly time between light and dark. A few tardy birds darted to the trees. The cicadas began buzzing. From the woods, nocturnal yips and rustlings sounded.

Tripp began packing up his supplies in the fading light.

"When will you leave?" I asked.

"Tomorrow. I'm on Friday's train for Harvard. You'll be off too. When do you start Brenau?"

College was on the horizon, but I felt no desire to go. "I don't know, exactly. Sometime in September."

"Good. You need to be busy."

"Please Tripp, if you tell me life goes on or some such I'll scream."

He tried to smile but it fell. "I won't say it. But it will."

I pushed from the tree and bent to pick up the fishing rods. "Please hurry back."

Tripp searched my face for his answer. "Is that an invitation? Can I come, even if it's not summer?"

"Don't be silly. You know you're always welcome here. Please come," I said more seriously. "You're my dearest friend."

"And you mine. We're blood brother and sister. My dearest sister." He paused. "Eliza, will you be all right? I worry about you. You don't have Covey—"

"No. She left," I said crisply. "But I'll be fine."

Through the fogged lens of his glasses, his eyes shone with concern. "I'll come to visit you, Eliza. As often as I can."

Fireflies were beginning to rise from the grass, hovering low, aglow with their love lights. Tripp looked out at the river again.

"You know, the beauty of fly-fishing is you don't need to be particularly good at it. You just want to get to the river. To stand under the sky, listen to the water, and accept whatever comes." He turned to look at me, his blue eyes sparkling. "To fish is to hope."

⊷

The Dog Star rose high in the sky and with it soaring temperatures and hellish humidity. The house was in an uproar as Mama packed for her move to Charleston. In another few days I would travel separately to Brenau College in nearby Georgia. Lesesne was returning to Charleston and Porter. But this year, Mama's move to Charleston was permanent. Heyward's death was the last straw for her. With him gone and Lesesne and me grown, she declared that she'd done her duty and was returning to Charleston for good.

A troupe of men were hired to load up carts with our suitcases and boxes filled with personal belongings. Sweat poured down their faces as they carried cartons down the stairs to the outdoors.

I walked through the house seeking refuge from the whirlwind of activity. My departure furthered my depression. I'd lost so much, I didn't want to leave Mayfield, where all I had left to love remained. I sequestered myself in the peace of the enclosed garden and idly snipped off dead rose heads. The camellias were long gone, and the stone urns, void of flowers, stood barren and gloomy.

It wasn't long before the August sun proved oppressive, so I retreated indoors. As I entered the foyer, a weary mover staggered under the weight of an enormous box, sweat beading on his brow. With a strained grunt, his grip slipped, and the box tumbled to the floor with a resounding thud. Shards of glass exploded from the dented box. There was a collective gasp as the poor man, horrified, gazed dumbly around him. Then mother screamed.

I ducked into the library and closed the door against the mayhem. The drapes were drawn from the glare of the sun and the air was marginally cooler. I meandered about, letting my fingertips glide across the spines of books on the shelves. The desk Mr. Coxwold once used had been taken over by my father. Daddy was usually careful about keeping his ledgers and papers organized. I was surprised to find his desk a shambles, covered with piles of unopened envelopes. On inspection, I saw they were dated as long as months earlier.

I heard the library door open and turning, saw Wilton enter. There had been an uneasy peace between us since Covey's departure. Our usual banter had ceased. I smiled nervously in greeting. "Come to hide out too?"

Our eyes met. He had a long face with expressive eyes and deep lines and creases that hinted at a lifetime of stories and emotions. He appeared to have aged in the past weeks. Not just the gray hair or the slump of his shoulders. It seemed that when Covey left, she took with her the essence of his vitality and optimism that had radiated around him.

"You miss her," I said softly.

He tilted his head and his gaze sharpened. "I do."

"I do too." I dropped my arms and said pleadingly, "Wilton, do you know where she is?"

"I do."

"Please tell me. I want to write to her. To apologize."

Wilton shook his head, slow but determined. "I can't do that. Covey asked me to not tell her whereabouts to anyone, especially you."

My cheeks burned but I understood and respected his loyalty. I knew hell would freeze over before Wilton betrayed his daughter. "I'm sorry, Wilton. I know this was hard for you too."

"It was. Is. Rawlins and I had words. Your father . . ." He paused. "He did his best to make reparations." Wilton's face hardened some and he crossed his arms. "I started working at this plantation when I was a boy, for your grandfather. Like you and Covey, Rawlins and I grew up together. I became his foreman after he took over Mayfield. When this happened with Covey, I was put between a rock and a hard place."

He reached up to rub his jaw in thought. "I've known Heyward all his life. He was a good man. And I know my daughter. I believe her when she tells me he loved her." He dropped his hand. "I read his letter, and in it I heard Heyward's intention for Covey was honorable. Still, he's gone, and my daughter is left with a child to raise alone." Wilton looked me in the eye with his answer. "Yes, it is hard that Covey's gone. But I trust my daughter to make the decision she must make for her own future."

I saw pain flicker across his face. "Mayfield is my job. My home. I'm loyal to the Rivers family. Have been all my life. But my first loyalty will always be to my daughter. Truth is, what's hardest is I can't do more for her."

The pain of these truths cut through me with a new freshness. "Thank you for explaining, Wilton," I said. I paused, collecting my emotions. "I owe you an apology as well. In betraying Covey's confidence, I also betrayed you. I will . . . I must . . . abide by Covey's decision. But it means your loss as much as mine. More. And for that, I hope you can find it in your heart to someday forgive me."

Wilton remained quiet for a long moment, then nodded his head. Finished with what he'd had to say, he lifted the papers in his hand. "More mail for your father." He walked over to set it with the others on the desk.

"Wilton, what is all this mail?" I asked, extending my arm toward the piled papers on the desk.

"Your father . . ." he began. I could see that he was choosing his words. "He's not kept up with the bills. Not since his boy died."

I stared at the disarray, shocked at my blindness. "I knew he was not himself. None of us have been. But I didn't know it had deteriorated to this point. How are the accounts?"

Wilton shook his head. "Abandoned. I've done my best ordering supplies and keeping things going, but I don't have the authority to pay bills or make the decisions he must. I've tried to reason with him . . ." He paused, straightened his shoulders and confessed, "But Miss Eliza, he's beyond reason. He took to the bottle before. And Lord knows, he had a good reason for it this time. But there has always been an end to it. I've never seen him this bad. He's like . . ." He stopped.

"Like what?"

"Like his daddy was. Old Mr. Rivers done lost his mind with grief after his sons and wife died. He drank round the clock, ranted at God, and took to wandering the woods until one day we found him lying by the river, at peace at last. I reckon Rawlins is lost too. He just don't seem to care no more."

"What's to be done?" I asked, my hand on my forehead. The heat was stifling, and I felt a bit dizzy.

"Mrs. Rivers made it clear she don't want to take care of business here. She's headed to Charleston and not looking back. Lesesne is, well . . ." He lifted his hands in a futile gesture. "He's young." Wilton left it at that. "Miss Eliza, there's no one left but you who can take the reins. You know this plantation as well as Heyward did. Love it as much too. Truth be told, I don't know how this place can continue if you don't."

I covered my face with my hands as panic struck because I knew he was right. "Wilton, I'm an empty shell. I don't feel strong enough. I don't know that I'm up to the task."

"Your daddy often remarked on how capable you were. Said he believed you could run this place on your own. I know you, Miss Eliza. I've always believed you were up to the task."

I was heartened at his words. "Daddy only told me he wished I was a boy."

Wilton chuckled and nodded. "That too."

"Would my father even agree to it?"

"I don't think he'd notice." His face looked unbearably weary. "That's the sad truth."

I leaned against the heavy wood desk, crossed my arms and studied him. "You've known me all my life. Do you trust that I will be able to manage this farm?"

"I do."

I took a sweeping glance of the library, the room where I'd spent hours in school being reminded daily in so many ways of the incompetence of the fairer sex. Now this weaker vessel was being asked to manage the plantation. It was up to me to prove them wrong.

"My ancestor, Eliza Pinckney, was asked at sixteen to run three plantations," I said. "I suppose I can manage to run one."

Chapter Thirty

⟫⟫◆⟪⟪

ELIZA LUCAS PINCKNEY (1722–1793) developed the indigo crop in colonial
South Carolina, one of the state's most important cash crops. She studied botany
and, at sixteen, managed her father's plantations while he was in Antigua. She
later married Charles Pinckney and gave birth to three sons and a daughter. Her
son Charles signed the United States Constitution.

1918

Another September arrived and for the first time in four years I
was not leaving Mayfield. The old adage *Life goes on* proved to be
true.

I awoke each morning to the calls of birdsong. Some mornings I
lay in bed just listening to the repeating chorus of the mockingbird,
the quarrelsome blue jays, and the lyrical song of the Carolina wren.
But not for long. I felt the call of duty to my marrow. I rose to survey
the property on Captain's back. Often, Wilton accompanied me,
teaching me water management crucial for rice cultivation, delivering water evenly across the field. As he did when I was young and
tucked my small hand into his calloused one, he guided me through
the tasks of managing the vast property with the same calm, deliberate voice he had when teaching me the patterns in the sand of a
rattlesnake, the roar of a bull alligator, or the green swards in the
midst of the field where feral hogs had been rooting.

Slowly my confidence grew. I had thought I knew every acre of
Mayfield. Now I felt I understood her.

———

Summer passed, and when the gold of autumn colored the landscape, I was ready to visit the Rhodes family. My nerves grew taut as I rode along the half mile allée of centurion oaks to the neighboring Magnolia Bluff Plantation. At the end of the shadowed lane, a grand, white house stretched out in a warm and inviting manner. I tied up Captain to the post, swept the dust from my skirt, and walked up the stairs to the red-roofed portico. No sooner did I arrive than Hugh's younger brother, Charles, opened the door. His face, so much like Hugh's, startled me.

"Welcome, Eliza," Charles said. "We were hoping you'd come when your illness passed."

I blushed slightly, hearing the excuse my mother must have offered the Rhodes family at my refusal to meet guests. "I received your flowers. It was very kind."

"We missed seeing you at Magnolia Bluff."

Charles appeared older than when I last saw him. Two years younger than Hugh, he'd grown several inches taller, but it was something more. The boyishness was gone, replaced with a new aura of maturity. Perhaps he had already assumed the weight of being the eldest son, I thought, and said a quick prayer that Charles would be spared from the war. Hugh's other brother, Chatham, was younger still. They gathered around me, a duo of handsome, blond-haired, good-natured boys.

"Mama's out on the veranda. She has tea," Charles said, politely indicating the way with his outstretched arm.

I walked onto the veranda and was met with a view of the vast, glistening pond shimmering like a mirror under the afternoon sun. Lush cypress trees, draped in Spanish moss, framed the water's edge, casting long shadows upon the tranquil surface.

"Welcome, dear girl." Mrs. Rhodes held out her hand to me from a white wicker chair under an awning.

I hurried to take it and was drawn lower to receive a kiss on my cheek. She was a handsome woman, slender, even frail. Her blond hair was streaked with white. When our eyes met, we saw the suffering of the past few weeks. Her hand clenched mine tighter in commiseration and support.

I sat in another white wicker chair next to the Rhodes boys, who were looking at me with sympathy and affection. I sensed communal grief in the Rhodes family and wondered, briefly, what it might have been like to be included in their warm bond. An unexpected wave of emotion swept over me, and I struggled for composure.

"Mr. Rhodes will join us shortly," Mrs. Rhodes said in way of apology. "He very much wants to see you. But let us begin our tea now, shall we? I don't think I can keep the boys from the pecan tarts any longer."

I faced a table draped in crisp white linen and adorned with delicate porcelain. The ice cubes clinked against the crystal pitcher as Mrs. Rhodes poured the freshly brewed sweet tea. On tiered platters were an assortment of petit fours, pecan tarts, and velvety pound cakes adorned with fresh berries. I watched the boys pile their plates with sweets and thought to myself how Hugh had a sweet tooth, as well.

We sipped tea and talked about everything but Hugh. The weight of our shared loss hung heavy in the air, as though Hugh was a specter floating on the outside of our intimate circle.

At last, Mr. Rhodes joined the group with his hearty apologies. Mrs. Rhodes's face lit up on her husband's arrival as she offered her cheek for his kiss.

"Miss Rivers!" Mr. Rhodes exclaimed, coming to take my hand. "Eliza . . ." He kissed it, then turned to search for a free seat. Charles immediately sprang to his feet and offered his father his chair. Mr. Rhodes settled, put his hands upon his knees, then turned his gaze again toward me.

"How are you, my dear?" he asked.

"I miss him," I said honestly. "Being here, I feel his presence."

Mr. Rhodes's face shuttered, and he looked out at the pond. "Yes, yes," he said softly.

Across the table, Mrs. Rhodes pulled a handkerchief from the sleeve of her dress and dabbed her eyes.

With a trembling hand, I reached into the pocket of my skirt and withdrew a small velvet bag. I spilled Hugh's signet ring onto my palm.

"I think you should have this," I said to Mr. Rhodes, holding it in the air. He appeared to waver, then accepted it. His gaze remained fixed upon the ring as emotions welled within him. Then he turned to Charles, who stood beside him. Clearing his throat he said, "Please give the ring to your mother."

A ragged sigh escaped Mrs. Rhodes as she reached out to accept the ring. She studied it with shaky hands, then clutched it tight and brought her fist to her heart. "You don't know," she said in a choked voice, "what this means to me."

"I think I might," I replied.

Mrs. Rhodes' smile trembled. "Hugh had come to talk to us, you see. He asked me to prepare my engagement ring. To give you." She paused. "When he returned."

"I would have married him before he left. I wanted to. But Hugh . . ." I couldn't continue.

"He wanted to do things right," Mr. Rhodes finished for me. "He told us." He attempted a smile but failed.

"But you must keep this ring," Mrs. Rhodes told me. "He wanted you to have it."

I shook my head. "It's your family's insignia. A treasured heirloom. It should go to Charles." I smiled at Charles. "Besides, I don't need the ring to remember him. Hugh will always be in my heart."

"Thank you," Mrs. Rhodes said. "You know, Eliza . . . I would have liked to call you daughter."

My emotions were spilling over. I rose, gathering my skirt as I did my wits. It was time to leave.

Mr. Rhodes stood and took my hand. "My dear, if there is anything we can do for you, please do not hesitate to ask."

I paused. "Actually, if it's not too much trouble, I would like to ask your advice."

Mr. Rhodes tilted his head. "Anything."

"Hugh often talked about your extensive agricultural efforts. I've long admired your success in truck farming. I could use your help at Mayfield."

Chapter Thirty-One

⊰⊱

THE AMERICAN ALLIGATOR (*Alligator mississippiensis*) is the only crocodilian native to South Carolina. It's estimated there are one hundred thousand alligators in South Carolina. It lives in coastal plain lakes and marshlands, with the ACE Basin being one of its most important nesting areas.

1924

Six years passed.

Daddy had his spells like his father before him. During the happier days he didn't drink as much, he would participate in the planning of crops, write a few checks, and approve my purchase and sale orders. It was more an act of consideration on my part than his factual understanding of what Wilton and I were doing on the farm. Then, without warning, he would go off on a drinking binge. I never knew what set him off. But whether it was from drink or illness, his mind grew dim and forgetful. With Wilton, I made the decisions for Mayfield.

In truth, I was born to it. I am industrious by nature and, as Mr. Rhodes once told me, I leaned toward creative thinking. Thankfully Mother had agreed to continue her family's support of Mayfield. With that boon and the wise guidance of Mr. Rhodes, I greatly expanded our truck farming business. The timing was right too. There was a big increase in demand for fruits and vegetables from the cities. The expansion of the railroads and improvements to the waterways among the islands gave the industry a boost.

I was careful to hire local workers for preparing, planting, and harvesting, all of which also helped the local economy. Our warm climate allowed for a long growing season, increasing profits. I felt pride greater than any I'd known at my accomplishments, regardless of whether my father gave me the property or not. By the end of five years, Wilton and I had doubled our production of lettuce, cabbages, peas, and beans. And God bless the cucumber. We couldn't grow enough of them. This year's crop was one of our best.

Come June, we were in good spirits for a celebration of the dual graduations of Lesesne from the College of Charleston and Tripp from the School of Veterinary Medicine in Alabama. Mama graced Mayfield with her presence for the festive gathering. Over the years, absence did not make the hearts grow fonder for my parents, though time seemed to have mellowed them. They treated each other with benign disinterest. Daddy curbed his drinking in Mama's presence. A relief to us all. But my practiced ear noted his slurred words.

It was déjà vu the night of the graduation dinner.

The memory of the previous graduation celebration for Heyward still hung heavy in our hearts. The candles in the heirloom candlesticks flickered. We sat at the same long mahogany table set with the family polished silver, crystal, and bone china.

Perhaps the biggest change was the length of women's hemlines. I wore a new gown of pale-yellow silk that gathered at my hip. My mother was resplendent in her favorite white with a wide red sash at her hips. My hair was cut in the new bob style; Mama refused to cut her glorious hair, streaked handsomely now with gray. Lesesne looked sleek and sophisticated in his new evening jacket complete with a white silk pocket square. He'd come to possess a dashing manner thanks to years of Charleston high-style living. Tripp's style was the understated elegance of pedigree. His navy cashmere jacket was conservative yet impeccably tailored. His time at Harvard seem to have given him confidence that was a far cry from the sweet, bookish, shy child. Even Daddy had dug his dinner suit from mothballs.

Mama reigned at the head of the table with Lesesne on her right. At the opposite end, I sat on Daddy's right with Tripp at my side.

"Aren't we a happy group tonight?" Mama said, her gaze touching each of us. "I look at you all and though I remember the children, see two fine men and a young lady. Do you remember how I used to scold you to sit up straight, or chew with your mouth closed?" We laughed lightly, appreciating the memory. "Tripp, or should I call you Arthur now?"

"Tripp still suits me," he replied amiably.

"Very well, Tripp," Mama continued. "You were such a little thing as a child. All freckles and cowlick. Look at you now! Why, I think you're taller than Heyward—" she paused, blinking hard, then quickly amended "—than he was."

Tripp was adept at table talk and smoothly covered Mama's faux pas. "We Chalmers men are late bloomers. I grew half a foot in high school and tripped over my own feet. My father jokes that I ate the beans from 'Jack and the Beanstalk.'"

Lesesne, who was still slight and barely five feet six inches, rolled his eyes.

"Eliza, darling." Mama turned her eye to me. "I do like your new hairstyle. So smart. Though you must come to my hairstylist in Charleston. She can do wonders. You know, I can't help but recall the time you cut your hair for that horse race. How old were you? Ten? Twelve? Do you remember?"

"Remember?" I replied. "I'll never forget. If I recall, that race led to my forced exodus to Charleston. All for the good," I quickly reassured her, not wishing to light that fuse during a family dinner. "But do you think I got this haircut for style? Hardly. At last, I can have the same freedom I did then." I reached up to touch the fringe at my neck. "It's so much easier when I work in the barn."

Mother's smile stiffened. *Touché*, I thought.

Tripp guided the conversation to another track. "Les, what are you going to do, now that you've graduated?"

"I prefer if you call me by my proper name, Lesesne," he replied with a chilly tone.

"No offense meant," Tripp readily replied.

"What am I going to do now . . ." Lesesne repeated the question. He insolently raised his eyes to Tripp. "By that you mean—work?"

Tripp held his smile. "Yes."

Lesesne shrugged elaborately. "I have no idea. I'm casting my bread upon the water, as it were."

Tripp's brows rose.

"You're welcome to work here," I said. "We can always use another pair of hands." I speared a chunk of beef and slipped it into my mouth.

Lesesne smirked. "Please. I leave farmwork to you, dear sister. You seem to like mucking about in the mud."

"I do," I replied cheerfully.

Lesesne turned to Tripp. "You like mucking around in the mud too, don't you? With the animals," he said in a teasing tone.

"That's right. I'm a veterinarian."

"Why, I'm sure Eliza can find work for you too."

Tripp smiled good-naturedly. "Indeed." He glanced at me with mirth then took a long sip of his wine. "I am unsure quite yet as to where I'll be practicing, but Eliza will be the first to know."

Lesesne looked from Tripp to me, his eyes glittering. "Ah, I see the way the wind's blowing. Perhaps you'll be farming together someday?"

Mama put her fingertips together and let them tap. "Wouldn't that be lovely? And to think, Tripp, your mother and I used to say you'd marry one day."

"Mama, please," I said, coloring. "Tripp just graduated and I'm busy managing Mayfield."

"Say again?" Daddy said, tilting his ear as though to hear correctly. "*You're* managing Mayfield?" He snorted. "A woman? Hardly."

I clutched my glass and stared back at him, fuming.

My father smiled at me with condescension. "I appreciate your help, of course."

"Everything comes together as it should in the course of time," Mama said placatingly. Then she spoke in way of announcement. "Speaking of which . . . tonight is a special night. We celebrate the graduation of our son." She reached into the bag at her side and pulled out a blue velvet sack enclosed by a slim gold rope. She handed it to Lesesne. "My darling son, this is for you. A *petite Cadeau.*"

"Thank you, Mother." Lesesne took the pouch and poured the contents into his palm. We leaned forward to see the gold pocket watch on a long chain. I recognized it immediately and gasped. Lesesne paled, recognizing it as well. He turned the watch around in his palm. His voice was flat. "It is engraved *Heyward Rawlins Rivers.*"

"Yes," my mother replied pompously. "And look, your name is engraved beneath it. *Lesesne Bissette Rivers.* My parents, your beloved Bissette grandparents, God rest their souls, loved you dearly. I know, had they survived that horrid Spanish Influenza, that they would have wanted to acquire for you a watch as fine as the gold watch they found for Heyward. Then it occurred to me that you should have that very watch. With that history, it would mean all the more to you."

Lesesne looked at the watch dispassionately, then slid it back into the pouch. "Thank you," he said in a dull voice. "I'll treasure it."

Mama raised a brow but let his lackluster response pass without comment. She rallied, raising her glass. "Hail college graduate! You're the first . . . and only . . . child of mine to achieve that distinction."

I lifted my chin, knowing that barb was meant for me. She was still upset that I'd chosen to work at Mayfield than go to college as she'd wanted.

"You've made me very proud. As for your future," Mama added, looking around the room to catch our attention, "I've been in conversation with several notable families about a suitable situation. You'll be well settled in Charleston soon, to be sure."

"Charleston?" My father's voice rose up. He had been leaning back in his chair, drinking the cabernet, idly listening to our banter.

But this comment had him sitting up straight, his eyes wide. "Not Charleston. My son won't be living in the city!"

I was startled at his outburst. I looked at Mother. She sat ramrod straight, her lips tight, and her dark eyes flashed at him in warning.

"He's a Rivers," Daddy said, his voice rising. "My eldest son. He will come back to Mayfield where he belongs. To take his place. At last. I've been waiting for him." He turned to Lesesne. "Isn't that right, Heyward?"

My brother's face paled. I met Tripp's worried gaze.

Lesesne leaned forward and said earnestly, "I'm Lesesne, Father."

Daddy paused, his rheumy eyes momentarily confused. Then he rose to his feet, holding steady on the table. He lifted his glass.

"Yes, of course. Lesesne. You went off to Charleston a boy, and you've returned a man. Ready to take on the responsibilities of your heritage."

Daddy looked around the table, his brows knitted in concentration, like a priest about to deliver the benediction. A memory flashed of just such a moment, six years earlier, at this very table. At Heyward's graduation from high school.

I paled. *No, he couldn't be . . .*

Daddy began in his slow drawl, "I stand before you with a heart brimming with pride. Tonight is a momentous occasion as we witness the continuation of a cherished tradition, the passing of the torch from one generation to the next."

He couldn't be doing this, I thought in denial. I looked at my mother. She met my gaze, equally incredulous. Clearly, she had not known about his intention.

Daddy weaved to the left but caught his balance and continued the toast. "To my dear son, I entrust you to continue the legacy and obligation of our generations. I entrust Mayfield to you, my son. May the Rivers legacy continue to thrive in your capable hands!"

We sat in a stunned silence. At length, Lesesne lifted his glass and drank. He was the only one to join the toast. The rest of us sat and looked at each other, disbelievingly. Mama clutched her glass, fuming. Tripp put his hand on mine.

"No!" I cried out.

My father sat clumsily in his chair and looked at me questioningly.

"You can't do this," I told my father. "*I* am the next in line after Heyward. *I* was the one who came running to your rescue. There was no graduation celebration for me because I was here, with you, to manage this property. For six years! Me!" I caught my breath, feeling my body shake.

"Eliza . . ." Father said in a condescending tone.

"How can you hand over Mayfield to Lesesne?" I railed. "To *him*? He has no management skills and knows nothing about running the farm. He doesn't even like farming. Or even being here." I shook my head. "This isn't right." I turned to my brother and pleaded. "Lesesne, you know what I say is true."

Lesesne was unmoved. He shrugged. "I will do as my father wishes."

I sat back, speechless. I saw it all clearly now. Lesesne only wanted his father's approval. He would do anything for it. Step over anyone to get it.

I tried again, gathering my calm. "Brother, I don't think you clearly understand what Daddy's gift entails. Maintaining this property is difficult. Hours of work every day. It's a life's commitment."

"You underestimate me," Lesesne replied. "You always have."

"But you don't want it!" I cried, feeling helpless.

Lesesne lifted his glass and studied the red liquid. "You forget there are legal constraints that hinder Daddy leaving Mayfield to you. Seeing as you are a woman."

"True," Daddy said. "Truly, if you had been born a son—"

"Stop," I said indignantly. "Don't say that to me. Not ever again. I am *not* a son. I am your daughter and as such I've proved my worth. As for legalities," I said to Lesesne. "Your education is lacking, Mr. Graduate. The Nineteenth Amendment to the United States

Constitution has been ratified. We are challenging and changing laws that discriminate against women." I turned to my father. "I *can* inherit Mayfield."

Daddy slowly shook his head with sympathy. "My dear Eliza. I do appreciate all you've done here. You are a dutiful daughter. But don't trouble yourself with these feelings. You've always done so. I am doing what my father did before me, his father before him, for generations. I can do nothing else." His tone changed to appease me. "Take heart, daughter." He reached over to pat my hand. "You'll soon have your own property to manage. When you marry Hugh."

My hand went to my throat. I couldn't speak. Frustration overpowered my anger as I saw the dimness return to his eyes. In that moment I knew I couldn't reason with a man without reason. The die was cast. I would never win this fight.

The room was suffocating. I rose from my chair and marched away, my heels clicking against the floor.

———

Clutching my skirt, I ran through the empty kitchen and out the back door. I sprinted to the paddock behind the barn. The sun was still bright in the sky and beyond in the green grass I saw a mare and her foal, lazily grazing. They ignored me. I took off again, running past the small enclosure to the bigger fenced pastures.

"Captain!" I called out, almost stumbling in the uneven earth. "Cap!"

I heard a whinny in the distance, and I ran toward the sound. The vibrant green grass was dotted with clover as I scanned the horizon. I spied my boy running toward me, his powerful hooves pounding the earth beneath him, his head high. It was as if he sensed my urgency. I reached the fence and climbed on the rung.

In a lunge I wrapped my arms around his great neck and buried my face against his velvety fur. "Oh, Cap . . ." When I opened the gate, Captain followed me, eager, his ears perked. I climbed on a higher rung, hiked up my skirt and, using the fence to boost me up, I hopped onto his back.

"Go, Cap!"

We took off along the dirt road at a trot, dust kicking up in the still air. The forest was cool and dim, the smell of composted leaves and earth prevalent in the air. On this evening it smelled to me of death.

We burst into the meadow at a canter. I nudged Captain with my heels, held tight to his mane, and felt the wind in my face as we raced across the open expanse. All the pain and sorrow I'd held inside bubbled up. As we galloped through the meadow, I lifted my chin to the sky and from my heart a scream erupted. I screamed until my throat was raw.

I fell limp against Captain's neck, and we came to a stop under the great oak. I didn't remember guiding him. I'll always believe Captain understood I needed to come to this spot. I slid from his back, let him loose, then without hesitation crawled into the womb of the tree.

The dark interior smelled of mushrooms and wood. I laid my head on the soft moss and curled up with my knees close to my chest and wept.

Chapter Thirty-Two

—◄═►—

THE WOOD STORK (*Mycteria americana*) is one of the largest American wading birds in the stork family, over one meter tall with a wingspan of more than sixty inches. The head and neck are bare of feathers, the plumage is mostly white with black flight feathers. The first recorded nesting of wood storks in South Carolina was in the ACE Basin.

1924

Eliza?"

I felt a gentle shaking and heard someone calling my name. As I slowly woke, a sense of déjà vu swept over me.

"Covey?" I called back groggily.

"Eliza, wake up. It's me, Tripp."

I blinked heavily and slowly rose upon my elbow. The light was dim, but I could see Tripp sitting beside me in his white shirt sans jacket and tie.

"You'll ruin your good pants."

"You'll ruin your fancy dress."

We chuckled as I sat up. Neither of us cared a whit for our clothing.

"How long did I sleep?"

"Not long. I came after you. I rode over to Sweetwater Pond first. When I didn't see you there, I knew where I'd find you."

"This was always our place. I mean, just ours. Yours, mine, and Covey's."

"The three in the tree," he quipped. "A trio." He smiled at me, and I was struck by how much he still looked like the ten-year-old boy. "Hey, my name has a second meaning. Tripp for being the third of our team."

"I like it." I slowly grazed my hand along the soft moss blanketing the earth. The twilight made the interior of the tree shadowy. "But it doesn't apply anymore, does it? Covey's gone . . ."

"She'll come back someday. She's our blood sister. She must."

I looked into his eyes. He seemed so sure. It gave me heart.

Tripp adjusted his long legs, ducking his head, trying to get comfortable in the cramped space. "But I don't seem to fit in here as well as I once did. It's a good thing the tree is continuing to grow or I'm not sure I would have made it in at all."

"Life's strange, isn't it?" I said giving my thoughts voice.

"How so?"

"I didn't see this coming. Tonight, I mean." I shook my head, still in wonder. "Les. Really? He chose Les over *me*. Because I'm a girl? Lesesne cares not one whit about Mayfield, other than the prestige it offers."

Tripp sighed. "Eliza, you have confronted this issue all your life. I hate to stand by and watch you get hurt, over and over. Perhaps . . . it's time to . . . let it go."

"Let Mayfield go?" I said with indignance. I couldn't believe he would suggest such a thing.

Tripp nodded. "It's like this tree. We fit into it perfectly as children. We shared the dreams of youth. But now—" he shifted uncomfortably "—we don't fit in it quite so well. Eliza, we've outgrown the hollow."

"Stop," I whispered, not wanting to hear this.

He paused. "I'm not a particularly religious man, but I've always appreciated the scripture from Ecclesiastes. I believe at this crossroads, the words have meaning for us. *For everything there is a season, a time for every purpose under heaven.*"

I glanced up sharply. "Is this a time for me to heal . . . or kill?" I asked him.

Tripp took my hands. "We will always have the memories of Mayfield. This place gave us an idyllic childhood. I'll always be grateful. But now it's time to put away the things of a child. Accept your father's decision."

"I don't know that I can ever let go. I belong here."

"Can you live here with Les as master? Can you abide with his decisions . . . or lack of them?"

I swallowed hard, not able to imagine that scenario after all I had done, the years I'd given to my father. "I could if it were Heyward," I answered honestly. Then shook my head. "But not Lesesne." I pulled my hands away. "I hate men."

Tripp laughed.

"Present company excepted."

"Thank you."

"What do I do? I don't want to live with my mother, but I have nowhere else to go." I covered my face with my hands.

Tripp reached out to put his hand on my shoulder consolingly. I felt the gentle pat of his fingers before they moved to take my hands again in his.

"Years back when I told everyone that we would be married one day, everyone laughed," he said. "But I never laughed. Eliza, I love the past we've shared. But now I'm looking to my future. One that I hope includes you. I know you don't love me . . . in the way you loved Hugh. But we have a lot of things in common, don't we? We like each other's company."

"Tripp . . ." I didn't like where this was going. I pulled back but he gripped my hands tighter.

"Come to Charleston with me. We can build our own home, our own life, together."

I felt my head swimming in his words. "What are you saying?"

His blue eyes shone with sincerity. "Eliza Rivers, will you do me the honor of being my wife?"

I pulled my hands away. "You can't be serious."

"Why not? You are my best friend. Friendship can be the best basis for a good marriage." He leaned forward, his tone persuasive. "I know we can be happy together."

Perhaps at another time in my life I might have believed that I had options. But now I was floundering in stormy seas. I had lost my love in the war. I had lost my home, my ambition. I had nowhere to go, no dream left to pursue. The man who sat across from me was my dearest friend. I heard Tripp's proposal as a lifeline. I believed we could make each other happy. He would be a much-needed comfort to me as I attempted to start over fresh, away from Mayfield, which was no longer my home.

"Yes, Tripp. I will marry you."

In the ambiguous glow between day and night, Tripp and I held hands and meandered through the woods toward the house. The temperature was lowering, and a gentle breeze stirred the leaves. Capitano trailed in the rear. We followed the worn path the horses had created, which made the walking easy. Twilight had always been a favorite time for me. Seeing the sky alight with sunset's colors both thrilled and soothed me. I was still feeling unsure about the huge commitment we had just made.

"Let's not tell anyone our news tonight," I said. "The debacle with the graduation dinner has cast a pall on the family. I'd like to keep our news for a happier time."

"It's your news to share, dearest Eliza," Tripp said.

"It is happy news, isn't it?"

"For me, the happiest."

"I will try to be a good wife."

"I've no doubt. And I, a good husband."

We walked in a pleasant silence as night deepened. Suddenly we heard an explosive crack in the air. We halted abruptly and swung our heads toward the sound.

"That's a shotgun," I said, eyes alert.

"It's coming from over there," Tripp said, pointing west.

Another shot fired and I heard the horrid thud of a bird hitting the ground not far from us.

"Who goes there?" called out Tripp.

We heard scuffling in the woods approaching and a moment later Lesesne broke through the foliage carrying a twelve-gauge shot gun. He was still dressed in his evening jacket though his tie was gone and his collar unbuttoned. He stopped, a lopsided grin on his face. "I should be asking that question," came the reply. "This is my property, after all."

His voice was slurred and on instinct I tensed.

"Hey, Les," Tripp called out amiably. He pointed to the gun. "Watch where you're pointing the business end of that shotgun."

Tripp smirked and obligingly lowered the muzzle to the ground. "Aren't you two the lovey-dovey couple?"

I warily studied my brother. I'd known for a long time that when he was angry or deeply upset he would get drunk and go out with his shotgun and shoot birds. He had a complete lack of remorse for the senseless killing. He killed indiscriminately, letting the birds lay where they fell. I'd told my father about it, expecting him to stop it, to reprimand Lesesne, but he only shook his head, set his jaw, and remained silent. He who had always taught us never to harm an animal. Still, I thought with disgust, Lesesne was the man my father chose to inherit Mayfield.

"Why are you angry?" I called out to my brother. "Tonight's your big night. You're the hero. You graduated from college. You're the master of Mayfield. You made your father proud."

"And what about you, sister? Are you proud?"

"Why do you care what I feel? You never have before."

"I don't. I know you'd rather it was Heyward who inherited. It was always Heyward you loved best. Not the one who was *less than*."

"Heyward is gone," I said.

"Is he? I still feel his ghost. He's always in my head." He twirled a finger around his head. "You think I took the property to make Daddy proud?" Lesesne weaved, shaking the shotgun in his arm back and forth like a waving finger. Tripp moved to step in front of me.

"Goddamn Heyward," Lesesne slurred. "*He's* the one I wanted to make proud. My perfect big brother. The one who could do no wrong."

"Lesesne . . ."

"Do you know what his final words to me were?" Lesesne cried out, as though in pain. "His damned last words in his last letter . . ." He shook his head. He spoke in a rote tone. "'If I die, it is up to you to assume the mantle of family and Mayfield.'" He paused and stared bleakly into the darkness. "It was Heyward. He told me to take over this place. I never asked for it. I don't even want it."

"That's ridiculous," I shouted. "You do not have to take over if you don't want to. Heyward wouldn't want you to do that. He would want you to be happy."

"Would he?" Lesesne roughly shook his head like a dog with a flea in its ear. "No, sister. You're wrong. Heyward loved Mayfield more than anything or anyone. He made me the sacrificial lamb."

"Stop it. Heyward knows I could take care of—"

"No, *you* stop!" Lesesne shouted. "Mayfield is mine now. It'll never be yours. Find yourself another place. Get married. I'm sure Tripp there will take on the job, won't you, Tripp?" He used his shotgun to point at Tripp.

"Lower the muzzle," Tripp called back sternly.

Lesesne and Tripp stared at each other in a tense moment, before Les lowered the gun again.

"Let's go," said Tripp, taking hold of my hand again.

As we walked away I called over my shoulder, "Stop shooting the birds! They didn't do anything to you."

It was hard to keep up with Tripp's long-legged stride through the grass. I could tell Tripp was angry, and I was relieved he had the sense not to challenge a drunken Lesesne. Suddenly a shot rang out again. I felt a rush of heat pass my arm and the wood of a tree very close to me exploded in splinters. I screamed and Tripp spun around, eyes blazing.

"You son of a bitch!" he called out. "You could have hit Eliza!"

My brother stood with the tip of the gun still pointed in our direction. His face was hard, and his eyes glittered with emotion, which made his grin all the more sardonic. "I wasn't aiming for Eliza."

Was he aiming at a bird? Or . . . Tripp? Or was that merely his macabre humor? With Lesesne, I couldn't be sure. My shocked mind spun with questions as I stood frozen to the spot, gaping at him. Beside me, I heard Tripp swear under his breath. I felt his hand tighten over mine, and with a tug, he led us away from the possible danger brewing with my troubled brother.

Part Five

THE WEDDING

I cannot promise you a life of sunshine;
I cannot promise riches, wealth, or gold;
I cannot promise you an easy pathway
That leads away from change or growing old.
But I can promise all my heart's devotion;
A smile to chase away your tears of sorrow;
A love that's ever true and ever growing;
A hand to hold in yours through each tomorrow.

—MARK TWAIN, "THESE I CAN PROMISE"

Chapter Thirty-Three

—◆—

FIREFLIES (*Lampyridae*), also known as lighting bugs, are a type of beetle known for bioluminescence, an ability to produce light within their bodies. The light serves to attract mates and warn off predators. Fireflies are nocturnal and hide in tall grass or other dense plants during the day.

1925

The wedding banns for the marriage of Eliza Pinckney Rivers of Mayfield and Arthur Middleton Chalmers III of Charleston were read in July at St. Phillips Episcopal Church. Wedding plans began in earnest.

My mother was never happier.

From the moment the banns were announced she embarked on a journey to create a celebration that would be forever etched in the annals of Charleston's finest. A year later, every detail had been carefully considered, from the decision to hold the reception in the ballroom of her East Bay Street house (at last she could use it in the style she'd dreamed of) to the exquisite floral arrangements.

I willingly slipped into the excitement of the preparations, allowing my mother full reign over plans that far exceeded anything I'd ever dreamed of, or wanted. Tripp and I would have been happy with a simple country wedding. But as Mama often pointed out to me, ours was a significant social wedding in Charleston, the wedding of the season, adding another level of grandeur and excitement to the event.

Mama engaged the services of the esteemed Parisian dress designer, Madame Estelle Dubois, renowned for her impeccable taste and style. On the day of my fitting, we strolled down King Street, parasols in hands. Overnight it seemed Charleston had become a hubbub of fashion. Jazz permeated the city and the styles. Women and men alike adopted glitz and glamour with shorter skirts for women and more casual suits for men.

I loved the new fashions. Not only did the style suit my slim, flat-chested body but I felt freer than I ever had in corsets and floor-length dresses with long hair bound up into fragile Gibson styles. Mama wore her long hair in a traditional chignon at her neck, but she was stylish under a saucy, tilted broad-brimmed hat.

In short, we were happy. At last, Mama could host a wedding, I was marrying a handsome young man from a good family, and I had left Mayfield behind to make my home in Charleston near her. Mama and I had our differences when I was a young girl. Some whoppers, to be sure. Yet, as women, a new bond had developed between us. An understanding, and dare I say, appreciation for each other as the women we were. I took some small pleasure in knowing that I was, at long last, the daughter she'd always wanted.

I looked over at Mama as we walked side by side along Meeting Street and thought how Tripp had been right that day in the tree hollow. How he'd said life was about change, and we either had to change with it, or get left behind.

The Bridal Salon entrance had an arching bower of colorful faux flowers. Beneath that, the scrolling letters of *Dubois* were encircled with gilt-edged roses. A Parisian cart overflowing with fresh flowers sat in front.

"Impressive," I said, stopping to take in the view.

"Since Madame Dubois set up her salon, all the Charleston elite are coming to her. Yours will be one of her first creations, so she is giving it her best effort."

I knew this meant a lot to her and nodded with enthusiasm.

She put her finger to her cheek in thought. "What do you call it when one promotes one's business in the papers?"

"Advertisement?" I replied. "The *News and Courier* is full of them."

"Yes, that's it. Well, Mrs. Dubois said your gown is her advertisement, as it were. And, since I was one of her first customers, she is giving your gown the utmost attention." I heard pride in her voice.

"Indeed."

Mrs. Dubois was waiting for us in the pink shop dominated by an enormous Venetian mirror. She was a slight woman dressed entirely in black. Her raven hair was slicked back with pomade, and with her dark, kohl-lined eyes and beakish nose, she reminded me of a crow. After greeting us with flourish, she clapped her tiny hands to alert her two assistants, then led me to the mirrored dressing room.

My wedding gown was indeed a testament to Madame Dubois's talent and the wedding's glamour and opulence. I stepped upon the platform as Madame and her assistants fluttered around me. The dress was a sheath of delicate satin adorned with intricate lace appliques, painstakingly handsewn by skilled artisans. The gown fell like water down my body with a cascading skirt that swept into a long train. My veil, a simple, long piece of intricate French lace.

Mama drew close, tears in her eyes. She reached up to gently touch the heavy veil of French lace that hung straight from my head to the floor. "I wore this on my wedding day. To your father."

"You were a beautiful bride, Mother."

She sighed as memories clouded. "As are you." She cupped my face. "My duckling has turned into a swan."

The memory of being scolded and called ugly after putting on Mama's makeup flashed in my mind. Today I received the gaze from my mother I'd always wished for.

Madame Dubois drew closer to walk around me, her face tight in concentration. She touched a rose applique, adjusted the veil, then stood in front of me, her head cocked to one side. We waited. At last, she exclaimed, "*C'est parfait!*"

Mama and I were in high spirits. The quaint restaurant Mama had chosen had once been a private house and was now a favorite spot for Charleston women to lunch. Paintings of local scenes covered the walls, the tables were draped in crisp white damask, and spotless crystal gleamed. The maître d' led us to a small, enclosed garden where the air was cooler and the sweet scent of roses filled the air.

"Well, here we are," Mama said, settling in her chair and removing her gloves. "Our last lunch together with you still a Rivers." Her gaze settled on me. "In two days, you will be Mrs. Arthur Chalmers."

I looked at my hands, focusing on the trio of stones on my left ring finger. The small round diamond set on either side with blue sapphires had belonged to Tripp's grandmother. This, like my marriage to him, was in keeping with societal expectations. I wasn't in love with Tripp. But I had given up on the notion of marrying for love. My heart had been broken and I was resigned that finding true love again was unlikely, or impossible. Tripp had advised me to put away the things of a child, and I had done so. Now I saw marriage as both a duty and a wise choice based on affection.

"I'm ready. It's been a long journey to find happiness with Tripp."

Mama's gaze rose from the menu in concern. "But you are happy?"

"I am content. I have accepted the notion that practicality outweighs matters of the heart. Marrying my best friend offers me companionship and security. We will build a life based on trust and mutual understanding."

"Wise. Passion in marriage is highly overrated. It's easiest to simply live in the present."

Our conversation was interrupted by the arrival of the waiter, and we placed our orders.

"Here's to living in the present," I offered as a toast, once the champagne had been poured. We clinked glasses. As I sipped, I wondered if I could ever really live my life that way. "I've always been driven to succeed," I said. "To have some goal, to cross the finish line a victor. Remember the horse race?"

Mother gave me a cold look. "That approach didn't prove successful."

I laughed without humor. It was the harsh truth. The past six years of my life, my determination to manage Mayfield, was for naught. "No," I conceded. "I suppose in the end I lost."

"Whatever are you saying? You are about to cross the finish line as Mrs. Arthur Chalmers."

"Quite."

I was spared answering further as lunch arrived. Over Dover sole we chatted about all things wedding—the gown, the flowers, which of the guests had accepted the invitations and which had declined. For the wedding of the season, those were few. The waiter arrived to refill our glasses.

"We'll be tipsy," I warned her.

"All the better. I am enjoying this time with my daughter before her wedding."

"Mama, we'll be living close to you in Charleston. We can have lunch together often."

She cocked her head. "Did you find a house?"

I nodded with relief. "At last. Most everything we looked at was far too grand for our budget. But Tripp's practice is doing so well," I added quickly. "I worried about the number of clients he'd have in the city, but since he opened his doors, it seems everyone in Charleston has walked in with a dog or a cat or some other sort of pet."

"Pets are all the rage these days."

"You should get one. A cat would suit you."

Mama put up her hand. "Spare me. I've had enough animals at Mayfield to last a lifetime."

I looked at the woman across the table from me. The tightness in her face had softened, and she laughed more often. A woman myself now, I was coming to appreciate how happy she was living in

Charleston and all she had given up to marry my father and live so far out in the country.

"So," said Mama, setting her silverware down, her lunch finished. "Tell me about this house."

I pictured the small brick house with its large window boxes. "It's a sweet house nestled among important houses on Church Street." I approached such discussions with caution and deference since Tripp didn't have much money of his own. I didn't want to shame him. "We are so grateful for the money you gave to us for our wedding. And Tripp's family has been generous as well," I hastened to add. "I admit, we were surprised at the expense of this neighborhood, but it's close to his practice. And, of course, family."

Mama tilted her head, listening, saying nothing.

"I want you to see it. The house is—" I groped for words to describe the cramped house "—charming. Sweet. Cozy."

"Those are words used to describe a cottage."

I held back a laugh. "It's the smallest house south of Broad Street, I'm afraid," I confessed. Then added brightly, "But that's what makes it such a find."

Mama paused in thought, then asked, "Did you purchase it?"

"No," I said, alert to the change of tone in Mother's voice. "Tripp is putting together an offer."

"Before you decide . . ." Mama reached into her reticule and pulled out an envelope, which she laid upon the table between us.

"What's this?"

Mama coupled her hands. "The graduation dinner for Lesesne never sat well with me," she began. "Not as a woman or a mother. I never held with the concept of primogeniture. I always felt it was a system that unfairly excluded daughters and younger sons from their inheritance, based solely on gender and birth order. Your father differs with me, as you know all too well. He fervently believes primogeniture is the only way to maintain the family wealth and land holdings over generations. The eldest son inheriting the family estate ensures continuity in the management of an estate as large as Mayfield." She gave a dismissive gesture with her hand. "It's all so intertwined in our culture with hierarchy, tradition, legacy. . . . I worried the pressure and expectations on Heyward's shoulders was a burden for him." Her face clouded with memory. "Yet it was one he clearly was suited for. He would have been a great steward of Mayfield."

"Yes," I agreed, feeling a twinge at the heart. I had never told her about Heyward's thoughts of leaving Mayfield and going with Covey to France. That was best kept in the grave with his memory.

"But when Heyward passed, I felt that a more egalitarian approach to inheritance would alleviate such pressures from Lesesne, who clearly was not suited for managing the estate. Or country living, for that matter. I argued with your father for equal distribution between the two of you. I know how you feel about Mayfield. The sacrifices you have made. I hoped too that sharing the estate would promote a healthier relationship between you and Lesesne."

She reached for her champagne and took a sip. "Oh, the arguments we had." Setting the glass back on the table she let her finger trace the rim.

"As you well know, your father did not agree with me. He felt only a son should inherit the family's property." She gave off a short laugh of disgust. "Which is rich, considering it has been his wife's fortune that has kept the farm afloat these many years. Another age-old tradition." She looked me in the eye. "You were the one clearly suited for managing Mayfield."

The old hurt roiled in my heart, but I tamped it down. "Thank you for that. I appreciated your continued support of Mayfield when I asked for it. I know it was hard for you to give."

"No matter now," Mama replied lightly. "I felt you earned it. You gave up college to run the farm when your father couldn't. You showed strength, loyalty, and vision. And, in truth, despite all the years of guiding you away from your dreams for Mayfield, I hoped things would end differently for you. That your father would see your worth and reconsider his antiquated position on primogeniture and leave it you."

She clucked her tongue in frustration. "But in truth, I am relieved you've escaped that fate," she said. "Let Lesesne inherit Mayfield. You were right, you know. He never wanted it. He was jealous of your brother. Everything came so easily to Heyward. He was the apple of your father's eye. I daresay Rawlins looked at Lesesne with disappointment." She cleared her throat. "No, Lesesne may not have wanted Mayfield. What he wanted was your father's approval. And God help him, he got it."

I realized my mother had not read Heyward's letter, or knew that he'd asked Lesesne to take care of Mayfield. Even still, my mother was also right. Lesesne wanted our father's approval as well.

She lifted her glass and stared at the amber liquid before adding, "My Lord, your father is a stubborn man. And . . . he's not well."

My heart hardened. "Not well? Mama, he's a drunk."

Mama's face was pained, and she quickly looked away. When she could speak, her voice was sad. "Heyward's death shifted something in him. He's . . . changed. Like his father was after the war."

"I don't know about my grandfather, but I do know that Daddy drinks all day, blusters and storms about, rudely making a mess of everything Wilton and I had worked so hard to achieve." I shook my head, brushing away the memories. "Daddy is not the man he was. You're right. That man died with Heyward."

Mama's gaze assessed me quietly. At length, she asked, "When did you become so hard?"

"I'm not hard, Mama," I replied soberly. "I'm a realist. I'm no longer the child with dreams." Then I added, "Were you hard when you left Daddy?"

"What?" she asked, startled by my boldness.

"Why did you leave? I had often wondered. You may have avoided scandal by not getting a divorce, but people still talk about your separation."

Mama blinked several times then said simply, "I was dying."

I was both surprised and intrigued by her candor.

"There was nothing left for me," she continued. "I could not stay at Mayfield to watch Rawlins wither away. And . . . yes. He is a mean drunk."

"Is there any other kind?"

My mother heard the accusation and looked away. There was no denying that alcohol made her angry and aggressive, as well. Their bitter fights remained scarred on my memories. To her credit, however, she'd curtailed her drinking since she'd left Mayfield. Whether it was the marriage or the place, free from both, I believed she had at last found peace.

Mama finished her champagne, then dabbed the corners of her mouth with her napkin and smiled with anticipation. "Eliza, I was my parents' only child. A daughter. You are my only daughter. The beloved granddaughter of your grandparents Bissette. As you know, I inherited their fortune." Her lips twisted into a sardonic smile. "So much for primogeniture, right?"

I raised my glass to her.

"That fortune included the house on East Bay Street. In this envelope—" she reached out to tap the envelope with her fingertip "—is the deed to that house."

"Mother, no," I gasped.

She waved my comment away with an elegant sweep of her hand. "It's done. It's not only my great pleasure to give the house to you, but also the right thing to do. Your father determined that only his son would inherit his property. Likewise, I've decided that my daughter would receive mine."

"But Lesesne. He always believed the East Bay house was his."

"He made his choice."

I had long accepted that Lesesne had been my mother's favorite. Or at the very least, she spoiled him and kept him close. While he lived with her at the East Bay house, Lesesne accompanied her to events such as the theater or art shows, proving himself a gallant and handsome escort. After he accepted his inheritance of Mayfield, however, Mama sent him packing. They'd had a fierce row about it. Mama was as unrelenting as my father had been with me. She would not let him return to her house except as a guest.

"I will share my wealth between the two of you, which should be enough for him to maintain Mayfield, should he choose to, and for you to maintain the East Bay house. Now, please, open it."

I reached across the table for the envelope. Unsealing it, I pulled out the legal document. On the first page, in bold print, Eliza Pinckney Rivers Chalmers was written as the owner of the great house on East Bay Street.

"I never expected this," I said in a soft voice.

"Which gives me all the more pleasure to bestow it," Mama said. She turned her head, caught the gaze of a waiter and discreetly lifted her hand. Looking at me, she sensed my hesitancy. "Darling girl, the timing is right. Don't you see? You and Tripp do not have to scrimp and save to buy a house. You can live at East Bay."

"But where will *you* live?"

Mama laughed lightly. "Why, with you, of course. It's a very big house."

I swallowed thickly, staring at the papers. I would never be able to think of that grand house as mine—especially not as long as my mother lived there. She would always be the lady of the house. I'd lived a lifetime as her daughter. Now I wanted to be Tripp's wife. I needed to be the master of my own home, no matter how humble. Slipping the papers safely back into the envelope, I placed it on my lap. The waiter arrived and refilled our glasses, finishing the bottle.

"Mama . . ." I said when the waiter left. "It's not that I don't appreciate this. Of course, it is so generous. But . . . Tripp and I, we will be newlyweds. We should live in our own house. We need time to be alone, don't you think? As husband and wife."

Mama was bringing her glass to her lips. She held it midair a moment, then set it back on the table. "It's very sweet, you wanting your own place as newlyweds." She reached over to put her hand over mine. "My dear, friendship with a man is a treasure. Marriage, however, is . . . complicated. Love is complicated." She sighed and tossed up her hands. "Men are complicated."

Then she leaned forward and spoke quietly. "Eliza, listen to me carefully. I'm your mother and I recognize my failures in the past. I want to support you in the future. This house provided me with a safe haven. It's important that a woman have her own money. It allows her freedom of choice. Independence. For that reason, I put the East Bay house in your name only, Eliza." Her lips curved in a wry smile. "Consider it matrilinear primogeniture. This is my gift, from mother to daughter."

Chapter Thirty-Four

⊶⊷

SPARTINA (*Sporobolus alterniflorus*) is a tall, smooth, perennial wetland grass that dominates tidal salt marshes of the South. Commonly called cordgrass, it is an important food source for many endemic and migratory birds. It also provides nursery and protective habitat for many aquatic species.

1926

On the first Saturday in June, I sat in the anteroom of St. Phillips Church surrounded by roses and lilies. Sunlight filtered through stained glass windows, casting colorful hues across my white wedding gown. This was a girl's greatest moment, if my mother were to be believed. It should be my happiest. Yet, I didn't feel especially happy. My gaze followed the elegant curve of the white stucco wall that reached high toward heaven. If fate had been different, I would be marrying Hugh today in this same church. Heyward and Covey would be at our sides. Lesesne would be living with Mama on East Bay. And Tripp . . .

I shook my head, feeling their absence. I couldn't allow myself to fall into the trap of memories. I was marrying Tripp today. Lesesne and I had made a kind of peace and he sat beside my mother in the church. This was a happy day, I upbraided myself, bringing my bouquet of white roses closer to my chest.

A knock sounded on the door.

"Miss Rivers." Father Johannes entered dressed in his black cassock. He smiled apologetically. "I apologize for the disturbance.

There's someone here who wishes to see you." He stepped aside and from the vestibule a tall figure entered.

My father stepped tentatively into the room then stopped as the great wood door swung closed behind him. I slowly rose to stand. I hadn't seen him since the day I'd left Mayfield a year earlier, not long after the fateful graduation dinner. I had packed my belongings and departed without another word to him, nor had I spoken to him or exchanged letters in all the months I'd been in Charleston. Not once.

We stood looking at one another in an awkward silence. Rawlins was dressed in a morning suit that was carefully tailored, still, the suit hung loosely from his gaunt figure and sloped shoulders. Alcohol had rendered him shockingly frail, and he was nervously fingering the top hat in his hands.

I licked my dry lips, my heart pounding. I had vowed I would not let this man walk me down the aisle. Not after his despicable disregard for me. I had not even invited him to the wedding.

"What are you doing here?" I asked, mustering my resolve.

He held out his arms in supplication. "Eliza, I'm your father," he replied, his drawl falling soft on my ears. "My little girl is getting married. Where else would I be? I dreamed of this day since the day you were born."

"Daddy . . ."

He straightened and said in the manner of a grand request, "It would be my greatest honor to walk you down the aisle."

Tears sprang to my eyes, and I looked around for a handkerchief. "I'll ruin my makeup."

Daddy pulled the handkerchief from his pocket and offered it to me with a gentleman's flair. While I dabbed my eyes, he hovered close.

"You look lovely."

I drew away from him. "You broke my heart," I said, choking on the words.

"I'm sorry," he replied, sounding sincere. He set his top hat on a chair and stepped near, then took my left hand in both of his. He looked at my engagement ring. "It's a beautiful ring." He looked at it a moment longer, then said, "What can I do to put things to right between us?"

I searched my father's sunken face. Once vibrant and so full of life, the change told a somber story. Instead of the hope of a new dream, his eyes were rheumy and pale. They were the eyes of a man with no more stories to tell. I had loved this man. Loved him still. That love compelled me to offer him one more chance.

"Daddy, I know that you always wished to leave Mayfield to a son." I sighed with exasperation. "Male primogeniture will out."

"Eliza—"

I put up my hand. "Hear me out. I have given up that fight. Today, I'm marrying Tripp and creating a new life in Charleston. Like you always told me I would." I took a shaky breath, willing myself to ask for the one gift that would mean the world to me. "But I will always love Mayfield. You know how much I love it. How much a part of me it is. If you could see your way to leaving me just a small piece of land. Perhaps the Sweetwater Pond property. I won that land back for the family, after all. Remember?" I could feel my heart rate accelerate. "If I could have any small piece of Mayfield to call my own, to bring my husband and children to in the future, I would be content. You know I would be a good steward. Just that, Daddy." Tears filled my eyes. "Please."

Daddy looked down at me from his height and straightened his shoulders. I caught a glimpse of the man who once stood tall at the head of the family table.

"I can never break up the property. You know that. I'm sorry."

The chill of his words caused my tears to crystallize. My blood froze in my veins and my spine stiffened. "I'm sorry too."

We were interrupted by another rapping on the door. Father Johannes appeared in a rush of excitement. His cassock rustled in the silence. "My dear, it's time."

Ruth, my maid of honor, entered behind him, resplendent in pale pink taffeta, carrying my bouquet. I thought, with a pang, of Covey. We had dreamed of this day for both of us, promised to be each other's maid of honor. Seeing my father, Ruth paused abruptly.

"Oh," she said in a high voice of surprise. Her gaze shifted from my father to me. "Has . . . has there been a change in the program?"

I stepped forward to take my bouquet from her. "No. There will be no change." I turned to address my father. His blue eyes watched me now with faint understanding. I went to retrieve his top hat from the chair and handed it to him. "You don't need to trouble your-self with a mere daughter. Go back to Mayfield. Please. You're not needed here. Unlike you, I don't hold to antiquated customs."

He stood motionless, his mouth drooped open, his eyes seem-ingly confused.

I gathered my train in my hand and, with a rustle of silk, left my father standing alone in the cold stone anteroom.

The church was charged with anticipation and excitement as my bridesmaids assembled in a line beside the groomsmen. Ruth arranged the long train of my gown so that it spread smoothly behind me, then took her place. Father Johannes nodded his head, and the heavy wooden doors opened wide. At the cue, the pipe organ thundered out Wagner's wedding march.

I paused at the threshold, my heart pounding. Ahead, fluted Corinthian columns supported the gallery, its boxed pews filled with the Charleston elite handsomely dressed in their finery.

Walking myself down the aisle would set the gossips fluttering. Had I made a mistake? Should I hurry back to fetch my father? I felt chilled and my feet would not move.

Then I saw Tripp at the altar. His fresh-faced smile elicited my own as all fear vanished. Tripp was always there when I needed him. And he was waiting for me.

I took a step forward, alone. I was ready to embark on this new journey.

Chapter Thirty-Five

⊰⊱

DRAGONFLIES (*Anisoptera*) are insects characterized by large, multifaceted eyes, two pairs of strong, transparent wings, and an elongated body. Their flight is agile and graceful, and they are often found near ponds, lakes, and streams. Predatory insects, dragonflies feed on other insects like mosquitoes, flies, and gnats, which is important in controlling insect populations. Dragonflies symbolize change and transformation.

1988

Outside, the sun had shifted in the sky. I turned from the window, took a long, deep breath, and exhaled slowly. I allowed my gaze to sweep the mural, ticking off in my mind the many stories that I'd shared over the past days. My eyes lingered on the scene of the great live oak tree with a large hollow in which three children played. There was Rawlins and Sloane's wedding, another with a pair of oxen pulling a plow in the rice fields, a young girl racing a horse, young teens at Sweetwater Pond, two blond-haired men in uniform standing shoulder to shoulder, and gravestones on a hill. It was a good start, I thought, feeling a weight lifted from my shoulders. The early years were finished.

My gaze swept across the multitude of other scenes and I sighed wearily. I knew these next told of other joys and other sorrows—adult and more profound. All chapters of the tale I had yet to complete.

The two women sitting at the table appeared as yet rapt with attention. But their faces looked tired. Cold coffee cups littered the table. The air felt stale. *Enough for now*, I thought. I rose and clapped my hands, startling them.

"We're going out," I announced. "We need to breathe some fresh air and feel the sun on our faces. And I know just the place."

<hr>

Sweetwater Pond glistened as dappled sunlight filtered through the dense canopy of trees. The light seemed to dance on the water with a mesmerizing play of light and shadow. Near the water's edge reeds and cattails stood tall, their slender forms casting elongated reflections on the surface. Dragonflies fluttered their iridescent wings as they performed their graceful aerial dances.

We carried a cooler and old Hudson blankets from the ATV and spread them out on the soft grass beside the pond. Norah opened the wine and poured glasses of chilled rosé.

We sat for a while gazing at the expanse of water that glinted in the sunlight like a huge jewel. After a while, feeling the wine, I set my glass aside and lay down on my back. The sky above was brilliant blue with white cumulus clouds drifting past. My body slowly softened.

"We've talked a lot about the past," I said aloud. "Let's spend some time focusing on the present moment instead of thinking about the past or future. I've learned that coming outdoors to the natural world helps me relieve stress and clear my head. And cheers me up. Tuning into what's happening around me helps create calm. Let's just sit quietly for a moment. Or lie down if you prefer. Become aware of your surroundings—the feel of the sun on your face. Use your senses. Sight. Sound. Smell. Touch. Taste. They link you to the world around you. Go on, now. Close your eyes." After a few breaths I asked, "What do you hear? What do you smell? What do you feel?"

With my eyes closed my senses heightened, I felt the softness of grass tickle my palms. Heard the gentle rustle of the wind in the leaves of the trees. From somewhere came the buzzing of a bee and warblers trilled from branches above. Pine and cedar, I thought as I caught their distinctive scent. In that moment, I felt very much alive, even as I understood at a cellular level that my health had diminished. Like the mural, I was in the final scenes of my life.

I gave them time to let the spell work. I looked to my side to see Savannah still sitting with her eyes closed, breathing heavily.

"Are you asleep?" I asked her.

She pried open an eye. "No. But close." She giggled and rubbed her eyes. "Actually, it was great. When I close my eyes, breathe in and out, and just listen, it's like you said. I feel . . . more connected. But it makes you sleepy."

"That's because you're relaxing. That's good."

Savannah yawned noisily. "I needed that."

"I try to get outdoors at least once a day," said Norah. "If only for a couple of minutes. Life can get pretty fast and hectic and I just need to take a break in nature. You could say it's my form of meditation." She looked across the pond. "I imagine that would be easy to do here."

"I've always found it to be," I replied. "As much as I love coming to Sweetwater Pond, in truth I haven't been in quite a while. I have to make time in my schedule, plan how to get way out here. Get the bug spray," I added with a light laugh. "It doesn't matter where I go, as long as I get outdoors. Even if it's just sitting in my garden."

"Do you still work full-time?" asked Norah.

"Yes." Seeing her astonished expression, I continued. "I've relinquished the reins of my corporation bit by bit over the years. Still, I shoulder the weight of the company and the direction it takes. At the shareholders meeting, when I announced my intention of letting the load go, I knew it was time. Past time. I was waiting, hoping for . . ." I paused. It was too early to discuss my plans. I had watched the two young women listen and absorb the family stories and was heartened. Watching them here and now, at this beautiful spot, I sensed they were forging an attachment to Mayfield.

"Changing the line of succession was not an easy decision for me." I looked at Savannah. "Your father was, understandably, upset. At another time, I'll explain my reasons."

"I don't need to know," Savannah rushed to say.

"I *want* you to know. It's important that you understand. And perhaps," I ventured, "agree with my decisions. Still, family strife causes a lot of stress, and my work has monopolized my time for many years. One thinks one can go chugging on like some train engine forever. It's hard to accept when one comes to the end of the track." I took a breath. "I had a heart attack recently."

"*Grandma*," Savannah said with alarm. She clutched my hand, eyes wide. "Why didn't you tell us?"

I was filled with affection for her emotion. "It was minor," I replied, patting her hand, making light of it. "I went to doctors, had countless tests, was poked and prodded. And I survived. I don't want you to worry. But it did convince me to retire." I laughed. "Your father should be pleased."

Savannah scowled. "He shouldn't have said those things. He's terrible."

"No, he's not," I chided. "But . . . maybe he needs to open his senses a bit." I steepled my hands under my chin. "You asked if I remembered Hugh. I do," I said honestly. "But Heyward, Hugh, and Covey are gone. Your grandfather too. Dear Tripp. And so many others. My ode to joy is having *you* here now."

Thunder rumbled softly in the sky, signaling it was time to head home. We quickly gathered our supplies and loaded the ATV. As the clouds overhead began turning gray, we headed back to the house.

We arrived at the house laughing. Slightly sunburned, our hair in disarray, we felt rejuvenated as we climbed from the ATV. Savannah assisted me and slid her arm around my waist as we walked to the rear door.

I felt the day's fatigue as we strolled along the brick walkway. I enjoyed my granddaughter's arm around me. Drowsy, I thought I might take a nap. Maybe a shower first.

A flutter caught my eye, and looking up I saw a bluebird hopping onto a green bough of a nearby live oak. I took the opportunity to pause and listen as he regaled us with this sweet melody. Bluebirds were considered a harbinger of good fortune.

On entering the coolness of the house, Savannah saw that the answering machine's light was blinking. She slid her arm away and dashed to the hall table to punch the play button.

"Hello, this is Hana. It's urgent. Mrs. Delancey, please call me back at your earliest convenience." After a momentary pause, there was a click of disconnection.

Hana's voice was monotone, but she rarely used words like *urgent*. I hurried to the phone and dialed her number.

"Hana? What is urgent?" I said when I heard her *hello*.

"Mrs. DeLancey. Thank you for returning my call." She paused, then launched into her report. "As you expected, there was great disappointment at the luncheon yesterday when you did not appear. And concern. Given it was your birthday, many of the family felt you would have attended if you could have. The message that circulated was that you are not well."

"Did you tell them I returned to Mayfield?"

"Yes, I did," Hana answered succinctly. "This did not deter Arthur. Rather, it seemed to fuel his argument. Arthur is undermining confidence in your ability to lead the business by reason of your health. He is pointing out the sudden—and he says dramatic—move to put thousands of acres into conservation as being affected by your illness. Arthur is also working to gain the support of other family members and key stakeholders by portraying himself as the solution to the immediate challenge of your illness. You should know, he has successfully rallied people against your proposal to change the hereditary succession."

"Of course he has." I took my son's plans in stride. I would not allow myself to get emotional. "I see now I shouldn't have left the fox in the henhouse."

"Ma'am," Hana said. "Arthur stated that he was coming to see you."

"Coming here? *To Mayfield?*"

"Yes."

"When?"

"I'm not sure, but soon."

"Is Bobby Lee now at Green Pond?"

"He is."

"Thank you, Hana. I'll call him."

I said goodbye to Hana and immediately dialed Bobby Lee's phone number, one of the few I knew by heart. He answered on the second ring. After pleasantries, he repeated Hana's account of the fallout after the shareholders meeting.

"He's coming loaded for bear," Bobby Lee drawled.

"Does he have the votes?"

"Not yet. The family likes the idea of having a vote in the election of the chairperson. And I'm sorry to say, given that he's your son, there is little confidence in Arthur's ability to manage the corporation."

"Bobby Lee, you are right. I cannot delay securing the final thousand acres of Mayfield. I've been formulating a new plan. Do you remember the young woman at the meeting who spoke out for conservation?"

"Yes. She was Heyward's granddaughter, am I right?"

"Yes. Norah Davis. She's highly qualified, with a PhD in environmental science and experience with the Nature Conservancy. And more . . . she's family."

"I see. Are you considering Miss Davis for chairman of the board of the Mayfield Foundation?"

"Indeed I am. She is perfect. The best of Heyward and Covey both."

After a pause, Bobby Lee said with an emotional tremor in his voice, "I'm happy for you, Eliza. I know you've been waiting for this moment."

I was grateful to my old friend. "Do you have the papers ready?"

"Yes. They're waiting for your signature."

"It's time for the next step."

I placed the receiver in its bed and took a deep breath. When I was a child, Wilton had affectionately said I had feral instincts. That extra sense that alerted me to change and allowed me to pounce in time. I felt those senses tingling now and hope surging in my blood.

The pieces were coming together. Norah had the résumé and the brains for advancement. Savannah had curiosity, a quick mind, and a good heart. They were each at a different stage in life, and they each would take what they needed from the stories I told. My task was to help raise questions in their minds. To help them visualize opportunities.

But it was Norah Davis who was a key to the future of Mayfield. I had to convince her of that.

"Everything okay?" Savannah asked.

I smiled weakly and nodded. "All is as expected."

The door opened and Norah came in with a gust of wind that smelled of rain.

"Made it in time," she called out, hustling into the kitchen.

Another gust whipped through the rice fields, sending the tall spartina grass swaying under the force of the wind, creating a mesmerizing dance across the landscape. Rumbles of thunder echoed, ominously, like a warning growl. Dark, roiling cumulous clouds were forming in the distance.

I walked to stand at the large windows. "Big storm coming," I said. "I can feel it in my bones."

Nature was both powerful and dangerous. Only a fool underestimated it. I thought of the next set of stories I would tell and wondered how the women would respond to them. Today I'd ended at my wedding to Tripp, akin to a sunny day. My stories were about to change eras and mood. In these, we were no longer children riding horses, falling in love, and playing in the wild. We had become adults and would begin navigating difficult decisions and changes of fortune. I looked at the ominous sky over the fields and shivered, thinking of the cold winds about to blow.

"Savannah, Norah," I called out, waving them closer. We stood shoulder to shoulder at the windows watching the approaching tempest. "Do you recall the year of my wedding?"

"Nineteen twenty-six," said Savannah.

"That's right. Now think about history. What was looming on the horizon like those dark clouds overhead?"

After a brief pause Norah said, "The Great Depression."

"Yes," I said somberly. I wrapped my arms around myself thinking of all the changes that harsh era had brought to Mayfield and the Rivers family. I had more stories to tell them: of joyous birth and tragic death, poverty and great wealth, divorce and marriage, hunting and killing, love and lies. And through it all, the fate of Mayfield hung in the balance.

The magnitude of the realization brought a stab of pain to my heart, quick and sharp. Gasping, I reach out for Savannah's hand, finding comfort in the connection with my granddaughter. As the pain ebbed and my breath returned, with my other hand, I took Norah's. I smiled, sensing the meaningful bond that was growing between us.

"This story is far from over," I said, squeezing their hands. "But for now, we rest. It is my honor to share all this with you. My greatest hope is that you, together, will carry on the history of Mayfield. And preserve its land, waters, and wildlife for generations to come." I looked out at the gathering clouds. "Tonight, a storm will brew. But trust that tomorrow the sun will shine again."

END OF BOOK ONE

Continue reading more of Eliza's story in
Book Two: *The Rivers' End*

Author's Note

For more than twenty years I have written novels that dwelt on Mother Nature and human nature. My modus operandi was to select a specific endangered species, do a deep dive into research, then finally, and importantly, roll up my sleeves and volunteer to work with the animals and organization. I created themes for the novel from what I learned about the animals first. Then the story.

Characters came to life, and their emotional and personal dilemmas mirrored the themes I was exploring. They, and their relationships, are what ultimately dominated the story. After all, I was writing a novel, not nonfiction. In this way I was able to bring to my readers not merely some knowledge about the animals in the backdrop, but hopefully, through emotion, a caring. I like to say *If you care, you take care.*

I'm eternally grateful to all readers who have written to me over the years or told me at events that they've not only learned about an animal in my novels, but later volunteered, offered donations to organizations, and became proactive in protecting them.

Researching and working hands-on with wildlife has been the greatest joy and privilege of my long career. After twenty years, however, I felt I had finished my personal mission. The increasingly profound impact of climate change caused me to shift my gaze and expand my focus not on one species, but rather the bigger picture of the health of our natural resources. I focused on my home state of

South Carolina and zoomed in on one extraordinary location that is so important to our state but relatively unknown nationally—the ACE Basin.

The ACE Basin is an acronym for the Ashepoo-Combahee-Edisto (ACE) rivers. This vast and ecologically significant area is located across four counties in southeastern South Carolina. A remarkable interlocking web of ecosystems comprised of pine uplands, hardwood forests, freshwater swamps, former rice impoundments, salt marshes, and estuarine tidal creeks that converge into the St. Helena Sound.

This landscape also provides a stirring history of human settlement that became the great rice plantations of South Carolina. Later, the abandoned rice fields created important waterfowl habitats. Along with those migrating birds came an influx of wealthy northern hunting enthusiasts that changed the culture and lifestyle of the area. There are countless stories of how people struggled to hold on to family property and how ownership of the land changed hands. The common theme in all of them—whether a *comeya* (someone who came here) or a *beenya* (someone who has been here) in Gullah dialect—is how this unique, special landscape fostered a deep love of the land and a desire to protect it.

This commitment led to the development of a relatively new phenomenon of protecting land for future generations of wildlife and people. Comprised of private landowners, state and federal wildlife agency representatives, and nonprofit land trusts, a conservation initiative was born. This effort provided plenty of conflict with county officials, loggers, and family members aggressively opposing the initiative, arguing it threatened jobs and hindered economic progress and future profits. Still, the ACE Basin initiative succeeded and became the model for other initiatives in South Carolina and elsewhere. It is an exciting history filled with personal drama and I was eager to tell this history of heroes and villains and human predicaments.

But how to tell the story of the ACE Basin, its history and the task force initiative, without slipping into a nonfiction narrative? Others have already written compelling accounts, both of individual people and properties, and broad histories. I especially note *Rice and Ducks* by Virginia Beach, *Baronness of Hobcow* by Mary E. Miller, *Turning the Tide* by Sally Murphy, and the essay *On Common Ground* by Dana Beach. I am a novelist. How could I reveal the heart of the issue—*why* people loved the land and fought so hard to protect it?

A woman came to life in my imagination. She was a strong, independent woman I named Eliza, whom I imagined to be a descendent of the great Eliza Pinckney (1722–1793). Born at the turn of the twentieth century, Eliza lived through an era of great change in the South Carolina landscape and its culture, and I could portray her love of the land that had been in her family for generations, her beloved home, and explore her fierce desire to protect it at any cost. Through Eliza, I could write the *why* behind the drive to ensure the gifts of clean water, productive forests, abundant wildlife, healthy soil, and heritage for generations to come.

In my novel Eliza comes of age and grows into the powerful woman we meet at the story's beginning in 1988. With a dual timeline, we hear the eighty-eight-year-old Eliza offer advice to the younger women in the novel. This brings me to the second reason I wanted to write this novel. As a woman of a "certain age," I could speak through Eliza to share my own, personal insights with contemporaries and younger women alike.

Covering eighty-eight years of a woman's life and including all the dramatic stories of the region and the era took up a lot of words and pages. To avoid delivering a huge tome to my readers, I divided the long saga into two books: *Where the Rivers Merge* and *The Rivers' End*. I hope readers will read this epic story to completion in book two where Eliza's tale comes full circle.

Though inspired by history and our natural world, this is a novel born in my imagination and fed by the research and stories I'd encountered over the past five years. I wrote the novel through the point of view of my heroine alone. This decision allows the reader to see the world through this one woman's eyes and avoids stirring the pluff mud. I had much to say and hope you enjoy the telling.

The true story of the ACE Basin is full of remarkable stories and people. It's an inspiring history of good people working together with a common love of this piece of the Lowcountry and the goal of conservation. I am honored to add my fictional account to the narrative.

Acknowledgments

=—⟨⟩—=

This is a story about conservation and love of land. In this arena there are many remarkable, inspiring people who fight the good fight and have fascinating stories to tell. It was my honor and privilege to meet many of them in the writing of this book. I am eternally grateful to:

Sally Murphy, my longtime mentor and friend who shared inside stories on the early days of the ACE Basin. Thank you, too, for reading and editing countless drafts, making sure the geography and science was correct, as well as for being a great copyeditor. There are not enough words to thank you for all you did.

Patricia Denkler, a great friend and supporter who joined me early in the quest and guided me to visit meaningful landmarks and plantations in the ACE Basin and for introducing me to important residents. In the ACE Basin I am sincerely grateful to Frank and Gay Fowler of Dean Hall Plantation who graciously allowed me to stay on the grounds and soak up the gorgeous landscape as I wrote the novel. So inspiring! Noel Garrett and the staff of Lowcountry Produce, Lobeco, who provided me with delicious meals and the chance to meet locals. Keith and Mindy Hiers for the spellbinding, educational tour of the vast Donnelly Wildlife Management Area and for answering my countless questions. Bob and Lucyle Copeland for a memorable visit to their beautiful home on Wimbee Creek where we shared a delicious supper and more stories.

Dr. Ernie Wiggers, past president and CEO, Nemours Wildlife Foundation, and Ms. Michele Barker, administrative assistant, for a tour of Nemours and for providing an understanding of the history of Nemours Plantation and the important research being conducted at the Nemours Wildlife Foundation.

Wise Batten, Sr., for kindly taking me under your wing as I began this book. Your generosity will be forever remembered. Brenda Batten for sharing your inspiring, beautiful poems. Betsy Melvin Batten for introducing me to your beautiful family and for taking me on a tour of the breathtaking Bonnie Hall Plantation. Michael Thomas for guiding us on the tour. Wise, thank you, too, for introducing me to your friends and colleagues who were fundamental in the foundation of the ACE Basin, in particular: John D. Carsdale for a treasure trove of personal experiences, Lane Morrison for the enlightening history, and Ken Caldwell for a memorable visit to Hog Heaven. Finally, I'll always treasure the memory of staying at the Gathering Shed of Black Swamp and observing the ducks flying in over the fields.

Dana Beach, founder and Director Emeritus of the South Carolina Coastal Conservation League, who offered me amazing history, facts, and insights on the ACE Basin and its creation as well as the complicated work of developing policies that promote sustainable development.

Jackie Hood McFadden, for reading the manuscript and offering guidance on our beloved Marsh Tackies.

Liz Stein, my brilliant editor who approached this novel with enthusiasm, ideas, and skill to guide the first installment of this epic story to fruition. And to the entire team at William Morrow who have given me immense support, expertise, and enthusiasm: Liate Stehlik, Jennifer Hart, Kelly Rudolph, Heidi Richter, Kaitlin Harri, Liz Psaltis, Mary Interdonati, copyeditor Mark Steven Long, and sensitivity reader Kayla Dunigan.

Faye Bender, my extraordinary agent, for reading early versions, for believing in my work, and guiding me toward the realization of this book.

Delia Owens, my dear friend and writing confidante, for memorable evenings in the cabin, long walks and endless phone calls talking about the craft of writing, our books, other books, and life. And for the joy of laughing.

Kayla Dunigan at Writing Diversely for your thoughtful and sensitive review of the manuscript.

Kwame Alexander, for reading the novel and offering me an important awareness and critique that I truly appreciated.

Signe Pike, my intrepid writing partner, for pounding the keys by my side as we strove for words. And for your wisdom and friendship.

Marguerite Martino, for graciously offering hours of enlightening discussion and plotting and reading early drafts.

Cindy Boyle for being a muse and gifting me with ideas, meals, tweets, and to John Boyle for introducing me to Capitano, that handsome boy, and for the book title. Thank you most of all for your friendship—and yummy wine.

Gretta Kruesi, who created the beautiful Southern Oak Tree that added art and a touch of grace to the book.

Marjory Wentworth for generously allowing me to include her beautiful poetry in my books.

My Home Team, upon whom I depend for every facet of the writing journey: Angela May, Kathy Bennett of Magic Time Literary Agency, Laura Anderson Strecker. You are the best and I'm forever grateful for your heartfelt support and friendships.

To my friends who supported and rallied around me during these past few years, keeping tabs on me and the book's progress. You know who you are and that I love you. And much love and gratitude to my writing friends who offered quotes for the book.

My family, children, grandchildren who brighten my days and send me the words, food, gifts, and hugs that sustain and encourage me as I write. This book was a long time coming and I am grateful for all your support and love. Finally, to my husband, Markus, for decades of support, encouragement, and love from the first time I told you I wanted to write a book, and you believed in me.

About the Author

MARY ALICE MONROE is the *New York Times* bestselling author of thirty books for adults and children. She has earned numerous accolades and awards including induction into the South Carolina Academy of Authors Hall of Fame; the Southwest Florida Author of Distinction Award; South Carolina Award for Literary Excellence; RT Lifetime Achievement Award; the International Book Award for Green Fiction, and the Southern Book Prize for Fiction. Monroe is a cofounder of the weekly web show *Friends and Fiction* and serves on the South Carolina Aquarium Board Emeritus, The Leatherback Trust, The Pat Conroy Literary Center Honorary Board, and Casting Carolinas Advisory Board. She resides in South Carolina and North Carolina with her family.